ISLAND FEVER

Jimjeran Book One

Sarah Carrell

To Kat —
Your encouragement
and questions made
this book so much
better!
   Thanks isn't
even enough!
   Sarah Carrell

Jimjeran (shĭm-shĕ-ŕon): n, Marshallese – a lifelong
companion

— MARSHALL-ENGLISH DICTIONARY

Island Fever (ī´-lənd fē´-vər): n, Colloquialism – the
claustrophobic sensation caused by living on an
island, created by being surrounded by the ocean on
all sides, resulting in the sense that you can't
escape.

ISBN-13 978-1-9804147-3-5

Dedication

This book is dedicated to the beautiful people of the Marshall Islands, whose land and lifestyle are endangered by climate change. They are losing the place they love because of the choices of people far away who may never know what a treasure they are destroying.

The Jimjeran series began as a work of fan-fiction. The *Outlander* story contributed Campbell's virginity and Carlie's nursing occupation and urged the story towards a rapid marriage. If you have read the *Outlander* series, you may find there are friends and relatives who resemble characters you know and love. However the distinct place, people, and events on Arno are from my own experience and imagination. I hope you find this story a respectful homage with refreshing and surprising echoes of the *Outlander* story, told in an original voice. I will **always** recommend you read the actual *Outlander* books, as Diana Gabaldon is a literary genius.

Island Fever would not have come to life if it were not for the writers and readers on *Archive of Our Own* and *Tumblr*—in particular the enthusiastic *Outlander* fans who gave feedback and encouragement, who provided a ready audience, and who made me believe my little story was actually something real.

My own life has been deeper and more fulfilling because of my time years ago spent with these amazing people on the peaceful island of Arno, who taught me the meaning of simplicity, generosity, and happiness.

Sarah Carrell

CONTENTS

Meester Mack 9

Miss Peachay 17

Alone 26

Pain in the Arse 33

Tuck-In Service 41

Night Noises 49

Dirty Laundry 57

Poor Me, Bore Me 69

Stitch Removal 78

Geckos, the Huntsman, and Campbell, Oh My! 85

Sunshine 99

A Beautiful Doughy Ball 111

Scar Stories 120

The Break Up 130

Consolation 139

The Proposal 147

Getting to Know You 159

Phoning Home 172

Restraint 179

To Have and To Hold 189

First Blood 199

The Morning After 208

Autle 214

The Storm 220

The Drop-off 228

The Visitor 236

House Warming 245

Feels Like Home..253

Division of Labor.. 262

Love Notes 271

Date Night.. 278

Getting Settled 290

The American 298

The Hotel 308

Hey, Uncle Ferguson! 317

I Choose You...323

Love Making...333

Island Fever Calendar 342

AFTERWORD.. 345

Chapter Notes... 349

CHAPTER 1

Meester Mack

"Miss Peachay! Miss Peachay!" I heard yelling from outside and rushed to the door of the clinic to see what was causing the commotion.

"Meester Mack is hurt!" one little girl called out to me. "Meester Mack is bleed!"

It was hard to determine what I was seeing. A mass of children—black hair, dark eyes, beautiful tan skin—was swarming toward the clinic, surrounding a hobbling adult, a tall man with furiously red hair.

"Help!" the children were crying out. "Help! Help Meester Mack!"

I propped the clinic door open with a rock, then waded through the crowd of kids to the man. When I got closer I realized that despite his impressive size he wasn't very old. He looked like a college student about my brother Seth's age and he was grimacing in pain.

I quickly inspected him for damage. He was wearing a tee shirt and board shorts, and the entire right rear side of his board shorts as well as the copper hair of his right calf were streaked with blood. I tucked myself under his arm and put my arm around his waist to help him hop the rest of the way into the clinic.

As we entered, he turned to one of the tallest boys. "Get Mr. Ewan and Mr. Graham," he said. "See if they can borrow the truck to get me home."

The kids would willingly have followed us into the clinic, but I shooed them away and shut the screen door. "Mr. Mack will be okay," I said, "But I need to help him and can't have extra germs around."

"*Sherms?*" the kids asked, looking around in confusion. "Where is *sherms?*" I turned my attention to my patient and figured the children would wander off in boredom.

"Where are you hurt?" I asked him, circling him to better see the tear in his swimming trunks. He had kicked off his flip-flops at the front door and his heel was leaving small bloody smudges on my floor.

"I dinna ken, exactly. It hurts like...*cack*...holy hell," he winced and panted. "But I think I've got a horrific cut on my arse." There was some accent to his voice, however strained it seemed. I couldn't quite place it but that wasn't the first order of business, anyway.

"We're going to need to get your shorts off," I said. "Do you think you can pull them off or shall I cut them off?"

"I dinna think I can bend to pull them off but it's not easy to get new clothes out here. Can ye help me, lass?"

Lass, I thought triumphantly. *Scottish. Goes with the hair, I guess.* I went over to the cupboard and pulled out a hospital gown that opened in the back.

"Over the shirt or take it off?" I asked.

"Off," he grimaced. "It's sweltering in here." He reached up to the neck of his tee and pulled it off, balancing on his left leg.

I was trained to keep professional no matter the body type I was working with, but in my professional opinion Meester Mack had an excellent set of pectoralis majors and a well-defined set of rectus abdominis muscles.

I helped him put his arms through the sleeves of the gown and then walked around to tie the back closure. He was tall, probably 6'4", so I had to stretch up on tiptoes to get the upper one tied beneath the flame-red curls at the back of his neck.

As I debated how best to remove his board shorts I glanced back toward the door, where I saw seven or eight little round faces peering in through the screen.

"We've got an audience," I said to him, gesturing at the doorway.

"*Jaab lale*," he said, shaking his head. "*Etal!*"[1]

The little audience quickly obeyed and disappeared. "What did you say?" I asked him, surprised at their immediate response.

"Don't watch. *Jaab*-don't, *lale*-look. *Etal* is go away."

"They *obeyed* you," I said.

"I'm their *teacher*," he explained, somewhat indignantly. "They'd better obey me."

With the audience gone, I walked around behind him. "I'm going to try not to hurt you or your shorts. But if you start screaming, I'm grabbing my scissors."

"D'ye have any whisky?" he asked hopefully.

"No," I replied. "Though I've got Advil or Tylenol."

"*A ghràidh*," he laughed. "Not nearly as much fun."

I was trying to pull out on the elastic waist of the shorts, when he gave a little grunt.

"Ah, lass, I forgot. The drawstring is tied in the front." He had been leaning on the examination table supporting his weight with his hands, and when he let go of the table and tried to pull up the gown to get at his shorts, he groaned and swayed slightly.

"Let me," I ordered him. "I *am* your nurse. I don't want you hurting yourself any worse than you already are."

I lifted his gown in the front until I could see the waistband of his shorts. He turned his head away as if to avoid eye contact while I was so close. The tie was just inside the waistband so I reached my fingertips inside and pulled at the end of the laces. When they resisted I tugged a little harder.

He chuckled ruefully, closed his eyes, and shook his head in disbelief. "It's *double-knotted*," he groaned, his cheeks flushing.

"No problem," I said as I finally bent to business and knelt in front of him, thinking I might as well distract him while in this awkward position.

---

[1] *Jaab lale*: chab loll´-lay, et-tall´ (don't watch, go away)

He held the gown up in front, revealing not only the waistband of the low-slung shorts but also enough of his firmly muscled abdomen with angular cuts at his hips that I felt flushed and slightly embarrassed.

"So, what's your name?" I asked, flipping down the front waistband of his shorts so I could see the tie and working on pulling the knot loose with my fingernails. "Did I hear them calling you Mr. Mack? Is that your name?"

He laughed, "Ah, no. I'm Campbell. Campbell MacReid."

"Carlie," I said, smiling up at him. "Carlie Beecher... I'd shake your hand, but I'm taking off your pants right now."

He guffawed and then groaned again. "You know in Scots, 'pants' means underwear, don't you? Can we hurry? I really need to lie down."

The knot finally untied, I again moved around to his back. Pulling the elastic as far as I could to avoid his wound, I scooted the waistband downward until it had cleared his backside and then I dropped the shorts to the floor. I closed the gown and helped Campbell lie face down on the table.

I picked up the shorts and tossed them into the sink, figuring I'd need to rinse out the blood before he wore them again.

"Okay," I said. "Let's have a look at this injury."

Leaving him as decently covered as I could, I pulled the right side of the gown away until I could see the angry red cut across his right buttock that showed little white sections where it had gone as deep as the fat layer. It was still slowly oozing blood. It was the strangest shape, though, the cut like a repeated "s" curve that rippled across his skin.

I removed the suture kit from the cabinet and brought over the lidocaine and a syringe. I figured I should give the numbing medication a chance to work before I began suturing. First, I laid a pre-soaked cloth with a numbing gel on it across the gash itself. While I waited for that to take effect, I rinsed the blood out of his shorts, wrung them out thoroughly, and hung them over the back of a chair. Then I injected lidocaine in several locations along the sides of the cut, my patient wincing but staying silent as I did. While waiting for the lidocaine to work, I grabbed his flip-flops and rinsed them, then used a Clorox wipe to wipe up the blood stains on the floor.

"Now, how did you do this to yourself?" I asked as I grabbed a basin and filled it with some slightly warm water from the tea kettle. I had just sat down on my rolling stool to begin cleaning the area when there was a clatter at the front door and two young men suddenly appeared. One of them had a scraggly beard and a sloppy man bun, and the other was just plain sloppy.

"Aye, and ye'd be the new UniServe nurse?" Man Bun said.

"Yes," I said, "I'm about to suture your friend's bum, so you can stay or go as you want to."

"Oh," Sloppy said. "Definitely stay. Are ye going to scream, Campbell?"

I heard Campbell mumble something, so I leaned closer to hear him. "Kick them out, please," he said.

"Okay," I said, moving toward the two gentlemen, then pulling the curtain around the bed to conceal Campbell from view. "You can stay in the waiting area." I motioned to the two folding metal chairs by the front door.

"Thanks," Campbell said, when I sat down next to him.

"You were about to tell me how you did this," I reminded him.

"I was going to go fishing with a couple of my students. They'd made a makeshift boat from corrugated aluminum. I was climbing in, but I made the boat top heavy, I guess, and it started to tip and made me lose my balance. Anyway I slipped wi' my right leg in the boat and my left leg still on the dock. I sat down on the corrugated metal and that's when it cut me."

"Well, that explains this strange pattern," I said, gently swabbing the surrounding area.

"Did it make ye a eunuch, Campbell?" a voice came from the waiting area. I thought it might be Man Bun, but I wasn't certain. "And before ye'd even got a chance to..."

"Hush your gob," said Campbell. "I'm serious, Ewan. If ye can't shut up, ye're just going to have to leave."

"I'll be back in a minute," I said, setting down the cloth.

I went back out to the waiting area and with my hands on my hips declared: "You know what, gentlemen, I really need to focus on suturing, and you are upsetting my patient. You need to go outside." The two seemed taken aback to be ordered around but got up hastily and apologized as they headed out the door.

When Man Bun and Sloppy left I went back, finished cleaning as quickly and gently as I could, and then began suturing. Eighteen stitches later, Campbell had a curvy line of sutures traveling diagonally across his butt cheek which I covered with gauze and affixed with a few pieces of sterile tape.

"Sorry about this," I said. "Your hair is going to make removing the bandage kind of painful."

"The hair on my arse, ye mean?" he mumbled into the paper covering of the exam table.

"Yes, sadly." I said. "So, be gentle with yourself when you remove it."

"Dinna just rip it off?" he asked. It took me a second to realize he was joking. "I hear the hairless look is in these days."

I chuckled at his attempt at humor. "Now, arm or ass?" I asked him, looking at the syringe that awaited on the metal tray with the suturing equipment.

He turned his head to look at me, startled. "Excuse me?" he said. "Obviously, my arse does not have armor. In fact, 'tis quite tender right now even with the thousand numbing shots you poked me with."

"Sorry," I said, feeling foolish. "That wasn't clear *or* professional. I need to give you a tetanus shot. It's given intramuscularly, so it needs to be in your deltoid or your glute. Do you have a preference? Because your injury is on your backside, I thought it might be easiest to give you your shot while you're in this position. Giving an injection in your arm would require you to stand up or sit, and I doubt it would be very comfortable right now. I can even do it in the side that's still numb."

"Arse it is," Campbell mumbled. "Go for it. Canna be much worse than I feel right now."

Tetanus shot complete and painkillers administered, Campbell was almost ready to leave, but not clothed. "I dinna think I can put my shorts back on," he said, still prone on the examination table. He swung his legs over the edge of the table and gingerly stood up.

"Yeah, you probably shouldn't," I answered. "But you've got to get home."

He looked down at the hospital gown. "Can I borrow this?" he asked. It was white and only went halfway to his knees. *Completely unflattering and somewhat indecent,* I thought.

"Wait," I said. "I've got a sarong you can borrow. I'll be back in a minute."

I headed next door to my apartment and found the blue batik sarong that I sometimes used as a swimsuit coverup back at home. Campbell eyed me skeptically when I showed it to him.

"It'll just wrap around you," I said. "Easy to put on and take off."

"How d'ye get it to stay up?" he asked.

"Are you a Scotsman, or aren't you?" I asked.

He scoffed. "I can put on a kilt," he said, "But I dinna have a belt here."

I demonstrated on myself, bringing the sarong behind my back, wrapping the left side around to the right, and then the right over the left, securely tucking the end of the fabric in at my left front waist.

"Thanks, lass," he said. I handed him his tee shirt and left him to wrap himself up in privacy. He was hobbling slightly when he emerged from the curtain, but looked oddly handsome in tee and sarong.

I finally handed the young man off to his two friends, who it turned out were Ewan (Man Bun) and Graham (Sloppy), the other two teachers at the UniServe International school on the other side of the village.

"Come visit us," said Ewan. "It's about a mile from here. The school is a long building with a metal roof and solar panels. On the left. We live in the apartments on the "yar" side."

"Yar side?" I asked.

"*Iar.* Lagoon side," clarified Mr. Man Bun. "And bring food when you check on Campbell. We havena been off this island in six weeks, so we're starving. 'Cept for Graham. Somehow he still manages to stay fat." Ewan dodged Graham's fist, as the two helped Campbell into the bed of a rusty pick-up truck.

"Keep it clean!" I admonished Campbell, uncomfortably resting on his left side. I could just imagine how painful the jostling trip back to their house would be, even if it was only a mile. When I came inside I saw his torn board shorts still drying over the chair in my operatory. I grabbed them and took them back to the apartment with me. I was pretty sure I had a sewing kit somewhere, and if I could manage with a suture set, I could probably fix a tear in fabric.

I was smiling to myself for the next hour, and then I finally realized why. I'd just had my first conversation fully in English since I'd arrived on the island of Arno and seen Laura leave me, flying back to Majuro on the plane.

CHAPTER 2

Miss Peachay

Twenty-four hours previously...

W*hat the hell was I thinking?"*

"Did you say something, Carlie?" Laura yelled over the roar of the airplane engines. At this volume her southern accent was barely distinguishable. I loved the slow drawl when Laura talked.

"No," I responded, shaking my head and staring down at the little green and white loop of shoe-string flung in the middle of the indigo Pacific Ocean, my home for at least the next 18 months.

I thought our pilot was trying to land us in the water as the plane began to slow and descend. I couldn't see anything beneath us, in front of us, or to either side.

"What's he doing?" I finally yelled to Laura, terrified. "There aren't pontoons on this plane!"

"Don't worry, hon. He's landing on the airstrip," she yelled back, smiling. Airstrip? It wasn't until we were merely hundreds of feet off the ground and the tall green coconut palm trees came into sight that I realized she wasn't kidding. We were landing on an airstrip, indeed—an airstrip that took up the entire width of the island. As the plane taxied bumpily on the grass runway, I looked in amazement at my surroundings. Water to my left, water to my right.

"You knew it was an atoll, didn't you?" Laura asked, grinning at the shocked look of terror in my eyes.

"I knew what atoll meant, but I didn't realize it referred to an island that is only like, five feet wide," I said, extricating myself from the cramped seat once the plane had stopped and the engines had sputtered until the propellers were still.

"Don't exaggerate," Laura laughed. "At its narrowest point, it's still at least 30 feet wide."

I'd stared at the little island of Arno on Google Earth, zooming in as close as I could when I'd first accepted the assignment, curious about this place I'd never been. I could see the wide treed portion where the clinic was in the village of Ine, and I'd followed the narrow strip with a single road down the center around to see where the main island ended but the shallower water continued along the edge of the lagoon, soon to become another little island in the circular chain that resembled an angular Mickey Mouse.

I had always dreamed of being in UniServe International, a multinational organization of educators and medical volunteers, serving in some remote community for a year or two after college. But Eric Anderson and I had met when I was just a freshman, and twitter-pated by the handsome, mature, intelligent English major's interest in me I had simply forgotten who I had wanted to be one day. Eric graduated that year, continued toward his masters' degree, and then taught in the English department my final year in the nursing program. When I graduated, he proposed.

Five years after graduating, Eric and I were still engaged and living together, just had never set a date. So on my 27th birthday I had announced to him that I was joining UniServe.

"You're kidding, right, Carlie?" he said, taken aback by my cavalier announcement.

"No," I said, shaking my head. "We're not married yet, we don't have kids yet, and you're doing research for your doctoral thesis. You can use the focused time to write, and I won't have regrets once I'm too old or too entangled to volunteer anymore."

"Eighteen months, though, Carlie?" Eric looked at me in concern. "You know fertility decreases with age, don't you?"

"And *you* know we haven't been using birth control for the last five years, don't you?" I responded. "If it was going to happen naturally, it would have happened by now." I'd stopped taking the pill when I finished my last day of nursing school, figuring if we got pregnant at least that might light a fire under laconic Eric's ass.

I'd dropped numerous hints about marriage; as sweet as my parents were about it, I knew they were disappointed that I'd chosen to live with Eric before getting married. Being the daughter of a chaplain came with its own store of guilt.

Thinking about Eric's disappointed confusion had me feeling emotional, but I blinked the tears away and whipped my hair up into a sloppy bun. It was humid, and not only did my naturally curly hair get ten times curlier, my neck and face were almost instantly glistening with sweat, and I could feel a single droplet traveling down between my breasts.

A pickup truck had rattled up to the plane, and Laura and I took turns handing heavy boxes down from the cargo hold of the plane and then putting them in the back of the truck, nearly filling the truck bed with boxes. When everything was loaded, Laura went to the pilot. Holding up two fingers, she said, "*Ruo awa.*"[1] Two hours. I almost had a panic attack at the thought.

Laura came smilingly back to the pickup, where it seemed as if the driver was asking Laura if we wanted to ride or walk. After the cramped half hour on the plane, I thought walking might be nice, but I was only wearing sandals and it sounded like the clinic was two miles away. I needed as much useful time with Laura as possible. With the anticipation of seeing the clinic and apartment as another motivator, I hopped up into the bed, found a sturdy box and sat down, tucking the skirt of my sundress around my legs so it wouldn't fly up in the breeze.

Laura smiled at my wide-eyed fascination as we rode along, attempting to point out different landmarks. I didn't need a travelogue, though; my brain felt full enough as it was. The airstrip had been in a completely clear grassy area with no trees, but we quickly reached the coconut palm tree "forest," if that's what you could call it, coconut trees scattered across the

---

[1] *Ruo awa*: Rue´-oh ow´-ah (two hours)

sandy landscape, interspersed with bushes, some places overrun with green jungle plants. The road was white gravel. At times it was smooth and looked like any other dirt or gravel road I'd seen, but at other times it faded to two narrow channels of rock with a grassy stripe down the middle.

After a few minutes, we began to see signs of life. Two little kids walked along the road barefoot, the girl in a skirt and tee shirt, the toddler in just a tee with a pair of bare brown buns below. They moved to the side of the road and waved and smiled at us, white teeth beautifully splitting their tan faces.

"They'll steal your hearts," Laura said. "Gosh, I'm going to miss them."

"Well, thanks for sticking around to give me an initiation," I said. "There's no way I would have known how to shop for six months at a time, and I can't imagine finding my way out here with my limited language knowledge." Laura had been a beacon of comfort in the unfamiliar surroundings. She had a matronly way of bustling about and putting everyone at ease. I could picture her in the pediatric hospital she was heading back to, providing comfort to parents and children alike.

Although many people spoke English on Majuro, I was very grateful Laura spoke Marshallese. I had tried, honestly, I had. But between having the stomach flu for three days during the immersive training in Hawaii and my chronic thick-headedness when it came to learning foreign languages, I had escaped from my language orientation knowing only "Where are you going?" "*Kwej etal ñan ia?*"[1] and "*Ejjab melele,*"[2] which meant, helpfully, "I don't understand."

Thankfully, I was going to have a translator for a few hours each morning during my basic clinic time, so I could learn about people's symptoms and better treat and teach them.

Laura had been the nurse on Arno for the previous 18 months. With her service time coming to an end, USI had sought a replacement for her, and I was the one chosen. An island with an area of a mere 5 square miles with only 2000 inhabitants spread throughout the 133 little islands surrounding the large central and two smaller lagoons was so small it didn't warrant a

---

[1] *Kwej etal ñan ia:* kway´ zhuh-tell´ ñan yah´ (you go to where?)

[2] *Ejjab melele:* eh´-chab mah lah´ lay (I don't understand)

huge hospital; but having a nurse practitioner at the clinic brought about an instant improvement to the quality of life for the locals. I would be responsible for basic health and sanitation education, family planning advice and medications, and general emergency care. For more serious injuries or trauma, the hospital on Majuro, 20 miles away, was able to send a helicopter to the airfield to pick up patients.

"That's the *Iroij's* house,"[1] Laura shouted over the rattle of the truck, gesturing at a utilitarian cement block structure a way back from the road on a slight rise. It was surrounded by a few other small houses, outbuildings, and shacks, and had a neatly kept yard covered with white gravel. "Mr. Timisen is the local governor. He speaks pretty decent English, and he has one of the two satellite phones on the island, if you need to get word to Headquarters in Majuro before your short wave radio appointment."

Where we were currently driving I couldn't see the ocean, but occasionally I would catch a glimpse of the turquoise water of the lagoon. It was surreal, beautiful, and humid. I scratched my leg; I think so far I'd counted sixteen mosquito bites, which made me grateful for the multiple cans of bug spray I had packed in one of my boxes.

As we went farther, there were more and more houses—gray brick buildings with low windows, shacks cobbled together of corrugated aluminum, plywood, and plastic sheeting, some with grass or palm branch roofs, and yards of the same white rocks.

Adults and children stared at us curiously. Laura seemed to get the lion's share of the greetings and smiles. "Miss Leenchah!" they called out excitedly. "Miss Leenchah, *iiokwe eok*!"[2]

"Leenchah?" I asked, confused. "Isn't your last name Lynch?"

"Yeah," she said. "Putting "uh" or "ay" at the end of your name is a Marshall term of endearment. You'll have to write and tell me what nickname they give *you*!"

---

[1] *Iroij:* ee-roych´ (ruler, leader)

[2] *Iiokwe eok:* yok´-way yook (I love you!). Iiokwe is similar to the Hawaiian "aloha." It means hello and goodbye as well as love.

Write. Now that was a new one. Write with pen and paper, envelopes, and stamps. Arno didn't have electricity, much less cell service or Wi-Fi. I was already panicking without my cell phone to look at for the time, the weather, the news and texts from friends. I shook my head as I looked around, barely believing this could be real. I was here, finally, on Arno.

And with that, the pickup pulled off to the side of the road, the tires making a crunching sound in the thick gravel.

There it was, my clinic! A nondescript building, boxy and white, it had an angled roof with solar panels on it and louvered windows with screens in the front. Laura hopped out and offered me a hand down from the truck.

Looking around, I saw that a small crowd had gathered. Laura spoke to the group in what sure sounded like fluent Marshallese, but of course I wouldn't know. Finally, she gestured to me and said, "Your new nurse, Miss Beecher." I could see them mentally processing the name. After a moment, a small voice piped up, "Welcome, Miss Peach-ay!"

Laura smiled. "Guess I don't have to wait to find out, Miss 'Peach-ay'!"

The crowd of men, women, and children gathered around the truck. With much greater speed than we'd loaded, the boxes were whisked out of the truck and into the apartment or the clinic as Laura directed them.

"House first, or clinic?" Laura asked. She had just been surrounded by a crowd of kids, and I realized she had been handing out chewing gum to her eager fans. "Bribery never hurts," she grinned. "I bought you some gum to share."

"Clinic, I think," I responded. "Seems more important."

Laura ushered me through the door into the clinic. Only about 20 by 20 feet, it held one small hospital bed at the back of the room and an examination table, both with curtains that could be pulled around them. There was a sink that had a pump-handled faucet next to what looked like a kerosene stove. A long counter with cupboards above and below was along one wall, and there was an old-school scale as well as an infant scale on a table next to it. One locked cupboard stood on the far wall. I assumed that contained most of the medicine which we would be able to replenish with the supply of new medications and bandages from three of the boxes we'd brought from Majuro.

"So, no running water, and no hot water?" I double-checked, still a little amazed that there were places without running water today. "Just the pump?"

"And a big tea kettle and kerosene stove," she said. "I always try to keep some water hot or warm for washing boils or cuts, but it's pretty quick to heat if you forget. They sell kerosene at Mr. Ogawa's store. Don't forget to keep yourself stocked. You've got solar powered lights, but they don't last forever, so you've got kerosene lanterns for another source of light."

Looking around the room for anything else she'd forgotten, Laura showed me the calendar and schedule on the wall. "First Monday of the month is Depo day. Depo Provera shots every three months for any women who are doing family planning. Infant mortality is higher if they don't wait long enough between pregnancies. Second Monday is well child check-ups. Third Monday is health day. You'll teach some sort of lesson on cleanliness, sanitation, or nutrition. And the fourth Monday afternoon is teen time. You can answer questions about safer sex, good dental health, things like that."

"How busy will I be?" I asked, feeling overwhelmed at the barrage of information. It wasn't like nursing was new to me, and I'd oriented on tons of different floors in hospitals. Having become a Nurse Practitioner, I was more independent and comfortable assessing and treating a whole variety of illnesses. My nervousness was exacerbated by the combination of heat, humidity, a new environment, and the underlying sense that time was passing quickly, and that Laura would inevitably be leaving me. Alone.

"Totally depends," she said. "Mondays are the busiest, of course. And you're "on" all the time, so be sure to leave a note on the door to let them know where to find you, but make sure you relax. Go snorkeling, learn to spearfish, visit families. That's probably where you'll do the best community health. Observe people in their environments and figure out which habits are causing poor health. And then, as they get to know and trust you, help them learn how best to improve their lives."

She passed the clinic keys off to me on a stretchy hot-pink curlicue cord to put around my wrist—one key for the medicine cabinet, and two keys for the door. We locked the clinic door and headed around the corner to the attached apartment.

As I stepped in the door of my new residence, I was stunned. This wasn't a house or an apartment; this was a *cabin*. A stark kitchen with open lower cabinets was to the right of the entrance. A set of shelves to my left held a can of spinach and a tin of some sort of canned meat...Spam, maybe. Beyond the pantry, a little closet area consisted of a stark bar with some hangers on it and a mirror over a chest of drawers. One twin bed and a bunkbed flanked the big window at the far end of the room which was floored with dark, unvarnished wood.

Stunned as I was by how plain the room was, I found myself drawn across the house to the window. I turned the dusty louvers to get a better view, and as I stood there, I took a deep breath. It was poster-worthy perfect. White sand melted into aqua water that deepened into teal at the center of the lagoon. Ghostly green bumps along the horizon showed where the other islands in the chain were across the lagoon. And the sky was a heartbreaking blue beyond blue, filled with white clouds.

"You will never find another place this beautiful," Laura said quietly as she came to stand by me. My nose was prickling, and my eyes were watering. "You're going to be okay," she said. I turned to her and crumpled into a hug as she patted my back. She was solid and soft, a motherly pillar of comfort.

Laura helped me unpack the cans and plastic bins of food into the pantry, helped me hang up my sundresses and make my bed with clean sheets. She showed me the well and demonstrated the best method for getting the tin bucket to fill with water; took me to see the little shower stall attached behind the apartment, open to the sky.

She took me to the outhouse, helping me use the bucket of water to flush the "real" toilet. She showed me the short-wave radio and wrote down the instructions for how to use it. As we finished each task, I could feel the passage of time and a sense of terror rising in my chest. Finally, it could be avoided no longer. A honk announced that Laura's ride back to the airport had arrived.

"Tomorrow will be awesome," she said. "You'll see all the little kids for well-child checkups, and the mamas will be sweet to you, even if they don't speak a word of English. Sharbella is supposed to show up at about nine... but realistically, she'll be here at ten. Island time, you know."

I walked Laura out to the truck and gave her a final hug.

"If you're dying for conversation in English, there are a few young guys teaching at the local school down the road that way," Laura said, gesturing indistinctly down the road. "They're also in UniServe, but they are…" she wrinkled her forehead, shook her head, and smiled. "Well, I'll let you decide how you feel about them."

She climbed into the passenger side, and the truck pulled away from the cabin, tires crunching in the gravel. I waved goodbye to Laura, standing on the doorstep of the clinic. And I spoke the words to myself again.

What the HELL was I thinking?

CHAPTER 3

Alone

S*sssshit*, that's cold!" I swore out loud as the frigid water splashed on my shoulders and streamed down my body.

"Nope. Nope. Nope. Nope..." I chanted, as I wrapped my towel around myself, grabbed my sundress off the hook, shoved my feet into my flip-flops, exited the little outdoor shower stall, and ran back into my apartment.

I hadn't thought I'd ever be cold again after the first sweltering day on Arno, after I'd sweated through the day and kept sweating through the windless night. I was obviously wrong.

I filled my cooking pot full of water and after two tries got the kerosene stove to light. Now what? I wasn't going to be pouring cold water over myself, so I needed to wait for it to boil. Standing there with my towel draped around me, I was freezing and feeling incredibly sorry for myself. I'd already taken the five-gallon bucket to the well this morning and spent a good half hour trying to fill it. Laura had said that the pump water in the clinic was from the catchment, which collected a limited supply of fresh rain water, only for drinking. For washing I needed to be using the well water.

Laura had shown me the technique to flick my wrist as I lowered the rope in the well so the coffee can "bucket" would turn on its side, sink, and fill completely with water, but I was terrible at it. I kept banging the bucket against the stone wall of the well, which was only succeeding in slowly crushing the can so it would actually hold less water.

I'd finally filled the bucket and then wrestled the forty-pound weight across the yard into my shower stall. I'd gotten undressed, trying to hang up my towel and the little sundress I had thrown on for coming outside, and then I'd grabbed the plastic bowl Laura said was to be used as a dipper and dumped the first bowlful of water over myself.

Laura had told me I could always boil some water to add to the cold well water. I hadn't thought I'd need that luxury since it was so hot on Arno. *I was wrong*, I told myself, *I totally need it.*

I could see a hint of pink in the sky over the lagoon, so I dropped my towel, pulled the dress back on, and headed outside to watch the sun rise. Certainly more beautiful than watching a pot boil, I told myself.

I strolled across the yard, approaching the beach. I'd come out here last night, when the tide was high. Now the tide was low, and the sand was pinkish white in the faint light of sunrise. Streaks of crimson, fuchsia, tangerine, and poppy filled the sky, radiating up from the horizon behind the islands on the other side of the atoll, which somehow looked closer now. In places I could see the shapes of coconut palm trees.

It was beautiful. I assumed I was alone, but then I looked off to my left. There was a dark blob on the beach a quarter mile or so away. The dark blob lengthened, and then walked back up off the beach. I glanced to my right and saw another dark blob in the distance, low to the sand, which then stood up and walked off the beach. I suddenly felt like I was intruding. I turned around and headed back to the cabin. *It was probably one of the most scenic places for a morning potty break I'd ever seen*, I thought.

I took the now-boiling pot of water out to the shower stall, poured it into my bucket, took the pot back to the house, grabbed my towel, and tried again.

This time the water was lukewarm but not unpleasant, and I gratefully rinsed the salty sweat from my body and hair before drying off and going inside to get dressed.

I made myself a disgusting and dissatisfying breakfast of instant oatmeal and powdered coffee and got ready to head to the clinic for my first day.

"Deodorant!" I exclaimed. I went over to the bunkbed and pulled out the big box I'd used for storing my extra toiletries. I'd bought enough for six months, even though I could probably get back to Majuro once or twice before then. "Deodorant... deodorant... deodorant..." I shoved different items aside until I found a three-pack of deodorant, cut the plastic wrapping, dropped the two spares back into the box, and shoved the box back against the wall. I wouldn't be smelly for my first day of work.

She had a sweet little name, "Sharbella," so I guess that's what I had expected. Instead my translator was wide and solid, middle-aged, and mannish. But she spoke English and fluent Marshallese, so that made her the most beautiful person I'd met on Arno thus far.

"Nice to meet you, Carlie," she said, as we entered the clinic. She'd brought out the white board and marker for the women to sign up for appointments, and she knew where Laura had kept the well-child records, so she assembled the binders, ready to fill with the newest figures.

When I poked my head out, the women greeted me with a cheerful chorus of "Good mo-ning, Miss Peachay!" I took a deep breath and slaughtered whatever name had been written first. "Jee-bon and Beh-tra?" I said.

The women, sitting with their babies in the grass in front of the clinic, smiled and laughed at my pronunciation.

"Shee-bon," Sharbella corrected me. "J says 'shh' in Majel."

Betra was an adorable little 11-month-old with brown eyes, wispy black hair, and a beautiful smile. She had several large circular bumps on her forehead, a centimeter or more in height. From the appearance and feel of the skin they seemed to be boils, but boils are often infected hair follicles and there was no obvious point of infection. I cleaned the skin with a warm salt compress, showing Jibon how to repeat the procedure at home, and gave her some topical antiseptic to use for cleaning Betra's skin for the next few days.

We weighed the little girl, measured her length and head circumference, and sent our first patient on her way.

When the second and third babies also had boils on their heads, I turned to Sharbella.

"Why do all the babies have boils?" I asked.

"Nutrition, and hygiene possibly? There aren't a lot of fresh fruits and vegetables available out here. Banana, papaya, breadfruit, sometimes limes, but not all the time. They don't wash babies very often. And babies can get mosquito bites, and then scratch their heads. It's very common here, and not only babies. If you look at the children's legs, you will see scars from boils. You have to make sure to wash with soap, and scrub your legs and arms with...like a *sponge?*"

"A loofah?" I asked.

"Yes," Sharbella answered.

The rest of the morning was a flurry of names and faces, adorable dark-haired babies and toddlers and beautiful mothers. Many of the women wore brightly colored polyester dresses with elasticized necklines. When they fed their babies, they just popped their whole boob out of the neck of their dress and kept on doing whatever they were doing, talking and laughing with their friends. No surreptitious covering of the baby and breast, no shuffling with nursing bras and cover-ups. Men and children walked by, and no one gave the nursing mom a second glance. It was refreshing and disconcerting at the same time.

When the last child had been weighed and measured and the record books put away, Sharbella stood and walked off heavily down the road. "See you tomorrow," she had said.

She left, and I was again alone.

After Laura had left the previous afternoon, I'd stood in bewildered paralysis in the center of my apartment for a full five minutes. But then I sprang into action. Before leaving for Majuro Laura had set off a bug bomb. *To try to cut back on the number of cockroaches*, she told me. But that meant that all the dishes stored in the open-air cupboard were misted with toxic dust. I started a pot of water so I would be able to wash them.

While the water was heating, I unpacked one of my boxes. Pictures first. One of Eric in his leather jacket and aviators in front of his '65 Mustang went on top of the dresser, joined by one of us together right after he asked me to marry him, me pointing delightedly at my ring. There was one of us cuddled up on the couch at my parents' house at Christmas, and another of us together on Guam, me in a bikini, Eric in low-slung swimming trunks with his hands on my hips. Looking at the picture, the way dark hair descended from his navel, I felt a pang of unfulfilled desire. *Suck it up, buttercup*, I said to myself. *You chose this.*

The stationery supplies went on the desk. I had stuck in a little lamp, so that went by my bed. It would be powered by the small battery that charged each day from the solar panels on the roof. A row of books would be my nighttime entertainment. I'd also brought along a box of medical resource books, but those were already in the clinic.

The water was close but not quite hot enough, so I looked through another box. Multiple bottles of shampoo and conditioner, eight boxes of tampons, boxes of soap, laundry detergent, dish soap, and *mosquito spray. Ah ha!*

I interrupted what I was doing to take the can outside and spray myself. In a few places the screens on the windows were torn, and I was continually nagged by the irritating high-pitched whine of mosquitoes flying around my ears. Sometimes I would sense the slight sting of a mosquito finishing its snack in time to kill it. More often than not, I wouldn't. Whether the mosquito earned the death penalty or not, the prick was always followed by a maddening itchy sensation and I had more pink bumps and white welts on my arms and legs than I could count. I was grateful that at least bug spray would keep the mosquitoes at bay.

I sprayed myself thoroughly, trying to turn so the wind wouldn't blow the spray into my eyes. "Tastes like evil Christmas," I muttered to myself as I accidentally got some of the "Back Woods" scented spray in my mouth.

When I looked up from violently spitting on the ground, I noticed a little girl watching me from the road. She grinned, then covered her face, slowly peeking out from behind her fingers. Finally, she seemed brave enough to approach.

"What's you name? What's you name? What's you name?" the little girl chanted rapidly three times in a row.

"My name is Miss Beecher," I responded.

"Hi, Miss Peachay!" she said.

"What's your name?" I asked her.

She pointed at herself. "Kay-tee," she said.

"Oh, Katie. Nice to meet you." I stuck my right hand out to shake hands, and she grabbed it with her left hand and swung it back and forth a few times, then dropped it.

She asked me a few questions in Marshallese, but when I couldn't answer her, she waved and meandered off. I stared after her in wonder. She couldn't have been more than four or five years old, and she was walking down the road without a parent in sight.

Back inside, the pile of dishes was next on my agenda. As I washed, rinsed, dried, and put away, my mind started wandering.

Seeing Eric's picture had brought one of our final conversations to mind. We were in our bedroom, and I was packing.

"Do you expect me to be celibate for 18 months?" Eric's tone was irritated and even slightly bitter. "I have never had the goal of practicing celibacy for a couple years when I turned 31. I certainly didn't choose the life of a priest, Carlie."

"Well, you didn't choose the life of a married man, either," I said, instantly regretting the words as they came out.

"Oh, so this is punishment, is it? Because we never set a date? Because we never signed a piece of paper, and you never wore a puffy white dress?" Eric stared at me as I came out of the walk-in closet with an armload of sundresses.

"I'm not trying to punish you, Eric. I just realized that if I don't do this now, I probably never will! And yeah, if we *were* married, I might *not* be doing it. What if we do get married and have kids? After they've been with us for 18 to 20 years and move out, we will be so settled in our lives that the thought of adventure and service will have long since faded from my memory."

Eric sighed. He'd heard this before. "I repeat," he said. "Do you expect me to remain celibate?"

I stared at him. "Well, don't you expect *me* to be faithful?"

He narrowed his eyes. "I don't think you *can.*"

"Now, what is that supposed to mean?" I asked indignantly, flopping clothes into my suitcase.

"Which one of us is it who can't seem to go longer than three or four days without sex?" he asked. "Which one of us is more likely to initiate sex?"

"I'm just an affectionate person," I protested, tugging on the zipper of the suitcase. "You're lucky I like to make you feel good, that you don't have to hunt me down, that I rarely reject you, and if I do, I make up for it. You don't seem to complain about it most of the time."

"Hmmm," Eric said, looking thoughtful. "I'm pretty sure you initiate for yourself, not just for my sake. You are too sexual for celibacy. I give you a month; and then you're going to find some dark-haired, dark-eyed, dark-skinned island man that you're dying to take to bed. And he'll take you up on it, too."

I stood there, dumbstruck, staring at him. What was I supposed to say in response?

"Just be sure to use protection," Eric said, threateningly. "We're getting tested when you come back, and I'm not sleeping with you unless you're disease-free."

I glared at him, horrified. "Do you really think so little of me? That I don't love you enough to be faithful?"

"For eighteen days, maybe," Eric said quietly, looking down at the quilt on our bed. "Maybe for eighteen weeks. But for eighteen months, Carlie, I don't think so. And if you're not going to be celibate, I don't want to be, either."

"I think you're wrong," I said. "But, let's just promise to be honest with each other. If we sleep with someone, we say so the next time we write. No details, just the word *sex*, or *not celibate*. I can write, "You were right." You can write, "Fuck you, Beecher.""

I had started crying then and Eric's face had softened slightly, though he didn't come over to hold me like I wished he would. He was too angry to take me to bed then even though I wanted him to, to show me that he forgave me, that he wanted me, that he trusted me; but later that night we made love with an earnest urgency that we hadn't had since our first year together.

It was going to be fine, I knew it. He was *wrong*. I would keep my distance from the locals. I would befriend women and children, and I would stay away from any man 18 or older, except in social situations. I would remember that I was planning to go back home, that I was engaged to marry Eric Anderson. That I loved him, and that he loved me, and that we were going to be together forever.

Still, as I finished up my packing in Majuro, I had packed one more thing—a small shiny black carton, now tucked into the cardboard box of toiletries, concealed behind the tampons and deodorant.

CHAPTER 4

Pain in the Arse

I began to wonder how my patient was doing as supper time approached that evening. Well, that wasn't the only thing. It was kind of a bummer to eat alone, and honestly I was just feeling lonely. As obnoxious as Campbell's coworkers had been they were harmless, and I just needed to be around people.

I eyed my pantry. I couldn't afford to feed other people all the time, but just once shouldn't hurt. I grabbed three cans of chili and a bag of Fritos, and then I took four of my precious apples and put them in my shoulder bag along with fresh bandages, antibiotic ointment, and Campbell's mended shorts. I threw in my flashlight in case I stayed past dark.

I felt jittery as I walked down the road. These boys weren't expecting some 27-year-old to come hang out with them at their house, though Ewan had told me I should come visit them some time. *Calm down*, I told myself. *They're boys, and you're bringing food.* I chuckled, remembering Laura's words. "Bribery never hurts," she had said. Of course, she was referring to the island children; I'd see if it worked with the island Scots as well.

A few of the kids came running out of their houses and stared at me as I walked by. Oh, that *was* the one other word I learned— "*Iiokwe!*"—Hello! I waved at the adorable little kids and called to them. Several covered their faces and giggled, but others were braver and called out, "*Iiokwe*, Miss Peachay!"

As I continued to walk, I realized I was being followed by a herd of gorgeous brown-skinned children. They trailed behind me, not close enough to engage but obviously interested in what I was doing and where I was going.

Then one little girl, probably 10 or 11 years old, came shyly up to walk by me.

"You go see Meester Mack? He is hurt?" she asked, trying out her English on me.

"Yes!" I said. "I will check his bandages. And I brought him food." I opened my bag to show her the cans.

"Is good," she smiled. "*Bōrañañ*, *Bujek* and *Koolol* are very hungry boys."[1]

"*Bo rawn' yawn?*" I asked, curiously.

"Um," she giggled. "The mamas name them because—their hair. *Bōrañañ* is mean curly hair. That is Meester Mack. *Bujek* means..." she wrinkled her forehead, then decided to show me what she meant, pulling her hair up and twisting it on top of her head.

"*Oh*," I said, "A bun. Like Mr. Ewan."

"Yes," she said, happy I had understood her. "Meester You-wan is *Bujek*."

"What was the last one?" I asked. "What do you call Mr. Graham?"

"*Koolol*," she responded. "Is mean very messy. And very hairy." She messed up her hair with her hands and smiled when I laughed.

"And what is *your* name?" I asked her. "Your English is very good."

"Riti," she said, smiling shyly. "Riti Botla."[2]

I had been anxious to visit my young Scottish neighbors just for some English conversation, but quickly decided I had found another person I could talk to. Riti was in the fourth grade, she said. And Mr. Mack was her teacher. She walked me all the way to the school and showed me around the side of the building to the guys' apartment. Then she waved and headed back down the road.

Taking a deep breath, I knocked on the door.

"What?" a grumpy voice called out. "We're off duty."

---

[1] *Bōrañañ*, *Bujek* and *Koolol*: Bo-rawn´-yawn, Boo´-check, and Cool´-ool (Curly, Bun, and Messy)
[2] Riti Botla: Ree´-tee Bot´-lah

"Ye better not be running away after knocking, ye wee urchins," came a second gruff voice. Footsteps came closer, and then Graham threw the door open so quickly it startled me.

"Oh, it's you!" he said. "Have ye come to check on your patient, then?" He turned and called out, "Campbell, the nurse is here to look at your arse." He turned back to me with a mocking smile. "He's in the back bedroom. Canna handle sitting at the moment, exactly."

He headed across the room to the couch, leaving the door open, so I came inside and shut the door.

"I didn't come to look at Campbell's arse," I retorted. "I brought supper, if you want it."

"Supper?" Ewan's head peeked around the corner, and Graham was back next to me in a flash.

"Food?" he exclaimed. "Why didn't ye say so in the first place? You wouldn't have brought us potatoes, would you?"

"Not this time," I said. "But have you ever had chili and chips?"

Ewan ushered me into their kitchen and happily provided me with a pan, a can opener, and his rapt attention as I heated up the chili, dished it into four bowls, and sprinkled the corn chips over the top. While Ewan and Graham eyed the steaming bowls skeptically, when I handed them each an apple to go along with it, they grabbed spoons, took their bowls to the table and hungrily dug in.

"Which room?" I asked, figuring I should check in with my patient, who wasn't appearing.

I knocked gently. "Come," said a husky voice. I opened the door, to find Campbell lying on his bed on his left side, still wearing the blue sarong, reading.

"It looks nice on you," I said, gesturing toward the sarong. "How are you feeling?"

"I've been better," he said, looking up from his book, then grinned and shrugged. "But I'm young. No worries."

"Have you taken any more Advil or Tylenol?" I asked. He shook his head.

"Hungry?" I asked. "Advil is better on your stomach if you eat first."

"Did I hear you brought us food?" he asked, gingerly sitting up and putting his pillow behind his back. "Ewan and Graham are pains in the arse. Ye didn't have to feed us, ye ken." He was smiling, though.

"I wanted to," I said, sitting down on the edge of the bed with my bowl as I handed him his.

Campbell crunched on a bite of the warm chili topped with corn chips. "*Yummm*," he groaned. "Salty. This something Americans eat? It's no' bad!"

"My family does it with lettuce, tomatoes, cheese, and ranch dressing on top," I explained. "We call it taco salad, an import from Mexico, sort of. Not having any of the fresh stuff, this was all I could offer."

"*Mmmm*," he murmured hungrily. "Lettuce. Cheese. Tomahtoes." His British pronunciation of the word tomatoes made me laugh. "Ye do start to miss fresh produce after a time out here."

Graham came to the door. "Campbell, are ye going to be selfish with our guest, here? First young white woman we've seen in months and ye keep her to yourself, of course."

Campbell rolled his eyes at Graham. "I can come out. Sitting isna as bad as I thought it would be." He moved to stand up, and I took his bowl from him so he had use of both his hands.

"While I'm here," I said, "I did think I'd have a look at it, just to see how the incision site and stitches are doing and to put a new bandage on. It was pretty deep in some places, and I tried to flush out any bacteria, but not having running water, I'm nervous about sanitation out here."

"See, I told ye she was here to look at your arse," Graham laughed, taking the bowls from me. "See ye in a few, but I'm coming back if you stay here too long. Honor of a lady, and all that." He closed the door.

"Graham, ye numpty," Campbell called after him, then turned to me, somewhat on edge. "Ye want me to drop my sarong?"

"*Your* sarong?" I asked, indignantly. "Are you stealing it?"

The joke set him at ease, but he was still blushing profusely.

"No," I reassured him. "I thought if you loosened the right side of the sarong and lay down on your stomach, I can have a look and keep you decent at the same time."

He followed my directions and only squirmed and grunted a little when I removed the original bandage. I inspected the incision site, cleaned it, and then applied some antibacterial ointment and a new bandage. "So far, it looks good," I said, standing up. He gently rolled off the bed and stood, and with his back to me, tucked the sarong back in at the waist again, and then turned back to me.

"The edges of the wound are all securely touching, and it looks like it's not leaking fluid. We will just have to keep an eye on it for the next few days particularly. I have no idea what might have made its way into the wound and could still be under your skin. If you start to have a fever, I'll need to give you a course of antibiotics to help fight off any infection."

I watched his gait as Campbell walked out to the front room. He looked sore but seemed to be able to put equal pressure on each leg. I grabbed an extra pillow from his bed, and then helped him arrange it underneath him so there was less pressure on his right side as he sat.

Once we were all settled on the two couches finishing up our dinners, Graham and Ewan looked at me expectantly.

"So," Ewan said, taking a big bite of his apple. "Is he going to be able to keep his arse?"

"*Wheessht,*" hissed Campbell, "I'm going to be fine."

"A day earlier, though," Graham offered, "with Miss Leenchah on Majuro, you would have been out of luck. They probably would have had to *amputate.*" He grinned at Campbell, and then smiled at me. Graham was a big guy, a little shorter and huskier than Campbell. Though his hair was slightly messy and it seemed as if his personal hygiene habits left a little to be desired, I liked his dry sense of humor.

"Is there no one else here who has any medical skill?" I asked. "That's a lot of pressure on me!"

"Not really," said Campbell. "If ye hadna been able to help me, I might have had to use duct tape." I glanced at the expression on his face to see if he was joking, but he seemed entirely serious.

I shuddered at the thought. "Well, fortunately, you didn't, and I think it's going to heal up very nicely. I'm pretty good with a needle." Thinking of that made me remember Campbell's shorts. I hopped up and went to my bag, coming back with the neatly mended pair of board shorts, as well as a cup of water and a couple of pain reliever pills.

"Wow, thanks!" Campbell said, inspecting the shorts after swallowing the pills. "Ye not only saved them, ye fixed them, too."

The three boys grinned and stared at me as I sat back down.

"You are making me *very* nervous," I said to them. "Why are you staring at me?" They looked back and forth at each other, as if they were waiting for one of them to talk.

"Well, Miss Lynch was nice," Campbell said, grinning. "But she wasna as young and bonny as you." He looked down in embarrassment as Graham and Ewan continued to grin at me.

"*Young?*" I scoffed. Laura was probably thirty-five, but at twenty-seven, I would not call myself young. "And *bonny*? I saw probably *ten* of the most beautiful women I've *ever* seen in my life today. And not *all* of them had babies," I laughed, remembering the circumstances under which I'd seen them at the well-child checkups.

"Aye, there are lots of bonny island girls here," said Ewan. "But Uncle Alastair has threatened us with death if we touch any of them."

"And just with *neutering* if we impregnate any of them," added Graham.

"*Uncle Alastair?*" I asked, incredulous. "Mr. Douglass is your uncle?" Alastair Douglass was the head of UniServe International in the Marshall Islands who was based in Majuro. I'd met the gruff, slightly fierce looking middle-aged man at the airport when I arrived in Majuro. Bald and bearded with bushy eyebrows, Mr. Douglass intimidated me from the beginning. He rarely smiled. I could see how even at a great distance, fearing his wrath could encourage better behavior among UniServe volunteers.

"Well," I said, flashing my engagement ring. "I hope you don't think that just because there's a white girl on the island that you're in any less danger from your uncle. I don't think my fiancé would like it if I got impregnated here."

It was a joke, but Campbell looked at me, stunned. I could tell he wanted to ask me something, but he stayed quiet. Ewan and Graham exchanged disappointed glances.

"Ah, well," said Graham, slouching down in his seat. "So, what do ye think of Arno?"

"It's beautiful," I answered hesitantly, taken aback by the sudden attention. "I've only been here a day, so I'm a little overwhelmed still. You've been here since the beginning of the school year at least. What do *you* think about island living?"

Graham and Ewan looked at each other giddily, and then launched into what was obviously a well-rehearsed riff.

"Well," said Graham, "I like it fine, but there *Arno* electric lights here."

"And," added Ewan, "there *Arno* running water faucets."

"Unfortunately," Graham mused, "there *Arno* flushing toilets."

"And it's kind of sad that there *Arno* refrigerators." Ewan concluded.

They laughed, but I shook my head, wide-eyed at them. "How do you survive without a refrigerator? There's no such thing as leftovers, I guess."

"Aye," said Campbell. "If you make it, ye eat it then, or throw it away. Get food poisoning once or twice, and ye learn not to eat things that have been sitting too long."

"Well," I said. "I have to admit this is all taking some getting used to. It's like stepping back in time to the days of the settlers or the Wild West."

"Settlers?" Graham asked, wrinkling his forehead.

"Oh, that's right, she's *American,*" said Ewan.

"You say that like it's a dirty word," I said to them curiously. "I've always felt positively about Scotland, even though I've never been there. Why would you hate America?"

"Says the woman whose country actually *succeeded* in winning their independence from Britain in the 1700s," said Graham.

"Aye," said Campbell. "Your minutemen and militia fought loud and fierce, exactly like the Highland army. *You* just happened to have enough trees and forests for cover. Ambush doesna work on a wide, flat field."

I looked beyond Campbell and saw that the sun had gone down and it was dark outside.

"Well, gents," I said, standing up. "I should probably be getting back to my shack."

"Thanks fer dinner," said Ewan, putting his feet up on the coffee table.

"Yes, lass, thanks," said Graham, lounging in a similarly relaxed fashion.

Campbell was looking from one of them to the other with an irritated expression on his face.

I shook my head, gathered up my bag, and walked to the door. I heard a few noises, whispering, and rustling behind me, but figured it was nothing.

I was about to close the door behind me when a hand stopped it. It was Campbell. He had on flip-flops, and as I stepped away from their doorstep, he came outside with me.

"What are you doing?" I asked.

"I'm walking you home," he said. "Graham and Ewan are lazy arses."

I shook my head. "You can't do that. You have a huge wound and lost a good amount of blood today. I'm fine. I've got a flashlight. It's not that far for me to walk, but you should definitely not be walking two miles with a recent injury!"

"Ah, lass, ye stitched me up fine," he said, taking a few slow steps forward.

"I *can't* let you do that," I said, standing firmly in place as he took another step forward toward me. "This is chivalrous of you, but I am your medical provider, and I cannot allow it."

"And I appreciate your concern for me," Campbell said, equally tenaciously. "But I know this place. There are different cultural mores here. And a lass walkin' by herself at night, now, that's just asking fer trouble. I *canna* let you go home alone."

We stood, facing each other stubbornly. Then Campbell walked toward me, passed me on the sidewalk, and kept going, calling over his shoulder. "Well, ye dinna have to walk *with* me, but I feel like taking a wee walk in the night air. I think I might go so far as the clinic."

"You are an *ass*," I said finally, "And it's *your* ass that is going to hurt tomorrow, you dimwit."

Campbell's laughter traveled back toward me through the darkness, and I hurried to catch up.

CHAPTER 5

Tuck-In Service

His flip-flops and my sandals crunched on the gravel of the road. It was dark. There was no moon. After the second time I accidentally bumped into him, Campbell put his arm over my shoulders and pulled me to his side.

"Can I use ye as a crutch, then, Miss Beecher?" he asked. I could feel him leaning some of his weight on me. He was solid and warm, and the part of me that had been hungering for contact and desperately missing Eric suddenly felt calmer as I slipped my arm around his waist.

"It's *Carlie*. And Campbell, really, if you're hurting you can go back."

"No, Carlie, I can't," he said firmly.

"Why?" I asked.

"Did they not tell you about the sexual culture in the Marshall Islands? I spent days in culture immersion when I first joined USI."

"Well, I did have the stomach flu for three days," I admitted. "Right in the middle of training. I might have missed something."

He grunted.

"Are you okay?" I asked, certain he was in pain.

"Aye," he answered. "I just dinna understand why they have a young white girl out here all by herself."

I stopped short again. "What? Campbell, that is so sexist!"

Campbell pressed me forward with his hand on the small of my back. "No, lass," he said, "It's *protective*. Their culture isna the same as ours."

"But why would that make you have a problem with a single white woman being here?" I asked.

"They assume things about foreigners, particularly about Americans. Their only exposure to American culture is through videos and DVDs. I've had students ask me, 'In Amedka, do they kiss all day?' 'In Amedka, do they fight all day?' because that's what they see on screen."

"Really? They're offended by seeing kissing onscreen? Is that so bad?" I asked.

Campbell sighed. He seemed slightly exasperated. "Okay, some background here. People in the Marshall Islands don't show affection publicly. Boyfriends and girlfriends, husbands and wives don't walk around holding hands. You might see boy students holding hands with their male friends, and girls with girls. But they don't hug, and they definitely don't kiss in public, at all."

"So they're overwhelmed by American PDA, then?" I asked, indignantly.

"Yes. And they make assumptions based on their own cultural background. Like, if anyone were to see us right now, they would assume we were sexually involved."

"What?!!" I exclaimed heatedly. "That's ridiculous!"

"In your opinion, but that's the way it is here. If they see a boy and girl walking on the beach together, they will assume they are sleeping together as well. So you have to be careful what you do."

"If that's true, then why are you walking with me? Won't that make people assume things about *us*?" Campbell was patting my shoulder as if trying to calm me down, so I took a deep breath. "Okay, explain away. I'm the outsider in this culture and I missed my cultural sensitivity training. What don't I know?"

"Yes, the locals might see us and presume certain things. But my concern is more that they assume things about *women* based on their choices. And walking alone at night is not something ye are going to be able to do, wi'out having people think that ye're a loose woman with loose morals."

"Okay, so I shouldn't walk alone at night if I want to maintain my reputation. But that's the worst thing that could happen?"

"They are a gentle culture," said Campbell. "But there have been rapes in the past. And they might not think of it as rape if you were walking alone at night. They will view your choices as *deliberate* attempts to seduce them."

Campbell couldn't see my face, so he couldn't know how furious that made me. "This is *exactly* the thing they are fighting against so hard in America. To make it clear to men that no means no, and that just because a woman is drunk or clothed in a sexy way, that it's not permission to take advantage of them."

"I will tell you this now," said Campbell soberly, "And I will probably have to tell you this again in the future. You are *not* in America. Things are *different* here. And there may be some things that seem completely black and white to you, but here, they're still gray."

"And are we supposed to just stand by and let this backwards culture stay backwards?"

"Carlie, not everything here is bad. Not everything in America or Scotland is good."

I huffed in frustrated response.

"For example, do you know what the Majel people call Americans?" he asked.

"No," I retorted hotly.

"*Ri-pālle*," he said. "Do you know what it means?"[1]

"Of *course* not," I said grumpily.

"It means selfish white person, basically," he said. I tried to pull away from him, but he had enough weight resting on me that it was impossible. "In your cultural training, did they mention that you should never compliment something when you are a visitor at someone's home?"

"No," I said. "Why not? There's nothing rude about that!"

"Because in this culture if you admire something they will *give* it you. Just give it to you. A compliment isn't just a compliment. They are generous to a fault and if you like something of theirs, it's yours."

---

[1] *Ri-pālle*: rrrri-pol´-lay (European in nationality)

"Well, that's just *weird*," I grumbled.

"To you," he said. "Not to them. Ownership is much more fluid here. I saw one colorful floppy sun hat travel from student to student in my class one week. I had *no idea* who owned it."

"That's got to be terrible for keeping lice in check!" I said.

"Aye. They don't even try," he responded, a smile in his voice. "But after a while, you're going to start to realize that in developed countries we have way too much and we're not grateful for any of it. And the simple things here are amazing. Just remember that you've come here to help them, not completely change them. Arno does not need to *be* America."

We walked in silence, and slowly my agitation faded.

"I'm sorry if I'm being whiny, Campbell," I said finally. "Everything here is so new and foreign."

"*Dinna fash*, lass," he said. "It's your second day here. Of course, you're feeling overwhelmed. I willna take anything you say personally right now."

"Well, how long have *you* been here?" I asked.

"Alastair is my uncle, and I came to Majuro from Scotland when I was eighteen. I was getting in trouble back at home, ungrateful little wretch that I was, so they shipped me off to help me learn to be grateful for what I had."

"Did it work?" I asked.

Campbell gave a scoffing laugh.

"And Arno, and teaching?"

"Well, I finished my schooling at the College of the Marshall Islands on Majuro, and once I turned 21, I was old enough to officially join USI. This is my second year of teaching."

"So that makes you..."

"Twenty-two," he answered. "How old are you?"

"It's not polite to ask a lady her age," I said jokingly. I could tell he was waiting, but I didn't answer.

"Now, ye said ye're engaged," he said. "What's your bloke's name?"

"Eric," I said.

"And where is he?"

"Back home, in Denver."

"And he doesna mind his fiancé being gone from him for 18 months?"

"Depends what you mean by '*mind*,'" I said. Wisely, Campbell stayed silent.

The little solar-powered external light of the clinic was ahead. Campbell walked me the rest of the way to my apartment door, waited as I got my key out and unlocked it, and smiled as I entered my apartment.

"Good night, Miss Peachay," he said with a wink.

"Goodnight, *Bōrañañ*," I said.

His eyes widened and he smiled in surprise. "The *mamas* call me that! 'Curly', right? How did ye know it?"

"Riti helped me find the school," I said. "She said, *Bōrañañ*, *Bujek*, and *Koolol* were hungry boys!"

His face brightened. "She's my favorite, that one. So smart!" Campbell turned back towards the school, wincing slightly.

"You're a gentleman, Campbell MacReid," I said. "Goodnight." I watched him as he walked away, until the darkness swallowed his muscular, skirted form.

I entered my empty apartment and sighed. For just a little while I had forgotten everything. For a moment I hadn't felt so horribly alone.

I opened the louvers of the window that faced the *iar* and looked out at the sliver of moon that was rising over the islands on the other side of the lagoon. A slight breeze came in as I peeled off my clothes and pulled on a tank top and shorts for sleeping. Once I was dressed, I flicked on the little lamp by my bed. Laura had told me lamps didn't seem to drain the solar batteries like the overhead lights did.

At first, I didn't hear it. The second time, I recognized the sound, a light tap on the door.

I walked over to the door, and the taps came again. "Carlie? It's just Campbell," a voice said, muffled by the wood.

I opened the door. Campbell stood outside, a sheepish smile on his face. He stood there for a moment, looking down at me. Then he said, "I had the feeling—no worries, just send me away if I'm wrong—but I had the feeling that ye could use a hug."

My nose and eyes stung, and I could feel my eyes filling with salty tears. "Yes," I nodded, stepping toward him. I cried as he pulled me to his chest, overwhelmed by the stress and the newness that had been weighing on me, the fear of being alone, and the gratitude for a real friend here.

Campbell was warm, both solid and soft at the same time. He encircled me with his arms and held me close. I could hear his slow, steady heart under my ear. For the first time since arriving, I felt myself release my breath fully. I felt safe.

It wasn't a casual, keep-your-distance side hug, or an awkward A-frame barely-touching hug. It was a warm, affectionate, loving hug, the kind of hug I used to get from my mom when I'd had a horrible day at school. It was both familiar and foreign at the same time; Eric wasn't one for frequent hugs.

I was still quietly crying when Campbell released me from the hug and led me over to my bed by the hand. Were it not for our recent conversation I might have been very wary, but all he did was sit down, draw me onto his lap, and put his arms around me again, patting my back and murmuring in some strange foreign language—*is there such a language as Scottish?*—while he held me. "It's okay, hen. *Dinna fash, mo chridhe.*"

"Campbell, I don't want to hurt you," I sniffled, attempting to stand.

"I barely feel it, lass," he responded. He drew my head to his shoulder and ran his fingers through my hair. Somehow the tender gesture and his gentle touch made me cry even harder.

When I had finally stopped weeping, he still held me. I knew I should at least get off his lap and sit next to him, that I should think about his injury; but I could not leave his arms.

"What is it that you're grieving most? Are ye missing your Eric?" he asked.

"Yes. And I'm just...I'm scared. I have never...lived *alone*," I said.

"Never?" he asked in surprise.

46

"I've never even slept in a room by myself for more than a week. When I was growing up, I shared a room with my sister. In college, I always had a roommate, and then Eric and I moved in together. I just feel so lonely here."

"So back in America ye live with Eric?" he asked.

"Yeah," I responded.

"Ye arna married, though?"

"No," I responded defensively. "But we're *engaged*."

"Huh," he grunted. He looked at my cleavage, and then saw me looking at him looking at me and flushed in embarrassment. "So that means ye..."

"Sleep together?" I offered. "Yes. Kind of judgy, aren't you?"

"I'm no' trying to be," he said, slowly shaking his head. "I just grew up with a devout Catholic mum. I *ken* people live together nowadays."

"Are you *still* Catholic?" I asked.

"Aye," he said with certainty, looking at me as if that was a ridiculous question to ask. Then he chuckled and shook his head. "If ye had grown up havin' to confess to Father Kelly, as I did, ye wouldna ever choose to live in sin."

I scoffed at his word choice, but he continued, confused. "I just wonder, if Eric is used to living with ye and *being* wi' ye... he canna be too happy to have ye leave him for 18 months, ye so bonny and..." he had been looking at my body again, and he looked away, blushing, as his voice trailed off.

As Campbell spoke of living in sin, I had become increasingly aware that I was in a skinny strapped tank and tiny shorts, and this young man wearing a sarong with nothing under it was having a distinct response to my nearness, state of undress, and the current topic of conversation. I was feeling warm and alert myself; the prospect of spending eighteen months celibate suddenly striking me with its full gravity.

I gingerly got up off his lap. "I think it's time for you to go," I said, holding my hand out to him to help him up.

"Aye," Campbell responded, nodding, eyes wide, his hands resting on his lap.

I stood there expectantly, and he flushed.

"I'm no' trying to be disrespectful," he said. "And I *am* going to go. But I need a minute."

I looked at him, realized what he meant, and suddenly burst out with a hiccupy laugh.

"What?" he asked, looking slightly offended.

"I'm sorry," I said. "I just thought of a joke."

"Aye?" he asked.

"It's a pun."

"I know what those are," he said, exasperated. "Are ye going to *tell* me?"

I shook my head apologetically. "I'm sorry. It's silly. It's late. I'm *tired.*"

"I can take a wee joke," he said, one side of his lips rising in a lopsided grin. "Even if it's at my expense."

I smiled and pointed at the sarong around his hips.

"I was just going to say... I think it's **sarong** time to be wearing that." I grinned.

He stared at me, then looked down at himself. Then as the light dawned on him, he shook his head and chuckled.

"Ye are a cheeky one, aren't ye?" He finally stood and drew me in for another hug, resting his chin on my head.

"The thing I miss more than anything leaving Scotland?" he said. "Hugging my sister Isla. She's just your height. Wee and feisty like ye, too." He paused, then spoke good-naturally, "Though hugging her doesna affect me the same way, thankfully."

"I need hugs, too, so we may have to be hug buddies, then," I said. "We'll just have to keep it in private. And hug for shorter periods of time." I squeezed him, and then let go.

"Thank you so much, Campbell," I said, as I saw him off at the door. "I really needed a friend here."

I sighed, locked the door, turned off the light, and curled up in my bed, sleeping as peacefully as if I was still held in Campbell's strong arms.

CHAPTER 6

Night Noises

At night in Denver, the sounds we would hear were city sounds: cars and buses, sirens, machinery, and music. And when he was asleep, but I wasn't, I would hear Eric's gentle snore.

Eric and I still lived in the townhouse we had been able to afford on his teaching salary. Though we now made more as nurse practitioner and professor than nurse and adjunct, we had worked to pay off school loans, assuming when we married, we'd permanently commit to a home as well as each other.

It wasn't an expensive townhouse, and yet it effectively muffled those city sounds with double-paned vinyl windows, venetian blinds and drapes, carpeting to curb echoes, and always a fan or white noise machine to cover up the sound remnants that made it through.

There was no such barrier on Arno. For one thing, the only source of cooling was the breeze off the *iar*, so the louvered windows were opened, especially at night, to let the air in. Even when closed, louvers did little to block sound.

The first night as I lay in bed, I was struck by the eerie lack of the sounds of civilization. No cars or public transportation, no music, save for the random child carrying a guitar down the road, nothing in the house powered by electricity—no refrigerator humming, no fan, no pumps or toilets running.

In the silence I started to hear other, softer sounds: the lap of small waves on the lagoon shore, palm and pandanus branches rustled by the wind, the low murmur of my nearest neighbors talking.

My brain worked to catalogue unfamiliar sounds: the high-pitched whine of a mosquito buzzing around my ears, the random crack and creak of my unfamiliar apartment.

One strange sound I could not place, though. It sounded like the chirp of a small bird, and it was coming from the rafters above my bed. From a similar location, I heard a strange slapping. It seemed to follow a pattern: *Chirp, chirp, cheep, cheep, slap-slap-slap-slap-slap.*

Finally, my curiosity piqued, I went and turned on the light. It didn't illuminate the rafters entirely, so I added the beam of my flashlight. When I found the source of the noise, I laughed. Two huge amber-colored lizards were mating on my rafter. They would chirp and cheep, sweet talking each other, and the slapping was caused by their tails beating against the metal roof as they lost themselves in the throes of gecko passion.

I turned off the lights, reassuring myself that while they might drop little offerings of poop down (so *that's* what I'd found on the table at supper time!) at least they'd be up there catching mosquitoes.

It had gotten easier to fall asleep in the past week. The sounds were becoming familiar, and the lapping ocean waves were the best white noise machine I'd ever had.

I was currently lying in bed trying to think through the events of the past six days. I had flown out with Laura on Sunday, moving my stuff into the apartment and clinic, watching Laura leave, and then cleaning and unpacking.

On Monday, I had met Sharbella and done well-child checkups in the morning. In the afternoon I'd had my first emergency case when Campbell had arrived with his corrugated tin boat wound. That night I had taken food to the UniServe boys at the Ine school. Campbell had walked me home, and I'd made my first friend out here.

On Tuesday I had stitched up the hand of one man who cut himself with his machete attempting to split coconuts. This man had gotten distracted, the blade had slipped, and he had a deep cut in the pad of his thumb.

On Wednesday, I had focused on re-organizing and familiarizing myself with everything in the clinic. I spent some time sanitizing the surfaces, and then read up on tropical climate skin ailments and treatments. That was most of what I saw: people dealing with rashes, boils, burns, cuts and scrapes.

On Thursday Jibon had brought Betra back because the boil had come to a head from the daily salt compresses. I lanced the boil as close to her hairline as possible, drained it, and then applied a sterile dressing with a warning not get it dirty or wet.

But now it was finally Friday night, and after an exhausting week, I was looking forward to not having clinic hours on Saturday—of being able to sleep in, explore the island, brainstorm some better meals, and possibly do my laundry. I was feeling a little anxious about that process, having never washed clothing completely by hand before. I had the big round red tub, the washboard and the scrub brush, plus a laundry line and clothes pins for drying everything. I would need to draw water from the well, and then it would just be an investment of time.

I had fallen into bed mentally and physically exhausted, with a sweet sense of anticipation knowing I would get rest and relaxation the next day. I was almost asleep when I heard a new sound, one that instantly made my heart rate increase and my muscles tense. Outside the window right next to my bed I heard quiet footfalls and a rustling sound.

And then I heard singing. Sort of. It was a tune so distinct, I could plunk it out on a piano if I needed to. It was in a sweet voice, singing a sweet tune, but it made me feel more like I was hearing the haunting little kid voice singing a nursery rhyme in a horror movie trailer.

"Miss Peachay, I want to talk to you," sang a heavily accented male voice. "Miss Peachay, I want to talk to you..." I froze in my bed, the throb of panic in my chest, breathing shallowly.

A different voice came closer, nearly in my ear, just speaking this time, softly, enticingly. "Miss Peachay, do you want to go to shungle with me?"

Go? To the jungle? I lay in my bed, petrified.

"Miss Peachay! *Kwo lukkuun likatu!*"[1]

---

[1] *Kwo lukkuun likatu:* kwoh loo´-koon lee´-kah-too (You are very beautiful)

"Miss Peachay! *Kwo kōnaan bwebwenato?*"[1]

My troubadours began serenading me again. "Miss Peachay, I want to talk to you...Miss Peachay, I want to talk to you."

I didn't want to say anything. What could I say? Go away? I don't want to go to the jungle with you?

I was about to announce that I had no intention of talking to them or going to the 'shungle' with them when I heard another voice. A deep, resonant Scottish brogue, hearty, confident, and calm, speaking fluent Marshallese.

"*Enana kainne*, Abner.[2] Miss Peachay *ejab kōnaan etal ippam.*[3] *Ta ne kwoj jerbale*, Samson?[4] *Kwoj jooko ne ej kadek.*"[5]

The other men answered, talking back and forth. I heard all the voices retreating, traveling farther and farther down the road toward the UniServe school, and then it was silent. I listened to see if Campbell was coming back, but I heard nothing. I couldn't understand why I was disappointed. I had already gone to bed. I hadn't wanted the company of the men outside my window. Why would I want Campbell?

I was just relaxing, on the edge of slumber, when I heard a different noise. The crunch of gravel, then rubber slapping on wood, paired with a creaking sound. Flip-flops? On my steps? A long moment of silence, then another creak and a rattling sound. Someone was on my doorstep, and he was trying to turn my doorknob.

I was *almost* certain the door was locked. I knew I'd locked it when I came in from going to the bathroom before bed. Hadn't I? Frantically, I thought

---

[1] *Kwo konaan bwebwenato:* kwoh koh-non´ bway-bway-nah´-toe (Do you want to talk?)

[2] *Enana kainne:* in-nah´-nah kine´-nay (What you're doing is wrong).

[3] *Ejab konaan etal ippam:* eh´-chab koh-non´ eh-tal´ eep´-em. (She doesn't want to go with you).

[4] *Ta ne kwoj jerbale:* tah´ nay kwoh jer-bah´-lay? (What are you doing).

[5] *Kwoj jooko ne ej kadek:* kwoh shoo´-koo nay edge kah´-deck. (You do bad things when you are drunk.)

over everything I owned. Did I have anything in here that would be a good weapon? Sundresses, shoes, a towel? A book. A frying pan!

I sat up in bed, ready to run if I needed to. Where would I go? Could I run a mile to the UniServe school? I threw my feet over the side of the bed and crept across the floor, scrabbling for my sandals at the door. I was panting, nearly hyperventilating. "*I can't run in flip-flops!*" I whimpered to myself, not realizing I'd spoken out loud.

"*Ri-pālle?*" The deep voice came through the door. "Carlie, is that you?"

"Campbell?!! Dammit, Campbell!" I exclaimed, opening the door. "You gave me a freakin' heart attack!"

"Sorry, lass," he chuckled, stepping away from the door. "I escorted your drunk friends away but thought I should check your door to make sure it was locked in case any of them tried to bother ye again tonight. I thought ye were asleep, and I didna want to bother you."

"I'm quite awake, thanks to you," I said, looking around. "Do you want to come in?"

"Sorry, *Ri-pālle*," he said. "I think ye should close the door."

I moved to come outside, and he shook his head. "No, Carlie. Shut the door—wi' you on the inside, and me on the outside."

"*What?*" I asked, confused.

"I dinna want the island men to think if they just stay longer, they'll get invited in." He reached for the door knob and started to pull the door closed.

"But Campbell, my heart is still pounding. I'm not going to be able to go to sleep."

"Ye dinna need to be afraid," he said reassuringly, as he inched the door the rest of the way closed. "I'm no' going home yet. I will sit on your doorstep awhile 'til I'm sure they won't come back."

I stood inside my apartment with the door closed in front of me for a frustrated second, and then I turned around, leaned against the door and slid down until I was sitting with my back against it.

"Why were they here? What did they want?" I asked. For a moment I wondered whether he'd be able to hear me, but quickly realized the door was hollow faux wood, with a gap at the bottom—and the two louvered windows to either side were completely open to the night air.

"What did they say?" Campbell asked. The door moved slightly against my back as he sat down on the other side.

"They said they wanted to talk to me or go to the jungle with me," I said. "They asked nice, but it freaked me out."

"Both mean about the same thing..." Campbell said, the door vibrating from his husky voice. "And I'm sure you can guess what that is."

I *could* guess. "What did *you* say to them?" I asked.

"Dinna remember, really. That what they were doing wasn't good. That you didn't want to go with them. And I told them they make poor choices when they're drunk."

"They were drunk?" I asked.

"Most definitely," said Campbell. "They wouldna be bothering ye if they were *sober*. Abner and Samson are decent enough men. They came stumbling by our house and told Graham they were going to visit ye. I didna want to confront them if they decided better, so I walked along the beach, matched their pace, and came out here when it was obvious they werena leaving ye alone."

"Thank you," I said. "That was weird. I hope that doesn't happen again."

"Well," said Campbell, slowly. "I canna promise that. I'm surprised Laura didna mention the nighttime visitors."

"That happens a lot?" I asked, stunned. "What do I do next time, when you aren't here to send them away?"

"I could teach you what to say.   Do ye want to learn some Majel?" Campbell asked.

"Okay," I responded agreeably.

"What do ye ken already?"

"I know '*eh jab' ma lay' lay*,'" I said.

"Okay. 'I don't understand.' That's a good one to know, but not helpful here. What else?"

"Um. *Kway' zhuh tal' non yah'*!"

"Hmmm. Excellent, if you want to ask them where they're going, though they already announced they would like to go to the jungle," he laughed.

"Okay, then what should I say?" I asked.

"*Ijab kōnaan* is pretty easy," Campbell said. "That means 'I don't want to,' or 'I don't want it.'"

"*Ee jab coh non*," I repeated. "*Ee jab coh non.*"

"That's really good," he said encouragingly. "Another thing you could say is *Kwō etal wōt*. That means 'you should go away.'"

"*Kwo' eh tall' what.*" I said, repeating it several times to try to get it in my memory.

"Good," Campbell said. "But you should say *something*, even if you say it in English. They're kind of persistent."

"So, let me get this straight," I said irritably. "I can't walk alone at night, though now I'm pretty sure I don't *want* to, but guys can just come to my house and try to seduce me through the window?"

"Or door," said Campbell. The door jiggled as he laughed. "I'm just joking, *Ri-pālle*," he murmured.

"You called me that *again*," I said. "Isn't that the word that means selfish white person?"

"Aye, *Ri-pālle*."

"*Rrrri pol'-lay?*" I repeated. "You're *really* going to call me selfish white person?"

"I dinna truly *mean* it that way," he said. "And are ye saying ye arna one?"

I scoffed. "Well, maybe I am, but why call me that?"

"It's a pretty word. I get to roll an 'r' at the beginning."

I laughed with a sudden realization. "That's why you Scots feel so at home in the Marshall Islands," I said. "You're the only two cultures I know that roll their 'r's' so often!"

Campbell laughed. "You wouldna think we were on exact opposite sides of the globe, would ye? So, you've finished your first week here. Is it like you thought it would be?"

"Yes and no," I said. "Some days I'm barely busy at all, while other days I almost can't catch a breath between patients."

"What do you see most of?" he asked.

"Boils and other skin ailments," I answered. "I end up giving stitches quite often as well. I'm getting even faster at it."

"What's the worst thing you dealt with this week?" Campbell asked.

I chuckled. "Well, I had this one patient... he like, fell on some corrugated tin and got this *horrific* cut across his ass."

Campbell laughed. "Are ye serious? Sounds like he must be an incredible klutz."

"He must be," I responded. "It took 18 stitches to close up the wound."

"Eighteen stitches across his hairy white arse?" Campbell suggested.

"I don't know that *those* are the first words that come to mind," I joked back, unable to keep from picturing sculpted muscle.

"Nurse *Beecher!*" he responded in shocked horror.

"Speaking of which," I said, "how does the wound seem to be doing? You should probably come in on Monday for me to check it. That will have been a week."

"Should I bring along a chaperone?" he asked. "Since you're going to have me take my trousers off?"

I scoffed. "Sure, Campbell, *bring* Ewan."

"I was just askin'," Campbell chuckled. "But I dinna think I'll bring him. I think I can place my arse in your hands with confidence."

"My interest in your arse is *purely* professional," I assured him.

From the other side of the door I heard an unmanly giggle, followed by a huge yawn. "Well, *Ri-pālle*," he said. "I'm tired. What are ye doing tomorrow?"

"Laundry, I think," I said, his yawn contagiously spreading to me. "And you?"

"Can I come visit ye in the light?" he asked.

"That'd be nice," I said. "Goodnight, Campbell."

"Goodnight, Carlie." I got up from the floor and listened to the sound of Campbell's flip-flops crunching in the gravel, my young protector heading home.

CHAPTER 7

Dirty Laundry

In our five years of living together since becoming engaged, Eric and I had fallen into a comfortable division of labor. Eric, having more of the business acumen, took care of the budget. I had more of a talent for cooking, so I did the lion's share while Eric was an excellent doer of dishes, pots, and pans. He took care of the vehicle maintenance, and I took care of the home. And somehow doing laundry had fallen to me; sorting clothing, switching loads, hanging up shirts out of the dryer, matching socks and neatly folding underwear, and putting tee shirts and jeans into our drawers.

When I woke up Saturday morning, the wind was whipping the curtains away from my window. I peeked outside. Though there were a few clouds moving quickly through the sky, it was sunny and already warm.

"Laundry time!" I said, to psych myself up. I had a plastic laundry basket already filled with the clothes I had worn so far this week, so I pulled out the laundry soap and carried my basket to the grass close to the well, where I found a place in the shade to set up my laundry room. On my next trip I brought out the red wash tub, the one by two-foot[1] scrub board made of wood, and the stiff scrub brush.

Once I'd put my laundry into the tub, I went to the well and wrestled with the coffee can bucket until I'd drawn my first five gallons, which I poured over the clothes and soap. I swished everything around and then sat down cross-legged facing the tub, pulling the skirt of my sundress to cover my knees. I leaned the scrub board against the side of the tub, grabbed the first

---

[1] 30 x 60 cm

item, which happened to be a pair of panties, slapped it onto the board, and then scrubbed it a little with the brush. I didn't want to completely wear out the fabric, so I kept my motions reasonably gentle, but I could see how the brush and board got the soapy water thoroughly through the fabric.

I had just picked up the panties to wring them out, when a deep male voice behind me said, "Well, hello there, *Ri-pālle!*" I thrust the panties back into the water.

"How're ye going to know which ones ye've already washed?" Campbell asked curiously, squatting in front of me. He grinned at my flushed cheeks. "I've *got* a sister," he said. "Those arna the first knickers I've ever seen."

"I wouldn't think they would be," I said. "I'm just not used to doing laundry out in the open." I pulled the panties out of the water, wrung them out, tossed them into the laundry basket, grabbed the next item of clothing, and continued the operation.

"A sister?" I asked. "How many kids in your family?"

A slight shadow crossed Campbell's face. "Just Isla, now," he said. "I had a younger brother Matthew, but he died five years ago."

"Is Isla older or younger?" I asked, scrubbing away as we talked.

"Older by two years, but she thought she was the boss of me from the time I popped out of my ma."

"Where does she live?"

"Still in Scotland," he said. "Married to my good friend Duncan. And how about you? Sisters or brothers?"

"I'm the second of four," I said. "Older sister Amy, younger brother Seth, and little sister Shelly."

"But not Catholic?" he asked curiously, smiling over at me.

"No, my parents just like kids," I said, focusing on scrubbing.

Campbell was smiling at me when I glanced up at him.

"What?" I asked.

"Ye're concentrating so hard," he said. "It's funny."

"Hey, this is new to me," I said. "When I go shopping, if an item says, 'hand wash only,' I put it back on the rack. This is like being in 'Little House on the Prairie!'"

There was no recognition on his face. "You know, '*Little House on the Prairie*?'" I repeated, then suddenly realized, "Oh, that's totally an *American* kids' book. It's about the westward expansion and a pioneer family who lived on the prairie."

"What's a prairie?" he asked, glancing beyond me to the lagoon, where the wind was whipping the waves into white caps.

"Oh, a grassland, in the middle part of America where it's pretty flat. They call it the 'breadbasket' of the states because most of the grain is grown there."

"Ah," Campbell said. "We dinna have prairies in Scotland, but we have the highlands. And moors."

"What books did you grow up reading? Is there *Scottish* literature?" I asked.

Campbell smiled. "Really? D'ye think we Scots are *completely* uncivilized? When we were growing up my mum always read us the Katie Morag books, about a little lass wi' ginger hair from Scotland. Because Isla was older I had a lot more books about girls than boys read to me. And Robert Louis Stevenson is Scottish, so I read Treasure Island. J.M. Barrie, who wrote Peter Pan was Scottish. J.K. Rowling wrote the Harry Potter books while living in Edinburgh."

"Oh, I read those, too—but I hadn't heard of Katie Morag..." I watched him squat there, almost sitting on his heels, his elbows on his knees. "Hey," I asked, "aren't your legs getting tired?"

"*Ejab*," he said.[1] "I mean, no. This is the way people sit here. Keeps your bum from getting dirty."

"Really?" I said. "Looks extremely uncomfortable."

"Try it," he said.

---

[1] *Ejab*: eh´-chab (no)

"I can't squat in a dress," I answered skeptically, "Wouldn't be decent!"

"Aye, ye can," he said. "Ye stand up, gather your skirts tight behind your legs, and then toss the extra fabric down between your knees in the front."

"And *you* know about how to squat in dresses because?"

"First, because I'm a Scot," he said, bright blue eyes twinkling. "Any self-respecting Scot has had a kilt on a time or two at least. And second, because I've seen almost every Majel woman here squat that way."

Game for a challenge, I stood up, gathered my skirts up tightly and dropped them between my knees as I squatted. It was very decent, but not a particularly comfortable position to maintain. After a minute or so I went back to my seated location on the ground, only to discover that my washtub appeared to be leaking and I'd just sat down in some sudsy dirt. *I should probably have kept squatting*, I thought.

"Ye'll figure it out with some practice," Campbell said encouragingly. As I continued to scrub, he watched me. "Can I get you some rinse water?" he asked.

"That would be helpful," I responded. "I don't have the knack for drawing water from the well yet." Campbell smiled, grabbed the big bucket, and left me to get the water. While he was gone I scrabbled for my other panties and bras in the water and washed them as quickly as I could. I was almost ready for the rinse water, scrubbing and sloshing my towel around, when Campbell came back.

When I was about to toss the towel into the laundry basket, Campbell reached out his hand. "Ye should wring it out," he said. "Ye dinna want all the soap getting into your rinse water." I stood, and Campbell took one end of the towel while I held the other, twisting in opposite directions to get as much of the water out as possible.

To rinse I just sloshed the clothes around in the clean water and then drained them, pulling them out of the water and slopping them into the laundry basket. Campbell picked up the laundry basket while I dumped the water out of the wash tub and then followed me as I walked around the house to the two laundry lines. Without asking if I needed help, he started grabbing clothes from the basket and wringing them out, taking the dresses, shirts, and skirts and hanging them up on the line with the clothespins. He kindly left the bras and panties to me.

We worked in companionable silence as the wind whipped the laundry around. Finally, I looked at him curiously. "Is it weird that we're not talking?" I said.

"I think it just means we dinna feel nervous around each other," Campbell said, shrugging his shoulders as he clipped another dress to the line. "Sometimes people prattle on to fill silences. I think it's a better measure of friendship if ye can be quiet together, too."

His musings made me smile, and I went back to the calming monotony of twisting, wringing, hanging, and handing things to Campbell. The whole process was very therapeutic, and when the job was done, with the clothes bobbing away on the line in the wind, I smiled at him. "Thank you, Campbell," I said.

"So, you want to go *bwebwenato* with me?" he asked.[1]

"That's what one of those guys said last night," I said, narrowing my eyes at him. "You're not asking me to go to the 'shungle,' are you?"

"Nah," he grinned. "*Bwebwenato* means talk or visit. I thought we could go for a walk and visit some different families today. D'ye have any other chores you needed to do?"

"No, just need to wait for the clothes dryer," I said, gesturing toward the clothesline with a smile. "Who should we visit?"

"Have you met your next-door neighbors?" Campbell pointed through the palm trees and bushes to the house we could see there.

"Not yet," I said, somewhat embarrassed that a week had gone by without introducing myself to anyone but the patients who had come to the clinic.

"Well, then, that's a good place to start." Campbell led the way to the road, the few steps to the next property over, and then he called out, "*Iiokwe, Anni? Kona?*" as we walked toward the house. A girl, probably in her mid-to-late teens, came out of the low door.

"Meester Mack!" she said. "Hi, Miss Peachay."

----

[1] *Bwebwenato*: bway´-bway-nah´-toe (talk, visit)

Well, we might not have met, but she knew who I was.

"This is Anni," he told me. "She's graduated from the school. Her father Kona is a fisherman who works out on the docks."

The girl smiled shyly at me. "You want some coconut?" she asked me.

"Sure," I said. One thing I had gained from my cultural training was that it was rude to refuse hospitality in the Marshall Islands.

"Meester Mack, can you climb?" she asked, pointing up a coconut tree to the large green oblongs up at the top. They looked nothing at all like the small round brown coconuts I'd seen at the grocery store.

Campbell eyed the tree, then gripped the trunk with both hands on the far side of the tree from him and basically walked up the tree, advancing his hands up the trunk at the same time. I had no idea how he did it and exchanged glances of astonishment with Anni.

Anni was smiling at me. "Meester Mack is *lakatu, dipen, y aetoktok*,"[1] she said. "Handsome. Strong. And tall. Yes?"

"Yes," I said, watching him as he reached the top, clutched the tree with his thighs, and then tossed down three coconuts.

"*Ej jeram?*" she asked curiously.[2]

"*Ejab malele*," I said. "I don't know what that means."

"*Jeram* means boyfriend," Anni explained. "Is he your boyfriend?" she again asked, eyeing me curiously.

"No," I said, with a chuckle.

"I see him helping you *kwakol nuknuk*. Washing clothes. *Ej jerbal in kora*.[3] That's woman's work. And he help you."

"Not my boyfriend, though," I said, trying to mask my discomfort. "He's just a friend."

---

[1] *Lakatu, dipen, y aetoktok:* lah´-kah-too, dee´-pen, ee eye-tok´-tok (handsome, strong, and tall)

[2] *Ej jeram:* edge share´-ram? (Is boyfriend?)

[3] *Kwakol nuknuk:* kwah´-call nook´-nook. *Ej jerbal in kora:* Edge sure´-ball en core´-uh (wash clothes, is work for women)

"I hear him talk to you," she said with a skeptical smile and raised eyebrows. *"In boñ. At night."*[1]

"Not a boyfriend," I repeated, smiling and shaking my head as Campbell approached, three smooth green coconuts in his arms.

Anni walked a few paces, grabbed a machete, and came back with it. Campbell took the machete, held one coconut at an angle in his hand, and repeatedly hacked off little bits of the outer fibrous husk until it exposed a section of pale brown. Then with one final slice, he exposed a gelatinous white substance underneath. Taking the tip of the machete, he cut through the white material, and handed the coconut to me.

"It's young coconut," he said. "Try drinking the coconut juice."

Hesitantly, I lifted the coconut to my mouth. The liquid inside was cool, sweet, and almost fizzy. I couldn't decide whether I liked it, but after mostly drinking water, it was more interesting, to be sure. I handed it back to Campbell, who guzzled it down and then completely cut the coconut in half.

"You can scrape out the meat," he said, demonstrating how to use a fingernail to free the flesh inside from the shell. Again, this was nothing like the brown store coconuts, with their thick, hard coconut meat inside the solid shells. This stuff was more like Jell-O, only a quarter of an inch thick or less, just a sweet, soft, jelly-like substance. I'd never really liked coconut, but I liked this. Campbell opened the other two coconuts, giving one to Anni, and offering me another sip from his before he drank.

After visiting with Anni, we wandered down the road, stopping to visit people along the way. I couldn't remember half of the names, and while some of them spoke English, other ones did not. We were fed banana bread, roasted breadfruit, salted fish, and more coconut. Then Campbell showed me Mr. Ogawa's store, where I could find some basic canned goods if I ran out as well as candy bars in the refrigerator if I had a chocolate craving. The store was one place on the island that used a generator for constant electricity. I felt jealous of their refrigerator.

From there we walked out to the dock on the ocean side. The water was much darker there than the lagoon. When I asked Campbell why, he said,

---

[1] *In boñ*: In bong (night)

"You remember them talking about the drop-off in *Finding Nemo*?"[1] At my nod, he explained, "The outer edge of an atoll has a steeper drop-off than the lagoon. We can take you snorkeling out here some time to show you, if you want. Of course, this is where tiger sharks have been spotted, so we tend to snorkel in the lagoon more." I shuddered at the thought.

Campbell turned and looked at me as I gazed across the open ocean in silence. "Are ye missing your Eric, then?" he asked.

"Yeah, it's strange to have been away from him this long," I said. "But I've been too busy for missing, I guess."

"So, if ye dinna mind me asking," Campbell said, "why USI? And why now? When you've been virtually married for five years?"

"It's just something I've wanted to do forever. We hadn't gotten pregnant and we weren't married yet, so I figured now was the time."

"But you love him, don't you?" Campbell asked.

"We've been together for seven years," I answered.

He looked at me silently for a moment. "That didna answer my question," he said, but he didn't press me again.

The wind was picking up even more, and the clouds in the sky were becoming more ominous, so Campbell suggested we head back.

"Can we walk on the beach together if it's not night time?" I asked. From Anni's comments, it was obvious our friendship hadn't gone unnoticed. However, Campbell didn't seem to think it was a problem, so we crossed to the lagoon side of the island and started walking down the beach back toward the clinic.

Over the islands on the far side of the lagoon, the sky began to darken. Soon, I could see the rapid approach of a rainstorm toward us across the lagoon, the water below the approaching clouds roughening in appearance as the rain hit it.

"My laundry!" I exclaimed. We were nearly back to the clinic when the first drops of rain began to fall. Campbell and I rushed from item to item, unclipping the clothespins and tossing the clothes into my laundry basket.

---

[1] Pixar Animation, 2003.

When the laundry was all off the lines, I stuck the basket inside my house. But I stayed out, as the warm rain pelted down in drenching sheets. Huge droplets soaked me to the skin, and yet I didn't go inside. I'd never been in warm rain before. Campbell had taken shelter on my porch and watched smilingly as I danced around in the water. Finally, dripping wet, I joined him on the stoop, squeezing in under the small amount of shelter provided by the overhang. Now that I was wet to the skin, I started shivering.

Campbell put his arm around me. "You're a silly girl, *Ri-pālle*," he said. When I glanced up at him, I was disconcerted by the intense look in his eyes, especially when his gaze seemed to drift down towards my lips and he subtly pulled me closer. I realized I was biting my lip, and I glanced toward Anni's house. I thought I might have seen a dark-haired form entering their cabin, but I couldn't be sure.

I swallowed, glancing past him at the storm and then back up at his face. God, he was warm and muscular. His face was delectably scruffy; Eric was always clean-shaven. I wondered how it would feel to kiss him, and the thought gave me shivers.

"Are you cold?" he asked. I looked back up at him. He hadn't looked away from my face.

"Just a little," I said. I couldn't deny it. I was trembling, though I was certain it was as much from being close to him as from being cold. The rain was pouring out of the sky, such big droplets that it hid houses and trees across the street from view.

"Do you want to come inside?" I asked. "Your legs are getting wet from the rain. I'm soaked and getting your clothes wet too." I pulled away enough to see the darkened, damp outline of my body on his tee shirt and shorts from underarm to knee where we had been pressed together.

"Dinna think I should, lass," Campbell said. "But I dinna ken how long this storm is going to last."

"We can leave the door open," I offered. "No one would think badly of you for taking shelter from the rain!"

"Aye," he said hesitantly. We stepped far enough away from the door to swing it open, leaving it ajar as we entered.

I grabbed my towel and began to dry my hair as Campbell looked away, his face flushed.

"I'm not going to change," I said, trying to set him at ease. However, he remained awkwardly at the apartment entrance.

I sighed, grabbing the empty hangers from my closet rod and starting to hang the mostly-dry dresses up. I couldn't tell what it was, but something was different from how he'd acted the previous day.

I bustled around, hanging my bras over the kitchen table benches. Glancing back at Campbell I could see he looked incredibly uncomfortable.

Honestly, I felt uncomfortable too. During that split second on the porch when he was looking at my lips, mentally I had already kissed him back, pulled him inside, and taken him to bed. What was *wrong* with me? Yes, he was sweet. And super-hot. But obviously I was missing Eric and I needed to reestablish an appropriate level of distance.

The rain storm was beginning to die down when I had emptied the laundry basket. I turned to face him. "Well, it looks like you can head home now. Thanks, kiddo. I really like hanging out with you; it's like being with my little brother Seth. You're his age."

He nodded back, narrowing his eyes.

I cheerily patted his arm as I grabbed the door knob in a clear signal that he was to leave now. "Thanks for keeping me company today."

"I'll see you later, then," he said quietly.

My stomach felt funny, and I didn't watch him walk away.

Saturday night I was just getting ready for bed when I heard rustling outside my window again. It was disturbing; I'd just been getting dressed.

"Miss Peachay, I want to talk to you," sang a disconcertingly strange voice.

"*Ejab kōnaan*," I said, proud of myself for remembering the Marshall words. "I don't want to talk to you."

"Miss Peachay, I want to talk to you," the voice repeated.

"*Kwō etal wōt*," I said. "Go away!"

"Good job, Carlie!" said a voice that was distinctly *not* Marshallese.

"Graham!" I exclaimed irritably. "What are you doing outside my window?"

"Oh, Campbell has us doing night watch duty," he said. "Until your visitors stop coming, or at least for the next week or so."

"That's nice of you," I said. "And I guess it was good to practice my Majel. Did I say it right?"

"Good enough," he said. "They would understand you."

"Okay," I said. "Well, good night, Graham. How long will you be staying?"

"Half-hour," he said.

I grabbed my book and was going to lie down on my bed to read.

"Um, Miss Peach," Graham spoke hesitantly. "Ye might no' want your light on when ye get dressed for bed at night."

"*What do you mean?*" I asked with a sudden rush of embarrassment.

"As much as I liked what I saw, so did all the other men out here at the time."

"All the other men??" I exclaimed. Frantically I started thinking, *did I take my bra off before or after I put on my tank top?*

"I'm just jokin' with ye," Graham chuckled. "Far as I know, I was the lucky one."

I groaned. "So you can see through the curtains?"

"Quite clearly," said Graham. "Ye can come out and see for yourself. We can trade places."

I could hear him coming to my door, so I opened it for him with Graham coming inside and me going outside the house to look through my window. Sure enough, having the light on made the polyester curtains virtually see-through. Graham slowly lifted his shirt to reveal his solid, hairy belly, gyrated sensually, and then lowered the shirt back down to end his strip tease.

As we passed each other at the door, Graham grinned at me.

"Yeah, I saw *all* that," I said. "It was *amazing*. Thanks."

"It was very pleasant for me, too," he said as I closed the door. "Ye do have some very cute knickers, and, ye know, a nice body as well."

"Last you're going to see of it," I said.

"I know someone who will be *verrrra* jealous of me," Graham said, enthusiastically rolling his r's.

"You mean Ewan?" I said. I could only imagine how happy it would have made Ewan to be outside watching me get dressed.

"Oh yes, him too," Graham responded.

It took me a moment to get what he was saying. "Why are you guys *constantly* teasing Campbell?" I said. "I mean, we're friends, but I'm engaged and five years older than him."

"Yes, but ye're bonny. And white."

"I am sure there are countless gorgeous island girls here ready to throw themselves at him," I said.

"He isna interested in just anyone," Graham said. "He's kind of particular."

"Particular? Why?"

"Oh, ye dinna ken?" Graham asked. "He's still a virgin."

CHAPTER 8

Poor Me, Bore Me

"Come on, dammit!" I swore at the bucket. I couldn't understand it. In the past eight days since arriving on Arno, I'd had a lot of practice drawing water from the well. I'd started to master the little wrist-flip required to get the coffee can to turn on its side and sink into the well water, filling quickly so I could pull it up, empty it into the five-gallon bucket, and lower it down again. But that morning, the bucket kept running into rock, and it wasn't sinking into the water. I peered down into the well, and I felt a surge of concern. There was barely enough water in the well to cover the pebbles at the bottom. What was I going to do if I ran out of water?

I had two sources of water on Arno. There was a well, and there was a catchment.

The well was at the center of our property. A wall of cement blocks built up in a square stood about three feet tall, and the well had been dug down through the coral rock that formed the atoll. Well water was brackish—slightly salty and bad tasting. Laura had clarified the distinction between my two water sources when she helped me move in. The well water was good for washing dishes and clothes, taking showers, and flushing our toilet.

The toilet was one bit of civilization I was grateful for. The locals used the sand of the lagoon beach in the mornings and the jungle the rest of the day for their bathrooms. A few people had outhouses. But when UniServe International had built the clinic, they dug a septic tank and installed a toilet in an outhouse structure across the yard from the clinic. With no running water, you had to pour a bucket of water into the toilet to cause it to flush. Because of the effort it took to draw water, I tended to wait through a couple of uses before flushing.

For drinking water, there was the catchment. The catchment had been dug into the ground and built with brick and mortar, and then up from the brick tank was built a wooden structure with a corrugated aluminum roof. The catchment was filled by rain. Instead of the gutters from the clinic and my apartment sending the run-off from rainstorms onto the ground, the downspout went all the way into the soil, where the pipe traveled across the yard to the catchment, spilling the fresh water into the tank. The hand pump in the clinic fed from the catchment, but I had a bucket specifically for drinking and cooking that I would fill, either by pumping water in the clinic or by drawing water through the door of the catchment. That bucket I would keep in the house, along with a separate bucket of well water for doing dishes.

I continued to swear at the bucket as I lowered it, only succeeding in filling it halfway most times, which made the process that much slower.

"What's wrong, Miss Peachay?" Anni had wandered over at the sounds of my frustrated language. I kind of hoped her English knowledge didn't extend to many of the words I'd been muttering under my breath.

"I think our well is leaking," I said. "The water level seems to be really low."

"*Ejab*," said Anni, shaking her head.[1] "It's not leaking; it's the moon."

"What?" I asked, confused. "The moon? What do you mean?"

"When the moon is full and when the moon is dark, we have highest tides of the month. When moon is half, we have the lowest tides, like right now."

"But what does that have to do with the water in the well?" I asked.

"The water in the well is fresh. It floats on top of the salt water below," Anni explained. "So when the moon is full and close, the tide is high, and the water in the well is high; and when the moon is only half-light, the tide is low, and the water is low. It won't be always. In one week, it will be high again, then low again."

"Huh." I said. "What do you know! Well, at least I don't have to worry about a leak in the well."

---

[1] *Ejab*: eh´-chab (no)

"*Ejab*," she said, smiling. "So you don't need to bad word the well anymore."

"I'm sorry," I smiled apologetically. "How do you say that in Majel?"

"*Jōlok bōd*," she said

"*Joe' lock burrrr*," I said, trying and failing to roll the r very well. "Sorry for my bad language."

"*Ejelok bōd*," she said, grinning back at me kindly. I assumed that meant, "It's okay."[1]

"Does the moon affect anything else?" I asked her, curious now.

"Oh, *aolep*...all things," she responded. "The full moon is when the pigs and people make babies. And womans bleed."

"What?"

"*Bōtōktōk*," she said, indicated her private area generally with her hand.[2] "I think the English word is *period?*"

"The moon makes women have their period?" I asked, wrinkling my forehead.

"*Ayet*," Anni nodded confidently.[3]

"Really?" I asked skeptically.

"You will see," she answered, shrugging her shoulders. "See if you change and start to bleed with the moon."

"That seems *very* strange to me," I said.

Anni smiled at me patronizingly. "Uh. You are *ri-pālle*." She shrugged again and strolled off toward her house.

Well, I thought, as I watched her depart. *Nice to know that Campbell's name for me not only means selfish white person; it also means **stupid** white person.*

I had felt like a stupid white person that afternoon as I stood in front of a group of island women to talk to them about health. I was grateful

---

[1] *Ejelok bōd*: eh-chel´-lock burrr (No more mistake)

[2] *Bōtōktōk*: bow-talk´-a-talk (bleed)

[3] *Ayet*: eye-yet´ (yes)

71

Sharbella was translating for me, and I had a feeling she was adding information to make me seem more intelligent, because I would talk for only a little while, and then she would talk for the next two minutes.

When I considered which topic I should address for my first community health meeting, I felt like it was important to encourage cleanliness and nutrition. But the responses I got from people reminded me I was not in the states anymore. Sure, they should bathe more frequently, but water was limited. They ran out of soap quickly, and it cost money.

They should eat more fruit and vegetables, but not much grew naturally on the islands, and some crops were seasonal. You'd get a gigantic bunch of bananas, and you'd eat banana bread and banana pancakes, and just plain bananas. But that quantity of bananas, Sharbella explained to me, blushing, could end up causing severe constipation. There might be an occasional papaya, or a few limes, but in general, the local diet consisted of fish, coconut, refined flour, and white rice, with a healthy dose of Crisco which was the frying oil of choice.

Once the bucket was full I tromped across the yard, weighed down by the forty-pound bucket, water sloshing out with every step. I put it in the shower and brought the empty shower bucket back to the well to fill to have in the house. I preferred to do my water-drawing all at once, because no matter how careful I was I always got wet, whether in the process of drawing the water or in carrying the unwieldy bucket to wherever I needed it.

The day was particularly humid, and it was extra work to draw the water, so by the time I was finished filling my second bucket I felt like I was damp all over.

I kept on thinking about food. It had only been a little more than a week that I'd been on the island, but I felt like I was starving for a massaged kale salad. Avocados on toast. Roasted Brussels sprouts. Carrot sticks, cucumbers, a green juice or smoothie. Just thinking about food made me salivate. Burritos, broccoli beef stir fry, Vietnamese pho soup, Thai pad-see-ew noodles, Indian curry.

But then I entered my apartment. On the shelves of my pantry were canned corn, canned peas, canned green beans, canned peaches, applesauce, and canned pears. There was pasta; I had flour and pancake mix. I had cans of tuna and corned beef and soup.

"I don't want *any* of this crap," I whined to myself. I wanted Whole Foods. I wanted a supermarket. I wanted something fresh. I wanted to go to a restaurant. I just wanted to *be* somewhere else.

In no way did I feel like a twenty-seven-year-old woman. I felt like a grumpy six-year-old. I was lonely, bored out of my mind, and incredibly unsatisfied. I wanted to stomp my feet, cry, throw things, and take a nap. And my period had just finished, so I couldn't blame PMS.

Then there was a knock on my door. I patted my cheeks to get them as pink as my red eyes, then went to open the door. Campbell and Graham were standing there, and they held out a plastic grocery bag to me.

At the question in my eyes, Graham said, "Why, it's mail day, lass, ye ken. Here's your mail."

"Thanks," I said, with a brief smile. It was hard to choke out the word over the lump in my throat, and I tried to not look too eager to slam the door with them outside, particularly since they were both beaming at me. I cleared my throat. "Really, thanks. I needed something today." Graham had turned to go, but Campbell kept his eyes on me, his face compassionate. He raised his eyebrows as if to ask me if I was okay. I nodded and closed the door.

It felt like Christmas, as I sat on my bed and opened the grocery bag, gently untying the knot instead of ripping it open. There was a small box— that was from Eric. There were several envelopes, and a couple of post cards as well.

I opened the package from Eric. Inside there were three envelopes. They said, "Open today!" "Open Thursday!" and "Open Saturday!" And underneath the three envelopes, there were three bags of M&Ms. Chocolate! I started crying, ripped open one of the bags of M&Ms and popped a few in my mouth as I opened the first envelope and flopped on my stomach to read the letter from Eric.

Dear Carlie,

You probably arrived in Arno today as I write this. It was amazing to hear your voice yesterday from Majuro. You sounded nervous and excited at the same time. What's it like? How has your first week of work gone?

Greg called the other day, wanting to know your contact address. He says they're going to miss you at the clinic, but the new hire seems to be a good fit, and she is grateful for the opportunity to work for such a great group.

I've started jogging in the mornings. My schedule has changed in your absence, and I find I'm doing more things that would have seemed selfish to me in the past. I'm going to bed earlier and waking up earlier, so some morning exercise feels good.

The trees look amazing. I've enclosed a few leaves for you to remember Denver by. This was always one of your favorite times of year. Sorry you're missing it!

Well, I can't say I'm not a man of many words, but this doctoral thesis is really monopolizing my thoughts right now, so this will be it for this letter.

Love,

Eric

The rest of the cards and letters shared news from home, and I could hear familiar voices as I read. My sister Amy enclosed a picture of her kids on their first day of school, all four of them staring off into space in different directions, the little goobers; though she did get one picture of them all smiling at the camera for "Auntie Carlie."

Mom said they'd had a tropical storm on Guam, but that nothing really got hurt except for their avocado tree which lost three of the largest branches, already loaded with fruit.

"It doesn't really matter, though," she said. "Your dad and I always gain five pounds when the avocados are ripe, so it's probably best that there will be fewer this season."

Seth filled me in on his latest adventures in his senior year of college. He still hadn't found a wife, he kidded, but considering that I was 27 and hadn't yet married, he wasn't too worried for himself.

And the youngest Beecher sibling, Shelly, currently a sophomore at the University of Guam, tattled on Seth—that he was dating way too many different girls, and it was like he was trying to experience an ethnicity sampler. The last four had been, in order, Korean, Japanese, Filipino and

Chamorro. She couldn't decide which young lady she liked the most, and apparently, neither could Seth.

Finally, there was a postcard from Greg, telling me I was missed, but that they were going to be fine in my absence. "Remember," he signed off, "You're there to get your sparkle back."

My best friend Greg was one of the reasons I had even decided to do this thing. We had met in college and traveled through the practitioner program together, becoming fast friends in the process. Greg had told me that it seemed like I'd been an empty shell lately, and when I talked about joining UniServe, that was the first time he had seen me sparkle in a long time.

When I'd read all the letters, I sprawled on my back on the bed, surrounded by the pieces of paper like tiny hugs all around me, and I cried.

Through the evening, as I ate my intensely boring dinner, read my boring book, did some boring yoga, and got dressed in my boring pajamas (in the dark), I grabbed different letters and read them again, laughing as I imagined those familiar faces and heard those familiar voices in my head.

But when I turned the lights off, I felt devastatingly alone. No one to talk to in the nighttime darkness. No one to laugh with as I fell asleep. No one in the bed beside me. No soft breathing from the other pillow.

"Hey, Carlie?" The husky voice spoke quietly from outside my window.

"Campbell. It's your night?" I asked. I sat up, turned on my lamp, and swept the curtain to the side. The gentle glow of the lamp lit his face slightly as well as creating golden highlights on his coppery hair.

"Ye seemed off this afternoon," he said. "Is everything all right? Did mail help?"

"I just feel dumb," I said. "I'm telling the locals that they need to eat better and wash themselves better, and they already know that. It's not like I have some great wisdom they don't have. They just don't have the wealth to vary their diets. They have to buy what's economical, and that's white rice and white flour! They can't afford soap all the time."

I could see Campbell's head nodding while listening to me. He stayed silent, waiting to make sure I'd finished my thought.

"They really are just subsistence farmers, most of them," he said. "Some of the men earn an income by harvesting and smoking coconut for copra.

And the women can make a little money by creating handicrafts. But most of them dinna have a career or any real source of income. Sometimes they send family members to work in Majuro and send them money just so they can live out here."

"Oh," I said. "You're right. But still I felt really dumb."

Campbell made a sympathetic sound, but he didn't contradict me. "Ye didna seem okay this evening," Campbell said. "What's wrong?"

"I don't want to whine," I said. "I'm just so bored and lonely and tired of canned food. Of not knowing the language. Of having only three real patients in a day and not feeling like I'm making a difference here at all. I'm missing home, and though I was so excited to get mail today, now I just miss everyone more."

I heard a little snicker, which irritated me for a second. "For not wanting to whine ye're pretty skilled at it," Campbell chuckled. Then his tone changed. "I'm sorry, though, hen. I ken it can be lonely, at first. Ye miss everything that was familiar. But it will become more comfortable with time."

"I want to believe you," I said. "But right now, I'm so lonely, it aches. I don't even know if I'm going to be able to fall asleep tonight. My mind is whirling with all the voices and faces I remembered all afternoon."

"Ah, lass, I'm sorry," he said.

I sighed. Somehow just a little sympathy made me feel better. There was another moment of silence.

"I have an idea," Campbell offered. "Can I bore ye to sleep?"

"What in the world do you mean?" I asked.

"I can tell ye about Scottish history," Campbell offered. "And since ye're American and, sorry to say it, *extremely* self-focused, you'll get so bored that ye'll fall asleep, and I can leave ye once I hear ye snoring."

"I don't snore," I insisted indignantly.

"Ewan says ye do," he responded. "He was on last night."

I sighed, exasperated. "Sure, Campbell. *Bore* me."

I heard the noise of something being dragged underneath my window, and then a faint thunk, which I guessed was Campbell setting down a section of log for himself to sit on.

Then he blazed into a rambling description of early Scotland. Primitive farmers, the Picts, Roman and Viking invaders, as well as a multitude of leaders like Duncan and Macbeth. Macbeth, contrary to my attempt to offer some input, was apparently *not* the character from the Shakespeare play.

Campbell's voice was rich and resonant. I loved listening to his accent, the way he pronounced words both familiar and unfamiliar to me. I found myself smiling, pulling my sheets up to my chin and rolling onto my side, closing my eyes as I listened to him. The subject matter may have been tedious, but his voice was nearly as comforting and warm as Campbell's arms could be.

Next Campbell told me about the Highlanders and the Rising of some Trilobites or something like that, and a princess named Bonnie or a prince named Charlie, I'm not sure which. I think they were married.[1]

Occasionally I would ask him questions, but as his deep voice rambled on, sure enough I found myself missing parts of stories, until I finally told Campbell through a gigantic yawn that he really had succeeded, and I was *so* bored, sleeping was going to be no trouble at all.

He chuckled, and I heard him moving his log seat away from the window. He came close once more, and through the haze of near-sleep I thought I heard him whisper something before he left.

"*Iiokwe eok, Ri-pālle,*" he murmured.

At the sound of soft words in a deep voice I nestled more firmly into my pillow, wrapping my blanket over my shoulder. I sighed again with a faint smile, grateful for Campbell's creatively sweet gesture.

It took a few additional moments for my brain to translate.

Campbell had said, 'I love you.'

---

[1] Oh, Carlie, he was telling you about Charles Edward Stuart, Bonny Prince Charlie, the leader of the failed Jacobite Rebellion of 1746.

CHAPTER 9

Stitch Removal

D ear Eric,
I miss you. I'm so far away here! It would be one thing if we had cell phone access, but it's strange to not be able even to just text or call you. It feels like a hundred times a day I'm reaching for a cell phone that's not there, wanting to tell you about something or take a picture to text you.

*But what's more disturbing is how much I **don't** think about you. I can go hours wrapped up in my life here, and when I walk into my apartment and see your picture, suddenly I remember that I'm engaged, that you're back in Denver, that really it used to be almost like we were married. I feel like I'm forgetting what you look like; what you sound like.*

The island men find me fascinating, but I doubt I'll be sleeping with any of them. I'm the only white woman on the island, so I am a bit of a celebrity. I've had nighttime visitors proposition me, sweetly inviting me to 'go to the shungle' with them, but they don't realize it's not that appealing! I have a night watch that's started patrolling so that my nighttime guests stay away, three guys from Scotland who are the teachers at the UniServe school down the road. It's nice to have friends who speak English. I just need to make sure that I'm also getting to know the locals, which I definitely plan to do—just during the day, not at night.

You weren't too far off. Thirteen days in and I'm really missing sex. I think that's why I've got a crush on one of the UniServe guys, though he's a baby in comparison to me. I took the stitches out of a wound on his butt today, and it took everything in me to keep from putting my hands on him and propositioning him there in the clinic. But that would be cheating on you in addition to violating all sorts of medical ethical guidelines.

You should be impressed. I did my laundry completely by hand this week. Water from the well, scrub board and scrub brush, and clothespins on a line. A rainstorm came, but we were able to get the clothes off in time.

Off the line, of course. 'We' is said young man Campbell MacReid and me. He asked me if I loved you. I didn't say yes right away; I never said yes at all. And when I was soaking wet from running around in the rain, he put his arm around me and pulled me close when I was cold, even though it got him all wet. He was looking at my lips like he wanted to kiss me, and honestly, I wanted him to. My clothes were glued to my body and I thought about what it would be like to invite him to come inside, take them off me, and take me to bed. I wish you were closer. If I could make love to you, I think I'd feel like I had my head on straight.

While I do feel like I've been able to help people, there is a challenge in being so remote. I don't have colleagues with whom I can share ideas or ask questions. One of the things that is the most frustrating to me it that the little babies and toddlers here get boils on their heads and foreheads almost all the time. They're adorable, with their big brown eyes and tan skin, but the boils look so incongruous and painful. I'm trying to decide what preventive techniques could help them, because once a boil has formed, it has to run its course.

I wonder what I've done by separating us like this; I worry that I've started us down a road that leads us apart. It wasn't my intention to break up; I just wanted an adventure. I was bored with our rituals, bored with our location, bored with my life. I thought one day we would have a houseful of children who looked a little like you and a little like me. But after five years, I'm wondering if kids are even in my future. And if they're not, if "Mommy" isn't one of the job descriptions I will hold, then I need to know what is important to me, what makes me feel alive. And that's why I'm here.

How are your studies going? How many pages do you have written, or are you planning on doing a thorough outline first before you start writing? I'm guessing this is going to become another fascinating read. Do you think you will publish eventually? I hope the quiet is helping you write more.

*It's quiet here, but in a different way. I'm having time to think. And I've started wondering, why did we become exclusive? I mean, you're kind and calm. But what made us decide we really **belonged** together? And why didn't we ever get married? Why didn't I force the issue more? Was it really going to take me getting pregnant for you to **finally** be willing to set a date, as if somehow only a baby would legitimize our love and make it necessary to commit further?*

Well, I need to finish this up. The guys said they would stop by and pick up the mail from me to give to Mayor Timisen. He's heading to Majuro today, and will probably bring mail back with him in a day or two. I hope I can write more next time. There's just so much going on, I'm really overwhelmed anytime I sit down and put pen to paper.

Love,

Carlie

* * *

"Next!" I said, coming out of the clinic door and checking the white board. "Um, looks like..." I grinned. "Young Master MacReid," I said.

Campbell had been sitting in the crotch of the sprawling tree out front, and he got up and came inside, closing the door behind him.

When I turned around, I was met with an eyeful—the top half of a pair of nicely sculpted buttocks peeking out above the waistband of his shorts and black boxer briefs.

"*Hell-O!*" I said, taken aback. "You're not wasting any time, are you?"

"*Please* tell me you can take the stitches out," he begged. I moved closer. Campbell stood with his back to me, holding the open front of his shorts up as I gently tugged the back of his shorts and boxers below the stitched-up cut on his right buttock. "They itch like crazy, and they're constantly getting stuck on my clothes. I've obeyed your orders not to swim or spearfish, and it's been almost two weeks."

"I think you are in luck, Meester Mack," I said, pulling the waistband of his boxers and shorts back in place. "Today is the day! I'll give you a hospital gown, so you can stay decent while I remove the stitches." He had turned back to me with an utter lack of embarrassment, shorts still unbuttoned. I could see the angular cut beneath his hip bones and the trail of hair leading down toward his fly. I felt my breath catch.

"I really dinna care, Carlie," he said, grinning. "I could just drop my drawers."

"Can you *please* let me feel like a professional?" I asked. "I know we're friends, but that would just be weird for me."

"Sure, *Ri-pálle*, but you're already quite intimately acquainted wi' my backside."

I rolled my eyes, returned the gown to the shelf and grabbed a sheet instead. "Okay, well, take off your shorts, but then at least cover yourself with this," I ordered, closing the curtain around him for him to undress.

"Ready!" I heard the muffled sound as Campbell called me in. He was covered by the sheet, laying on the table as I brought over the suture removal kit and antiseptic wash.

After cleaning the healed wound and surrounding skin, I set to work, gripping each suture with the sterile forceps to pull it away from the skin slightly, then quickly snipping the stitch with the surgical scissors and setting the suture aside on a piece of gauze.

Campbell groaned as I took out the first stitch. "Are you okay?" I asked. "It shouldn't hurt!"

"No, it feels good. It has just itched like hell," he said. "I'll keep my groans to a minimum from here on out."

"And you'll be able to scratch to your heart's content when I'm done," I said. "Though propriety encourages one to wait for scratching their butt until they're alone." He laughed.

"This is quite the scar," I chatted as I worked. "I've never seen anything like it before. I'm glad it didn't get infected. I saw some little boys playing in that boat or one like it, and there were some rusty regions that seem like they could really do some damage!"

"Aye, they probably should retire that boat. And next time I will use better judgment," he said, shaking his head disgustedly.

"Well, we would all have a lot fewer stories if we didn't make stupid mistakes." I dropped another suture onto the gauze.

81

"You'll have to show me one of *your* scars," Campbell said, turning to look at me. "And tell me the story that goes with it. It's only fair, I think."

"Sure, sometime," I said. "Last stitch!"

Campbell reached his hand back, rubbed it across the stitch-free scar, and sighed. "I'm glad that's gone," he said.

"And it's not really in a prominent place," I said with a grin, pulling the sheet up to cover him. "Only your girlfriends will see it." Campbell's eyes flickered over to me and a strange look passed over his face—shyness, embarrassment, desire. I wondered what *my* face was telling him.

"Well, thanks, *Ri-pálle*," Campbell said, gripping the sheet to him and sitting up. "I've been thinking—I can literally say ye saved my ass." He snickered.

"You're welcome," I said casually, turning to pack up the suture removal materials. "See you around?"

Campbell sighed, cocked his head, and looked me directly in the eyes. "Carlie, you're acting strangely. Did I make ye uncomfortable the other day?"

I tried to play dumb, but I could feel my cheeks flushing. Could he tell I had wanted to kiss him, too? I felt lightheaded and took a deep breath. "It *was* a little awkward," I said.

"I know," he said, smiling ruefully and dropping his gaze to the floor. "I'm sorry for pressing ye on the point. Your relationship with Eric isna my business. And I know that long-term relationships go through times when you dinna feel as connected, but you are still committed to each other and that gets you through."

Oh, I realized with some relief, *he's talking about asking me if I loved Eric.*

"It's okay, Campbell," I said, putting my hand on his knee so he'd look back at me. "It did make me think about my motivations for coming out here. And I realized there *must* be something deep down in my relationship with Eric that I need to explore."

"But it wasna my place to question or confront you," he said, his forehead furrowing, putting his hand over mine and stroking my fingers absentmindedly. "I think I wanted to make Eric look bad, for whatever reason." He shook his head, frowning. "It wasna kind."

My eyes were tearing up.

"Oh, Carlie," Campbell said with concern. "Have I hurt ye?"

"No," I shook my head. "True friends don't need to be afraid of each other," I mused. "I actually think your questions came out of concern for me and a desire to seek the truth. I *will* try to be honest with you when I can, and if I'm ever offended, I'll let you know."

Campbell hopped off the exam table and smilingly offered his arm—he was gripping the sheet firmly with his other hand. I stood and stepped close to him and again found myself sinking into him as he stroked my back, ran his fingers through my hair, and murmured foreign phrases to me. Again, I started to sense his physical response to me, but I didn't let go, pressing myself more firmly to him, running my own hands over his back, creeping surreptitiously downwards toward the rise of firm muscles. The pace of my breathing was increasing, and Campbell's heart under my ear had sped slightly as well.

"You're not ending this, are you?" Campbell asked finally.

"Nope," I said, snuggling my head against his chest.

"Well, *I'd* better, then," Campbell said, laughing as he released his grip. I cleared my throat, feeling the warmth of arousal in my lower abdomen, and then blew out my breath as I left him to change.

"Goodbye, *Jimjeran*," Campbell said as he departed from the clinic. Sharbella had been translating as I interviewed my next patient.

"*Shim share'-on*? What's that mean?" I asked accusingly. "Weird lady? Evil American? Stinky foreigner?"

"I'll tell ye sometime," he said with a wink, patting me on the arm. "See you later, Carlie."

Sharbella was smiling at me when I looked back at her. "*Jimjeran* is bery good friend. A friend for all of life," she said.

* * *

Dear Carlie,

The house seems empty and blank without you here. I'm still struggling to understand why you decided, at this stage in life, to leave an established relationship and career and run halfway around the globe. I've already made it clear how your choice has made me feel.

I am trying not to be selfish, though. I realize that we started dating when you were just nineteen, and I was already four years older and farther on in life than you. It's possible that by beginning to date me at such a young age, you ignored your need for adventure and put aside your heart's desires. But I do wonder, if you really loved me, would you be doing this?

I still remember when that girl with curly brown hair walked into the English office. You didn't like the way I'd graded your essay, and you had come to argue your case. I remember thinking that you were fiery, articulate, and beautiful. When you reciprocated my attention, I couldn't believe my good fortune.

Now, I'm just feeling deserted. It makes me a little angry, but I know how excited you are about this. I am glad the clinic was willing to let you take a leave of absence without a fear of losing your job when you come back. You certainly will have a lot of practical, in-the-field experience after this time.

This writing letters thing will take some getting used to, but I always loved getting mail from you that summer you were a camp nurse. Write me soon.

I do miss you, but I'm trying to keep busy, and I'm being social—going to mixers and university functions. Just because you're gone doesn't mean I have to sit at home. In fact, I think I'm out a lot more than when we were together.

Make good choices and keep yourself safe. We've invested a lot of years in each other, and I would hate to lose you.

Love,

Eric

I wondered, as I read Eric's letter, what *he* had left unsaid.

CHAPTER 10

Geckos, the Huntsman, and Campbell, Oh My!

L iving in the islands was not for the faint of heart. For every gorgeous beach scene and sunrise, there was something startling, harsh, or gross. Though I wasn't sharing my space with Eric or a roommate or sister anymore, I was sharing it with countless living things. Besides the geckos, who would happily mate with each other on quite a regular basis as well as leave little white splats on my kitchen table, there were ants. If I made the mistake of leaving a crumb or dropping food in the kitchen and not picking it up immediately, a little trail of black bodies would soon be marching across my floor, carrying as much as they could back to their nests.

And it wasn't just the food I accidentally dropped that was at risk of being eaten by scavengers. I quickly discovered that a bag of flour I'd brought had weevils in it, as did the bag of pinto beans. The flour I was able to sift to remove the offending critters, but the beans were a loss as the weevils had burrowed into many of them and I didn't have the time to inspect each bean individually.

The humidity also had a way of making it into almost anything. I'd bought some "ship biscuits" on Laura's advice, thick hard crackers about 2 inches square that were decent with peanut butter but were so dry they required a lot of water to wash them down. The ship biscuits came in a square tin with a tight tin lid. Those seemed to escape the humidity well. But if I opened a package of cereal or crackers, even if I rolled over the top of the interior bag and clipped it securely with a clothes pin—or three—the humid air would find its way in and turn the food stale or soggy in nearly no time.

I had brought along a lot of sealable plastic containers, knowing that plastic provided the most impenetrable barrier to humidity, and re-packaged most of my food items other than the canned goods once I opened the boxes.

The most hideous housemates, though, I had not met until that morning.

I was happily getting ready for work, paging through my dresses on their hangers to decide what I wanted to wear, when on the wall at the back of my hanging clothes I caught just a glimpse of a geometric design, about the size of my hand. When I stopped and parted the dresses so I could see what it was, I screamed. It *was* the size of my hand, yes. And it was a *spider!* A gigantic spider with a large body; thick, slightly hairy jointed legs; and beady black spider eyes.

I jumped away from the clothes, screamed again, and danced around even though I hadn't touched it. I may also have shrieked a few more times for good measure. Slightly thereafter, there was a hesitant knock at my door. Still wearing just bra and panties, I went over to the door.

"Yes? Who is it?" I asked.

"It's... Campbell," said a deep voice. "I was out for my morning jog, and I heard you scream. Are ye all right?"

"Ah..." I said, looking down at myself. "Yes, but there is a *gigantic* spider at the back of my closet. It's horrifying. It's as big as my hand... It's as big as YOUR hand!"

Campbell laughed. "Oh, dinna worry about it. That's a huntsman spider. They're good, 'cause they eat mosquitoes and ants. You shouldna kill it."

"*Kill* it?" I exclaimed. "There's no way I'm getting *close* enough to it to kill it. But I don't know if I can stay in this house if it's here!"

"Do ye want me to take it out of your house, then?" he asked, genially. "I'm no' afraid of them. They're harmless, really."

"Yes, please," I said. "Let me get something on." I grabbed the dress on the closest end of the closet rod, slipped it on over my head, and opened the door.

"Sorry," Campbell apologized, stepping quickly away from me as he entered the apartment. "I dinna smell very good after a run." He was shirtless, sweat glistening on his chest, his long, loose-fitting athletic shorts riding low on his hips. "So, where is this foul beast?"

I gestured toward my clothes, and with Campbell there, got up the courage to part the dresses to the place I'd seen the spider. It wasn't there.

Campbell searched the back of the closet and the floor around it, to no avail. He pulled a few items off my dresser to check there, and when he turned back to me, he raised his eyebrows and looked down at his chest and abdomen.

"Is there something on me?" he asked.

"What?" I responded.

"Ye're staring at me strangely," he said. "I dinna ken what you're looking at."

"Oh, God," I blushed. "Was I staring at you?" I shook my head. "I'm sorry, it's just you're shirtless and a man, and there's no TV or movies or magazines out here..."

"A *man*, am I?" he asked with a playful wink. "Ye lustin' after me then?"

"Sorry," I said, unable to meet his eyes and chuckling uncomfortably. "Let's get back to locating the spider."

Campbell appeared to be blushing as he reached up to the shelf above the hangers to check for the spider.

"He might have gone behind your dresser," he suggested. "They're not that brave. They're more likely to come out at night..."

I stared at Campbell, hands on my hips. "Are you trying to be funny?"

"Nah," he said. "But they'll no' be trying to eat ye at night. They'll be busy hunting mosquitoes!"

I shuddered. "Well, I do like the thought of fewer mosquitoes."

Campbell grinned, then glanced back at my closet one more time. "Sorry. I think we may be out of luck. I dinna think I'll be able to find him, so I'd better get along. Got to shower. Dinna think my students would want me to stink like this all day. And I dinna think *you* can handle me being around much longer," he said, looking askance at me as I again zoned out on his chest.

I shook myself out of my reverie again. "I'm so sorry, Campbell. I'm not trying to make you feel awkward. It's just early in the morning, and apparently my self-control hasn't woken up yet..."

"Ye dinna need to explain, lass," he said. It looked like he was about to hug me, but then it seemed he thought better of it, not wearing a shirt as he was.

"You don't *really* smell bad," I said, sidling up for a quick side hug anyway, "Ugh! but you *are* sweaty!" I exclaimed when my hand contacted his back.

"Sorry, lass, it's humid, and I just jogged to Jabo and back. One more mile to go!" Campbell grinned as he left the apartment. I didn't mean to, but I followed him to the corner of the house, observing the muscles in his back ripple as he jogged down the road.

I shook my head in wide-eyed admiration as I watched him lope away, sighed, and then returned to my apartment.

Eric and I had occasionally had to be apart through our relationship. Several times he went away on sabbatical and I had remote clinicals and practicums. When we were apart without the option of being intimate together, I was quite comfortable taking care of business myself.

Right now I felt short of breath and agitated, the buildup of desire heavy in my gut. Campbell was so damn hot. Closing my eyes, I could picture the swell of his chest muscles burnished with copper hair. I shivered as I pictured the delicious contours of his abdomen, the defined six pack, the sexy way his hipbones made a 'v' that pointed downward. From being held and hugged by him I already knew the athletic shorts clinging to his form concealed something significant. Spiders or no, I was quite positive I felt aroused enough now to take care of some of the pressures of not being with my fiancé.

I turned the cabin light off—there was still a little light coming in through the curtains, but no longer the harsh glare of fluorescents. I lay down on the bed and closed my eyes.

Eric had a secretive smile on his face. "You want to spend a little time together, babe?" he asked. "You look really sexy tonight."

"Of course," I said. "Just let me finish doing these dishes."

Dammit, I thought. *Not sexy enough.* Maybe that weekend in Breckinridge, when we rented the cozy log cabin with a fireplace. The snow thickly frosted the landscape, making the fir and pine trees droop under its weight. But it was warm inside, no matter the weather on the mountain.

He walked toward me in his boxers, his slender shoulders, lean chest, and pale white stomach glowing golden in the light of the fire.

Huh. That wasn't good either. *And not nice, Carlie,* I thought to myself. *You're really white when you're naked, too.*

I closed my eyes and concentrated again.

*"You're a virgin? You've never done this with **anyone**?"* Campbell was *alert and ready, wide-eyed and astonished, as I unbuttoned my dress and let it fall to the floor.*

"Oh, ye're gorgeous, Ri-pālle," he said, reaching his hand out to me, his sculpted muscles rippling. "I dinna ken how to do this. Will ye be patient wi' me, please?"

"Don't worry. I'll take care of you," I said. I walked to him, straddled him on the bed, and ran my fingers through his wild mop of red hair.

"Oh, Campbell, I want you so bad..." I said, as he tentatively reached his hands toward my breasts. He touched me gently and then with more desperation. I could feel his desire growing in intensity beneath me.

His eyes widened. "Please, Carlie. Can I take you now? I've waited so long for this."

I suddenly realized there was a knocking at the door.

What the fuck? I thought, feeling frustrated and thwarted. I shook my dress down over my legs, walked across the apartment, opened the door, and stuck my head out, fully expecting a neighborhood child or someone who had shown up early for clinic.

"Why're your lights off, *Ri-pālle?*" Campbell asked, confused. "Are ye trying to lure the spider out of his hiding place?"

Even though there was no way for Campbell to know what I had just been doing and I knew he couldn't see my thoughts, I felt a sudden flush come across my face.

"Ye all right, Carlie?" Campbell asked. "Ye're very red, and ye seem out of breath! Did you find the spider?" he looked past me as if to see. "Do ye need me to get it for ye?"

"No. How can I help you, Campbell?" I finally had the presence of mind to ask. "You *just* left."

"Oh, I forgot to ask if you wanted to come to our *Samhain* party tonight."

"*Sow' waan?*" I asked, stupidly.

"*Samhain,*" he repeated, as if he was correcting me, but it sounded exactly the same to me. "It's a Scot holiday. Like your American Halloween? They dinna do anything here on Arno, but we like to have a bit of fun, and thought ye might like it, too."

"Sure," I said. "What time? What should I bring?"

"Five? Come before sundown, anyway. As for what to bring, we're going to fry up some breadfruit to make chips." At my empty expression, he said, "French fries, *Ri-pālle?*"

"Oh, yeah," I said, with a deep breath. "That sounds good, Campbell."

I sighed. Real Campbell was hot. But he was also innocent, sweet, and a good friend. I doubted I'd be able to get myself back where I had been just a few minutes before.

He was walking away but turned back to me. "Do ye have any apples still, *Ri-pālle?*"

"Yeah," I said. I'd been hoarding them in the two weeks since I arrived. "Only five left, but I guess I can bring four of them."

"Well," Campbell said, "Ye can use the peel to divine who ye're going to marry. Should be fun."

"Okay," I said. "And I just had a thought. I can make a batter for fish, if you catch any big enough to filet. We could have fish and chips."

"Now that is a good idea," he said. "Do ye have more oil? If we're doing all that frying, we'll need it."

"I'll bring it along," I said. "See ya later, MacReid." I tried my best to roll my "r" so his last name sounded authentically Scottish.

Campbell froze and stared at me strangely for a moment. "*Oh!*" he exclaimed finally, shaking his head with a sheepish grin. "*MacReid*, not '*mo chridhe.*'"

"What's the difference?" I asked, yet again confused by his Scottish pronunciation.

"You Americans say 'muh' instead of 'maah.' You said my last name, but for a second, I thought you'd called me '*mo chridhe.*' In Gaelic, that means 'my heart.' It's a pet name for family. That's what my parents called me when I was growing up, what my sister calls me. '*Mo chridhe,*' not MacReid."

"Sure sounds the same to me, MacReid," I grinned. "Take it as you will." His eyes twinkled in response, and with a smile he headed off toward school.

As I closed the door behind me, I sighed and smiled. Campbell's ironically timed arrival had interrupted the moment. It was probably better not to fantasize about him. He had saved me from a little bit of emotional unfaithfulness, and though I felt extremely unsatisfied, friendship was probably preferable to lust.

Yet throughout the day, I kept picturing the flash of raw emotion on Campbell's face when he thought I'd called him "my heart."

When I arrived at the boys' house that evening, I went around to the side yard. Graham was piling up a bunch of wood and branches, and grinned and waved at me. I went into their house after knocking briefly. Campbell was in the kitchen already, slicing breadfruit into long rectangles with a sharp knife, then dropping them in batches into a tall-sided pan on the stove, partly filled with sizzling oil.

Ewan directed me proudly to a baking dish filled with pale pink fish filets, which he declared he had *personally* boned and filleted. Campbell produced a second pot to which I added my oil, letting it heat up while I stirred together the batter mix with some water, and made quick work of frying up the fish.

"At a real Samhain celebration, we'd have to recite poetry before eating," Graham said, coming in to the delicious smells of fish and fried breadfruit, "But there's no way I'm letting these delights cool down before eating them!"

We gathered around their table, and with lots of salt and malt vinegar enjoyed the *almost* Scottish supper.

"So," said Graham, leaning back in his chair and patting his stomach. "Now that I'm full, it's time for dinner entertainment. Ye don't happen to have any poetry in your memory, do ye, Carlie?"

"I have most of one memorized," I responded. "It's 'Two Roads' by Robert Frost." The boys looked at me blankly. "Well, he's an American poet, so I guess you might not be familiar with his name, but you might recognize the poem... Two roads diverged..."

"Stop!" said Ewan. "Ye need to stand."

I rolled my eyes, walked over to the kitchen, and turned to face them. "I don't know it perfectly, and I can't guarantee I've memorized it all."

"Get on wi' it," teased Campbell. "None of us are professional orators."

"Okay," I said, closing my eyes to try to remember how it started.

> "Two roads diverged in a yellow wood,
> And sorry I could not travel both and be one traveler
> Long I stood, and gazed at one as far as I could
> To where it bent in the undergrowth
> Then took the other as just as fair
> Though having perhaps the better claim
> Because it was grassy and wanted wear
> But as for that, the traveling there
> Had worn them really about the same..."

"So," I said, "Notice that the poem really says the roads are about the same. But people tend to remember the last stanza, not realizing that what the poem says is that which choice you should make isn't always clear!"

"We dinna need an interpretation. Finish it, now," said Ewan impatiently.

"I think I may have heard it before," Graham said encouragingly.

"I shall be telling this with a sigh Somewhere ages and ages hence," I pronounced.

The boys joined me on the last lines:

"Two road diverged in a wood and I...
I took the road less traveled by
And that has made all the difference."[1]

Graham, Ewan, and Campbell clapped as I made a deep curtsy and went back to my seat.

"My turn!" exclaimed Ewan, getting up and clearing his throat. He squared his shoulders and looked off into the distance as he recited:

There once were three men from Loch Garry
Named Harry and Larry and Barry.
Now Larry was bare
As an egg or a pear
But Harry and Barry were hairy.

The rest of us groaned but clapped all the same. Graham got up with similar fanfare, bowed, and performed with extreme flourish:

Catriona, a pretty young lass
Had a truly *magnificent* ass.
Not rounded and pink
As you possibly think
It was grey, had long ears, and ate grass.[2]

"The best one of *all*," I exclaimed as I clapped, and Graham grinned.

"I havena gone yet," said Campbell. His face looked a little flushed, but the apartment *was* hot from all the frying we'd done. "This one is by Robert Burns, Scotland's own poet. And for Carlie's sake, I'm going to translate it into *American*."

I rolled my eyes in response.

"It's called 'Oh Wert Thou in the Cauld Blast,'" Campbell said. He started his poem, speaking quietly, his gaze often landing on me.

---

[1] This is my actual memory of the poem. It's not quoted correctly—don't memorize it from this version! It and Robert Frost's "Mending Wall" are the two poems I managed to commit to memory during high school.

[2] "Scottish Limericks." Rampant Scotland. Retrieved January 2018.

O wert thou in a cold blast,
On yonder lea, on yonder lea,
My plaid to the angry airt,
I'd shelter thee, I'd shelter thee.

Or did misfortune's bitter storms
Around thee blow, around thee blow,
Thy shelter should be my bosom,
To share it all, to share it all.

Or were I in the wildest waste,
So black and bare, so black and bare,
The desert would be Paradise,
If you were there, if you were there;

Or were I monarch o' the globe,
Wi' thee to reign, wi' thee to reign,
The brightest jewel in my crown
Would be my queen, would be my queen!

I stared at him as he finished. "That's like, something you would read at a wedding," I said, and thinking of Eric, I teared up. "Robert *Burns*, you said?"

"Now, Lass," said Graham. "We didna bring ye here to make ye cry... where are those apples?" I went looking for them as Graham grabbed four paring knives from the kitchen.

"Okay," said Graham. "Now we will peel the skin off the apple in one long spiral, and don't let it break! We're going to tell the future."

"There was one line in your poem that I didn't understand, Campbell," I said, as we sat back down at the table. "It said, 'my plaid to the angry airt.' Is it talking about a kilt? Like plaid fabric?"

Ewan shook his head sadly. "Ye are absolutely Scot illiterate, young lass."

"You guys are teachers, so *teach* me," I said.

"*Tartan* is the fabric," said Campbell. "And each clan has its own special tartan. MacReid, and Douglass, and Stuart. All different."

"But isn't that what *plaid* is?" I asked.

94

"A 'plaid,' lassie, is like a wool tartan blanket," said Campbell. "It was often pleated or gathered and buckled in with the kilt and could be loosened to wear as a cloak or jacket. And "airt" means direction, like on a compass. So the line in the poem, 'my plaid to the angry airt,' means that he'll wrap his love in his plaid with him, and turn his back in the direction of the angriest wind, to shelter her.'" He raised his eyebrows and stared at me.

"That's really sweet," I said, choking a little, breaking eye contact and picking up my apple. "So now we do some fortune telling? Samhain is a complicated holiday!"

We all focused on peeling our apples, and Ewan quickly gave up after his peeling broke three times. "I think that means I'm going to marry three lasses named Ingrid, Isabel, and Irene," he said, critically eyeing the three short straight sections of peeling on the table in front of him.

Campbell, Graham, and I fared better. Graham was the first to throw his apple peeling, and it came out looking like a Q. We could only think of "Quinn" as a possible name, and as Graham wasn't acquainted with any Quinns, the teasing couldn't go far.

"Throw yours over your shoulder, Carlie," said Graham. I obeyed, and then turned around to cock my head and peer at the peeling.

"That doesna look like an E, Carlie," said Graham. He didn't say it, but it most definitely looked like a C.

"No, it looks like a lower case 'e,'" I argued. "The top is looped around so it's almost touching."

Ewan squinted and cocked his head to one side. "If ye say so, but I still think it looks like a fancy script C."

I couldn't meet Campbell's eyes.

Campbell was last to go, tossing his peeling in the air, after which we all looked behind him. His peel had flung outward and unrolled almost completely into another gigantic 'C.'

I needed to get out ahead of this. "U," I announced confidently. "Ursula? Uma? Unique?"

"Ah," said Campbell. "Definitely Ursula. Ye remember, boys—the one we used to see at St. Mary's... in Inverness?"

Graham and Ewan were filled with lustful memories apparently, and Campbell made grateful eye contact with me. It was obvious neither of us appreciated being teased about the other.

After our fortune-telling, we went out to the yard, where Graham built up the bonfire and we gathered on the grass around it. Campbell had brought a quilt out from their apartment, and he scooted to one side so I could sit next to him.

"So, now's the time for scary stories," said Ewan. When none of the rest of us volunteered, he said, "Culloden Moor is the place where the Highland culture died. The bloody Battle of Culloden took place there, just miles from Inverness, where nearly two thousand Highlanders died in less than an hour. And on every April 16, should ye go there, you'll see visions of ghosts, even a highland warrior in a kilt, and people swear up and down that if you are still, you'll hear the sounds of swords clashing."

"Highland culture died there?" I asked, knowing instantly as the words left my mouth that I'd created another opportunity to be ridiculed.

"Aye, after the Jacobite rebellion," answered Campbell.

"What was that?" I asked, inwardly kicking myself for not just nodding and smiling.

"I *told* you about it the other night. That was when the Jacobites wanted to restore the Stuart monarchy," he explained, but then smiled. "Though, if I recall correctly, you might have been snorin' by then."

"What would restoring the Stuart monarchy have meant?" I asked, then shook my head as the guys exchanged wide-eyed glances of disdain. "I'm *sorry*! I just don't know anything about Scotland!"

"Ah, we'll forgive ye," said Graham. "Ye're sweet enough to look at that we'll keep ye around, even if ye're thick as a post."

Campbell grinned down at me.

"So, what legend do *you* have?" I asked him.

"I always liked it when my dad told me about the Selkies. In Scottish folklore, Selkies are seals when they're in the water, but they're humans when they're on dry land. So astonishingly beautiful, that they'll leave you pining after them, lovesick for the rest of your days." His gaze lingered on me an instant longer than necessary.

"Aye," Graham called my attention away from Campbell's riveting turquoise eyes. "I read somewhere that the Selkies are 'eternally lustful.'" He shook his head slightly. "That did make it a little disturbing for me to visit St Andrew's Aquarium, or to holiday at the seaside. I didna quite know how I should feel about those cuddly little seals!"

"Do you have any American legends or scary stories, Carlie?" Ewan asked.

"Well, my mom and dad didn't care for ghost stories or things like that, but my older sister Amy and I did tell scary stories to our little sister Shelly."

"How so?" Campbell asked. I couldn't tell if it was my imagination, but I could swear he was sitting closer to me than he had been a few minutes before, and now as he leaned back on his hands, his arm was quite clearly in contact with my back.

"Well, Amy hid up on the top shelf of the closet, and I told Shelly that the boogeyman lived in her closet. And while I talked to her, using as scary a voice as I could, Amy pushed and pulled the door open and shut, so that Shelly totally believed us. She still won't forgive us, and she's twenty. She was afraid of the dark for *years*!"

"You're cheeky," said Campbell, bumping me with his shoulder. "That's funny, but what a horrible thing to do to a wee lassie!"

I was yawning at that point, so I got up. Campbell was quick to volunteer to take me home.

We walked in silence most of the way, the stars above us, the sound of the gentle waves of the *iar* off to the right. As we passed various homes, we could hear people talking and laughing, could see the glow of lanterns.

Again, we kept bumping into each other as if drawn together by a magnet.

"May I?" Campbell asked. I gently slipped my arm around his waist as he put his around my shoulders.

"You know we shouldn't be walking together alone at night," I said to him.

"I ken it," he said, quietly. "But what I know, and what I *want*, are two very different things."

I said nothing, but I knew exactly what he meant.

When we reached my door step Campbell embraced me. We were around the corner from the clinic light, so the stoop was in darkness.

"What would you be doing for hugs if I wasn't here, wee one?" Campbell whispered, stroking my back and hair as I threaded my arms around his waist and felt myself relax into him.

"I'd be dying of deprivation," I said, my voice muffled by his tee shirt.

We embraced a long time, standing there in comfortable silence until he shifted awkwardly. I could guess why and I wasn't surprised; my own body felt like it was glowing.

Finally Campbell breathed deeply, kissed me on the forehead and bid me goodnight. "Sleep tight," he said. "Don't let the spiders bite."

"Campbell!" I groaned, as he disappeared into the darkness.

In the nighttime darkness of my apartment, my thoughts were drawn back to Campbell. To the sparkle in his blue eyes when he looked at me; to the soft warmth of his body against mine, the strength of his arms, the gentle touch of his hands stroking me. To his body's obvious response to holding me close, and to my own response to being held.

As I undressed for bed, I imagined Campbell's hands helping me, gently removing items of clothing, caressing my curves, grasping me firmly. I ached for it to be true, to have his lips on my neck, to be able to run my own hands over his muscles. To kiss him, not just look at his mouth. To feel his response to me and to bring him pleasure.

I might have been interrupted earlier in the day, but no distractions barred me from following through with my fantasy this time.

Afterward I slept uneasily. My own touch had been sufficient; but it was not *enough*.

CHAPTER 11

Sunshine

A fter clinic today, I will visit my sister in Matolen," Sharbella said. "Do you wish to come with me and do home visits? It is five miles, but the truck will take us and it can also bring us back."

I debated inwardly for a moment. In the past weeks since arriving on Arno I had ventured out from Ine several times. I had walked to Jabo, a mile and a half to the west, which was where Sharbella lived. I had also walked at least a mile past the UniServe School which was already a mile in the other direction, searching for a place I could sunbathe. That had failed, for as soon as I peeled off my sundress and lay down on my towel in my bikini, excited little voices announced that I had been discovered. I pulled on the dress just in time to be surrounded by a whole group of kids, excitedly chattering at me and showing me a huge coconut crab they had found in the palm forest.

Matolen was all the way at the eastern tip of the islet, and though some of my patients had traveled that distance to come to the clinic, I had never been that far in that direction.

"I need to be back by seven to call the UniServe office in Majuro on the short-wave radio," I said.

"Oh, we will be back by then," she assured me. "You will like to visit Matolen. They have lime trees there, and many kind families."

I locked up the clinic after making sure my bag was packed with all the incidental supplies I might need for house calls. Soon after one, the town truck rattled up and Sharbella and I climbed aboard, finding a place to sit in the truck bed.

As we jounced along down the road, I smiled, my hair whipping wildly around my face. I had forgotten a hair tie, so I swept my hair up, wrapped it into a bun, and twisted my hot pink curlicue key chain around it to keep it in place, the keys jingling as I did it. Sharbella grinned at me, holding her long hair down with one hand.

It was too loud to talk, so I gazed around, noticing how the coconut palm forest seemed to be thicker and deeper on the southern side of the road. Generally the road stayed close to the *iar* side, and the lagoon was often visible, though in places the trees and underbrush were thick enough that we couldn't see it for a time.

My heart quickened a little as we passed the UniServe school, but I saw no sign of Campbell, Graham, or Ewan.

It was silly how exciting it felt to be whipping along the island road at a mere fifteen miles per hour, but it was practically a roller coaster thrill in comparison to the typical two-miles-per-hour, flip-flop pace I typically traveled.

In 20 minutes we reached the first houses of the village, and soon we arrived at the main village center. If Ine was a city, Matolen was a suburb. There was no store, no school. It was simply homes, gardens, and copra smoking ovens.

The truck came to a stop in front of a nicely maintained house with a well-swept gravel yard and brightly painted sleeping windows. I had asked Campbell on our *bwebwenato* why Majel houses had long, low, horizontally hung plywood window covers that they propped open with sticks. He had told me that the Marshallese people slept on pandanus mats on the floor. The windows were low so that the breeze could blow over them as they slept. Typically there were no screens on the windows, so open or closed, they were no protection from the prolific mosquitos.

"*Iiokwe*, Miss Peachay!"

I had been recognized, and quickly I was whisked from house to house by a woman Sharbella introduced as Jelōñ Botla, one of the matriarchs of the village, well-versed in the ailments and challenges each resident faced.[1] She

---

[1] Jelōñ Botla: Shell-long´ Bot´-lah

knew enough English that she was able to concisely express their needs, and for the better part of two hours, I was kept busy with patient after patient, occasionally being offered coconut juice to quench my thirst or salty dried fish which made me thirsty once more.

Finally Jelōñ brightly said, "*Emōj kiiō.*"[1]

"*Bwe?*"[2] I asked. I had learned that meant, "What?" and was an easier thing to say than *Ijjab malele* (I don't understand).

"We are finish now," she said. "You come our house, eat."

I followed her back to the house I'd seen on arriving, and she brought out a mat for me to sit on in the yard.

"*Kottar jiddik,*" she said.[3] "In a little time will be ready."

I sat there awkwardly for just a few minutes, but then a familiar little face came around the corner.

"Miss Peachay!" exclaimed Riti. "You are at my house!" She was followed by two other girls of similar age, whom she introduced as Hemity, her cousin, and Kabet, her sister.

"*Itōk,*" said Riti. "Come with us, Miss Peachay. We make..." she wrinkled her forehead, obviously trying to think of the word in English, then shook her head. "We show you."

The girls led me across the road to a wide green field that on closer inspection was scattered liberally with delicate pink flowers. They ushered me to a spot in the middle of the field and we all sat down.

"What kind of flowers are these?" I asked.

"*What,*" said Riti cheerfully.

"The flowers," I said. "What are they called?"

"*What,*" Riti responded, furrowing her forehead and nodding at me.

"These," I said, pointing down at the little bits of pink. "What are they called?

---

[1] *Emōj kiiō*: em-mozshe´ key´- oh (finished now)

[2] *Bwe*: bway? (what?)

[3] *Kottar jiddik*: coat´-tar chee´-dick (wait a little while)

"Oh!" Riti, Hemity, and Kabet dissolved into peals of giggles.

"No, Miss Peachay," Riti said, picking up a flower and pointing to it. "This flower is called *wūt*. W-U-T. *Wūt*,"

"But isn't that the word for *rain*?" I asked.

"*Ejjab*," Kabet replied. "Rain is *wōt*. W-O-T. Flower is *wūt*."[1]

I put my hands to my head and shook it, making my key chain hairband jingle. "I can't hear the difference!" I exclaimed. As far as I could tell, both words sounded exactly the same.

The girls giggled at me and then each picked a flower.

"*Lale*, Miss Peachay," said Hemity.[2] "Watch now."

They pinched the petals off at the base and gently lay the five pink ovals on their skirts, stretched out in front of them. Then picking up a single petal, they licked it and then pressed it to their fingernail where it stuck, like a delicate little press-on nail.

"You do, too, Miss Peachay," said Kabet, gesturing toward the flowers in front of me. I smiled, picked a flower, and began the fragile task of trying to get new petals to stick on my fingernails without making the previous faux nails fall off.

I relaxed in their presence, not feeling the need for constant conversation, focusing on the task, on the warmth of the sunshine on my back, surrounded by beauty both floral and feminine.

My manicure was almost finished when I heard a horrible clanking squeal. I looked up to see a rickety, rusty bike traveling up the road. And on the bike was Campbell.

"Meester Mack!" called out Hemity. "*Itōk! Lale* the fingers of Miss Peachay."

Campbell dismounted his junk heap and gently picked his way through the flowers to where we were sitting. He squatted down next to me.

---

[1] I still can't tell the different between them. Whit, whut, what, whot, they all sound the same to me. That one word with slightly different vowel sounds means five or six different things in Marshallese.

[2] *Lale*: lah´-lay (watch or look at)

"Let me see, Miss Peachay," he said, holding out his hand, palm up. Though the three girls were right there I extended my hand and gently placed it on his.

"*Aiboojoj*," he said, gently squeezing, then releasing my hand.[1] At the question in my eyes, he translated, "Beautiful!"

"Why you come to Matolen, Meester Mack?" Riti asked.

"I needed to tell the parents about their naughty children," he joked, running his fingers through his hair and grinning back at her. "About how badly they are doing in school, how they aren't finishing their work, how they talk all the time, and how they do not respect their teacher."

Riti pouted at him. "Meester Mack. *Kwō nana*.[2] You like to tease us bery much."

"*Kwōn mōña ipem*," the girls told him firmly.[3] "You will eat with us." They got up from their spots.

"We must help my mother," Riti said. "You come soon."

The three girls trailed off, holding their arms out stiffly with their fingers stretched wide, like a trio of women leaving the nail salon.

"Campbell MacReid," I said, meeting his eyes and then looking away. It had been a couple of days since Samhain, and since then my night watchmen had been Graham and then Ewan. Samhain, when Campbell had walked me home with his arm around me; when he had held me just a little longer than necessary on my doorstep.

When I glanced back at him, he was blushing and looking at the flowers around him. "Do you get your nails done in the states?" he asked.

"Not often," I responded. "A nurse is constantly washing her hands, using latex gloves, holding things. My fingernails get chipped too quickly if I get a manicure, so it's a waste of money. I do pedicures more often." I extended my feet to look at them. "Though my toes are looking woeful these days. It's been six weeks at least, I think."

---

[1] *Aiboojoj*: aye´-bow-zshush (lovely)

[2] *Kwō nana*: kwoh nah´-nah (you are bad)

[3] *Kwōn mōña ipem*: kwon mung´-aye ee´-pem (you eat with us)

Campbell looked at my feet, then back at me with a small smile quirking his lips.

"My sister Isla used to do that to me. And then force me to paint her toenails as well."

"My little brother Seth had his nails and make-up done a time or two, I admit," I replied.

"How old is he? Your 'little brother'?" Campbell asked.

"I thought I told you," I said. "He's twenty-two."

Campbell flushed again. "How old were you when he was born?" he asked casually, gazing away from me over the flowery field.

"Old enough to help change his diapers," I offered, biting my lip teasingly.

"You were a very talented one-year-old, then," joked Campbell. "Two-year-old? *Three*-year-old?"

I shook my head and rolled my eyes.

The girls were waving to us from a distance, so Campbell got up and offered me a hand.

Throughout supper something seemed off. The little girls gathered around me, wanting to be with me and ask me questions, while Campbell seemed perfectly happy to carry on serious conversations in Marshallese with the other adults, paying absolutely no attention to me at all. I tried to tell myself I was being petty for wanting to monopolize Campbell's attention, but I did feel oddly envious.

I got distracted from my jealousy by my delightful little companions, though. They took me out to their orchard and let me pick a small woven basket full of tiny green limes, a nearly-ripe papaya, and then gave me a small hand of the tangy petite bananas that grew on Arno.

"The limes are bery good with salt," said Kabet. When we got back to the house she cut one lime into wedges which we sprinkled with salt and then sucked. I grinned across the house at Campbell, whose eyebrows were raised.

"Where's the tequila?" he joked, then went back to his conversation.

After that I played a game with the girls that was remarkably like jacks but involved tossing a handful of small pebbles up and trying to catch as many of them as possible on the backs of our hands. I realized with a start that the late afternoon shadows were no longer stretching across the yard. It must be at least six, and I needed to get back to the clinic by seven.

"Oh!" I exclaimed. "I need to catch the truck back to Ine." Several faces turned to me with apologetic expressions.

"I'm sorry, Miss Peachay," said Jelōñ. "The truck is gone already."

"Well, fuck," I said, instantly realizing my error when the word came out. Fortunately the only one who realized I'd sworn was Campbell, who winked at me.

"I'd better start walking, then," I said. "It's going to take me a couple of hours to get home."

"You can ride the bike and I'll jog," said Campbell, getting up. "*Iiokwe, aolep.*"[1]

We left amid cries of "*iiokwe,*" out to the field where Campbell had left the rusty bike. He pulled it up by the handles and gestured for me to take it.

I eyed it skeptically, then looked down at myself. I was wearing one of my longer, looser dresses.

"You could tie the front and back of your skirt together between your legs so it doesn't get caught in the chain," Campbell offered. I followed his instructions but ended up with what looked like clown pants that didn't allow my feet to move enough to pedal the bike.

Campbell stood back, looking at me and then at the bike. There was a metal basket attached to the handlebars. He looked at the basket, then at my ass, and then up at me.

"You don't really think..." I said.

Campbell took my tote bag from me and placed it in the basket, spreading the edges of the fabric over the metal. I stopped him, pulling the fragile papaya and bananas from the bag. He climbed onto the bike and then offered me a hand. "Make sure your skirts don't catch in the front wheel," he said.

---

[1] *Iiokwe, aolep*: Yok´-way aw´-lep (Good-bye, everyone)

I sat on the handlebars, my legs extending over the basket, which made me lean backward, almost against Campbell's chest.

It was incredibly awkward until Campbell picked up speed and then the bike, noisy as it was, provided a speedy ride. It was jiggly, though, and realizing Campbell's view over my shoulder I felt awkward which inspired me to start singing, the rutted road providing a trilling vibrato. "You are my s-u-u-u-un-shine, my only su-u-u-un-shine..."

From beside my ear harmonized a perfectly-pitched bass voice.

"You sing, Campbell?" I exclaimed happily, then continued our impromptu duet. "You make me ha-a-a-a-appy, when skies are gra-a-a-ay..."

After a mile or so, he brought the bike to a stop. "I'm getting a neck ache from trying to see over ye. Hike your skirts up, Carlie," he directed. When I stared at him in response to the odd request, he explained. "So you can bike for a while, and I'll jog."

That seemed to work for probably two miles, and then we came to a stop again. I couldn't handle any more uncomfortable seated positions, and the rust on the bike chain made pedaling twice as hard as it should have been.

"It's less than two miles from here," I said. "You go on. I can walk."

"Nah," Campbell insisted. "Don't ye think it's more interesting to experiment with different positions?" He blushed, shaking his head as he realized what he'd said.

I noticed then that the bike had pegs on the back wheels. "I could try standing on those and hold onto your shoulders," I suggested.

It worked. I was able to perch on the pegs while Campbell sat on the seat and I leaned forward with my hands on his shoulders. In almost no time at all we went speeding by the school, and five or ten minutes later we were pulling up in front of the clinic. The last glowing rays from the sunset were visible over the palm trees on the ocean side.

"Have we made it in time?" I asked. "I'm supposed to call Alastair on the short-wave radio at seven."

"Aye," Campbell said glancing at his watch. "With minutes to spare."

"Now if I can just remember how to use the radio," I mused. I had walked several steps toward my house and Campbell had turned his bike toward the school when I impulsively exclaimed, "Don't leave yet. Come hang out with me. Help me call Alastair."

Campbell looked at me, a frown on his face.

I sighed. "Is it really going to hurt anything for us to just hang out?" I gestured toward my neighbors' house. "Anni went with Kona to Majuro. No one will hear us talking."

"Well, you shouldna speak to me when you're with Alastair on the radio," Campbell warned me.

"Sure," I agreed. As I stood at my door, I had a moment of panic. *My keys.* I picked up my bag and started to look through it.

"Are ye looking for something, *Ri-pālle*?" Campbell asked.

"My keys," I said desperately. "I can't get into my house without them."

Suddenly I felt a tug on my hair, heard a jingle, and my hair started falling out of its bun. I put my hand up to keep it in place and turned to Campbell crossly, only to see him standing there, amused, his hand reaching out to me holding my hot pink curlicue keychain. I took it from him, rolled my eyes, and unlocked the door.

"Remember," Campbell said nervously. "Don't talk to Alastair as if I'm here."

I nodded and with another look around to see if there were any people to see us, we entered the apartment. Campbell fussed with the knobs and dials of the shortwave radio, and in a few minutes I heard the staticky sound of Alastair Douglass's voice.

Our conversation was brief. I reported on the number of patients and the amount of money paid for services. Payment was optional in this impoverished community, but still people would bring change or gifts of food. I shared a quick list of needed supplies, and then signed off.

When I turned from the radio, Campbell was looking at me. I almost thought he was looking at me *hungrily*, but I didn't want to misinterpret his expression.

"*Ri-pālle*," he said. "I ken ye think it's silly, but I dinna feel comfortable being here in your apartment at night."

"Can we talk outside, then?" I asked. "I don't want you to leave yet. My evenings are so empty."

107

He smiled compassionately. "Aye. But we'd be devoured by mosquitos. They're out in force until at least an hour after dark."

I went searching through the boxes under the bed left by previous occupants and came up with a large mosquito net. Looking around the apartment, Campbell eyed the two benches flanking the kitchen table.

"Do ye have a quilt?" he asked. I carried the bulky net and blanket while Campbell stacked the benches atop one another and carried them out together as if the heavy wood weighed nothing. We located a level grassy spot in the middle of the field beside the clinic. I spread out the quilt, and Campbell placed the benches on either side of it. Then we lay the mosquito net over the benches, tucking it underneath the legs of the benches so that it wouldn't slip.

Then, trying to quiet our laughter, we crawled into our makeshift tent from the foot end, lay down on the quilt, and looked up at the night sky, our view of the stars only slightly occluded by the mosquito net.

"So, Miss Beecher," asked Campbell. "Where are you from?"

I laughed. "That's a tough one. I was born in Germany. My dad's in the Air Force. I lived there, then in Japan, then on Guam, and finally settled in Denver. I guess I would call that home now."

"And you told me once about your family. You have—two sisters and one brother?"

"Yes. There's Amy, who is two years older than me. Seth is younger, and then Shelly is the youngest. She's nineteen, almost twenty."

It was getting chillier. I wasn't touching Campbell at all, but I found myself scooting nearer so I could feel the heat radiating from his side.

I turned over and tried to push the quilt into shape where my head had been. "Stupid rock," I said. "I can't seem to escape it."

"Use my arm," Campbell offered, extending it out to my side of the quilt.

It was what I wanted in my heart, but for a moment I hesitated. *Alone with boys at night,* my mom always had said. *That's a recipe for disaster.* My heart was thudding in my ears as I reclined against him, snuggling into his side, my head nestled on his chest. Unintentionally I hummed a contented sigh.

Campbell sighed as well, pulling me closer.

"The girls asked why you came to Matolen today," I mused. "You never really told them, and then you left when I did."

Campbell was silent. I could hear the whine of mosquitos hovering around the net, desperate to get at us, and the faint sound of the waves lapping on the sand of the lagoon beach. "Because you were there," he said quietly.

Now it was my turn for silence.

"I think my heart must be pounding, Carlie," he admitted. "I canna hide it, and I want to be honest with you. But I also know you're engaged and I ken you aren't free. I'm sorry that what I know to be true doesna stop me from... wanting you."

"I understand," I sighed, turning toward him slightly. I snuggled more firmly toward him, pressing into his warmth to escape the chill of the night air. *Stop messing with his mind!* my logical side screamed at me.

"I like being close to you," he murmured.

"I like it too, Eric," I said.

The silence was deafening.

I was embarrassed, amused, mortified, yet unsurprised. I'd spent enough time thinking about being with Campbell; no wonder my mind had mixed him up with Eric.

Campbell came up on his elbow and stared at me, his face impenetrable.

My heart was racing. *Kiss me, dammit,* I begged inwardly. I tried to telegraph the message with my eyes. Couldn't he see it? I knew he wanted me. If *he* kissed *me* I wouldn't be cheating, would I? —not as *much* anyway...

Campbell was breathing shallowly, his forehead wrinkled. He inched closer to me, then reached out his hand to stroke my cheek. With his thumb he gently traced my bottom lip. That one touch sent shivers up my spine.

"*Mo ghràidh*," he whispered. "*Tha mo chridhe a 'buntainn riut.*"[1]

---

[1] Scottish Gaelic—My love. My heart belongs to you.

"What does that mean?" I asked. His pupils were wide. I could almost sense that it was taking superhuman strength for him not to kiss me.

"I canna tell you," he said sadly. "You're *engaged*. You dinna want to know. You *can't* know." Finally Campbell sat upright, lifting the mosquito net with him. He sat with his arms draped around his knees, his back toward me. "Oh, Carlie," he finally sighed. "I need to go. I can't be doing this. What kind of man am I being?"

"We can still be friends, can't we, Campbell?" I begged, propping myself up on my elbows. "I didn't mean to call you that. It's like a parent calling their kid the wrong name. I know who you are. I know Eric is my fiancé. But I appreciate you too much, I *need* you too much for us not to be friends at all."

Campbell put his fingers on his temples and massaged his forehead. He sighed, then set his shoulders determinedly. "Yes, Carlie. Friends," he responded in a resolute voice. "We can be friends."

I stood up, wrapping the mosquito net into a messy ball as Campbell folded the quilt. He handed it to me and silently picked up the benches. We walked to my apartment, Campbell returning the benches to their spots beside the kitchen table. Then he turned and looked me up and down one last time.

I stepped toward him. "Will you hug me, at least?"

"I can't," Campbell said, slowly shaking his head. "Not tonight. And perhaps we shouldna be alone, at least not for a while."

With a sad half-smile lit by the faint light of the clinic, he turned to leave, picking up his bike at the side of the road. As he retreated, I heard him slowly whistling the tune we'd sung together earlier in the evening.

"You'll never know, dear, how much I love you. Please don't take my sunshine away."

CHAPTER 12

A Beautiful Doughy Ball

My third clinic week was at an end and I was scrubbing the counters when I heard loud male voices getting closer and the crunch of gravel under flip-flops.

"We are feeding you tonight, Miss Peachay," said Ewan, grinning at me. "Are ye done? We can walk ye to our house."

"Campbell is a master at making pizza crust," offered Graham. "Ye'll think you died and went to Italy."

"We'll wait for you," said Ewan. "Put on a swim suit under your dress and bring shorts and snorkel gear. We'll take ye spear fishing, too."

"*Fish* and pizza?" I asked skeptically.

"Don't knock it till you've tried it, lassie," said Graham, grinning at me. "And ye need to eat more. Ye're getting too skinny; we'll work on fattening ye up."

"Aye, if ye lose too much weight you'll... lose too much... *weight*," said Ewan, eyeballing my chest.

"Well, I won't say no to pizza," I said, ignoring Ewan and locking the door to the clinic. "Can I bring anything?"

"D'ye have a can of olives?" Ewan asked. "Sausage? Pepperoni? Mozzarella cheese?"

"You're making pizza without cheese?" I said.

"We have parmesan," Graham answered.

"That's not pizza!" I said skeptically.

"Well, if ye dinna have it, ye canna use it!" Ewan shrugged. "Really, it's good. Ye'll like it."

"I'll like not cooking," I answered. "I still have no idea how to cook for just one person when I don't have a refrigerator."

When I returned from getting dressed, my beach bag in my hands (with my as-yet-unused snorkel, mask, and fins), Ewan and Graham were lazily resting in the grass in front of the clinic. They hopped up as soon as they saw me, and we headed to their house.

We chatted as we walked the mile to the school, our conversation frequently punctuated by enthusiastic children coming out to greet their teachers. Gruff Graham was a teddy bear when he saw his first and second graders, and Ewan kidded around with his middle schoolers. It made me smile to see these acerbic characters sweeten when they were around children.

"How long do you plan on teaching here?" I asked.

"Dinna ken," said Ewan. "'Tis a beautiful place and a good life."

"But what about marriage, family, kids?"

"I've already got kids enough," joked Graham, trying to shake off the three or four little ones currently hanging from his arms.

Watching the two, I supposed if they decided they wanted to be in some sort of extended adolescence, it was fine with me. They both seemed older than Campbell, maybe closer to my own age if I had to hazard a guess. And if I had responded to my desire to spend time in UniServe International earlier in my life, who knows whether I would have felt like going home, either.

As we approached their apartment, my heart started racing. True to his word, Campbell had avoided being alone with me for the last several days. I had tried to stop thinking of him too much, tried to lose myself in work and cleaning. Tried to think about Eric, being with *Eric*.

*Friends. Campbell and I could definitely be friends. We **had** to be able to be friends...*

"So where are you going to bake this masterpiece?" I asked curiously, as we entered their apartment. It seemed to me that without electricity, it would be kind of hard to bake anything. So far, I had only eaten things that I could fry or boil.

"In the oven, of course," answered Ewan.

"How do *you* have an oven?" I moved over to their kitchen to have a look at their set-up, which, it turned out, was quite a bit nicer than mine.

"Propane," said Ewan. "But we can make ye a little oven for your kerosene stove from a ship biscuit tin if ye have one."

"Or," said Campbell, coming around the corner, "ye can come here if ye need to bake something. And then ye can share it with us. I hear we're 'hungry boys,'" he said, grinning. "Hey, *Ri-pālle.*"

He was shirtless, wearing just my sarong. My heart jumped at the sight of him. Tanned and well-defined, he was delicious to look at. I tried not to stare.

"I'm never getting that back, am I?" I asked, gesturing toward the sarong.

Campbell looked at me apologetically. "I dinna think I *can* give it back to ye," he said. "It has put me in touch wi' my past, wi' my Highlander roots."

"A Scot never feels so manly as when he is wearing a skirt," Graham stated grandly.

"Yes," said Campbell, looking down. "Since my horrible injury, this sarong and I have bonded. I'm afraid it isna yours anymore."

"Well, you owe me then," I said.

"What payment will you be requiring?" he asked, eyeing me flirtatiously.

I narrowed my eyes at him. I wasn't quite sure how to respond to flirting. We'd said *friends*. Was flirting included in that?

And as far as payment went, I had a few thoughts, *none* of them appropriate. "Are you any good at building? I want to make some raised garden beds, so I can try growing some fresh produce."

"Aye," said Campbell. "That I can do. Then I willna have to feel guilty every time I see ye and I'm still wearing your sarong."

"I hear ownership is much more fluid in the Marshall Islands," I said, smiling at Campbell. "Don't be surprised if one day I show up and just take it back."

"Well, hopefully ye do that when he's no wearing it. Or at least wearing underwear," said Ewan. He looked thoughtful for a moment, and added, "Which is *never*."

My gaze flashed to Campbell's pelvis impulsively, and I looked away as quickly as possible. Unfortunately, as far as I could tell all three guys had seen me. I shook my head and laughed. "You boys are so nasty," I said. "Is it just that you can't talk like this with the local girls?"

"Aye," said Ewan. "Not the local lassies, and we definitely canna talk like this wi' our students. We have to play dumb with them."

"Play dumb?"

Campbell had been opening cupboards and taking containers and bowls out, but he stopped and turned toward me. With a smile, he crossed his arms over his chest and leaned back against the counter. Then with wide, innocent eyes, he said, "Meester Mack, what mean '*ba-shina*'?" He looked expectantly at me.

"I don't know that word," I said. "Bah shine uh? What is that?"

"Fanny?" Campbell hinted. I shook my head. "Honeypot?" he said. I shrugged my shoulders, continuing to shake my head. "A *va-gin-a*?" he finished, blushing.

"Your students *ask* you that?" I said, shocked.

"All the time. *You* might not have had to pretend ye didna understand, but I've gotten excellent at playing dumb," he said. "In Majel, the letters v, f, p, and b sound alike. That's why they call you Miss Peachay instead of Miss Beecher. Instead of having "fun," they have "pun." They will walk to the 'billage' instead of the village. So they will ask me, 'What mean '*puck*'? What mean '*ba-shina*'? What mean '*be-nice*'?"

"Be nice?" I said, confused. "I think I know what they mean by *puck*. I get *ba-shina*. But *be nice*?"

Ewan raised his eyebrows and with a subtle motion pointed downward toward his crotch.

"Penis?" I laughed. "Wow. They can*not* pronounce that one. Where are they seeing these words? Because they're definitely not *hearing* them."

"I don't know. Dictionary?" said Campbell, rolling his eyes. "They find themselves very amusing but get extremely frustrated when we don't understand them."

"And we *never* seem to," said Ewan, grinning innocently.

"I don't have the same problem with mine," Graham said grumpily. "They're still busy overusing the Majel words for poop, pee, and fart."

"*Pijek, raut, jiñ*," Ewan called out, teasingly.[1]

Campbell had gone to the cupboards and brought the ingredients back to the kitchen table where I was sitting. Like the host of a cooking show, he narrated as he added the ingredients and began to mix and knead the dough. It was quite enjoyable, watching his muscles ripple and flex as he moved, folding, stretching, and compressing the dough.

"And you add just enough flour to keep it from sticking, and then you knead it until it makes a beautiful doughy ball!" he ended with a flourish, holding up the finished dough in his floury hands.

"They really should have a show called the Shirtless Chef," I said enthusiastically.

Campbell looked over at me teasingly. "D'ye need me to put my shirt back on?" he asked. "Is that more than ye can handle? 'Twas just a hot day, and I'm in my own apartment."

"Nah," said Graham, looking at me with narrowed eyes. "I think she likes the view."

Suddenly I felt embarrassed. Was I that obvious? "No, I'm fine," I said. "I'm just starting to feel kinda celibate."

"I'd be happy to help you with that, lass," said Ewan generously, clearly staring at my breasts.

"If I need assistance, Ewan," I said, smiling, "You'll be the first to know."

Campbell put the dough into a bowl and covered it with a dishcloth. "Okay," he said. "Let's get ready to go spearfishing. Carlie, ye can change in my bedroom if ye want."

---

[1] *Pijek, raut, jiñ*: Pizhe´-eck, rout, jing (poop, pee, fart)

I ignored the suggestive smiles and went into his room with my bag, pulled off my sundress and put on a pair of shorts over my swimsuit. When I came out, Campbell stared at me. "Huh," he grunted with lowered eyebrows.

"What?" I said. Campbell's grunts always meant something, and this time it appeared to indicate I was doing something wrong.

"I dinna want ye to feel like I'm always correcting ye, but ye're not going to be able to wear those shorts outside," he said, frowning down at my legs.

"What? Why?" I asked.

"Women's shorts have to completely cover their thighs here," he said matter-of-factly. "Those don't even cover them halfway."

"You're kidding!" I said, astonished. "I don't get it. So far, I've seen countless women pull a boob completely out of their dresses to feed their babies in full view of everyone here. What's the deal with thighs?"

"Breasts are a sexual thing in American culture," he explained. "No' here. Here, they're just a source of food for babies. On Arno, the erogenous area is the thigh. Ye show your thighs, and that's like showing cleavage down to your waist in America. Ye need to be covered to the knee."

I scoffed. "Well, I guess I'm just going to have to stay here then. I didn't bring another pair of shorts."

"Ewan," said Campbell, eyeing me up and down thoughtfully, "Go get Carlie a pair of shorts."

"Why me?" Ewan whined.

"Because you're the smallest," explained Campbell. "Carlie wouldna fit mine or Graham's shorts."

Ewan wandered back with a pair of hideous orange things, so with one last glare at Campbell, I went back to his bedroom and put them on.

"Happy?" I grumped as I reappeared, the drawstring of Ewan's trunks tied firmly to keep them from falling off my hips.

"Ye look perfect," Campbell smiled, eyes twinkling as he retreated to get dressed.

When the guys had on their swim trunks, they grabbed several long metal poles with thin black handle loops from the entryway. Graham had a net bag and Campbell and Ewan each clipped an oblong metal carabineer to the belt loops of their shorts.

I was grateful for my beach bag, as Ewan, Campbell, and Graham all juggled their equipment in their arms. Finally, we reached the beach and dropped all the equipment. I watched and copied as the guys grabbed some green leaves from a bush, spit into their masks, and rubbed the inside of the mask with the leaves.

"What does this do?" I asked.

"Keeps the mask from fogging inside," said Graham.

Once the masks were on their heads, they dipped their swim fins into the water and then slipped their feet inside. They peeled off their shirts, grabbed their spears, and then started walking into the water.

"Here's yours," said Campbell, handing me a spear.

"Really?" I said, staring at him in disbelief. "You're just going to set me loose in the ocean with a spear that I don't know how to use?"

"Aye, *Ri-pālle*," he agreed with a grin. "I should at least show you how to use it. And the basic rule is, dinna pull it tight unless you're paying full attention, and dinna release it if there's a person in front of ye. Especially if it's me. Ewan and Graham, I dinna so much care about."

He showed me how to grip the rubber loop between the thumb and forefinger of my right hand. He was left-handed, so we were mirror images of each other as I watched and copied him by stretching my hand up the body of the spear until the rubber band was stretched tightly. When I let go of the spear, it sprung forward several inches.

"It works even better underwater," he said. "The tube fills with water, so it has more momentum and hits harder. Ye wait until ye have a fish just a few inches in front of the tip, and then ye release it."

Ewan and Graham were already chest deep in the water, but Campbell waited for me as I awkwardly flopped my way into deeper water. When we finally got up to waist depth, Campbell showed me how to put my snorkel into my mouth, and then I lowered my face into the water.

The first thing I noticed was a strange crackling sound. The ocean was noisier than I had thought it would be. I had no idea what the source of the popping, snapping, sparkling sound came from, but it was unfamiliar, nothing like swimming in a pool.

Our fins had stirred up the white coral sand underneath our feet, so when I put my face in the water I couldn't see a thing. I'd taken just a few breaths when I started panicking. I pushed myself out of the water, spit out the snorkel and stood, panting. Campbell had begun swimming away but looking back saw I wasn't behind him and stood up as well.

"What's wrong, hen?' he asked, sloshing back toward me, water dripping off the end of his copper curls and down his torso.

"I'm sorry, Campbell," I said, holding my hand to my chest as I tried to catch my breath. "I don't think I can go. Like, I started panicking. With my face in the water I can't see where I'm going and it's hard to breathe through the snorkel."

"You can practice," he said. "It will get easier."

"I've snorkeled before," I said, embarrassed. "But I used to go with my sisters and brother."

"Come on, Carlie," he said reassuringly, gesturing to me. "*Itōk, Ri-pālle.* I'm left-handed, you're right-handed. I'll hold your hand."

My hand firmly gripped in his, the ocean didn't seem so overwhelming. With swim fins on our feet we didn't really need our arms to propel ourselves speedily forward. Pretty soon the water deepened, and I began to see shiny flashes in the water ahead followed by the shadowy shapes of rocks and coral becoming clearer and clearer.

Within minutes we were surrounded by schools of beautiful fish, as if swimming through a tropical fish tank. There were bright orange fish, multi-colored striped fish, black angelfish with trailing yellow fins, and even a few tangs that looked remarkably like Dory from *Finding Nemo.* Suddenly I felt guilty; we were going to spear and eat these beautiful creatures?

I noticed that Campbell was tugging me off to the left, so I patted his hand and let go of him. I wasn't feeling as afraid, and I'd gotten used to breathing just through my mouth. I imagined we'd both be more successful if we weren't attached, but still I tried to keep him in my line of sight and followed him as he turned toward a large coral formation.

To prepare myself, I experimented with my spear a few times, seeing how far forward I needed to put my hand for the spear to spring about 6-8 inches when I released it. Then I swam over to the coral and started looking for my first target.

I decided to look for the ugliest, plainest fish I could find. Somehow it seemed like it wouldn't be as mean to eat the ugly ones. I was engrossed in my search, when a hand patted me on the shoulder, and when I looked, motioned upward.

The ocean wasn't very deep; in fact, I was able to balance on the tips of my swim fins and touch the bottom.

Campbell pulled his snorkel out of his mouth. "Think ye can do it?" he panted. I nodded, not wanting to chance getting water in my mouth. "If ye spear one, I'll help ye get it off and put it on my stringer."

I could see the metal ring hanging off his shorts with three bright fish strung on it. "You already have three?" I exclaimed, spitting my snorkel out.

"I'm experienced," he grinned. "I'll stay wi' ye. Once ye've got one, I'll start fishing again. We dinna need more than three or four per person. They don't keep long."

Knowing Campbell was watching me made me feel nervous, but I waited until a plain silver fish swam in front of my spear, and then I released my grip. The fish darted away, and the spear banged against the coral; I tried again with the same result. After three more failures, Campbell again motioned for me to surface.

"Ye've got to anticipate it a little," he advised. "Shoot where it's going, no' where it is now."

The sixth time was a charm. I launched the spear before the fish was right in front of the tip, and the sharp spear pierced it almost instantaneously. Of course, then I was excited, looked up to show Campbell, got salt water into my snorkel, breathed it, and started coughing.

As I sputtered at the surface Campbell gripped me firmly about the waist to hold my head above the water, grinning at me with affectionate joy. "Ye did it, Ri-pālle! Good job!" He slipped the silver fish off the spear and passed his fish stringer through the its gills, clipping it again. "Now, do it again."

"Aren't you going to fish more?" I panted breathlessly.

"I've done it plenty," he said, smiling. "And it's making ye happy."

CHAPTER 13

Scar Stories

I was giddy when we arrived back at the apartment, as I had caught four more fish. Graham and Ewan kindly admired my catch, though two of the fish were small and slightly mangled.

My experience with swimming in ocean water on Guam had been that salt water leaves a residue on your skin. By the time we got back to their house I was feeling kind of ratty-haired and sticky.

"I think I should go back home to shower and get changed," I said. "I feel salty and gross."

"You dinna want to have to walk an extra two miles just to be cleaned up for dinner," insisted Ewan. "Just use our shower."

Agreeably I grabbed my towel and dress, with the sudden distressing thought that I hadn't brought along any extra underwear. While I figured I could put my swimsuit back on, I didn't like the idea of walking around in wet clothes.

"Can I pop in your room for a minute, Campbell?" I asked.

"Aye," he answered from the kitchen where he was punching down the dough. I entered his room, then gingerly closing the door behind myself I tiptoed over to his dresser. In the top drawer I found a variety of briefs and boxers and finally chose a pair of black boxer briefs without the strange front hole.

Attempting a breezy greeting as I passed the kitchen, I went out to their shower. There was already a full bucket of water and some basic hair products as well, so I had everything I needed. When I got dressed after my shower it felt a little strange to put on Campbell's underwear, but it was better than the alternative.

As I returned to their apartment, I saw Ewan outside, slicing each fish up the belly with a sharp knife and scooping out the innards. Meanwhile, Graham had been gathering sticks and building a fire in a little fire pit. When I looked at him curiously, he said, "Fish taste best barbecued over a fire." It looked like he had a small metal grate with him, and a bottle of soy sauce.

Back inside, I went into the kitchen to watch the chef at work. Campbell was spreading tomato sauce and some thinly sliced pepperoni sticks over the pizza dough, which he'd rolled out to fit a rectangular pan. That finished, he sprinkled it generously with Parmesan cheese and Italian herbs, and then stuck it in the oven.

"Barbecue time," he said, smiling as he grabbed plates and gestured for me to follow him outside.

Just in front of their door was a small shaded patio. There were a couple of plastic chairs under the porch roof, and Campbell grabbed one to sit on by the fire. Looking around, on the far side of their yard by the fire pit I saw a funny sling-like hanging chair, supported by a thick rope tied to a huge tree. Settling myself in the swing, I watched as Graham turned the fish over on the grate, their skins looking brown and blistered, splitting to reveal white flesh inside.

I was staring up at the tree curiously when Graham said, "Breadfruit." He pointed with his fork up through the branches to the bumpy green balls high in the tree.

"How in the world do you pick them? They're so high up!" I asked, still leaning back in the swing from which I could see the tall branches, large leaves, and numerous fruit.

"A rock and slingshot," said Campbell, grinning. "And quite a bit of skill. That's one thing I've yet to master; it's quite impressive to see the locals take down a breadfruit with a single shot."

I tried to imagine how a person could use just a rock and a sling shot to get a huge round fruit from high up in a tree.

Graham used a fork to put a few of the perfectly-cooked fish on each plate. I inspected my first course with interest. Still whole, pretty colors blistered and blackened, the fish had diagonal knife cuts along each side through which I could see flaky white meat.

Watching other people had turned out to be an important social skill on Arno; by observing the boys I saw that they were pinching hot pieces off with their fingers to eat. My fish stared at me blankly as I grabbed my first bite. "Hey, thanks, buddy," I said apologetically.

My little friend was delicious and fresh, with a mild flavor accentuated by the salty tang of soy sauce. I began to feel less guilty for eating Dory and Nemo's friend, though I could have done without his eye staring at me accusingly.

With the coming of dusk, the mosquitoes arrived in force as well, so we retreated into the apartment just in time to eat Campbell's perfect pizza fresh from the oven. The boys were right; lack of mozzarella didn't detract at all.

As we settled on their couches after finishing dinner, I looked down at my stomach. "I've got a food baby," I groaned, frowning at the little bulge on my stomach. Campbell had occupied the seat next to me, and taking me completely by surprise, he reached over and gently stroked my belly.

"We'll name her Peshay," he said. At my confused expression he grinned and explained, "*Peshay*. P-E-S-C-E. That's Italian for *fish. . .*"

"Aren't you clever?" I laughed, scraping his hand off my stomach as subtly as I could. His thumb was dangerously close to my braless breasts, and I was already feeling a little too much just sitting next to him. He'd said he wanted to just be my friend, but it felt like he was toying with me.

It didn't get any easier as the evening progressed. Ewan started spouting off about how Arno was traditionally known to have a "love school."

"They would have girls lie in a canoe on the sea and feel the rocking of the waves. That's all the sexual education they would need to please a man," Ewan explained happily.

"Seems to me I know a few things that lying in a canoe would *not* have taught me," I said, frowning and shaking my head. When all three guys turned and stared at me with intense interest, I groaned and covered my face in embarrassment. "I'm sorry. You guys talk dirty, and it's rubbing off on me."

"I'd be happy to rub off on you," said Graham. Campbell reached over and punched him. "Ow," said Graham, rubbing his shoulder in surprise.

"So, let's not be sexist here," I said. "What happens if a man lies in a canoe? Does he learn anything valuable?"

"If it's Campbell, he gets seasick and starts heavering!" Graham said, glaring at Campbell. "And he wouldna have much opportunity to practice what he learned anyway."

Campbell glared back at Graham, and decided it was time to change the subject. "So, Miss Beecher, you said you'd tell me about one of your scars," he said. "Have you decided which one?"

I held out my leg and pointed at a small round white spot on my ankle. "Five years old, riding on the handlebars of my dad's bike."

Campbell turned and stared at me. "Your worst injury was from riding on handlebars?"

"Handlebar moustaches?" sniggered Ewan, earning an evil glare from Campbell.

"Then why did you...?" Campbell said in an aside to me. "Were ye afraid to ride wi' me yesterday?"

"I learned my lesson back then," I whispered as I shook my head and continued. "My foot slipped between the spokes, mangled my ankle, and crashed his bike. It hurt, and I remember my dad crying because he felt so bad, and that I got orange juice. We didn't have juice very often in my family," I explained, when they seemed surprised at my memory of such an insignificant thing.

"Your turn, Ewan," said Graham.

He opened his lips and indicated his teeth. "Two fake front teeth. Summer camp counseling," he said.

That one took me by surprise and I laughed. "One of your campers punch you in the mouth?"

"No, just broke them out going down the waterslide headfirst. Wouldna recommend it. And all I was trying to do was just be a fun camp counselor. That will teach me..."

"Graham?" I said.

He pulled his shirt up and then his shorts downward. When I looked surprised, he said, "Don't worry. It's just an appendectomy scar. Twelve years old. Almost died."

"Thought you'd just muscle through the pain?" I asked.

"Real men don't need hospitals," he joked.

"Campbell?" said Ewan.

"This all started because I told Carlie it wasna fair she was so familiar with the scar on my bum."

"I havena seen it," said Ewan.

"Neither have I," agreed Graham.

"Go for it," I said, averting my eyes, as Campbell stood and unbuttoned his shorts. He faced me as he dropped the back of the shorts down so Ewan and Graham could see the scar. Both guys took a sharp intake of breath.

"I didna realize how big it was," Ewan gasped. "Your arse, I mean. That's just a baby scrape."

"Good work, Miss Peach," exclaimed Graham, acknowledging the severity of the injury. "It willna disfigure him for the rest of his life as I feared. He *might* still be able to find himself a wife."

"Can I see how it's healed?" I asked, realizing I hadn't seen his scar since removing the stitches over a week before. Campbell frowned slightly, but slowly rotated to turn his back to me. For a moment I was completely in nurse mode, happy to see that the skin on both sides of the scar had already lightened from the previous week and the stitch marks were fading. I had reached out and palpated Campbell's skin to feel how thick the scar tissue was when I looked past him and saw both Graham and Ewan staring at me wide-eyed, and I realized that Campbell had frozen and was clenching every muscle.

I took my hand away, blushing. "Oh, God, I'm sorry, Campbell," I said. "I totally forgot that we're not in the clinic right now. I'm just proud of my work."

Campbell did his shorts back up, but when he sat down, he sat about a foot closer to me. It didn't escape Graham's notice. He looked at us thoughtfully for a moment, then spoke. "You know, there are rumors going around about you guys."

"What kind of rumors?" I asked, already knowing what the answer was going to be.

"That the two of you have been hanging out alone, at night, in your apartment," said Ewan. Campbell and I exchanged an awkward glance.

"We don't hang out inside my apartment at night," I said, realizing with chagrin as Campbell stiffened next to me that it wasn't completely the truth. The first time he walked me home he *had* come in, had sat on my bed, held me on his lap... and needed a moment to recover before leaving. And then of course, there was *yesterday*. "Graham has been in my apartment at night, though," I said to change the subject.

"Graham's been in your apartment?" complained Ewan. "You never let *me* in!"

"Just to show me how see-through my curtains were when I was changing with the lights on inside."

Ewan glared at Graham. "Ye *told* her?"

"We never peeked at Miss Lynch, but after I saw what I saw I thought I should let her know."

"Not fair at all," grumped Ewan, and Campbell gave me a sidelong glance.

"Well, on that note, I think it's time for me to go home," I said. I gathered up my swimsuit, towel, and snorkel gear and put them in my bag. When I got to the front door, Ewan was there, tennis shoes on.

My heart sunk when I realized it wasn't Campbell. I wanted to talk to him and I'd been missing his hugs. But I couldn't exactly express that, so I cheerily wished Graham and Campbell good night. At least as I met Campbell's eyes, I could see that he wasn't happy to relinquish his time with me either.

As Ewan and I walked down the road I kept my distance from him, afraid he might try to make a move on me. Finally, he stopped me.

"I can tell ye're scared of me, Miss Peach. What kind of guy do you think I am?" Ewan asked. "I may like a dirty joke, but ye can trust me not to lay a hand on ye uninvited."

We walked in silence for a time, and finally Ewan spoke up. "In all seriousness, Carlie, ye do need to be careful."

"Careful, how?" I asked.

"Wi' Campbell, of course," Ewan said.

I looked at him skeptically. "I need to be *careful* in my *friendship* with my *friend* Campbell?" I asked.

In the moonlight I could see his eyes narrow. "With how close you get to each other," he said. "With what you do and where you go together. With what people see, and what people don't see but guess at..."

"Come on, Ewan, we're just good friends," I said. I knew I was lying, that I felt more than that; but I didn't want to face the truth.

"He told us, ye ken," Ewan said.

"Told you what?" I asked innocently.

"That ye called him by your fiancé's name. That's why we invited you over. Because he's vowed not to be alone wi' ye, and the lad's been pining to see you somethin' fierce."

"It was just a mistake," I said. "I told him that." I was at once mortified that Ewan and Graham knew and endeared by how admirable Campbell was being.

"I see the way he looks at you, lass. And the way you look at him."

"We do get along really well," I agreed, trying to act nonchalant. "And we like being with each other. We just kind of bonded. Campbell's an awesome teacher, and he's been kind enough to introduce me to Marshallese culture and the language. So, yeah, I like hanging out with him. But I'm engaged, and he's like... my little brother's age."

Ewan walked a few more steps before responding. "You're not going to like hearing this, but that ring on your finger is possibly the only thing about you that's engaged."

My stomach dropped, and I suddenly felt sick.

Ewan continued. "Campbell got in enough trouble back in Scotland that he still doesn't want to go back there. This is a safe place for him to be, and he's grown up a lot in the past four years. For you, spending time wi' him might just be a harmless fling, and you've got something to go back to if it falls apart. But if the two of ye get in trouble, Campbell's got nothing to fall back on."

It took a few minutes for it to sink in. I might have still been hotly fuming inside, but I could see the truth in what Ewan said. Finally I responded, "Okay. What should I do then?"

"Make yourself scarce. Visit with the locals. As much as I hate to say it, don't visit. Don't bring us food. Graham and I will try not to pull you in with us for a while. Campbell needs time to get his head on straight. He could find a nice local girl to marry and just stay here forever. Somehow I can't see you settling down in a place like this. It's just a low-tech vacation for you. It's much more than that for Campbell."

"What if I don't agree with you?" I said bitterly, turning to face him in the faint light of the clinic.

"I'm serious, Carlie," Ewan said. "Ye must stay away from him. You dinna ken what you're doing to Campbell by flirting with the lad. You're toying with his entire future."

I felt nauseated when I got back to my house. I didn't even say goodnight to Ewan when I went inside, where I sat in the darkness in my room. I was trembling, but I wasn't sure with what. Anger? Embarrassment?

What the fuck are you thinking, Beecher? I asked myself. *You are engaged to Eric Anderson, and here you are playing pseudo-girlfriend to a young virgin. What is **wrong** with you?*

We *were* playing with fire. There was the increased intimacy of taking care of him and seeing him undressed; the silliness of sharing clothing (He still had my sarong, and I realized I was still wearing his underwear); the emotional intimacy of Campbell listening to me and the physical intimacy of him embracing and holding me. There was also my complete awareness of his attraction to me, the way I aroused him physically... and the depth of my own attraction to him. This wasn't how you started a platonic friendship. And it wasn't the way to stay faithful to Eric.

I struggled to fall asleep, the events of the day replaying in my mind. The sweet moments of spearfishing with Campbell, his smile at me as he held me tightly about the waist when I'd speared my first fish, his curls a wet auburn, his eyes as blue as the lagoon around us. And later the pressure of his palm on my stomach, caressing me as if I carried his child.

I felt sick and devastated. If I pulled away from Campbell I wasn't going to lose just a friend.

"*Mo chridhe*," I whispered to the darkness. *My heart.*

* * *

Campbell and I were in two separate canoes which were tied together on the open sea. We lay on our backs, feeling the movement of the waves until we became one with the ocean, until we melded with the life force of the earth. Finally, we sat up.

"Have you learned enough?" I asked him.

"I'm ready when you are," he said, gazing at me with eyes that mirrored the ocean.

"Well, this is how you lose your virginity," I explained.

Suddenly we were in a middle school hallway. I reached down and grabbed his hand and we walked down the hall, kids turning and looking at us, pointing at our hands, giggling and whispering as they turned away.

Then we were at a high school dance, our arms around each other. I was wearing a wrist corsage; he looked overdressed in a tuxedo. He leaned down and kissed me, a sweet, gentle pressure against my lips; our noses bumping awkwardly because we hadn't learned to tilt our heads yet.

Next, we were in the backseat of a car with steamed-up windows. He had his hand up my cheerleading uniform shirt, clumsily squeezing my breast over my bra while we awkwardly French-kissed in hesitant wet explorations. When I walked in the front door of my house, my mom commented offhandedly about my red lips and flushed face.

I saw my floral print bedspread in my room at home with the door halfway closed, his back to the door and his pants around his ankles, and me on my knees in front of him. I looked up at him and his head was dropped back, looking half-pained while I inexpertly tried to make myself and him feel good, gagging too easily and feeling ashamed afterward.

And then in a dorm room, lights off, trying not to disturb my roommate on the top bunk, I gasped through his first touches, astonished by the feel of his hand between my legs. And when I'd seen heaven during my first, shuddering orgasm, I had to hold him off. "Not now," I said, "maybe another time," unsure if 'another time' would ever come.

Finally, we were out on a date—the third one—to a nice Italian restaurant. We'd eaten, and walked, and talked, and laughed, and then we went back to his apartment (because he had one), and after looking at each other with a question and an answer in our eyes, we gently undressed each other and made love in his queen-sized bed. And when I bled he was compassionate and went to get a washcloth for me from the bathroom. And afterwards he drove me back to the dorm with toilet paper stuck into my panties since I didn't have a panty liner. When he dropped me off, he walked me to the door and kissed me goodnight gently, saying, "That was wonderful, Carlie. Thank you for trusting me with your first time."

"Goodnight, Eric," I said, blushingly smiling as I watched him walking down the sidewalk away from me.

I woke up sweaty and despondent, and cried myself back to sleep.

CHAPTER 14

The Break Up

"**M**iss Peachay...Miss Peachay!" Urgent knocking at my door woke me from my fitful slumber. I hadn't slept well at all since waking up in the middle of the night. I peeked out of the door to see a thin teenage girl standing there. "Miss Peachay, *niññiñ, kōn an nañinmej.*"[1]

A baby was sick. Sharbella had been working to teach me Marshall phrases in the times when we didn't have patients, and I knew enough to know 'baby', which sounded like 'ning-a-ning' and 'sick'— 'nang-in-mesh.' I held a finger up. "*Kōttar jidik*—wait just a minute."

I threw on one of my dresses over my pajamas and strapped on my sandals. Grabbing the keys to the clinic, I headed out the door.

I'd seen the teenage girl around before. "*Etam in?*" I asked her as I unlocked the door of the clinic to grab my travel kit.[2] "What is your name?"

"Karla," she said. "I know little English. Is my sister baby *kōn an nañinmej.*"

"Your sister's baby is sick?"

She nodded. "*Itōk ippa,*" she said desperately.[3]

Just the word "*Itōk,*" made me think of Campbell, reaching out his hand compassionately to me when I was frightened of snorkeling, saying "*Itōk, Ri-*

---

[1] *Niññiñ, kōn an nañinmej:* Ning´-a-ning, cone on nang´-in-mesh (baby, he is sick)

[2] *Etam in:* Ett´-tom een (What's your name?)

[3] *Itōk ippa:* Ee´-tok ee´-pah (Come with me.)

pālle." Come, Carlie. I had come to like Campbell's name for me, the way it rolled gently off his tongue, the way he looked at me with an affectionate half-smile when he said it. I swallowed hard to rid myself of the lump in my throat as I followed Karla down the road.

"Tiljek's baby?" I asked, as we arrived at the block building with low windows. She nodded, grabbing my hand and pulling me inside.

I felt a sinking feeling in my stomach when I knew it was him. Sharbella had whispered to me as Tiljek wheeled her baby away in a wheelbarrow that she had lost several children in infancy. Little Maxson cried wherever his mother went. Tiljek was simple, slightly empty-eyed. And whether there was something genetically wrong with her children, whether she lacked the ability to feed her babies or care for them well, this was her fourth baby. None of the others had lived.

They had a small kerosene lantern lit in the bare room with pandanus sleeping mats on the floor. Tiljek was holding Maxson on her lap, rocking back and forth. I held my hands out, and she placed him in them. He was hot to the touch, had a red tint to his sweaty skin, and I could hear him wheezing. He was exhibiting all the symptoms of pneumonia.

I pulled out my little cheat sheet of medical terms *"Ikkijelok?"* I asked.[1] "Is he having trouble breathing?" Tiljek didn't answer, just staring at me blankly.

"Aet," Karla said. "Yes."

"Ewi toon?" I asked. "How long?"

"Ruo raan," she said.

"Two days?!" I exclaimed. I tried to calm myself, but I knew that letting pneumonia go untreated in an infant could have devastating consequences.

I shuffled through my bag until I found the inhaler and spacer. The nebulizer was back at the clinic, but this would do for now. Shaking the inhaler, I put the mouthpiece over Maxson's mouth and gave him an albuterol treatment to widen his airways and relieve his labored breathing. Unfortunately, the raspy wheezing continued.

---

[1] *Ikkijelok*: Ih-kid´-jell-ock (difficult breathing)

"Can they boil some water?" I asked Karla. She wrinkled her forehead.

I pulled the little English-Majel dictionary out of the bag. "*Bōel aebōj*," I directed.[1]

"*Aet*," said Karla. "Okay." She left the house to go to the cooking shack. The steam from boiling water could help to ease Maxson's breathing.

I found the liquid acetaminophen and an eyedropper and gave Maxson a dose, then looked back at my medical term sheet.

"*Emmoj?*" I asked.[2] "Has he vomited?" Tiljek stared at me blankly. Her husband, who had been sitting in the shadows, moved forward.

"*Aet. Emmoj.*"

"How about diarrhea?" I asked. "*Biroro lojem?*"[3]

He nodded.

"*Ewi toon?* How long?" I asked.

"*Jilu raan*," he said.[4] "Um. Tree days?"

I felt sick. Vomiting and diarrhea would add dehydration to list of challenges I'd need to combat for Maxson to recover.

"Tiljek," I said. "*Kōkaajiriri.*" I handed Maxson back to her, gesticulating that she should nurse him.[5]

"*Ejjelok*," the father said, shaking his head.[6]

"She doesn't have milk?" I asked, confused. The baby was only four months old.

"*Ejjab*," he said. "*Emmat.*"[7]

---

[1] *Bōel aebōj*: Bo´-ell eye´-bodge (boil water)

[2] *Emmoj*: Em-mozhe´ (vomiting)

[3] *Biroro lojem*: Pih-dro´-ro lo´-shem (diarrhea)

[4] *Jilu raan*: Chee´loo rie´-een (three days)

[5] *Kōkaajiriri*: Coe´-kah-jah-ree´-ree (Nurse him)

[6] *Ejjelok*; Etch-chel´-lock (There's nothing)

[7] *Ejjab, Emmat*: Etch´-chab, Eh-mat´ (No, empty)

"What are you feeding him, then?" I asked, looking around and shrugging my shoulders in confusion.

He searched in the shadows and came up with a baby bottle and a can of evaporated milk. Not the best choice, I knew, but better than nothing.

I gave Maxson another treatment with the inhaler while the father prepared a bottle for him, but Maxson didn't seem to have much desire to drink; that was not a good sign. When Karla came back with the pot of boiling water, I took the blanket they had wrapped Maxson in and draped it over the pot and his head. I turned him on his side and patted his back, seeing if I could loosen any phlegm and get him breathing better.

The whole time, Tiljek sat blankly, no expression on her face. No tears, no concern. She didn't reach for her baby or come close to me to see how he was doing.

After the steam had dissipated, I rewrapped Maxson in his blanket and leaned against the wall of the house, patting him on the back. I fell asleep with the hot little body on my lap.

When I woke up an hour or two later to the faint light of morning and a neighboring rooster crowing, something didn't seem right. Maxson wasn't on my lap anymore. I looked around to see that he was on a mat in front of Tiljek, who was fanning him gently.

"How is he?" I asked, crawling over to place my hand on him. His skin wasn't hot anymore, and I felt a moment of relief until I realized he wasn't breathing.

"*Ewi toon?* How long?" I cried out, grabbing my stethoscope and listening for the heartbeat that wasn't there.

"*Juon awa,*" Tiljek said blandly, fanning away.

An hour. His skin had taken on a purple pallor. It was too late to do anything for him. Maxson was gone.

I stumbled from the house, and walked to the lagoon, where I sat on the sand and stared out over the water.

Compartmentalization. It's a talent a nurse must develop so that he or she won't be crushed by the constant barrage of sickness and death one deals with in the health care field. Somehow the clinical, sanitized nature of a hospital or clinic enables compartmentalizing.

A hospital looks nothing like where we live. Beeping machines and sterilized tools, people wearing uniforms, the sanitized color of white... a *hospital* is where death happens. Not a little house on a beautiful tropical island. Not when you've done your best. Not when it's a mother's fourth baby and none of them have lived.

I buried my face in my hands and sobbed.

And then I heard the sound that broke my heart.

"Carlie? Are you okay?"

He was barefoot on the beach, wearing that damn sarong and a tee shirt, looking muscular and innocent and adorable. I wanted to rush into his arms. I wanted him to hold me. I knew that was the one thing that would make this ache in my chest go away. But instead, I lied.

"I'll be okay. It's just... Tiljek's baby. Little Maxson just died." Campbell moved closer. "We can't be alone together anymore," I said to him. "If they're gossiping about us, we need to be more careful."

"What if I don't care what they say?" he asked. I could see his jaw clench, but his eyes were filled with compassion.

"You *should*. If you lose your reputation among the locals, they won't trust you to teach their kids."

He stepped forward again.

"It's more than just your reputation. *You can't be here*," I said, standing up.

"But you *need* me, hen," he said gently, reaching his hand out to my cheek and swiping the tears from beneath my eye with his thumb. He moved toward me as if to take me in his arms.

I stepped away from him. "I *can't* need you, Campbell," I shook my head as my chin quivered. "I'm engaged to Eric. I can't be so intimate with you. I'm sorry. I've taken advantage of your kindness and I've allowed my loneliness to fool myself into thinking this was okay. I've used my distance from Eric to justify this." I motioned back and forth between us. "We're not having sex, but this is *cheating*."

He was looking at me with an expression of such compassionate affection that I wanted to throw myself at him. I wanted him so bad I needed him to *hate* me.

"You're such a nice kid, Campbell," I said. He stiffened, and his eyes narrowed. "And I appreciate your friendship. But I've let my isolation in this place create a false sense of intimacy. If we were in the states, we wouldn't be friends. You wouldn't hang out with some older woman. You would never have noticed me, and I'm *certain* I wouldn't have noticed you." Yet another lie; with his bright hair and broad shoulders, Campbell was certain to draw attention wherever he went.

"I am here to focus on service to others, not some silly flirtation with a kid I could have babysat growing up." I could see that my words were finally working. Campbell's jaw was tightening, and his eyes looked at me with a fiery intensity that rivaled any strength of desire or affection I'd seen there before.

"I've already allowed myself to ignore the locals and shirk my responsibilities. If I had been doing home visits, I would have known Maxson was sick. I could have done more, and he wouldn't have died."

I covered my eyes with my hand. I could feel his continued closeness, even though I'd insulted him and tried to push him away.

"Please go away, Campbell. I'm not strong enough right now to fight with you."

When he spoke, his voice was low and measured. "Okay, *Ri-pālle*, I'm going. But I thought I'd tell you, when you come to a Majel funeral it's local custom to bring gifts of soap and dollar bills." The silence of bare feet on sand meant that when I finally opened my eyes, he had disappeared like a ghost.

There's no delaying a funeral in a tropical climate. Without a morgue or refrigeration, the decomposition process begins immediately. Word traveled quickly that in the evening, there would be a funeral at Tiljek's house.

I needed to not be alone, so I wandered next door to Anni's house. I found her sitting on a strange bench, holding half of a coconut.

"What are you making?" I asked.

"Coconut rice for the funeral," she said. I squatted near her, having learned the benefits of squatting instead of sitting ever since Campbell had shown me how to do it. I shook my head. I couldn't escape him—my Marshall Islands experience was *infused* with Campbell. Anni, coconuts, even being alone in my apartment made me remember him. After I'd insulted him and driven him away he was still teaching me, telling me what I needed to know so I fit in, so I did what was right.

I hadn't had a break-up since high school, but the nauseated ache in my gut took me quickly back. Being apart from Campbell? Remembering the look on his face? This was *torture*.

Anni held half of a fully-grown coconut, the kind with a dark brown shell and thick, hard meat on the inside. The stool she was sitting on had a grooved metal bar sticking off one end. Anni had a bowl underneath the bar, and she was leaning on the coconut, grating it into the bowl. I watched curiously as she finished grating that half and then the second half. Then she scooped up the coconut meat with her hands and put it in some cheesecloth, twisting the cloth to enclose the coconut inside. Next to her on the ground was a big black pot filled with water and raw white rice. Anni dipped the bag of coconut into the water, then removed it and squeezed milky liquid out of the cheesecloth. She repeated the process several times until the water coming out of the bag ran almost clear. Then she shook the grated coconut out into the pig trough, tossed the cheesecloth over her laundry line, and turned to enter the cooking hut.

"May I watch, Anni?" I asked, not wanting to be rude.

"*Itōk*," she said smilingly, inviting me in. Inside the cooking hut there was a fire ring with a metal grate. Above the fire the roof of the hut angled upwards to lead the smoke up and out.

There were already two breadfruits cut in half on the grill over a small fire. Anni took them off and put them on a pan, then added a few sticks to the fire and put the pot on top of the grate.

"What is a Majel funeral like?" I asked Anni. "What should I do?"

"You just sit with them—*jijet ipem*."[1]

"Do you say anything?"

---

[1] *Jijet ipem:* Shee´-shet ee´-pem (Sit with them)

"No, just sit and be...*sad* with them."

My eyes were tearing up at the thought. That I could do. "I want to be polite," I said. "I just don't know everything."

"Oh, they will forgive you," Anni said. She smiled kindly. "They know you are *ri-pālle.*"

I couldn't stop the tears. "I need to go home," I whispered.

Dear Eric,

I want to make things right between us. Will you please forgive me? Coming to the Marshall Islands was a cruel thing to do to you. I was selfishly only thinking of myself and my desires. I'm not sure what I expected, but this is not some tropical vacation. It's harsh and hard and lonely.

I lost my first patient today. He was a little four-month-old baby named Maxson who died of pneumonia. I did what I could, but I couldn't save him. There was no ER to take him to, no way to intubate him or give him a nebulizer treatment to help him breathe. I fell asleep with him on my lap, and when I woke up, he was dead. Tonight, I'll be going to his funeral, where they tell me I will just sit and be sad with the family. It's not enough.

I also need to confess. You are right; I am a weak person when it comes to resisting my impulses. But I have not cheated on you, not even with a kiss, even though my loneliness led me to get too close to the other white guys on the island, one in particular. I've stepped back from that closeness, and I am determined that I will be stronger.

*I have committed to UniServe, and I want to have the fortitude to stick with this. But if either of us determines that this is just too much for us to be apart, I am willing to end my commitment early. **Nothing** is more important to me than us.*

I love you,

Carlie

The sun was low in the sky when I put my sandals on and walked to Tiljek's house. I had a horrendous headache and felt sad and sick from crying. I'd written a letter to Eric that I wished I could teleport to him right this minute. I wanted reassurance that he still loved me. But the reality was, mail wouldn't go out until Monday morning with the plane, would take a week to get to Denver, and then it would take another week to get back from Eric to me. It would be two weeks until I received a reaction from him.

A small crowd of people were scattered around Tiljek's yard, sitting on woven pandanus mats on the ground. A table held an abundance of food—rice, fish, barbecued chicken, Spam, roasted breadfruit, bananas, and papaya. There was even red Kool-Aid with ice in it, and a woman was frying little round donuts over a camp stove.

I waited my turn to go inside and then sat next to Tiljek, who was still fanning little Maxson to keep the flies away. A white sheet over him covered his mouth. I handed Tiljek a bar of soap and two dollar bills, which she added to the pile next to her. Her eyes still looked empty.

I was cried out and weary, but I could sit and be sad with her, so I did that, watching Maxson's wispy black hair lifting in the breeze as she fanned him.

When I went outside, I filled my plate with small amounts of food. A portion of breadfruit, which made me think of Ewan and Graham. Barbecued fish, coconut rice, a tiny banana, a cup of juice, and two small round donuts. I looked around the yard, saw Graham, Ewan, and Campbell sitting on a mat on one side of the pebble-strewn yard, then turned and found Anni.

"You not sit with Meester Mack?" asked Anni as I sat down next to her on the pandanus mat.

"No," I said. "*Ej jab kōnaan.*"

"He doesn't want you?" she asked. I met his eyes across the yard. That obviously wasn't true. He was looking at me and didn't look away when I met his gaze; we stared sadly at each other until I finally looked down.

"No, *I* don't want *him*," I said over the lump in my throat. "How do you say that?"

"EE-jab, not eh-jab," said Anni. "But Miss Peachay," she shook her head, looking at me critically. "*Enana riab.* Is bad to lie."

CHAPTER 15

Consolation

Nothing felt right on Sunday. As I did my laundry I pictured Campbell squatting next to me, his eyes crinkling at the corners, a grin on his lips. A few times I heard flip flops on the road and turned, my heart racing, only to see a smiling islander walk by.

I hung my dresses up on the line and I could still see him, two clothespins gripped between his teeth, holding up a flowing floral dress in front of his body as if he was trying it on, raising one eyebrow at me suggestively. The dress had barely reached his knees.

"That is *definitely* your color," I had commented, and he had laughed, turning and pinning the dress on the line.

I went back into my house, and stopping momentarily on the stoop I ached to feel his strong arms around me.

While making my bed with fresh sheets, I thought of him sitting there in *my* sarong holding me, helping me feel safe and not alone anymore.

Everything reminded me of Campbell, and every time I thought of him, I felt more guilty and critical of myself. This young guy, my brother's age? And me, an engaged twenty-seven-year-old? Eric and I had talked about this. He *knew* my heart was flighty.

I re-read my letter to Eric and cried a little bit more. Then I put on my big girl pants, cleaned the clinic, and set out a home visit plan for post-natal care, writing out the questions to ask in Marshallese with possible answers and a few other helpful phrases. I wanted not to feel helpless, and if inadequate post-natal care was a cause of increased infant mortality, then I would do something about it.

I also took a few minutes to write to my best friend Greg. He had told me when I left that if there was any way the clinic could support me, I should let him know. With no fear of being judged, I poured out my heart about Maxson and my feelings for Campbell and how I didn't want to cheat on Eric and how I wished I could do more for the little children on the island.

The day was less breezy than it had been a couple of weeks back when Campbell had helped me, which meant my clothes were slightly crunchy when I took them off the line. I crossed my doorstep carrying my laundry basket, picturing a soaking wet girl, curls drooping, dress dripping, being hugged tightly, pulled into Campbell's sheltering side. I missed him so bad I ached.

I went for a walk in the evening, telling myself it would be okay to just bump into him by chance. I even walked past the UniServe school twice; on the road headed toward Matolen, on the beach headed back to the clinic, my heart pounding both times. But I saw no one, not Graham, not Ewan, not Campbell. I wondered if they'd scolded him, too, grounding him to his room...

That night I brought out my photo albums, trying to remember what it felt like to be with Eric.

But instead of warm memories, the pictures just created a stark contrast with the young man I'd seen just that afternoon on the beach.

You're so shallow, Carlie, I told myself. *Does a hot body and sweet affection count for more than years together?*

Sure, Campbell was energetic and enthusiastic. Since Eric was older than me by four years, that made him nearly ten years older than Campbell. *Of course* Eric was more settled. *Of course* he was less passionate. I tried to think back to when we met. Even then he was responsible. He was so much more mature and respectful than the other guys I dated that year.

When comparing him against the other options back then, Eric was a prize. Educated, articulate, with a job, his own apartment, and an actual car. He wore shoes, believed in showering, and offered to pay for me on dates. And when we were in bed together, he cared if I came. When I compared Eric to the boys around me, of course there was no comparison.

But I had never even considered that there could be so much more.

The world looked brighter on Monday. I got up early, took my shower, and went out to the beach with a mat to sit on as I watched the sun rise behind the islands on the other side of the atoll. I was certain I could fall back in love with Eric, and I thought journaling about him would help. I started writing a list of things I appreciated about him and memories I had of being together with him.

I tried to not notice what was missing from the list, the things that I craved—passion and affection.

When my neighbor Kona knocked on my door Monday evening and handed me a plastic grocery bag filled with mail, I could not have been more excited. That morning I had sent my mail with the driver of the pick-up truck as he went to meet the plane. I sighed with the thought that my letter to Eric was on its way.

There were notes from my mom and dad, a letter from my older sister Amy which had been scrawled on with crayon (probably one of my nephews). There was also a postcard from my college roommate. And at the bottom of the stack, there was a letter from Eric. I pressed it to my chest but decided to save it for last.

As I read the other letters, I kept finding myself looking at the letter from Eric. *Remind me why I love you*, my heart begged. *Be what I need.*

Through the letter from my mom, the little scribbled notes from my niece and nephew, through the slightly judgmental scolding from Amy, my eyes crept to the envelope with Eric's familiar handwriting on the outside.

I felt nervous to open it. There were so many things I needed it to say. "Have reasonable expectations, Beecher," I told myself as I finally used my letter opener to tear open the flap and bring out the letter from Eric.

I was about to start reading when a rapid knock on my door startled me. For a second, I felt a sinking sense of *déjà vu*. What was happening *now*?

It was a female voice, calling out, "Miss Peachay! Miss Peachay!"

I opened the door, and there was Anni. "*Itōk!*" she said. "Come see the miracle!"

"What?" I asked, confused.

"Come! Come! Put your shoes on! We run! Come see the miracle!"

I wasn't going to run in sandals, so I pulled on a pair of tennis shoes as Anni continued to urge me to hurry. Finally ready, I shut the door and followed Anni at a swift trot.

"Come see the miracle!" she shouted, heading toward the village of Ine, away from the UniServe school. We kept running, Anni calling out, "Come see the miracle," if I ever fell behind. Eventually I realized we were heading toward the fishing dock on the ocean side of the atoll. A boat? Visitors? A big fish? A shark? A whale? I had no idea what she was taking me to see.

We stopped, panting, on the edge of the dock.

"Look!" exclaimed Anni, "The miracle!" She gestured, and then I saw it. High in the dark, star-filled sky, was a full moon.

I stood in silence, staring up at the brilliant white circle. I could hear the pounding of my own heart in my ears and the gentle lapping of the waves on the shore. My nose pricked at the distinct, slightly fishy scent of the ocean. And I took in the stars, so vivid without the light pollution of the city. Tonight, I could distinguish the Milky Way, the brighter white stripe of stars showing the galaxy radiating out from our solar system.

And there was the moon, perfect and round, gray shadows of the craters so recognizable as the man in the moon I'd grown up seeing. He looked the same as always, just clearer.

It was a miracle. A miracle to be alive, a miracle to be here. I smiled at Anni. "How do you say 'Thank you?'" I asked.

"'Kommool,'" she said. "Is mean thanks. And 'kommool tata' is mean thank you bery much."[1]

I turned my face and gazed up at the glowing moon. "Kommool tata," I whispered.

I smiled all the way back to my apartment, this time noticing my beautiful island home. I sighed contentedly as I waved to Anni, taking one last look at the moon, now higher in the night sky.

---

[1] *Kommool tata:* Comb´-mole tah´-dah (Thank you very much)

When I got back inside, I changed into my shorts and tank top and then turned on my lamp, cuddled up in bed, and pulled out the letter, ready to hear from Eric.

Dear Carlie—

I won't waste time beating around the bush. I don't want to be engaged any more. I would like the freedom to live my life, and I don't feel it knowing my ring is on your finger halfway around the world. I haven't slept with anyone, but I don't like living my life with you as a shadow over it.

God, Carlie, I can't believe I'm having to do this. I have loved you for years. I thought I would be spending the rest of my life with you, but your choice to leave me has helped me see you don't value me in the same way. I can't commit to someone who won't commit to me.

You can try to blame this breakup on me, make me out to be the bad guy. Don't. You're the one who left. I am still in the same house, at the same job, with the same life. You are the one who wasn't satisfied with what we had, so you don't get to blame me if you suffer the consequences of your actions.

I've spent a lot of time considering this whole situation, and I have the strong suspicion you wanted to break up with me but didn't have the strength of character to do it. So instead, you put me in an untenable situation and forced me to break up with you, so that I look like the bad guy.

Goodbye, Carlie. If you want, I'll keep writing you, but as a friend. We can take stock when I see you in Denver again. Right now I won't rule out getting back together, but after eighteen months apart, I can't imagine that either of us will be in the same place.

Eric

I stared blankly at the page in front of me. I recognized the handwriting, but it couldn't really be from Eric. It seemed so cold, so unloving. As if he felt nothing. As if the years we spent together meant nothing.

Then I remembered my own letter. Heading to Eric, probably on Majuro or somewhere over the ocean between here and Hawaii, was a hopeful, loving, committed letter which would get to him in a week. He had sent this letter a week ago. It didn't matter that I had determined I was going to be faithful to Eric and end my friendship with Campbell. Eric had *already* broken up with me.

I felt nauseated, devastated. There was only one person I wanted to see, that I needed to see. And I didn't care what time it was. I pulled my tennis shoes on again and jogged down the road in the light of the bright full moon.

His window faced the *iar*. I tapped quietly on it, hoping I wouldn't disturb the others. He came to the window, and even in the shadows I could see he was just wearing boxer briefs. His hair was messy, sticking up in several places.

"Carlie, lass, what are you doing here?" he asked.

I couldn't talk. I just held up the letter in my hand and burst into tears.

"I'll be right out, *Ri-pālle*," he said, fading into the darkness of his room. I heard his toe hit something and the sudden sound of swearing, but in a minute, he was outside.

He eyed the backyard, took me by the hand, and led me to the swing, where he sat down and then invited me onto his lap. He'd pulled on a tee shirt and shorts, and he'd brought out a blanket. Campbell pulled the blanket over us, tucking me in under his arm with my cheek on his chest, and then he handed me a dish towel.

"It's all I could think of for a handkerchief," he said apologetically. I couldn't talk yet; I couldn't explain, but Campbell held me as I wept. Wrapped in his strong arms with his hand gently stroking my hair, I knew the world was not going to shatter around me.

Eric wasn't good with tears. He viewed them as manipulative and it made him uncomfortable if I cried. Unfortunately, I'd always been an emotional person, so he often viewed me as trying to make him give me my way. He would listen, certainly, but he wouldn't move toward me, and as much as I would wish to be held when I cried, it was unlikely.

But right now I had everything I needed with Campbell's arms around me, my cheek against his chest, and his heart steadily keeping time under my ear.

I was grateful to be close to him, to feel his warmth in the nighttime chill, to feel his body against mine. And faintly, in the back of my mind, past the part of me devastated that Eric had broken up with me, something small whispered: *If you love him, and he loves you, there's nothing in your way anymore.*

"You're okay?" I finally asked. "I'm not putting your legs to sleep?"

A chuckle rumbled through Campbell's chest. "Maybe a wee bit," he said, adjusting our bodies so that I was more beside than on him. "But I dinna care. I will hold you as long as you need to be held, *Ri-pālle*." He squeezed me with his arm, as if to convince my body as well as my mind.

"That may be a while," I warned him; he responded with a laugh and a kiss on my scalp.

Finally, I could speak. "The letter. Eric... broke our engagement. You were right, Campbell. He couldn't stand to have me gone. He thinks I've been selfish and he doesn't want to wait for me."

Campbell didn't say anything, just sighed and patted my shoulder.

I closed my eyes. I was cried out and exhausted. I just needed sleep, but I didn't want to be alone.

"Campbell," I whispered, "Can I sleep with you in your bed tonight? I can't be by myself."

He was quiet for a moment. "*Sleep* with me?" he asked.

"When you hold me, I don't feel like I'm going to fall apart," I said. "I need you. Can I please stay?"

When he spoke, I could hear the humor in his voice. "Do ye think that's a good idea? Ye just broke up wi' me, like two days ago. Do ye think I can be trusted, all night, wi' you dressed in this—*whatever* it is." He frowned skeptically and gestured vaguely toward my shorts and tank top.

"I trust you more than anyone else in the world, Campbell," I said.

"Then ye are even more tired than you realize," he teased.

I climbed off Campbell's lap and reached my hand out to him.

"So..." he said, standing up slowly. "In my bed? Wi' me? All night?"

"Just to sleep," I said tiredly. "I just can't be alone right now."

With a little shake of his head, Campbell led me inside. We tiptoed into his room and he turned down the covers on his bed, climbed in, and ushered me in next to him where I curled up in the curve of his body.

I woke numerous times throughout the night. Besides waking up with the horrible memory of Eric's letter and the embarrassing thought of my hopeful missive heading his direction, I was extremely aware of Campbell in bed with me, his warm bulk behind me. I think he was trying not to touch me, but whenever he was sleeping, he would flop his arm over me and pull me close, his body announcing quite clearly how he felt about having me in bed with him. After a while he would startle awake and retreat to his side of the twin bed with a muffled "Sorry!" into my hair.

However, if I began to feel despondent again all I had to do was lean back and I would feel solidity and warmth, and I could breathe again.

As I was creeping out of Campbell's room early the next morning, I tiptoed past the couch. And then I heard a voice speaking, slow and sad. "I told ye, Carlie, and I was serious. If ye willna listen to me, perhaps ye will listen to Alastair Douglass." Ewan stepped out of the darkness. "You continue to risk Campbell's future every time you use him."

"I'm not... I didn't," I protested. He was looking me up and down, making me aware that I'd run down to the school in my skimpy shorts and tank top.

"What kind of girl are ye, Miss Beecher?" He looked disgusted. "Lass, I *spoke* to you. I asked you, *specifically*, to stay away." Ewan's arms were crossed over his chest as he shook his head at me. "I thought if ye just let Campbell get over you, if you made him remember that you were engaged. If you *acted* engaged, for Christ's sake, then the lad could move on wi' his life. Then you would have been *welcome* to come back. But now, ye've *slept* with him? The lad's not going to be able to get over *that*."

Ewan sighed as he turned away and walked back into his bedroom. He stopped before he entered his door. "You leave me no choice, Carlie."

I didn't understand what he meant until a well-dressed man came to the door of the clinic mid-morning and handed me a chunky black phone with a thick antenna. I held the satellite phone to my ear, and heard a gruff Scottish voice say, "Miss Beecher, pack a bag. You're coming to Majuro on the Jolok boat today."

CHAPTER 16

The Proposal

A re you really wearing that?" I asked Campbell, as he stood, took my duffle bag from me, then offered me a hand to help me up into the bed of the pick-up truck.

"Aye," he said, looking down at the sarong. "It makes me feel confident— ready to go to war. You know the Scots fought in kilts, don't you?"

Campbell was joking, but I could sense that he was nervous. I was nervous, too. Though we hadn't done anything to deserve Evan's disapproval, I *had* jogged home in a tank top and shorts. Since I hadn't seen many people, my guess was that Ewan must have radioed Alastair. It wasn't like we talked or made a lot of noise, but somehow Ewan had known we were together. I figured we were about to get a stern talking to, and I'd be told by yet another person that I needed to stay away from Campbell MacReid.

There were others in the pickup truck already, so I squeezed in next to Campbell. It confused me when he didn't settle next to me. He seemed lost in his own thoughts, but it wasn't like him to be so standoffish.

"I'm really sorry, Campbell," I shouted in his ear above the din as we rattled down the road. "I didn't mean to get you in trouble!"

He shrugged and looked away. I scooted closer to him hoping he'd respond to contact, but he frowned, shook his head, and gestured toward the other riders. I figured he was probably mad at me for getting pulled into this. It wasn't his fault I came to him, and I was the one who asked to stay the night.

The truck stopped in Jabo where I was pleasantly surprised to see Sharbella exit a boxy house, followed by a burly Majel man carrying a small suitcase. Campbell and the man helped her up into the bed and Campbell stowed Sharbella's suitcase, then sat back down by me.

"I have a doctor appointment in Majuro," Sharbella explained, with her hand on her stomach. I wondered what was wrong; she hadn't told me she wasn't feeling well.

As more people got into the truck, it necessitated squeezing together to make room, and *finally* I felt Campbell relax against me, his arm behind my back, hand firmly grasping the side of the truck. I felt like crying in relief as I settled into his warm side.

The boat wasn't yet ready to leave when the truck reached Arno Arno and unloaded passengers and baggage onto the dock.

"Will you walk with me, Campbell?" I asked, pointing toward the beach. He followed me, and we made our way over the coral sand in silence for a few minutes. Finally, I stopped and looked at him. "What's going on? I can't stand you not talking to me, Campbell. This is making me miserable."

"*You're* miserable? How do you think I've been feeling, Carlie?" Campbell looked at me accusingly. "After Maxson died you refused my comfort, insulted me, pushed me away, and then you came to me last night. You asked to sleep *in my bed with me*," he said, looking around beforehand and lowering his voice as he said it. "And it may not have been sexual, and I didna touch ye inappropriately, but I have *never* slept wi' a woman before." He blushed. "And you canna help but have noticed me responding to you... *physically*."

I nodded, flushing slightly, not meeting his eyes.

"So, aye, I'm upset. What do ye want from me? I was trying to be respectful of you after our trip back from Matolen, trying to figure out how to be your friend. But then just a few days ago ye did your best to insult and alienate me, to make me stay away from you, and then ye *use* me when it's convenient for you!"

"*Use* you, Campbell?" I retorted. "Come on. You *know* why I pushed you away. For the same reason you pushed *me* away! I was becoming too dependent on your friendship, too connected to you. I thought we both agreed that it was inappropriate, especially since I'm... since I *was* engaged."

Campbell rubbed his face with his hands, then met my eyes. "I care for you, Carlie. I think you ken how much I do. But I *love* these people. I *love* this island. It is my *home*, and I canna let ye take this from me."

We could see the passengers loading onto the boat. Campbell turned and walked away from me. "I'm sorry," I said again, but he didn't respond.

The Jolok boat had no seats or chairs, so passengers sat on the wooden deck of the small boat as it was tossed about by the waves. The thought of facing the fierce Scotsman made me nervous, but it was the rolling ocean that made Campbell sick to his stomach. I scooted closer to him and patted him on the back as he threw up over the side of the boat.

Meanwhile, I terrified myself by looking at the near-black water and pondering the separate world under that surface. Invisible to me were whales and sharks, giant squid, innumerable fish, and an underwater landscape of which we could see only the coral rings surrounding remnants of the peaks of old mountains.

I also terrified myself with other thoughts. What would my life look like if I had to return to Arno and no longer be friends with Campbell? He was currently facing away from me, trying to steady his eyes on the horizon to keep his stomach settled.

I pictured those vivid blue eyes, almost as bright as the turquoise of the lagoon, the way they crinkled at the corners when he looked at me, the way his lips would curve in a smile when we shared a joke. The look of affection he would get on his face when I was talking to other people, or the deep curiosity in his eyes, glancing down at my body when he thought I wasn't watching.

He was leaning back with his large hands splayed on the deck behind him. Looking at those hands I thought about the way Campbell touched me, stroking my back, my hair, putting his arm around my shoulders.

Visually I traced his strong shoulders and muscular back, the curls at the nape of his neck, the draped sarong over the curve of his... I stopped myself.

*I know I'm attracted to him. But do I **love** him?* I asked myself. *Is that why I went to him last night? Was it just the sadness and disappointment at Eric breaking our engagement? Or was it that without my ties to Eric, there was no longer any reason to stay away from him, and I wanted to be with Campbell more than anyone else?*

I felt myself trembling internally as I looked at him, and it wasn't just from the fear of what would come when we met with Alastair Douglass.

I was grateful when we traveled under the bridge on the island of Majuro and landed on solid ground, though on the taxi ride to the USI headquarters I still felt nauseated.

"D'ye understand why you are here?" Mr. Douglass lowered his eyebrows as he stared across his desk at the two of us sitting next to each other in two chairs. Campbell was still a little green from the boat trip, and I was still reeling from Eric's letter and the sudden fear that not only did I not have anyone to go back to, I could lose my position here as well.

Alastair was glaring at me.

"Sorry, what did you ask?" I felt scattered and embarrassed that I was starting the whole conversation out wrong.

"Why are you here?" His voice was gruff; his face angry.

"I'm pretty sure it's because I spent the night at the boys' house, after my fiancé broke up with me by letter yesterday."

"You spent the night at the boys' house? On their couch?" Alastair asked the question, but it wasn't for clarification; he knew full well what the answer was.

I exchanged glances with Campbell; he shrugged, shook his head, and looked away like it was my question to answer. "Well, I slept in Campbell's bed with him, but we didn't like, *sleep together*, sleep together."

"And how would anyone know that?" Mr. Douglass asked. "Ewan and Graham saw you coming out of Campbell's room early in the morning, wearing some version of nighttime attire, with tousled hair and sleepy eyes. You live a mile away, so every single family along that road had the opportunity to see the same thing as ye walked home."

"Uncle," Campbell said, but at Alastair's glare he corrected himself, "I mean, Mr. Douglass. Carlie's fiancé broke up with her. She needed to not be alone. We didna do anything sexual. I held her, that's all."

Alastair glared. "Ye see what a difficult position ye put me in, though, young lady. *What* were you thinking?"

"I'm sorry, Mr. Douglass," I said. "I guess I wasn't really thinking at all. Without a roommate or a female friend to talk to, without the ability to call my family, I needed *someone* last night. Campbell's been a good friend to me, and I trust him. I never feared for my honor, and I guess I didn't think about other people's perceptions if I were coming back from their house early in the morning. I just knew I couldn't be alone."

Alastair pulled out a sheaf of papers. "D'ye ken what these are?"

I looked across the table and read upside-down, *"UniServe International Volunteer Code of Conduct,"* I said.

"Recognize your signatures?" he said, pushing two more sheets of paper across the table at us. We nodded, and I glanced over at Campbell. This sure felt like being sent to the principal's office as teenagers. Next, Alastair handed us another piece of paper, with addendums and numbered policies, two of which were highlighted in yellow.

"Carlie," said Alastair, "Would you read section 3.13 and 3.13.1, please?

I leaned forward and read the highlighted portions.

3.13 Sexual Behavior

While the matter of Volunteer sexual behavior is a highly personal one, Volunteers are required to follow legal and policy requirements of UniServe International. Failure to do so may be grounds for disciplinary action up to and including administrative separation.

3.13.1 Host Country Sexual Mores

Because of the legal, social, and political implications of inappropriate sexual behavior, it is important that UniServe International standards be clear. To this end, Country Directors shall ensure that volunteers both understand and honor host country sexual mores, including ideal expectations about dating, pre-marital sexual experience, and single parent maternity and paternity. Volunteers will be made aware of the consequences for themselves and the UniServe International program if these mores are violated.[1]

"Campbell," Alastair said. "Ye've had the most experience in the Marshall Islands. How would you describe the mores of this country?"

---

[1] Adapted from Peace Corps 2017 guidelines: MS 204 Volunteer Conduct, and MS 284 Early Termination of Service.

"Honestly, Mr. Douglass, they assume that sometimes young people will be sexually active when they are not yet married. Of course, they'd prefer they didn't, just as parents would in most other countries."

"Is the same thing expected of UniServe volunteers, however? Remember, the guidelines ask for even better behavior from our volunteers. *Ideal* expectations."

"You have made it clear, sir, that we should not enter into sexual relationships with locals." Campbell paused, but as I glanced at him I could see a spark of defiance in his eyes and a stubborn jut to his chin. "However, Uncle, you hadn't clarified the policy regarding other volunteers. And even if you *had* clarified it, I will state again, Carlie and I do *not* have a sexual relationship."

"Now," said Alastair, completely ignoring Campbell's last comments. "It doesn't spell it out in these guidelines, but the basic reason for being terminated from UniServe, which is called 'administrative separation,' is if your behavior diminishes the effectiveness of you as volunteers or the UniServe program as a whole." He looked up at me under lowered eyebrows. "For those reasons, I am leaning very heavily toward administrative separation for you, Miss Beecher."

"What?" I sputtered. "Why? How does what happened—what *appeared* to happen last night diminish my effectiveness?"

"Let me ask you, Miss Beecher. On which population on Arno do you feel you have the most impact?" Alastair's eyes glinted fiercely.

"Probably the women and children."

"How are the women going to act toward you if they think you're a whore?"

I recoiled at the word. "I'm not a whore, sir. I have only been with one man—*my fiancé*—in the last eight years."

Alastair ignored me. "But if they think ye are, are they going to bring their children to you? Are they going to trust you near their men? Are they going to feel safe asking you questions about their illnesses and ailments?"

I had a sinking feeling in the pit of my stomach.

"There are *reasons* for our cultural sensitivity training. We have come into the Marshallese world. We will educate, and we will heal, and we will support the physical and social health of their community. One thing we will not do is to try to put our culture on them."

"They know I'm American, though," I insisted. "Surely they can understand I'm not trying to put my culture on them if they assume, *incorrectly*, that Campbell and I are in a relationship."

"Anytime we live by or try to force them to live by the mores of another country we do them a disservice by disrespecting their culture. For example, early missionaries did a lot of damage here, unintentionally, of course. They didn't like seeing women's breasts. That was their own cultural bias which they attempted to impose on the Marshallese. So they clothed them. But when the natives didn't dry off as quickly after a rain storm because they were wearing cotton that got soaked and stayed wet, they got skin ailments and they got sick. Just by making islanders wear clothing, missionaries killed them."

I wasn't about to further irritate Alastair by pointing out his ridiculous comparison between causing the deaths of islanders and what Campbell and I had done.

"Mr. Douglass," I said, appealing to reason. "I'm a good nurse. I'm doing a good job. I've already developed relationships with people. I'm learning Marshallese. Surely you don't want to have to find and train someone else. What if this never happens again?" For a moment I thought I might have seen acceptance on his face.

"Word has already gotten out, Miss Beecher. They willna respect ye. And they will either not trust ye, or not come to use the clinic services at all."

I was beginning to shake from stress. "Mr. Douglass, I didn't do anything wrong." I said, but I couldn't keep my chin from quivering. "Am I not allowed to be human, to need people?" Campbell might well have been angry at me earlier, but in response to this reaction, he reached over and grabbed my hand.

Alastair ignored my question. "To be honest, Miss Beecher, it's your reputation with the men that troubles us most. You're already alone on Arno, which was certainly not ideal. But if they think you have loose morals, the night time visits are just going to increase. And my *nephews* are not out there to provide you with night watch service."

"I'm gonna kill Ewan," Campbell muttered under his breath, shaking his head.

"And you, Campbell," Mr. Douglass continued. "How can I punish her and not you? It will come across as nepotism, me treating my family with extra favor. What am I to do with you?" He paused and shook his head. "I could relocate you, I guess. Or maybe it's time for you to go home to Scotland for a while."

"*Alastair*," Campbell said, slowly releasing my hand in shock. "How could you *do* that?"

I stared at Campbell, seeing the deep pain in his blue eyes, feeling incredible guilt for putting him in jeopardy, for putting my own position in jeopardy. The deepest pang of emotion I had, though; the thing that stunned me more than anything was the thought that suddenly entered my mind—*I don't want to lose him.*

Still, when the words came out of my mouth I couldn't believe I'd said them.

"What if we got married?"

Mr. Douglass and Campbell turned and stared at me.

I looked at Alastair, took a deep breath, and spoke again. "Seriously. What if we got married? While the Majel culture frowns on premarital relations, surely they care less if the couple gets married. Wouldn't that fit within the guideline of the policy? They might not respect us if we were just messing around, but if we're then married, they'd have nothing to object to. They'd just see us as horny fiancés who jumped the gun a little. That way we both stay on Arno. Campbell can keep teaching, and I can keep being a nurse there. Problem solved."

"*Ri-pålle*, how can you propose such a thing?" Campbell half-laughed as he exclaimed in astonishment. I hadn't looked at him as I was talking, but now I could see his face was flushed and his lips were pale. "You don't mean it, do you?"

Alastair simply sat behind his desk, his face displaying interest instead of horror. He shrugged. "I can't argue with your logic. Whether it's a *reasonable* solution, though..."

I turned back to look at Campbell. "I care about you," I said earnestly. "I don't want to lose you. And I don't want you to lose all *this* because of me."

Shakily, Campbell said, "Can I speak to ye alone, Carlie?"

When we entered the other room, Campbell grabbed my hand and led me over to the couch where he sat and pulled me to sit down next to him, not releasing my hand. He looked down at our interlocked fingers for a moment and then he looked up at me.

"Are you *serious*, Carlie?" Campbell's eyes blazed with an unfamiliar intensity. Yet he also looked fragile somehow, as if something barely below the surface was about to break.

"What do you mean?" I asked.

"We joke a lot, *Ri-pàlle*. I want to know if you're serious. Are you really suggesting that we get *married*?"

I smiled, slightly embarrassed. "Yeah," I said, shrugging my shoulders, "I could marry you."

He sighed. "You know that's not what I'm asking, Carlie... Do you *want* to *marry* me?"

I felt short of breath. He was making me spell it out, and the thought of rejection was terrifying.

Campbell continued. "Ye see, I don't believe in divorcing. When I get married, my plan is the 'til death do us part' kind of marriage. I dinna want a fake marriage. If we married each other, I would want to stay married, have children wi' ye, get old wi' ye." He paused, red creeping into his cheeks but a mischievous smirk on his face. "And I'd want to bed ye. Frequently." At those words, my uterus spasmed. "I *already* want to make love to you," he said intently, blushing as he looked down at our hands. "It would be torture if ye married me, but ye didna mean it; if ye didna truly want me that way, or if you only planned to stay married until your term was up. Do you *really* want me?"

How could he not know? I thought. *Isn't it constantly written on my face?*

I took a deep breath. "I do, Campbell." My voice caught in my throat. "I want you, too," I said, earnestly meeting his eyes. "I've missed you so much the last few days it hurt *physically*. I want to be around you. I love talking with you, laughing with you. I trust you. I feel safe with you."

Campbell released his tight grip on my hand, but covered it with his other hand, stroking my palm softly with his fingers as I continued.

"But hasn't it been clear?" I continued. "I don't think I've been able to hide how I feel. I'm not satisfied at just being friends. I want *more*. I want to be *with* you. I want your body, naked, next to me."

I could see him jerk in visceral response to my words. He put his hand up to stop me. "Ah, *Ri-pàlle*, unless ye want me to attack ye here and now, you should stop talking like that." His face was flushed.

I didn't obey him; I leaned over and whispered in his ear, "I want your weight on me, I want you...*in* me."

With a subtle shake of his head and widened eyes, Campbell's face demonstrated exactly the effect I was having on him. Then he squared his shoulders and narrowed his eyes.

"Carlie, that does *not* completely answer my question," he said, leaning back and folding his arms across his chest. "That's just *sex*. People have sex with *anyone* these days. I dinna want to be married just so I can make love to ye." He looked away from me, his forehead wrinkled. "At least, that canna be the *only* reason."

I realized then what he meant. "It's not just that, Campbell. I came out here because I was ready for my life to change. It has. And during this change you've become someone I *truly* care for. I don't think I'm fooling myself that there's something special between us, Campbell. It's not just attraction. It can't just be affection. There's something here... isn't there?"

Campbell nodded in agreement, still staring at the floor.

I continued. "Eric broke up with me, but I am not going home. There is *one* open door I see in front of me. And it's *you*. You ask if I can imagine being married to you forever. Well, maybe I can't exactly picture it. But I'm ready to be married. And I can imagine life with you being very satisfying. *You're* the one who is going to have to decide if that is enough."

Campbell had continued to look away from me as he listened, and as I finished, he sat silently. From the parade of emotions on his face, I could tell he was thinking furiously. Finally he again took my hand in his and hesitantly met my eyes.

"And if that's enough for me?"

I shrugged my shoulders, looking at him with a tentative smile.

"So, shall I ask ye, then, Carlie?"

"Ask me what?"

"Will ye marry me, Carlie Beecher?"

This was truly surreal; my heart was pounding. But Campbell was gazing at me with his ocean-blue eyes. He stroked my hand and there was nothing else I could have said.

"Yes, I will, Campbell MacReid," I exclaimed, standing and pulling him up to his feet. He gripped me about the waist, crushing me in an embrace, pressing his lips to mine. He tasted like salt, a sweet kiss full of both hope and desire.

I sunk into the sensation that I had imagined countless times, feeling faint.

"I couldn't sleep last night," he said, pulling away from me for a moment to look at me in wonder. "You were with me, next to me, all night long, and ye never reached for me. Eric had broken up wi' ye. I thought ye might kiss me. But then I thought, maybe you didna want me like that."

I wrapped my arms around him, urging us together. I'd said I wanted him; that was an understatement. He wanted me, too—that was instantly certain.

We kissed as if we'd been starving, finally able to act on the attraction we had been feeling for weeks. Campbell's arms were firmly around me, pulling me up towards him. All those weeks of celibacy had me lightheaded at the sudden abundance of stimuli; at the taste of him, the softness of his lips, his closeness, his muscles against me, his body clearly responding to me. As if drawn by a magnetic force I lowered my hand and put it on him, feeling the size of him through the thin folds of his sarong. He groaned, kissed me harder, and skimmed his hand over my breast in my sundress; and then both of us froze.

"Alastair's in the other room," I panted, eyeing the couch and wondering how long it would take a virgin to finish.

"Aye," he said, pushing me away and taking a deep breath. "I think we should wait until my Uncle's no' in the next room, and probably until we're married to consummate our marriage."

"We're already at second and sort-of-third base," I joked, still short of breath. "It wouldn't take long," I felt myself being drawn back to him, and he could see it.

"No, Carlie," he said, shaking his head and laughing. "We should restrain ourselves."

"Why?" I groaned. "We already got in trouble as if we had sex…"

"Hen," he said, gently. "Would it be so bad for me to be a virgin when I marry? It's a rarity in this world."

I looked at him, and realized he was right. I had to close my eyes and breathe for a moment.

"You know the only thing helping you keep your virginity right now is the fact that Alastair is in the next room, don't you?" I asked.

"Good thing he is, then," Campbell said with a grin.

"You're not any fun at all," I sighed, bitterly accepting continued celibacy.

"Not right now. But I *will* be," he said, one side of his lips twisting up into a wry smile. "I promise."

I *believed* him, and the thought send a warm flush through my body. It didn't make things easier, as I was already combusting.

"Shall we tell Alastair, then?" I asked.

"I think we should, *Ri-pālle*," Campbell said, nodding at me with a slightly stunned expression.

I released my breath slowly. "Do I look okay?" I asked. Campbell reached out and smoothed the hair that had been tousled in our enthusiastic embrace, gently brushing a strand out of my face.

"How about me?" he asked. His hair needed a small amount of smoothing and straightening as well. He was about ready to leave the room when I nodded toward the front of his sarong and then looked away politely. "I think you need a minute."

"It's not going to help me to stay here in this room wi' ye," he said, looking me up and down hungrily. "I think we might need to not be *alone* wi' each other until our wedding day."

"Well, when will that be?" I asked.

"Tomorrow or the next day, if I have anything to say about it," Campbell said. He stepped close to me, gently took my chin in his hand and kissed me.

CHAPTER 17

Getting to Know You

Alastair Douglass was waiting when we came out of the other room. I wondered how much he had heard. I wondered how much our faces and bodies told him.

"So?" he asked.

"We're getting married," I said, feeling incredulous as I met Campbell's eyes. He looked about as shocked as I felt.

Alastair glanced from one of us to the other, bushy eyebrows lowered and forehead wrinkled.

"Campbell?" he asked, a question in his voice. "Son, are you certain?"

My brain was swirling, my thoughts telling me I was being foolish and insensible. Crazy. Impulsive. Ridiculous.

"*Definitely*," said Campbell, his voice confident. "I'm sure." At his words I reached out to him, slipping my arm around his waist. He sounded more certain than I felt at this instant, but in the act of touching him I could feel myself calming and when his arm went around my shoulders I relaxed.

Alastair still looked skeptical. "This is not just to be an engagement," he said. "You actually plan to be married, correct?" Both of us nodded. "Well," Alastair continued. "I don't want you to delay indefinitely. Beyond a couple of weeks and I'll begin to think I've been made a fool. You won't try to wait very long, will you?"

"No," insisted Campbell. "I don't want to wait at all. I'd get married tomorrow if we could. Thursday... Friday? But how do we arrange for a wedding?"

"Well," Alastair leaned forward in his chair, putting his elbows on his desk. "You'll need to see the Secretary of Foreign Affairs at the government office. That should probably be done today, as there's at least a three-day waiting period after applying for a marriage license to be married. That would make Friday the earliest you could be married."

My heart started pounding, and I was quite certain Campbell's grip around my waist tightened.

Alastair continued, "You're an American citizen, Carlie; Campbell's Scottish, and we're here in the Marshall Islands. They'll be able to get you the proper forms at the Foreign Affairs office. You can't head back to Arno until the Jolok boat leaves tomorrow afternoon. Since there are shops here, you can get a wedding ring and a dress if ye want it. I can phone the Iroij by satellite and arrange for the local reverend on Arno to marry ye. Ye might want to buy some extra food while you're here to provide for a party."

"We also need time for a *honeymoon*," said Campbell firmly. I looked over at him in surprise. He winked at me. "There's no privacy in town, and despite your doubts, I believe in the sanctity of marriage, Uncle Alastair. I've waited for marriage and I intend to take the time to *fully* enjoy my new wife." I tried to disguise the fact that his words had given me shivers, but Alastair noticed. He shook his head and scoffed. Campbell noticed too, and he subtly caressed my arm, which just made it worse.

"So, this is what we are doing the next few days," said Alastair. "Making certain the two of you are really serious about this damn foolish plan, and if you are, preparing for a wedding and a," he glared at Campbell, "SHORT honeymoon, and then figuring out the logistics of the two of you living together on Arno."

"Logistics?" I said. "Won't he move in with me?"

"Your cabin's not very nice," said Alastair.

"I think I should still be near the clinic," I said. I looked at Campbell to see if he agreed, and he nodded. "It was fine for me alone, and it's got room for more than one."

"I can see to improving it, if needed," said Campbell. "I dinna see that much else that we'd need to deal with, logistically."

Alastair seemed mollified that marriage would not instantly make us more demanding. He leaned back in his chair and crossed his arms over his chest. "Well, then?" he said. "I guess we have your papers here for safekeeping, don't we? You'll need your passports for the application."

Alastair had his secretary find our files, and then he drove us to the government offices.

"Have ye eaten since arriving?" he asked as he prepared to drop us off.

"Not since breakfast," I said.

"Well, when you're done here, call me. I'll pick you up and take ye to my home, then," he said generously, a gesture which completely took me by surprise. "Moneo[1] and I will feed you, and you can stay with us for the night as well."

The clerk managed to find the correct paperwork for us in his cluttered office and we walked down the hall to the notary's office to finish filling everything out.

Campbell sat close to me as we wrote on our forms, his knee against mine. At one point he chuckled, and then at my questioning look said, "We're lucky to be marrying *here*, I guess..."

"Why is that?" I asked.

"Because in Scotland, we'd have to register our license in the council area we were to be married, at least 29 days before the wedding."

"There's no waiting at all in Colorado," I said with a grin. "Maybe they figure if you've waited in lines at the court house long enough, you deserve to get married."

We looked at each other then, small smiles on each of our faces.

"We're doing this?" I asked him.

"Aye," he said, smiling in disbelief and looking down at the official papers in front of him.

Alastair was finished with work for the day when we had completed the process around 5:30, so he picked us up.

---

[1] Moneo: Muh-nay´-oh

Majuro was astoundingly busy and urbanized. It made me glad to live on an outer island, seeing the lack of trees and the massive quantity of homes and buildings here. Alastair drove us beyond the edges of the city to a place where more trees seemed to conceal houses set back from the single road. He parked in front of a small but nicely kept up home and led us inside.

"Ye'll stay in here with my daughter Revka," Alastair said, pushing the door of a small bedroom open. "And Campbell, you'll sleep on the couch."

A Marshallese woman came out of the kitchen; she had long black hair and a sweet smile.

"Ah, and this is my wife, Moneo," Alastair said, smiling down at her. She shook my hand but reached out and hugged Campbell.

"Auntie Moneo," he said, "this is my fiancé Carlie."

"Welcome," she said with a smile. There was no surprise on her face, so I wondered if Alastair had already told her the news. "I look forward to getting to know the girl Campbell has chosen."

"May I help?" I asked. "*Jiban?*"

"*Aet*," she said, smiling gently. "You can cut up the vegetables."

"Vegetables," I groaned. "I've missed vegetables. I really need to grow a garden on Arno."

"Oh, I have seeds that grow well on the islands," Moneo said. "Remind me to share some."

Soon we had the table set with coconut rice, barbecued chicken, and fresh vegetables—beans, peppers, and cucumbers. Teenager Revka appeared, a lovely girl with lightly tanned skin, light brown eyes, and brown hair. She gave Campbell a hug, and then we ate.

"Be careful about how much of the vegetables ye eat," said Campbell. "They may not agree wi' ye if ye havena had any in a while."

Sadly, Campbell was right. Not long after dinner, I started having to spend some quality time in the restroom. I was extremely grateful they had a flush toilet, and fortunately after about an hour of violent stomach pains I was able to rejoin the family as they visited in the sitting room.

Not long after, Revka went to bed and then Moneo and Alastair seemed to be retiring for the night as well.

I changed into my night clothes in Revka's room where Moneo had set up a pallet for me on the floor, but I wasn't ready to go to bed. It seemed like such a huge decision and we hadn't had much time to process in the rush of the afternoon. I peeked my head back out to the living room, where Campbell had taken off his shoes and had stretched his sarong-covered legs out on the couch.

He looked up the instant I opened the door and gestured for me to join him. "Uncle," he called to the kitchen, where Alastair was doing dishes. "Carlie and I would like to talk. D'ye mind if she stays out here to visit wi' me, even after ye and Auntie go to bed?"

"Ye're twenty-two, Campbell," Alastair said, in amusement. "You're an adult. I'm not going to tell you when to go to bed or who ye can talk to."

"But it is your home, and I dinna want to be disrespectful," Campbell said.

"Aye, thanks, lad," said Alastair. He pointed over to an organizer on the wall. "There's a blanket for you for tonight, Campbell. And if the two of ye, well..." he eyed my shorts critically then looked back at Campbell, "If the two of ye decide to get familiar wi' each other, for God's sake, be *quiet* about it."

"You still don't believe us, sir?" I said, chastely sitting down by myself.

"Oh, aye, I believe you might not have been having sex last night...but wi' my knowledge of the young and the way women respond to getting engaged, I wouldn't take any bets on what happens in the next few days." I peeked at Campbell, who was blushing profusely.

Alastair went out to the kitchen, and Campbell and I looked at each other from our spots on two separate couches with a coffee table in between them.

"Is this crazy?" I asked him.

He shook his head in amusement. "I dinna think that's a helpful question to ask, *Ri-pälle*," said Campbell. "By asking it, ye're already saying ye think it is crazy." He paused for a moment and smiled gently. "And, it *is*. We don't *have* to get married, ye ken. Now that Uncle Alastair has had a chance to calm down, he might rethink the severity of the consequences he wishes to give us."

"I *want* to get married," I said hesitantly, realizing with surprise that I truly meant it. "I just want to feel like I know you better."

Campbell raised his eyebrows at me with a grin. "What do you want to know about me, then?"

"Politically..." I said. "how would you describe yourself?"

"I dinna ken. We're not like the Americans," Campbell said. "Not divided like that. For one thing, we have more than two main parties. But I agree with most of the policies of the Scottish National Party. We believe in nuclear disarmament, we wish to be part the European Union, and we want Scottish independence. We're on the liberal side, more like the American Democrats," he explained. "There's not a lot for us to rally for, though. Scotland already has socialized medicine. We canna believe the hubbub in America over health care and guns. It's ridiculous. Although those of us with Highlander roots can understand the fears about being disarmed. The British actually did that to us after Culloden." He looked at me with a question in his eyes. "Yourself?"

"Me? I believe in social justice," I said. "I believe that human beings matter, no matter how much money they have. I believe people are a product of their upbringing. And I believe that everyone should have access to health care."

Campbell smiled. "Hmm," he grunted shortly. "I think you are who I know you to be already. You have a generous heart. And I assumed that's why you're here."

"What would *you* like to know?" I said.

He looked over at me shyly. "I knew that you *liked* me," he said, eyebrows furrowed. He wrinkled his nose and laughed. "I was nearly *certain* ye found me to be attractive."

I sighed and chuckled sheepishly as I bit my lip.

"I ken how I feel towards you." He appeared to be pondering his question very deliberately. "But still, why did ye ask me to marry you?"

"'Cause I don't want to go back to Eric, to America. Because I want to stay on Arno. Because I care about you. And when I thought about never seeing you again it nearly broke my heart."

"Truly?" he said. "Because the day of the funeral you made it quite clear you felt I was beneath you." He raised his eyes to look at me.

I shook my head at the horrible memory. "Couldn't you see how tortured I was to say all of that? I was trying to get my heart back where it belonged, Campbell," I said. "I didn't want to be unfaithful to Eric, no matter how attracted I was to you. He was my fiancé."

"Aye," Campbell agreed. "And ye ken I did try to be respectful of him. I didna ever touch ye in a way that seemed wrong, did I?"

I shook my head. "No, you've always been very good. Incredibly good. And incredibly sexy..."

He grinned at me, "I still canna believe how lucky I am that you asked me."

"Oh, I think I'm luckier that you said yes," I responded. "You have such a good heart, Campbell. I've never been around anyone who makes me feel as safe as you do. Except maybe my parents."

Campbell laughed. "Yet, I hope you dinna feel the same way towards me as you do towards them."

"No," I said. "But strangely, there are times when you've taken on a role of parental authority towards me. It seems like you like telling me what to do... or not do..."

Campbell shook his head sheepishly. "Aye, but ye ken all I was trying to do was protect you."

I put my toes up on the edge of the coffee table. "And I *didn't* listen, and here we are. You must think I'm ridiculously irresponsible."

"No!" Campbell insisted, shaking his head. "I dinna feel that way at all. I'm proud of you, so professional and capable—a *nurse*," he said. "You impressed me the first time I met you."

"Well, you're an excellent teacher, Campbell," I remarked. "I can't go anywhere on Arno without seeing something that reminds me of you teaching me things. You have no idea what a talent that is."

"Will you stop being so damn sentimental!" said Alastair, finally coming out of the kitchen. "Carlie already spent enough time in the loo. I don't want to have to go vomit in there."

Campbell and I chuckled as Alastair disappeared down the hallway.

165

"So, *Ri-pālle*," Campbell said, sitting up and leaning forward with a curious smile on his face. "Now that Alastair is gone, I do have another question. What were you talking about when you said we were at second and almost-third base today?"

I covered my face with my hands in embarrassment. "I'm *sorry*," I said. "That was really rude of me. I wasn't showing any sort of self-control, and I shouldn't have..."

"*Stop*," Campbell interrupted. "Ye didn't see me fighting ye off, did ye? I wasna looking for an apology. I just want to know what you meant by 'second' and 'third base'."

I laughed. "It refers to American baseball, but it's a euphemism for the steps towards sex. First base is kissing. Second base is above the waist touching; third base is below the waist touching, and a home run is sex."

"Ye're *blushing*," he said, grinning at me.

"Well, I'm talking with my virginal husband-to-be about sex."

"So," he mused, forehead wrinkled, "I was at second, and *you* were at almost-third?

"We were kind of both there together," I said teasingly.

"Now, what made it 'almost' third?" Campbell asked, looking confused.

"*Over* the clothes," I said, grinning.

"Well, then I wasna all the way at second, either," he said suggestively as his gaze drifted downward over my body. Reluctantly he pulled his eyes away and smiled over at me. "Did you have any other questions you wanted to ask me? What I believe, what I like?"

I stared at Campbell for a moment, and then a strange sense of panic filled my gut. "There's so much I *don't* know about you," I said. "And so much that I've just assumed because of where we are and the kind of person you seem to be. But you're young. Are you a club hopper? Do you smoke? Do you use drugs? Do you drink a lot?" I could feel my heart beating faster. "Will you want to live in the Marshall Islands forever, or do you think you might live elsewhere—Scotland or America?"

Campbell had been shaking his head through my whole barrage of questions and laughed when I stopped.

I took a deep breath. It was one thing to propose marriage, another entirely to consider the long-term consequences of such a commitment. My brain was swirling with questions and thoughts about what the future could hold; how the two of us could be different, how conflicts could arise. I'd been so wrapped up in the immediacy of being dismissed and the possibility of losing my friendship with him that I hadn't considered what it truly meant to propose marriage.

"Come here, hen," Campbell said, motioning to the couch beside him. "I'm no' going to attack you, no matter what my uncle thinks; no matter how much I might want ye, and I *know* I can calm you down."

Stretched out next to him, feeling his warmth, with his arms clasped around me and my head tucked under his chin, I could feel my breathing and heart rate slow down.

"How do you do that?" I asked, turning my face up to him. "How do you know what I need?" Campbell stared down at my lips and sighed.

"I dinna ken, *Ri-pálle*, I just do. And right now, ye need me to kiss ye," Campbell whispered with a teasing smile. "I want to, as well. But I can only do it if it's no' going to make ye molest me. Do ye think you can handle it?"

"Cross my heart," I said, as he gently lowered his lips to mine. I sighed, almost a little whimper.

"I like that," Campbell whispered against my lips.

"What?" I asked.

"That wee sound ye made just now," he smiled. "Save that one for future reference."

"What do you mean?" I asked.

"It makes me feel things," Campbell said. "It should come in handy."

Sighing, Campbell leaned his head back against the couch. "So, *Ri-pálle*, ye asked lots of questions. Club hopper? No. Dinna have many clubs here, but they seem loud and shallow to me, and beside that, I've been told that I'm a *terrible* dancer." He grinned as I laughed. "Smoking? No. Drugs? Not anymore. Drink? Yes. A lot? No. As to Scotland or America, I guess I've thought of going home. I love it here, but it is very primitive," Campbell said. "And I wasna getting married when I thought of the future before. What ye want matters to me, too, Carlie. I think we can decide together. Seems to me teaching and nursing are both flexible careers—we could work anywhere."

"But what if we find out we don't like the same things, or we have different interests, or you think I'm boring or I think you're irresponsible?"

"Carlie." Campbell shook his head and squeezed me a little to stop my talking. "You're overthinking it."

"How?" I asked.

"I've been here long enough that the locals call me *ri-majel*. That's means I'm a local, I'm not a *ri-pālle*—I'm simple, not selfish. I dinna need much. Have you seen the people who live on Arno? Would ye say they were happy?"

"Happier than anyone I've ever known in the states," I said.

"And yet they have so little material wealth. But they have an abundance of what they need: food, water, a place to sleep. Friends, family. Work. Laughter. Beauty around. I'm already happy, *Ri-pālle*. Now, if ye add to that a woman I can laugh with, who happens to be very bonny," he smiled and kissed me again. "Who has lots of curvy bits I want to touch," he said, running his hand over my hip. "And if she happens to want to put her hands on me, too; why, I am a lucky man indeed. So ye see, I wasna offended today. It made me happy to know ye want me."

I sat up straighter and put my hand behind his neck, pulling him down to me for an affectionate kiss.

He grunted, a little husky sound in his throat. "I like that," I said, smiling teasingly. "You should save *that* one for the future."

He chuckled. "And more than that, Carlie, ye can fix me when I get hurt and I can hold ye when you're sad. I'd say that's all a pretty good place to start."

I reached up to him again and melted into more sweet affection that grew in intensity until Campbell finally chuckled and drew away, letting his breath out with a whistle.

"I've done this with lasses before," he marveled. "Somehow this feels *different*." He trembled as he inhaled and then exhaled slowly.

"What do you mean?" I asked. I already understood, as I was having the same heady rush myself.

"Like it's going somewhere." He bit his lip. "Like it means something." He sighed again. "But perhaps we should talk more and maybe touch less. Especially as this is a rather large decision. I dinna want desire to fog our minds to the truth of whether this is the right choice."

I knew I'd seen that often enough with some of my conservative Christian friends who were trying to wait for sex until marriage, who blazed forward in relationships that were wrong for them because they couldn't see through the haze of yearning.

And if I was being honest, I couldn't know for sure which emotion had led to my crazy proposal. Rejection, sadness, fear, desperation, attraction, guilt, affection. I'd felt all of those in the last two days. "Do you think desire is clouding *your* judgment?" I asked.

Campbell met my eyes, then furrowed his eyebrows in thought. "No," he said finally. "Not at *all*." He smiled then, a confident, affectionate smile that warmed me to my toes.

I sat up and scooted away from him, grabbing a pillow to hold on my lap as I sat cross-legged on the couch. "So. Tell me about your parents, Campbell."

He shook his head sadly. "Sadly, my ma's gone, and I've not seen my dad for years. He went away after she died. Don't even know where he is right now."

"I'm so sorry," I said, for a second wishing I hadn't even asked.

"*Dinna fash*," Campbell said, seeing the look on my face. "I want you to know me, and that means my hurts as well as my happiness."

"So it's just you and Isla then?"

"Our Uncle, Ferguson MacReid, looked out for us after they were gone, but I left soon afterwards. Isla moved in with her boyfriend's family, and then they got married. They were pregnant with my nephew, Brian, ye see." Campbell smiled, pulling his wallet out of his pocket. I scooted closer to him as he showed me the little photos. "So Brian's nearly four, and then there's Ellie, their daughter. She's two and a half." I loved the way he pronounced half "*hoff*." Isla was red-haired, like Campbell, but more auburn, and less curly.

"That's Duncan," he said, pointing at Isla's dark-haired husband. "God bless the man for putting up wi' that firebrand."

Campbell sighed as he stowed the photos back in his wallet. "I havena been home for quite some time now. Thankfully, there's Facetime and Skype, so at least the wee ones recognize their Uncle Cam."

"Can you tell me about your parents?" I asked.

"My ma was a devout Catholic," Campbell said. "She prayed over me when I was young. Took me to mass. Made me memorize the catechism. She's the reason I'm still a virgin. She said once that it was easy for a man to give himself to anyone. But that my da had given her the gift of himself when they were married. And she worshipped him for it, because she never worried if his heart was with someone else."

It was a beautiful story, but somehow it made me feel guilty. "Well, Campbell, would she think *I* was good enough, then?" I asked. "I'm not a virgin. I'm older than you. I've had other men. I haven't saved myself for you."

"Doesna matter, Carlie," Campbell said. "Being with ye will be gift enough. But, you said, 'Saved yourself?'" Campbell looked confused. "Ah, that's right. You're Christian. Sometimes I forget ye arna Catholic, *Ri-pálle*."

"Does *that* bother you?" I asked. "Because it seems like your faith matters."

"Doesna bother me," he said. "And aye, my faith matters, but that's between God and me, and your faith is between God and you." He met my eyes again and chuckled. "As long as you can respect that it's as much a part of me as my red hair."

I bent over to kiss him. "And just as beautiful," I said.

Campbell swept my hair away from my face and dug his fingers into my curls. His grip intensified as we continued to kiss, and I found myself scooting closer to him, pressing myself against him, running my fingers through his hair as well, tracing the lines of his arms. Finally Campbell pulled away, closing his eyes and breathing out slowly. "So, ye said ye willna molest me," he chuckled; I could almost swear he sounded disappointed.

"No," I said solemnly, though it took every ounce of self-control in me to mean it.

"What if I said I changed my mind, and that it doesna matter?" he asked, raising his eyebrows, running his fingers up my arm and giving me shivers.

"I would say, 'Too bad, buck-O! Not gonna do it.'" I grinned at him.

"What if I wanted to go to almost-second base again?" he asked, slipping his hand up my ribcage from my waist.

Denying my automatic urge to grab his hand and show him the way, I gently pushed him away and smiled. "I know how to be a good girl. *You* need to stay out of the bathing suit area!"

"But I like swimming *naked*," he said, kissing my neck under my ear. "Then there *is* no bathing suit area."

"Campbell," I pushed him away again, beginning to feel irritated at the mixed messages I was getting. "Are you *testing* me?"

"No," he said, shaking his head seriously. "You're so sexy when you're holy. Now I *want* to be naughty. Must be the Catholic boy in me, who figures he might as well have something to confess."

"How much have you had to confess?" I asked him nosily. "Have you been on any of the bases before?"

"All the way to second when I was 16," he said, blushing. "First time at almost third—today."

"You're kidding! So, you've never even had a *hand job?*" I exclaimed in astonishment, instantly regretting it because it seemed to embarrass him. "Or had a girl go down on you?" I asked, biting the inside of my lip.

He blushed furiously. "*No.*"

"So you have no preconceived notions about what it's going to be like with me?"

He nuzzled my neck again, then pulled my hand to his lips and kissed my fingers. "No. But I have a feeling I'm going to like it. So, what if," he whispered, toying with the hem of my tee shirt, "I said I wanted to go *all the way* to second with ye?"

"I would say, 'Goodnight, Campbell,'" I said, pulling myself reluctantly away from him.

"Are ye serious, *Ri-pālle?*" he asked, eyes hooded, his voice husky.

"Yes," I said with a sigh, then smiled. "We are waiting until we get *married.*"

CHAPTER 18

Phoning Home

Revka woke up early, needing to get ready for school. After she spent a few minutes having to repeatedly step over me as she first went to the shower and then got dressed, I folded up the sleeping pad and went out to the living room with my blanket to get out of her way. Campbell was sleeping on his back, his blanket twisted around his legs, his arm bent, hand by his face. The early morning sun glinted off his copper chest hair as his stomach rose and fell with each breath. I watched him for a moment, then went and knelt by him. I stroked his arm gently, wondering if he was close to waking. His lips curved into a slight smile, but he went on sleeping. I tiptoed back to the other couch and curled up in my blanket.

When Alastair and Moneo came out to the kitchen and started talking and preparing breakfast, it was impossible to sleep further. Campbell woke and smiled at me. We got up to get ready for the day. One significant event of the morning was the incredible pleasure of a hot shower, even though I minimized my time to save water.

I was feeling nervous as we ate breakfast. Alastair and Moneo headed off to work; Revka had taken the bus to school. I had charged my very dead cell phone through the night, and now there was no excuse not to call my parents.

"What's the time difference between here and Denver?" Campbell asked, as I picked up the phone.

"Oh, my parents don't live in Denver," I said. "Hadn't I told you? My dad's in the Air Force; he's stationed at Andersen Air Force Base on Guam. That's just 2 hours earlier than here. Since it's 8:30, it'll be 6:30 there. They're usually up by now."

"You did mention that your father was in the United States military," Campbell said, "But you hadn't mentioned where."

"Well, he's a chaplain," I said. "So he's not a fighting airman."

"Your father is a pastor? A Reverend?" Campbell seemed to find that amusing, though I didn't know why.

"Not a pastor as much as someone who provides spiritual and emotional counsel."

"What do people call him?" Campbell wondered.

"Well, he's Major Beecher," I answered. "But I call him Daddy."

His eyebrows rose in amusement. "*Daddy?* Exactly how old are ye?"

I was too nervous to laugh at his joke. As I stared at my phone, Campbell got up and came to sit by me, putting his arm around my shoulders. "No need to be nervous, *Ri-pálle*. Or are your parents scary people?"

"No," I shook my head. "I just have no idea how I'm going to explain this." I took a deep breath and pressed the send button.

"Daddy!" I exclaimed when he answered the phone, Campbell making a face at me in the background. I turned away from him. "How are you and Mom doing?"

"Carlie Anne!" said my father. It was good to hear his familiar voice over the line. "We didn't expect to hear from you so soon. We thought you wouldn't be able to get to Majuro for a month or two. We have gotten letters from you, though."

"It's Carlie?" I heard in the distance. Seconds later, my mom picked up the other phone—landline, of course. My parents couldn't live completely in the present. At least their phones no longer had those curly cords attaching the phone thingy to the other part.

"Hey, kiddo," she said. Campbell smiled, hearing her voice over the line.

"She sounds like you," he whispered.

"So, what's up?" Daddy asked. "It sounds like you had a pretty tough weekend."

"My letter about the funeral got to you already?" I asked.

"Just yesterday, in fact," Mom said. "I hurt for you, Carlie. After such a fun day, too, snorkeling with the Scots. Losing Maxson must have been incredibly hard. I'm really sorry that you weren't able to let Campbell comfort you," she said. "He sounds like such a nice guy, but Eric *is* your fiancé. You need to be careful."

"Speaking of which!" I exclaimed, as Campbell looked at me, an amused expression on his face as he realized that I had written my parents about him. He scooted closer to me so that he could hear better.

"So, this is all going to come as a shock to you," I said. "But it's better to just say it. Mom, Dad…. Eric broke up with me…"

My mom gasped, "Oh, honey, no! Are you okay?"

"Yes," I said, "but I'm not done with what I have to tell you yet. Eric broke up with me, but I'm engaged again… Um, Campbell and I are getting married." There was absolute silence on the other end of the phone. I waited. Nothing. "Hello?" I said.

"Carlie Anne," my dad said compassionately. "Are you *pregnant?*" Campbell's eyes widened, and he blushed slightly.

"No, Dad," I responded with a rueful chuckle, stammering as I explained. "We haven't, I mean, we're not at that… Um, no, I'm not."

There was more silence. "Do you need me to call you back?" I asked. "Obviously you guys are shocked."

"We need time to process," said my mom reassuringly. "I mean, Eric's been part of the family for almost seven years. That's a lot to… that's *fast*… Honey, you haven't even been there a *month*. How long have you known this boy?"

"Long enough to know how I feel about him," I said, feeling flushed and embarrassed.

"You care enough about him to marry him?" my mom asked.

I looked at Campbell's rugged face, his gentle eyes, his smile. Without realizing it, I think, he had begun holding me tighter.

"Yes," I whispered. I had to hold the phone away from my ear as Campbell took my chin in his hand to kiss me.

"Are you still there?" my mom was asking as I put my ear back to the phone.

"Yes."

"So, have you set a date?" she asked.

I closed my eyes and blew out my breath slowly. "We're thinking, like, *Friday*."

More silence.

"Come on, Carlie, seriously," Mom laughed. "When?"

"Seriously," I said. "I'll explain the reasons in a letter, but we are getting married. As soon as we can."

"Without even giving us a chance to see if we could come?" said my dad. He sounded disappointed. "It's only eight hours by plane if we take the island hopper, Carlie. I want to be able to walk you down the aisle . . . or beach."

My mom spoke up, "Jeff, it's going to be okay. Carlie, this does seem impulsive. But you're a grown woman, and this is your life, and we trust you. But if you're going to get married Friday, Daddy and I will look at getting flights and we can let you know if we can make it. When do you head back to Arno?"

"Today," I said, "If we can get everything done we need to. If we go tomorrow, we'll have to charter a boat."

"Call us before you leave, then, hon," said my dad. "And whether or not we can come, we love you, and we wish you all the best."

Campbell reached his hand for the phone, a question in his eyes. "Hey, dad?" I said. "Campbell would like to talk to you."

"Just a minute, sir," Campbell said, as he put the phone to his ear. He left me and walked back into Revka's room, shutting the door.

A few minutes later, Campbell came out and returned the phone to me.

"Daddy?" I put the phone to my ear.

"Okay, Carlie," Daddy said. "I give you my blessing, baby girl. He seems like a fine young man—if he keeps his word. I'll talk to you soon."

"What did you say to them?" I asked, as I hung up the phone.

"I'll tell ye sometime," Campbell said. "For now, we need to get things done."

It was a hectic day. We stopped at the bank first, where we proceeded to have our first fight. It started with me saying, "Well, I have money in savings if you need it," when talking about Campbell buying me a wedding ring.

"No, I willna be borrowing money from ye to buy you a wedding ring," he said stubbornly.

I stood in front of him and put my hands on my hips. "Okay, Campbell MacReid, if you say that you want the kind of marriage that's forever, then here's the deal. A nurse makes more than a teacher, period. Do you have a problem with that? Because I'm not going to be a separate bank accounts kind of girl. I had enough of that for the past seven years, and see how easy it was to break ties with Eric? If we want to stay married forever, we need to entangle ourselves so separating is next to impossible. And that means what's mine is yours."

"But can't you see, Carlie," Campbell retorted, "That a wedding ring is different? I'll happily use your money to buy food and clothes and go on vacations. But this is going to be from me to you, and I willna be using your money, even if it means it's a simple band because I canna afford more. Can you simplify your desires, or do you *need* a gigantic diamond, *Ri-pàlle?*"

His pet name for me had never sounded so snide and mean. I stopped and put my hand on his chest and stared at him.

"Ye're still wearing your engagement ring from Eric," he said, forehead wrinkled, as he put his hand over mine. I looked down at my ring finger, stunned. The white gold ring with a princess cut diamond, probably several thousand dollars in value, was still there.

"I'm so sorry, Campbell," I said, pulling it off my finger and dropping it into my purse. "I hadn't even... I didn't think... I'm sorry. Simple is fine. I'll love whatever you choose."

After drawing out cash from the bank, we scribbled down a list of things to take care of. I wanted better curtains for the apartment, and Campbell said he needed to get a few things for the house as well. We planned our last stop before heading home to be a grocery store where we could buy rice and canned meats like tuna and Spam for the party, as well as beverages and flour for the ladies to create whatever form of dessert they could. It was a little strange to think of a wedding without a cake.

And we wanted to get it all done by four when the Jolok boat left.

For two hours we separated, each working on our own to-do list.

For my part, I found a salon where I could get a pedicure, and then decided to get waxed. I left a bit of nature—no need to stun the poor boy, but I wanted to make it easy to find what he needed to.

I also found a little shop that had a lovely white lacy sundress that would work for my wedding dress, as well as some lingerie—pretty chemises and some clingy beach cover-ups. I liked the way they let my breasts move, concealing some of my body, but revealing the shape of my breasts and the rise of my nipples. In the changing room I looked at everything with a young virgin in mind. I felt like I was giving him a gift, and choosing lingerie was like buying special wrapping paper. He was right; there was something to be said for knowing I would be his first.

And only, a little voice in my mind said. For a moment, my heart stopped. How could a young man be satisfied with a woman five years older than him? How would *Campbell* ever be satisfied with *me*? He wanted this to be forever. Could I really commit to him? What if we found out we didn't like each other? I was almost hyperventilating with panic.

I took a deep breath, thinking. *This is Campbell. He's already your friend— strong, funny, good-humored, and sexy. You trust him, you feel safe with him, you love him, you're attracted to him. Other long-lasting marriages have started with less.*

When we met back up again, Campbell looked giddy, but I must have had a similar expression on my face, because he asked me, "What have you been doing, *Ri-pálle*? Ye look like ye're keeping a secret."

"So do you," I said, which made him grin and hug me.

Our last stop was the supermarket, where we spent a crazy amount of money on food and drinks, and then we lugged everything to the Jolok boat dock.

While we waited for the boat, I called my parents again. They were still working on it, they said, but if we could wait til Friday evening, they would try their hardest to come for the wedding.

The tiny boat pulled up to the dock and was quickly loaded with our boxes as well as a large crate of some kind. With the boat riding low in the water,

I wondered whether we'd make it to our own wedding, much less be able to be joined by my parents.

On the boat I watched Campbell—his seasickness relieved by a healthy preventive dose of Dramamine—carrying on a conversation with a wrinkled little *jibū*, listening to her and talking to her with bright eyes and a big grin.[1] As he talked, she threw her head back and laughed, revealing toothless gums.

Running through my mind were my dad's final words on the phone. He was choked up as he said goodbye. "Carlie, sweetie," he said. "I know he's young; I know this is fast, but I see why you're doing it. This one's a keeper."

Daddy shared the gist of what Campbell had said to him: "It would crush me, but if ye say no, sir, I will not marry your daughter. I vow to ye, sir, I will love your daughter well. I know to the depths of my soul that she is the woman with whom I want to spend my future. I will keep her safe; protect her at the cost of my life. And I will love her, when you are no longer able to."

I turned my eyes toward Arno. The ocean, blue sky, green trees, and white sand swirled in front of me, and I lifted my hand to wipe away the tears. I felt terrified and certain at the same time.

In seconds, a warm body was behind me, an arm wrapped around my shoulders, lips kissed my cheek, and a voice in my ear said, "I'm here, hen. *Dinna fash.* Let's go home, and then let's get married."

---

[1] *Jibū*: shee´-boo (grandma)

CHAPTER 19

Restraint

Our day had been so busy, filled with stress and decisions and a long boat trip over the rolling ocean, that when the pickup dropped us off at dusk in front of my house with countless boxes and bags—and that mysterious crate— I stood in paralyzed silence on the gravel.

"*Itōk, Ri-pālle,*" said Campbell, grabbing me by the hand and leading me toward the beach. The pickup had jolted off with people that needed to travel on to Matolen; it was getting dark outside.

"I've been wanting you all day, Carlie," he said huskily. "I need you in my arms."

We had reached the beach, standing on the grassy lip of sand that had been eaten away by the high tides. Pale pink light still emanated from behind islands on the other side of the lagoon, but the sky was becoming progressively darker, slowly filling with stars. Campbell sat down on a level spot carpeted with short salt grass, and I moved to sit next to him. He swept me into his arms and kissed me until I was breathless.

"Oh, God, I want you so bad," he said. "I want to take you back to your cabin and have you naked and touch your body," he whispered in my ear, kissing my neck.

"Your breasts, and your gorgeously round arse," he groaned, his hands heading there as he spoke. "I can't wait."

I reluctantly urged his hands away, though I had absolutely no desire to be a source of restraint and very little confidence that either one of us was going to make it until Friday night. "It's just two more days," I said reassuringly.

"Two days too long," Campbell groaned again. "Every time I looked at you today, I had such *thoughts* about you. Whenever you walked in front of me... Whenever you brushed up against me... How do engaged people wait until they get married?"

"Most of them don't," I said, laughing. "You said it yourself. Virginity 'til marriage is a rarity. I think it's 5% or less of women. And who knows what percent of men?"

"Guess I'm just an oddity," Campbell scoffed.

"No," I kissed him firmly, "You are *exceptional.*"

"I like that," said Campbell with just a trace of pride in his voice, then shaking his head. "But I'm not sure of the point now. Maybe it's not so important to wait anymore."

"Not important?" I said. "To have your wedding night be exciting and fresh? I kind of wish I was still a virgin, so I could experience it with you."

"Nah," said Campbell. "But it canna hurt for you to know what ye're doing!"

I smiled and kissed him thoroughly, displaying evidence of my expertise.

"Now, it's not sex if I just do this," Campbell suggested, his hand creeping back toward my breast. I didn't stop him this time. "Oh, Carlie," he groaned when he had me against his palm.

I responded with a gasp, twining my fingers through the hair at the back of his neck. It had been too long since I had been touched and kissed passionately. I had been lusting after Campbell for weeks now, and we were in the dark, by the beach. We were engaged. No, we weren't just engaged; we were actually getting married. He wanted to touch me... well, I wanted to touch him too. As we kissed, I ran my hands over his shoulders and down his arms, then across his chest. I returned the favor and put my lips to his neck, traveling up to nip his ear.

It was like waking a beast. He groaned, laid me on the ground and lowered himself over me. "Christ, Carlie," he said, pushing my skirt up as he kissed my neck. His hand was warm as he slid it up my leg till he reached my upper thigh. He had just run his fingertips along the edge of my panties when he gasped. "Oh, God, you have to stop me, *Ri-pálle*," he begged. "Please. I..."

"*I* have to stop *you*?" I panted between kisses, feeling instead like I wanted to guide his hand exactly where I ached to have him touch me. "I'm ready to drag you into my house and have my way with you."

Finally, Campbell groaned and pulled his hands away. He flopped on his back next to me.

"I've always prided myself on my self-control," he sighed. "I dinna seem to have even a bit of it right now."

"Making out just makes it harder," I said. "To wait, I mean," I added, as he looked at me, confused. "But it will do *that*, too." I grinned.

Campbell grimaced. "I dinna think it's possible for it to be harder than it is right now."

I resisted a very strong urge to see if I should believe him.

Finally, Campbell sat up and squared his shoulders. "I *did* just talk to your da today," said Campbell. "I should definitely keep my hands off Major Beecher's daughter, if only out of respect for her father."

"What about what Miss Beecher wants?" I asked, snaking my hand out and stroking his thigh. He groaned, then reached down and grasped my hand with his to remove it from his leg.

"I think Miss Beecher would appreciate a strong and principled man as a husband," Campbell said, slowly standing up. "One who knows the value of restraint and delaying gratification."

He reached out his hand to me. "*Itōk, Ri-pālle*. Let's get the packages into your house. Once we're done, I'm gonna go home, punch Ewan in the face, and then I'm gonna hug him. After that, I'm going to go to bed, to have verra inappropriate dreams about my wife-to-be."

It was very strange to return to clinic work in the morning. Fortunately, few emergencies had occurred in my absence. There were several sores and rashes to attend to, a cough, an eye infection. I even got to pull out a rotten tooth, which was *definitely* outside my comfort zone.

After school finished, Graham, Ewan, and Campbell showed up at the house, carrying Campbell's dresser from their apartment, along with a bunch of hand tools. I worked on hanging the new curtains as they took apart the bunk bed and reassembled it as a king-sized frame. In Majuro we had purchased a thick mattress pad and king-sized sheets, so we were able to put the twins side by side to make a bed that would fit both of us.

It was so hot in the house that eventually all three men pulled off their shirts, revealing a striking variety of physiques and levels of hairiness. Graham was the chunkiest, barrel-chested and hirsute not only on his chest but also his back. Ewan was pale and scrawny with a tiny patch of black hairs in the center of his concave chest. Campbell, now... he was something else altogether. I loved that his shorts could never seem to stay up, the way they rode low on his hips—revealing every muscle group of his abdomen, exposing the waistband of his briefs. I tried to act busy in the kitchen, but I snuck as many peeks as I could of my handsome fiancé. I amused myself by thinking of them as the three bears: one was too small, one was too big, and one was *just right*... And the one that was just right was going to be *mine*.

As the boys continued to work, I went outside for a minute. They didn't realize I could hear them very clearly through the windows.

"So," asked Graham, "Have ye popped your cherry yet, man?"

"No," Campbell responded, "But I know she wants me, maybe as much as I want her. Dinna ken how I'm going to keep my hands off her 'til tomorrow. I'm not being very successful so far."

"Don't tell me that," groaned Ewan. "Her breasts? They're soft, aren't they?"

"Hush, man, dinna talk about my wife-to-be like that," Campbell scolded. "But, *yes*."

I heard Graham mumble some unintelligible curse words.

"I still can't believe ye got up the courage to ask her," said Ewan. "Wi' Alastair there, and everything."

"But I didna ask her, not at first," said Campbell. "It was her idea."

Graham scoffed. "Jammy bastard."

"I am, that," said Campbell. "I canna believe she wants to marry me."

I stood outside the window smiling, and finally headed in.

I cooked dinner for the boys as thanks for their help. Ewan and Graham took up residence quite happily on the bed Campbell and I would be consummating our marriage in the next day.

"This should be interesting," said Ewan. "I've not been to a *ri-Majel* wedding before where there were two white people getting married."

"Have they given ye the *nuknuk* yet?" Graham asked.

"What's a *nuknuk*?" I asked.

"The virginity cloth," said Ewan, as if that was the most normal thing in the world. I stared at him, confused.

"Aye, after ye get married, the party will come back here; the two of you will come inside, and...*you know*," said Graham. "And then you'll toss out a cloth with Campbell's boaby on it."

"What is that?" I asked, afraid I already knew what it meant.

"Evidence. To show if ye are a virgin. To see if there's blood."

"But I'm *not* a virgin," I said, shocked. "That's *obscene*. And my *parents* might be here."

"That's the way it's done here," said Campbell, shrugging his shoulders in resignation. "Whether it's obscene or not." [1]

"But, Campbell, what will that mean for you, for us? Does it matter?"

"Not too much," he said. "If my family were here, and if they cared whether ye were a virgin, then it might. But wi'out a groom's family to object, it willna be a problem."

"Except for the fact that everyone on the island will know that I wasn't a virgin when we got married."

"They already assumed it," said Ewan. "*Dinna fash.*"

"Wait a minute," I said, suddenly horrified further than I'd already been. "Did you just say they expect us to come in here and... *have sex*... while everyone is outside?"

"Aye," said Ewan. "It's your wedding night! They expect Campbell to give ye a right poundin'!"

Graham and Ewan made quite a show of bouncing on the bed vigorously enough to make the whole apartment rock, groaning and panting for effect.

---

[1] See "First Blood" chapter notes.

I looked at Campbell, who was blushing and shaking his head, but grinning an incredibly cheeky grin.

"You're lucky you're hot," I said to him. "Otherwise, I would just call this thing off."

Campbell headed home with Graham and Ewan sometime after dark, which was probably a good idea. He'd been eyeing me hungrily, and I was quite certain I would not be a good influence if I were left alone with him. We did hug at my door after Graham and Ewan went outside, and Campbell kissed me chastely. "Tomorrow," he whispered in my ear.

"It's good you're leaving. I don't want to wait," I whispered back. He sighed, increased the intensity of his kiss for a few seconds and then pulled away with a groan.

"I'm surprised it's even five percent," he said as he left.

Friday afternoon when I was done with clinic, I strolled to the school to visit Campbell. I couldn't be bothered about the whole 'Don't see your bride-to-be on your wedding day' superstition. I just needed to see him so I could calm myself down. The children were still in class, and I peeked into his classroom.

Campbell had his back to the class as he drew a diagram on the chalkboard. As he sketched, he explained in Marshallese. I slipped into an empty desk and crouched down slightly behind the student in front of me. When he was done drawing, he turned and explained it again in English.

"So," Campbell said, pointing to the picture of a mountain with a ring around it and some bumpy waves surrounding it. "Atolls begin as volcanoes, pushing up from the ocean floor. If the volcano lasts long enough, coral begins to grow on the sides of the volcano, becoming a fringing reef."

He turned back to the board again and drew a picture of a small hill in the middle of a ring, explaining in Marshallese as he did, then turning and explaining in English. "Over time, the volcano goes dormant and begins to sink, or subside, back toward the ocean floor. If the coral grows fast enough, it keeps pace with the sinking volcano, continuing to stay right under or up to the water. A lagoon forms between the reef and the volcano, and dirt carried by the wind begins to create sediment that fills the lagoon and drops on top of the coral as well, building up the island."

The children were turning and pointing at me, giggling and whispering. Campbell turned around and gave the class a teacher glare before drawing his final picture on the board, explaining in Majel.

He looked confused by the noise as he duplicated his explanation in English. "Finally, the volcano has completely subsided, leaving a crater where the lagoon is, but the coral continues to grow, protecting the island, and sediment continues to be laid down, making the islands higher above the ocean surface."

When the whispering and giggling continued, Campbell began to look irritated. "*Jab konono*," he said firmly.[1] "Stop talking." The kids continued to giggle and whisper. "*Jaje manit ñak manit*," he said.[2] "You are being *very* rude."

"*Jolok bōd*, Meester Mack," a voice spoke out.[3] I looked and saw that it was Riti, who smiled at me and then addressed Campbell. "We're sorry. It is Miss Peachay. She is *jijet*—ah, sit in your class."[4]

I peeked my head out from behind the student in front of me, and Campbell shook his head at me.

"Miss Peachay," he said sternly. "*Itōk ije*.[5] Come here." He motioned for me to come up to his desk, then lectured me crossly. "You're causing trouble. You will have to stay after school today." The kids broke out in outrageous giggles.

"Meester Mack," said one adorable little girl. "You and Miss Peachay will marry tonight? *Komro kōmiro palele buñniin?*"[6]

---

[1] *Jab konono:* chab kah-ngo´-no (stop talking) This one is strange to me, because I could swear the phrase for be quiet was jab keroro, with rolled r's—at least it worked with my students when I taught!

[2] *Jaje manit ñak manit:* shah´-shay mon´-it ngot mon´-it (You are being very rude—in Majel, repeating a word (in this case, manit twice) means *very*.)

[3] *Jolok bōd:* joe-lock burr, with a rolled 'r' (I'm sorry)

[4] *Jijet:* shee´-zshet (sit)

[5] *Itōk ije:* Ee-tok´ ee-shay´ (Come here)

[6] *Komro kōmiro palele buñniin:* comb´-row comb-me´-row pah-lay´-lay boo-ngeen´ (You will marry tonight?)

"*Aet*," said Campbell, smiling down at me. "*Ej lukkuun likatu?*"[1]

The kids all shouted yes in response to whatever he'd asked. "That's not fair," I complained. "I don't know what you're saying."

"He say," said one little boy in the front row, so embarrassed he was unable to meet my eyes, "That you are bery pree-ty." The children giggled again.

Trying to be respectful of the Majel cultural mores, I kept my distance from Campbell by sitting in a chair by his desk at the front of the room as he sat down, finished up the class period and excused the children from class.

He leaned back in his chair when all the children were gone.

"Meester Mack," I said. I sat gingerly on the edge of his desk, facing him. "I'm impressed with your expertise at speaking Majel."

"I *have* been in the Majels for four years," he said. "And my Auntie Moneo, obviously, is Marshallese, so I had lots of practice."

"I wish I was fluent in a second language," I said. "We Americans tend to be pretty terrible about foreign languages."

"Well," said Campbell, "This isn't just my second language. I know Majel, German, obviously English, and a wee bit of the Gàidhlig."

"Gay lag?" I asked (saying it with a terrible American accent). "What's that?"

"The mother tongue of the ancient Scots!" he exclaimed. "Ye didna know that?"

"Really?" I asked. "Scotland had a different language before English?"

Campbell was so angry his eye was twitching. With his fierce voice rising so that I wasn't quite certain whether he was joking or not, he exclaimed, "Just goes to show you that Britain *succeeded* in destroying Scot culture! They took our swords, our dirks, our tartans. And apparently, they took our language as well!"

---

[1] *Ej lukkuun likatu*: edge loo´-koon lee´-kah-too (she is very pretty)

"I'm sorry I didn't know," I said. "Now I do. So that's the language you speak in when you cuddle me? Scottish Gaelic? I like it; I like the way it sounds."

Campbell narrowed his eyes at me and shook his head. "I dinna think I can marry ye anymore, *Ri-pàlle.*"

"Oh, *no,*" I said flirtatiously. "And here I was *really* looking forward to being married."

He continued to look at me, silent, eyebrows raised.

"Well," I said. "Maybe I can make it up to you." I attempted to look as penitent as possible.

He looked me up and down. "And how d'ye intend to do that?" he asked, grinning.

With a glance at the classroom door, I sat down on his lap.

Several minutes later, feeling lightheaded and thoroughly man-handled, with the evidence of my arousing effect on him beneath me, I paused to catch my breath. Campbell finally stopped, took his hand off my breast and looked up toward heaven as if begging for help to escape temptation. "I want you too much," he breathed. "This is *ridiculous.* Surely I have the self-control to wait just five or six hours..."

"Did you drop something on the floor just now?" I asked, losing the flirtatious tone. Campbell looked around, confused, but as I lowered myself to the floor and retreated under the desk in front of him, his pupils dilated.

"Oh, my God, Carlie! *What* are ye doing?" he asked, raising his eyebrows at me.

He was wearing the sarong, with nothing under it.

"Hey, Campbell!" The voice was Graham's; Campbell sat up sharply and his legs stiffened. "Have ye seen Carlie? Someone said they saw her come this way, and I thought maybe she was with you."

Campbell leaned forward in his chair and cleared his throat. "She stopped by, but she had... lots to... do." He grabbed my hair to make me stay still. "Why did you... need her?" His voice sounded a little labored. I wondered if Graham noticed anything strange.

187

"Oh, it's just— her parents are here." Graham said. "Maybe you want to go greet them, then? Sounds like they like ye okay."

"Aye, I'll finish up here in a minute or two and head down. Are they at the clinic, then?"

"Aye," said Graham. "How're ye feeling, Virgin? Are ye excited yet?"

"More than you could possibly know!" Campbell exclaimed, sounding strained.

Allowing Graham a few moments to leave, I emerged from under the desk to find my fiancé sitting, looking dazed.

"You're *stopping*?" he asked breathlessly.

"Well, yeah, my parents are here!" I said. "C'mon, Virgin," I joked, grabbing him by the hand.

"I'm no' satisfied at *all*," Campbell said, following me, "But I dinna feel much like a virgin anymore either, *Ri-pālle.*"

I turned back to him. "Welcome to virginity in the 21st century, Campbell." I pulled him down for a gentle kiss, but lightly licked his lips halfway through, making him gasp. "And don't worry, after tonight, Graham won't be able to call you that anymore."

CHAPTER 20

To Have and To Hold

T hey were standing out front of the clinic when Campbell and I arrived. By then we were flushed from the brisk walk instead of our recent behavior. My mom, petite and brunette, her brown curls generously interspersed with white strands, immediately approached and gave me and then Campbell a hug.

My father was more reticent, hanging back and eyeing Campbell with critical curiosity. I had hugged him, and Campbell reached out his hand, which Daddy shook firmly, but then he took Campbell by the arm. "Let's walk a little, son," he said, as they headed down the road toward Ine. Campbell looked back at me with wide eyes, and I shrugged my shoulders helplessly, mouthing, "Sorry!"

"How did you get here so fast?" I asked my mom. "The Jolok boat doesn't arrive on the island until six."

"We went ahead and chartered a boat," Mom said, gesturing toward my apartment, "with Alastair and Moneo." It was then I noticed Campbell's aunt and uncle, hanging back to allow us time for greetings with my parents.

"Where will you stay?" I asked, suddenly wondering how we could accommodate so many guests—on our *wedding night*. "The closest hotel is in Arno Arno."

"Alastair Douglass is friends with the Iroij," Mom said. "That's the local ruler, right?" I nodded in response. "He is able to host us in his palace," my mom explained. "Though Mr. Douglass assures us that the term 'palace' is used loosely here."

189

I hugged my mom again and got a little choked up as I felt her arms around me. "I still can't believe you're here!"

Mom wrapped her arm around my shoulders. "We're all feeling just a little surprised right now," she winked. "But I am here for you, baby. Now tell me about my new son-in-law."

The local women had divided the extra food we brought on Thursday morning, parceling it out to prepare rice and banana bread and donuts at home ahead of time. As we stood there, they were bringing pots and wood to Kona's house next door and to Jibon and Kabua's house on the other side. Men carried stringers of fresh fish, and several also brought the newly plucked bodies of chickens. Children skipped up with rolls of pandanus mats which they laid out in the grassy area on the clinic property. A few men came carrying sawhorses and boards, and soon some makeshift tables had been set up as well.

I took my mom out to the *iar*, where we'd decided on having an open-air wedding. "Oh, Carlie," she said, squeezing me again as she looked out over the turquoise lagoon toward the islands on the other side, "It's so beautiful." She sat down on the sandy grass, ironically in the same place Campbell and I had been making out two nights previously. Just seeing the spot made me shiver in anticipation.

"I'd like to help you fix your hair and get dressed," she said, glancing at her watch. "It's 4:15 and the wedding is planned for 6:30. But please tell me you have ten minutes to tell your mama how in the *world* you got engaged so quickly?"

"Sure," I said, sitting down next to her. "I think I told you that I met Campbell my second day here, because he had a huge gash on his butt," I said, "and I had to give him stitches."

She looked at me with a smirk. "Oh, Carlie," she said, "That's always how it always starts—looking at their hineys!" I rolled my eyes at her. "I could tell you liked him a lot from your letters. You already told me that he was Scottish, and a teacher, and that he was really sweet."

"From the very beginning," I agreed, nodding.

"He hugged you, didn't he?" she asked. "Even in that first letter it was obvious how much you liked him already." Mom was looking across the water, her forehead wrinkled. "I wondered, when you decided to come out here, if everything was okay between you and Eric."

I took a deep breath. "I thought it was fine," I said. "But under the surface, I wasn't happy. And as much as I didn't want to be unfaithful, my heart was drawn to Campbell."

"You've always needed affection, kiddo," she said, putting her arm around my shoulders. "It seems like Campbell is an affectionate guy."

"He is," I said, "They never show affection in public here, so he's been the one who gives me hugs and holds me when I'm sad. He's been my best friend here."

"But 'best friends' is still a long way away from marriage," Mom said.

"Well, I felt more for him than that, Mom," I said. "Even when I was still engaged to Eric, I started to have feelings for him."

"Why get married so quickly though?" she asked.

"My incredible cultural stupidity?" I offered. "Along with Eric breaking up with me. I was so devastated after getting his letter, I went to Campbell to be comforted. But it was nighttime, and afterward I just didn't want to be alone, so I slept in his bed with him." My mother said nothing, just raised her eyebrows at me.

"We ended up getting in trouble because I walked back in the morning in my pajamas and Mr. Douglass believed my ability to be effective was damaged because the locals wouldn't respect me. He said he should probably terminate my service and send me home. And he didn't feel like he could punish me and not Campbell, which meant Campbell was in danger of losing his position, too. So, I proposed."

Wide-eyed, my mom shook her head at me. "You did? Just to avoid going back to the states?"

"I know it seems fast, Mom," I said. "I know he's young. I know Eric just broke up with me. But there is just clarity in being with him. I feel safe and loved when I'm around Campbell, and he doesn't hold himself back from me. He wants to be married forever, and I just knew."

"So," Mom looked confused. "You fell *in* love with him and *out of* love with Eric. Eric broke up with you and then you slept with Campbell?"

"I slept in Campbell's *bed*," I said. "We haven't *slept* together."

My mom raised her eyebrows. "No?"

"He's never had sex before," I said in a low voice. "We're waiting... or, we've been *mostly* waiting."

She scoffed. "Good thing you're getting married tonight."

"Yes," I nodded, agreeing with her. "Because I do want him, Mom. And I think we're going be good together."

"Oh, Carlie," sighed my mom, "I can tell you really do like him, but it still seems so sudden to me! Does *he* know what he's signing up for?"

"Neither of us do," I said. "But we've talked, and both of us feel okay about it."

"You know, kiddo," she said. "Even if your dad and I thought we knew who we were as people and as a couple, we had no idea what life would hand to us. And you're right. It's been okay." She cocked her head and gave me a look of blessing and permission, as if she was finally satisfied with my answers.

"Come on, Mom," I said, hopping up and reaching a hand down to her. "Let's go visit the ladies and see if we can help."

With an hour left, Mom and I retreated to my apartment. While I had squatted and chatted with the ladies who were cooking, she had wandered around the property, finding some delicate pink and white flowers. Having the same ridiculously curly hair as I did, my mom had plenty of practice getting it to obey. She pinned my hair up, and once I'd put on my simple white dress, she wove flowers into the hair around the bun.

I hadn't typically been wearing much makeup because the humidity made it run too easily, but I put on some mascara and eyeliner, and a little bit of lip pencil and gloss.

Campbell and I had decided we'd keep the ceremony pretty laid back and traditional. Traditional vows, ring, kiss the bride. The sun would be going down on the ocean side, so the sky would be pretty, but no glaring sun behind us.

We had considered writing vows to be shared in front of everyone but based on our short courtship and considering that half our wedding attendees weren't even English-speakers, we decided to each write something to the other that we could go out to the water and read to each other alone. Campbell heartily agreed to the idea, so I had spent some time writing my thoughts the night before. I took the time to read it over once more and rewrite it neatly. My draft was a mess and even a little tear-stained.

The time was approaching, and I became more and more anxious. My mom could see it, and even though the two of us were virtually the same size she pulled me down on her lap.

"Baby, what's going on?" she asked.

"How can I promise forever, Mom?" I asked. "I don't even know if I could have promised forever to Eric."

"I think that's partly the point, Carlie," she said. "You yourself told me that something in your heart recognized something in Campbell. He loves you well, doesn't he?"

"He holds me when I'm upset," I said gesturing toward her arms around me and gingerly dabbing around my eyes with a tissue. "And I guess I was used to that, growing up. The thought of having him close, whenever I need him, of not having to say goodnight, of not having to send him home..." I sighed longingly.

My mom held my face in her hands. "It will be wonderful. But Carlie, there may be times when he won't be able to give you what you need, though, and that doesn't mean it's over. It just means he's human. . .You're going to have to give him grace, just like Daddy and I have given each other grace, just as we have been forgiving with you."

"Oh, Mom," I said, leaning over to hug her. "I'm so glad you responded to my crazy decision and came to be with me."

She grinned. "We love you, Carlie, and we would do anything for you."

I heard guitar and ukulele music coming from the lagoon beach. "Where's Daddy?" I asked suddenly. "Isn't he going to walk me down the aisle?"

"Oh, didn't he or Campbell tell you?" Mom said. "Campbell asked him to do the ceremony for you kids so it would be in English. And I get to walk my baby down the aisle."

I slipped my feet into my sparkly flip-flops, lifted my skirts with one hand, took my mom's hand with the other, and headed down to the beach.

The islanders were all gathered along the pathway, and as we walked closer to the *iar* they followed us, settling on the grass and mats on the sand where they could see us. Moneo and Alastair sat with the *Iroij* and his wife.

My dad and Campbell stood halfway to the water. I realized we hadn't even considered what height the tides would be; we were very lucky that it was low tide, so there was a sandy swath of beach to be married on.

Campbell turned and watched us approach, a wide smile brightening his face. Up until now I'd only seen him in shorts and tee shirts—and occasionally the sarong. Now he was wearing khaki pants and a blue button-down shirt with a dark blue blazer. His ruddy red curls which had been combed for the occasion now were nearly burgundy in the fading pink light of sunset. He was heartbreakingly handsome, and he had eyes only for me.

My mom walked me all the way to Campbell, who held his arm out to me. He paused, though, to hug my mom, and to give her a hand as she sat down with Alastair and Moneo.

My brain couldn't internalize much of what my dad said. I only saw the look of love on my daddy's face, and the adoration for me in Campbell's eyes, and I spent most of my time trying not to cry.

Our vows were traditional... for better, for worse; for richer, for poorer; in sickness and in health, to love and to cherish, to have and to hold, from this day forward, until we are parted by death.

And then we brought out our rings for each other, both of us having chosen simple gold bands. As we in turn placed a ring on the other's finger, we repeated words spoken by countless others before us: "With this ring, I thee wed; With my body, I thee worship; And with all my worldly goods, I thee endow."

I looked at Campbell, anticipating for a moment being worshiped by and worshiping that particular body.

And after that, Campbell and I walked to the water's edge. He was hesitant, his eyes concerned.

"Are you okay, Carlie?" he said. "You seem so sad and serious."

"I'm just trying not to cry," I answered, proceeding at that precise moment to completely fail at my efforts.

Campbell moved toward me, tucked me up under his chin, and held me close.

"Everyone's watching," I said. "The Marshallese don't show affection publicly."

"I think they'll excuse us today," Campbell said, with a kiss on my forehead. "and I think I should keep holding you, because if this doesn't make *you* cry, it might do it for me." He pulled a piece of paper from his pocket, and in the fading evening light, he read to me.

My Turn

It could have been when you brought us food,
Or when you showed me how to wear a sarong,
Wrapping it around the curve of your hips.
Or when you stitched up my injury so calmly and capably,
Maybe it was when you sent Ewan and Graham away,
And they obeyed you.

Perhaps it was when I first focused on you,
The wild-haired new nurse
Who put herself under my arm
And authoritatively walked me into the clinic,
Put her hands in my trousers to undo the drawstring
And took off my shorts.
Or when you made dirty jokes and surprised all of us.

Whenever it was, at some point I realized
That independence isn't all it's cracked up to be.
That it was okay to need someone, to want someone.
And I wanted you: brown eyes and wild, curly hair.

What cemented "us" was when you needed me, too.
That you cried in my arms when I came back to hug you goodnight.
When you talked to me through the door because I couldn't come in,
And you didn't want to be alone after the drunk villagers visited you.
When you held my hand to go snorkeling,
So you wouldn't feel alone and afraid.
When you needed me to talk to you

So you could fall asleep.

I knew you needed me.
I could see it in your eyes at Tiljek's baby's funeral.
It was killing you to be apart from me.

He should have dropped everything and come with you.
Or if he had loved you well enough, you wouldn't have left him.

When you came to me, devastated by him,
It was being with me that comforted you.
It was my arms, my body, my heart, that sheltered you.
I loved you already.

When you said you wanted to marry me,
With your hand in mine,
I couldn't believe how lucky I was.

When I was a young man,
My ma pulled me close to her.
"Campbell," she said, "Promise me, son,
That you will only ever give your body
To someone who looks inside you and *sees* you.
Ye're braw and bonny, and lots of girls
Would give anything to lay claim to ye.
It's easy for a man to give himself to anyone who will have him.
But your da gave me the gift of himself when we were married.
And I worshipped him for it,
Because I never worried if his heart was with someone else."

When my ma died, my da had sobbed,
"I willna ever love another woman like I loved her."
And I knew he was telling the truth.

That's the reason I waited for love.
I had plenty of opportunities,
Girls who would drop their knickers or get on their knees for me,
But I couldna do it. Not with my ma's face before me,

Saying, "Being with you is a gift, sweet boy.
Give yourself to someone ye love."

It didn't keep me from theft, drunkenness, or brawling,
Which is why I'm not welcome in in my home town right now.

But when I realized I loved you I was grateful,
And tonight, I'm giving myself to you.

He wasn't lying. His eyes were wet, and mine could barely read my own
words for him. But he held me close as he listened to my hesitant voice.

Enough

I didn't expect to fall in love
Not with anyone but him, not so fast
But something in you spoke to my soul
And somehow you could hear my heart,
Even when I didn't speak.

You have *freely* given me what I needed
Without me having to ask
Comfort, affection, attention, time
Security, protection, assistance, help

This seems sudden, and at times I worry
That I am just using you to fill the empty spaces
The space left by disappointment,
The space left by a five-year engagement
Without a wedding
Without a baby

The space left by aging,
Of not being where I thought I'd be by now
The space left by loneliness,

I don't want to just *use* you
So I hope that somehow I can fill your spaces, too

197

That somehow, you'll need me
That in some way my arms will be long enough
My body big enough
My heart strong enough
To hold you
When you need to be held.

"Oh, Carlie," Campbell said, pulling me to him. "You *are* enough." He turned and called out to my dad, "Can I please just kiss her here, Major Beecher?"

"I now pronounce you husband and wife," my daddy called back to us. "Okay, Campbell, **now** you may kiss the bride. And you, Carlie, may kiss the groom."

And so we did.

CHAPTER 21

First Blood

O utside, the village men were laughing raucously. Children ran around the property on the *iar* side, screaming, probably hopped up on the red dye from the punch we'd provided.

Over the crowd, I could hear Campbell's rich laugh. He was still not coming. I was aching to have him with me, eager to finally have my hands on his firm muscles but at the same time extremely self-conscious about what this would be like—having sex with Campbell for the first time with a crowd of people waiting outside. I tried to calm myself by walking around the house.

It was amazing the difference made by a hardworking man and his friends. The bunk beds had been disassembled and then reassembled into a king-sized frame which now held two twin beds side by side. King-sized sheets and a good mattress pad camouflaged the seam between the mattresses, and with the secure frame we wouldn't be falling in between the beds accidentally any time soon. I trailed my finger along the covers; I wasn't going to be sleeping alone anymore.

Above the bed were our thick new drapes covering the window. I had wanted privacy, and these would provide it.

"Maybe the best purchase I made in Majuro," I said, stroking the fabric of the new curtains.

"Or the second best," I corrected myself, looking down at my body. I'd chosen a cream-colored camisole to wear for our wedding night, with a plunging neckline between lacy triangular cups, skinny satin straps, and a gauzy skirt, with a pair of lacy panties underneath. Until Campbell came in and shut the door from prying eyes, though, I'd thrown on a satin robe and tied it at the waist.

The lighting of the house was harsh, so I turned off the fluorescents and went old school—lighting a bunch of hurricane candles in clusters around the room. Their gentle glow was calming and lovely. I stood in the middle of the cabin and looked around. "I guess that will have to do," I said.

"Ye talking to yourself, *Ri-pālle?*" the voice behind me asked. I hadn't heard the door open. Campbell closed it behind himself.

He stood there shyly, still wearing the linen button-down shirt and khaki slacks; he had shed the jacket some time ago because it was so warm, though the sun had gone down several hours before.

He had something white in his left hand, which he set down quickly, facing me with a hesitant smile.

"The party's still going strong," I said, motioning toward the clear crowd sounds that were coming from outside.

"Aye," said Campbell, "It won't be over for a long time. And right now, they're just waiting for what comes next." He halfheartedly indicated the white cloth that he'd come in with.

I must have looked worried, because he was next to me in three steps, wrapping his arms around me. "*Dinna fash*, hen," he whispered into my hair. "I'm here."

"Thanks for the reminder," I sighed, murmuring into the front of his shirt. "This, at least, feels right." I looked up and met his eyes, still held in his arms. "I'm not sure why, but I feel so nervous."

"Ye canna see my knees knocking and hands trembling?" said Campbell with a small smile. "I think it's a combination of terror and excitement."

I lifted my face to be kissed, after which Campbell lightly put his hands on my cheeks, turning my head to press his lips to my forehead.

"Shall we?" I said.

"Unless you want to talk for a bit," he said, the intensity in his eyes making it clear which he would rather do.

"We might as well just get it over with," I said, shaking my head. I stopped, though, at the crestfallen look on Campbell's face. "It will be *good*," I assured him, "But I *still* think this is just about the weirdest thing ever."

Campbell looked me up and down. I could tell he was flushed and embarrassed, but his eagerness was stronger than his reticence. "Can I... undress ye?" he asked, looking me in the eyes.

Suddenly the crowd sounds seemed to dim into the distance, and I was observing Campbell with a heightened awareness. His eyes, still as blue as ever, looked darker because of his dilated pupils. He was so handsome, and he was my *husband*. I nodded, almost timidly, feeling desperate for him to touch me.

He reached his hand toward the front of my robe, asking permission with his eyes. I relaxed my arms to my sides, so he could access and untie the sash. Then he slipped his fingers under the lapels of the robe by my neck and slid the silk fabric off my shoulders, his fingers tracing the curve on my skin.

I could see the pace of his breathing increase as he looked at me in the lingerie, his eyes darkening with desire; his chest shuddering upward and then falling as he exhaled.

He reached his hand out hesitantly, brushing his fingers across my clavicle. He sighed. "Oh, God, Carlie, you are so beautiful." He lifted his hand to my cheek and bent to kiss me.

I stepped closer to him, relishing the soft pressure of his lips on mine.

"You're still wearing a lot," I said, reaching up to the buttons on Campbell's shirt. After I'd unbuttoned the first few buttons, I ran my finger lightly down the deep indentation between his pectorals, making Campbell tremble. I unbuttoned the rest of the buttons, pulling the shirttails out of his slacks, and then pushing the shirt off his shoulders as he shrugged out of it.

I stepped back and looked at him. I'd seen him shirtless before, but not when I could touch him or kiss him however I wanted to. I stepped forward, and as I put my hands to the button of his pants, I kissed his chest and then gently licked one of his nipples.

He acted like he'd been electrocuted, startling and then grabbing me firmly by the upper arms to kiss me thoroughly. "*Ifrinn*, Carlie, you're going to drive me mad!" he whispered. My own lips were tingling, and I was aching for him to touch me, surprised that he wasn't as bold in his caresses now that we were married, now that he could actually make love to me.

I'd continued to unzip his trousers as we kissed, and as I reached inside the waistband to push them off his hips, I realized he wasn't wearing underwear. I met his eyes, making sure he didn't mind being naked, and quickly got my answer. He reached his own hands to the waistband of his pants and pushed them off, kicking them to the side once he'd shaken them off his ankles.

I didn't want to seem too eager, but I let my eyes take in all of him. I must have groaned, because he grinned. He was muscular, big and lean at the same time. I was about to reach for him, and he shook his head.

"I need to see *you*," he said. I looked down. The chemise and panties were quite sheer, but I could understand his desire to have nothing between us.

Campbell stepped toward me, and then hooked his finger under one strap and pulled it off over my shoulder. He bent to kiss my neck and breast, then removed the other strap. I helped him push it downward over my hips, and then stepped out of it. Campbell eyed me appreciatively, then knelt before me. He gently kissed me below my navel, as he pulled my panties down over my hips, his hands tracing my curves as he drew them to the floor.

By then I was about to jump out of my skin, about to reach my hand out and force him to touch me. Instead I reached to help him up.

"*Itôk*," I begged. "Come to bed, Campbell."

"Wait a minute," he responded, standing. He gazed at me until I felt goosebumps peppering my skin and my nipples hardening; I wasn't cold but I was shivering. I would have felt conspicuous and embarrassed if Campbell didn't have an equally visible response to me.

"I love you, Carlie," he said. "I canna believe how lucky I am. Come here."

I came toward him, and he took me in his arms. I felt virginal and fresh, my softness against his rugged muscles, his strong hands caressing my back, hips, and breasts. While we had begun touching each other with a strange hesitance, he was becoming bolder, his hands strong and insistent, his touch and kisses enthusiastic and urgent. When I felt like I was going to faint if I didn't lie down, I finally was able to pull him to the bed.

Campbell reached for the *nuknuk*, and for an instant I was horrified. But when he lay me down, his beautiful body stretched at length by me on the bed, I forgot everything but him.

"What do you want?" he said huskily, as he lay on his side next to me, propping himself up on an elbow. I didn't need anything but him inside me. Instead of answering, I took his hand and led him to the silky warmth between my legs.

I whispered. "This says I want you and I'm *ready*."

"Already? I still want to... touch you for a while," he said. His forehead wrinkled as he explored my curves, a smile playing about his lips as he continued to caress and kiss my body.

"Please Campbell, here," I said, pulling his hand back down to stroke me more intimately. I could see him watching my face for my reaction as he explored and discovered how aroused I was, and he groaned as he sensed my readiness.

His touch was inexpert but gentle, and he responded to each breath, moan, and sigh as if it was a directive. It had been so long since I'd been touched by a man that I did feel virginal, more and more desperate for him to enter me.

"Campbell, we can... It's fine... it's time," I gasped as he kissed my neck and continued to touch me.

I truly had not expected to climax our first time; I hadn't thought it a reasonable expectation, but Campbell beamed with pride when I cried out, squirmed and gasped in response to him, and he kissed my shoulder when he knew I'd come.

"I tried to be quiet," I panted. "It didn't work."

Campbell laughed.

"I did *not* expect that," I gasped. "You're a virgin. How do you know anything?"

"I *may* have found a book in Majuro," Campbell said, grinning. "I didn't want to be a selfish, clueless virgin when I got married—just a virgin."

I got up on my knees, kissing his chest and neck. Though he seemed to enjoy it he finally said, "I can't wait any longer. Are you ready for me?"

"Yes," I said. "Do you want me on top?"

"Not for the *first* time," Campbell smiled, shaking his head, so I lay back as he moved over me, and I watched his face as he entered me, his eyes widening in wonder. My own eyes widened as well for an entirely different reason.

He was right; he did not need any more turning on. Nor did he need much time. It might have been a minute, tops, and he was gasping over me, and then he fell, spent, next to me on the bed.

I felt flushed and feverish with quenched desire, and hugely embarrassed that a crowd of people outside had just heard me and then Campbell pant, cry out, and moan, and were about to have a cloth thrown out to them containing the evidence of our recent intimacy along with the evidence of my non-virginity. It seemed obscene.

I turned to Campbell who was lying next to me, wide-eyed, stunned, and adorable. Suddenly I forgot everything else.

"Well?" I asked him, moving to kiss his chin. "How was your first time?"

"Stop," he said. "Lay back. Put up your legs."

I was confused. So soon? The explanation came very quickly.

"Virgin blood, *Ri-pālle*," he said, kissing me with a smile. He reached over to the table and grabbed his fishing knife. Bending his knee to bring his thigh closer, he quickly sliced across his inner thigh, and a line of burgundy blood sprung from the wound. The nurse in me thought, *I hoped he cleaned the knife*, but my eyes teared up when I realized what he was doing. I reached my hand behind his neck and pulled him to me for a kiss.

He waited for the blood, then swiped it with his middle finger. Looking at my face, he kissed my lips, then reached down and touched me.

I didn't expect to enjoy it, and I doubt that Campbell had planned to linger, but his hand on me so soon after climax had an unexpectedly stimulating effect. I buried my face in his shoulder, so they wouldn't hear me outside.

"Again?" he exclaimed in astonishment, a proud smirk on his face when I lay back on the pillow, panting. "I'm a better lover than I thought!"

"Or it has just been too long since I had sex," I said. At Campbell's crestfallen expression, I smiled. "Oh, you did good, Campbell—but I am looking forward to having sex when there's not an entire village waiting outside to look at your semen and my blood."

"Okay," said Campbell. "Time to sit up." He held out his hand to me.

Wrinkling my nose as I took his hand and gingerly sat on the wedding cloth, I said, "May I just say, this is a *strange*, strange custom."

When I got up, I grimaced at the blood-splotched fabric critically, but when I looked at Campbell, he was gazing at me.

"Carlie," he said. "You are so beautiful. I could just stare at you all day."

"Do we go back out?" I asked. "It's weird, but I want to see my parents more before they leave tomorrow."

"Aye," Campbell said. "As much as I want to climb back in bed and touch your body again, I think we should get dressed." We cleaned ourselves up, Campbell pulling on his khaki slacks and shirt, as I grabbed a bra and panties and put on a short-sleeved maxi dress—I figured I'd feel less embarrassed if I were thoroughly covered. I peeked in our mirror, but other than a few more curling tendrils falling around my face, I still looked fine. Campbell came up behind me and put his arms around my shoulders, hugging me as he kissed my neck. He looked jubilant and proud and I felt blissfully high, if a bit embarrassed.

He grabbed my hand, picked up the virginity cloth, and we headed to the door. Before he opened it, he kissed me firmly. "My wife," he said. "Carlie MacReid."

"I kind of like the way that sounds, husband," I responded.

We opened the door to shouts and cheers, especially when he handed the cloth to Alastair and Moneo, who held it up to show the splotch of blood. Alastair had married Moneo in a typical Marshallese wedding as well, so he seemed nonplussed by the experience. Then Campbell and I headed out to food and merriment and Marshallese dancing, as the community celebrated our new marriage with us.

As a small band of musicians played guitars, ukuleles and bongos, a group of little girls wearing green leafy skirts did the native Marshallese style of dance. The dance was like a cross between the hula and belly dancing—they would do this little stepping movement where they rocked their hips from side to side, sometimes focusing on just one hip, squatting lower and lower to the ground as they did so. I was awed by the way they could move their bodies.

Among the girls were Hemity, Rita, and Kabet. When they had a break in their set, they came up and sat with me by my parents.

They were giggling and elbowing each other, and finally Kabet spoke shyly.

"Miss Peachay," she said then stopped herself, looking at the other girls and then me with forehead wrinkled. "Or, are you Missus Mack now?"

"Miss Peachay is fine," I responded.

Riti grinned. "We knew Meester Mack love you a long time ago."

"Ayet," said Kabet. "The way he look at you."

"And talk about you at school," offered Hemity, putting on a deep voice as she mimicked Campbell. "'Miss Peachay is a smart girl, like you.' he tell us. 'She have to go to school a long time to become a nurse,' he say."

"He's been so happy at school," giggled Riti. "He say you are his *Jimjeran*."

Responding to a signal from their troop leader the girls got up reluctantly.

"You come dance with us, Miss Peachay," ordered Kabet, pulling me by the hand.

I went up and tried to do it with them, eventually dragging Graham and Ewan up with me as well to the great delight of the locals. I looked over and saw Campbell watching me with an amused smile as he ate and visited, and then lost myself in the fun of movement and laughter until I felt like I was actually doing justice to the dance moves. I felt sexy and happy and any time I looked over at Campbell, stunned again to think that we were really and truly married. My dad had pulled us to the side after the ceremony to sign the marriage certificate with the Iroij and Alastair as witnesses, so it was official.

As the party wound down and Alastair, Moneo, and my parents prepared to head to the Iroij's house, I saw my father pull Campbell aside again. I shook my head, thinking, *why in the world does my dad keep terrifying my new husband?* But then I saw my father embrace Campbell tightly, and when both men turned back, I could swear they seemed misty-eyed.

"Carlie Anne," my dad whispered in my ear as he hugged me goodnight, "I've said it before. There's something about this boy—Campbell has a pure heart and he loves you. I truly trust you with him." He sounded choked up. "What he did for you tonight was just more evidence of his character."

"Congratulations, kiddo," my mom said, squeezing me as she eyed Campbell appreciatively. "Enjoy your new husband. He's quite a specimen! And I've always had a thing for redheads."

"Mom," I groaned, "You're married!"

"I still have eyes," she teased, swatting me on the backside. "And now you're married too!"

"So, Campbell," my mom said to him. "We will see you at Christmas on Guam, won't we?"

"If we're able to," he said agreeably. A brightness in his eyes reminded me of what he'd lost. I hoped my parents would continue to welcome him as much as they already had.

The crowd had dispersed, families heading home, *babas* carrying their sleepy children, *mamas* taking away leftover food platters, everyone fading slowly into the darkness, flashlights bobbing away from us down the coral gravel road.

Graham and Ewan had excused themselves with some ribald comments in Gaelic that made Campbell's face flush with embarrassment.

Finally, we walked into our apartment, closed the door behind us, and gazed shyly at each other.

"We're married," I said. "That's *crazy*. It almost doesn't feel real."

"I ken a way to help ye remember how real it is," Campbell said sheepishly, "If ye wouldna mind doing it again, so soon."

"Yes, please," I said, standing on tiptoes to kiss my husband.

CHAPTER 22

The Morning After

I'd been on Arno for only four weeks, but my body had acclimatized to the heat and humidity. I often went to bed hot, but in the middle of the night I could wake up shivering from the cold air blowing in the louvers from the lagoon, even if "cold" was probably still in the low 70s or high 60s.

It was only faintly light out when I noticed the chill of the morning breeze wasn't affecting me as usual, because I was being snuggled by a warm, bare body. Campbell's breath was hot in my hair, his arm draped over my hips, his arm hairs tickling as they brushed against my skin. His thighs contacted the backs of my legs, and I could feel his chest against my back. It seemed as if he was still sleeping, considering his softly raspy breathing which you could just barely count as a snore; however, certain portions of his anatomy seemed more awake than others.

As I rolled away from him onto my stomach, Campbell snorted shortly and then eased onto his back. I propped my chin up on my hand and gazed at him. Long eyelashes curled on his cheeks. He had a straight nose, and a strong jawline with just a tiny bit of scruff. *I hadn't noticed*, I thought. *He shaved for me yesterday!* Campbell generally ran around with 3-4 days' growth, which was quite sexy to me, but this was sweet, too.

His Adam's apple moved as he breathed. There was a deep dip at the base of his neck which I felt like kissing. His chest was muscular, with a fine carpet of reddish-brown hair. His abdomen was toned, too, though relaxed in sleep he looked soft and stroke-able.

Youth definitely has its perks, I thought, as my eyes traveled lower. Either Campbell had kicked off or I had stolen the blanket, and he was covered by just a thin white sheet, which currently was doing little to hide his substantial morning testosterone surge.

Seeing Campbell there in his fresh innocence, I thought about the joy of initiating him to all the kinds of pleasure he could experience. I could see why Campbell's mom worshiped his dad, probably with her body as well as her heart. There was inestimable value in being his first, in not having the specter of other women, other bodies looming over our bed.

I reached under the sheet and stroked down the length of Campbell's thigh. His eyebrows moved, and the corners of his mouth lifted in a faint smile. *Still asleep*, I thought; but I knew how to wake him.

It was effective; when he felt my mouth on him, his eyes flew open. "What are you doing?" he gasped.

"Shhh. Stay still," I said, though in the end it was fine that he didn't really stay quiet *or* still.

Afterward, Campbell was grinning foolishly at me and then chuckled. "I was disappointed when ye stopped yesterday because I didna expect you to be doing that after we got married," he said.

"Why ever not?" I asked in bewilderment.

Campbell looked sheepish. "Graham and Ewan said that Catholic girls kneel when they marry because they're giving thanks that it's the last time they'll ever be on their knees...for a particular reason."

"Well, I doubt that's true," I said, kissing him with a grin. "And I'm not Catholic, anyway."

I reluctantly pulled myself out of bed, musky with the smell of sex and sweat and feeling an irresistible desire for a shower.

As one of my going-to-bed rituals to simplify my mornings, I had finally taken to leaving a full bucket of water in the shower and a full pot of water on the kerosene stove, ready to turn on and heat up the next day. This way all I had to do was turn on the stove and I'd be 10-15 minutes from a warm shower.

After lighting the stove, I slipped a sundress over my head, emerging from the neck hole to see my husband eyeing me appreciatively.

"You *just came*," I said in mock astonishment. "Why are you looking at me like you want to eat me?"

"The fact that I couldna do anything with ye at the moment doesna make you any less gorgeous," Campbell said, "If you recall, I haven't been partaking of *any* of this. Not in the flesh, and not visually, either."

"Holy hell!" I said in astonishment at my realization. "You've even been protected from internet porn..."

"Kind of hard to access here when there's no electricity and no internet," said Campbell. He looked slightly embarrassed. "Though I canna say I've not seen *any*. I was in Scotland until I was 18, and Majuro has both internet and electricity."

"But a couple years' detox?" I said. "Praise the Lord and Hallelujah!"

"You're becoming very spiritual, *Ri-pālle*," Campbell said with a smile, as he climbed out of bed and walked over to the kitchen naked. I took a turn around him, appreciating the sight of his toned muscles and gorgeous ass, which I grabbed, kissing him in between his shoulder blades and making him shiver, just because I could.

"Are you cooking up some porridge... uh, oatmeal?" asked Campbell. "I'm starving, but probably dinna need *this* much." He gestured toward the huge pot of water.

"Oh, no," I said. "This is just for a warm shower."

Campbell turned to me with an eager smile. "I can help you with that," he said. "With the soap and washcloth and such..."

From my attempts at shower sex or even just joint showering with Eric, I knew that it was much less sexy than it appeared in movies, especially because you spent half the time freezing cold. But Campbell looked so excited, I couldn't burst his bubble.

With the water boiling, we grabbed a couple of towels, Campbell wrapped his sarong around himself and with a surreptitious glance in each direction we snuck out to the shower.

Campbell took great attention and care and apparently a lot of pleasure in washing my hair and body quite thoroughly. The slipperiness of the soap seemed to especially please him, and I finally had to tell him that my breasts and ass were probably clean enough, thank you very much, and I was getting chilly.

He wasn't done, though. Nuzzling my neck after he'd rinsed me off, sipping droplets of water off my skin, he said, "You're so clean and sweet-smelling." He wrapped a towel around my shoulders and his sarong around his waist, and then proceeded to kiss me thoroughly. I didn't understand what he was doing when he tossed the washcloth on the floor until he pressed me back against the shower wall, knelt on the washcloth in front of me, lifted one of my legs over his shoulder, and generously repaid my wake-up favor... twice over.

"Such an education I'm getting," he grinned, as he stood up, looking at me in wonder as I leaned against the wall with my eyes closed, recovering. "Can I ask you something?"

"Of course," I said.

"It seems like you really enjoy it. Sex, I mean." His face was innocent, hopeful.

"Um, *yes*! Probably more than I *should*," I said, which made him grin.

"I *thought* you might," he said, "Though Graham and Ewan tried to tell me you were probably all talk and no action."

I laughed and rolled my eyes. "Dipwads. They're just jealous."

"And I'm doing okay? I was afraid I might not be very good at it, in comparison..." Campbell said, looking vulnerable. At times I could forget our age difference, but at other times his youth was evident.

"Doing okay?" I stared at him in disbelief. "Campbell," I said. "I have had *five* orgasms in 13 hours. If you were any better, I don't think I could handle it... not that you can't still improve your skills," I continued, realizing what I was saying. I kissed him. "Now, I'm freezing, and I think I should get dressed."

As I exited the shower, Alastair was standing out in front of the apartment.

"Is Campbell up yet?" He asked, gesturing toward the apartment, his eyebrows rising as the man in question sheepishly came out of the shower stall after me.

"Get dressed, Romeo, and let's talk," Alastair said, rolling his eyes.

After dressing, I came back outside to hang up our towels. Anni called out to me through the trees, *"Iiokwe,* Miss Peachay. *Komro kōmman nana aolep boñ."* [1]

"Ij jab melele," I said. "What does that mean?" Anni giggled, and headed back into her cook shack, leaving me to try to remember the way the words sounded so I could figure it out.

I was worried what Alastair might be saying to Campbell, and he returned to our apartment with an expression on his face I couldn't interpret.

"Is something wrong?" I asked, concerned.

"Oh, nah, everything's fine," he said dismissively, giving me a quick hug. "Alastair just wanted to give us something. I'll show you some other time."

"Campbell, I need you to translate something," I said. I repeated what Anni had said to the best of my ability. Campbell's smile grew wider and his face redder as I talked. "So," I said. "I think I remember a few words. Is 'comb-row' *you guys*? And 'comb-mon' is *make*? And 'nah nah' is *bad*. What's 'all leb'?"

"All," said Campbell, grinning.

"And 'bong'?"

"Night," he said, nearly giggling.

"What was she saying?" I asked, though I had a pretty good idea. "You guys make bad all night?"

"Ever heard of sex being called 'doing the nasty?'" Campbell asked. "Well, one of the euphemisms in the Marshalls is '*kōmman nana*,'" he laughed.

"Anni said we were having sex all night?" I exclaimed, horrified. "We weren't that loud, were we?"

"*Some* of us were," Campbell said innocently, looking away from me, then acting like he was quoting a completely normal conversation. "Yes, yes, oh Campbell, harder, harder, yes, yes, oh God, yes..."

---

[1] *Komro kōmman nana aolep boñ*: Comb´-row comb´-mon nah´-nah all´-leb bong (You make bad all night)

I blushed furiously and determined to change the subject. It was apparent from the look on Campbell's face, though, that my enthusiasm had bolstered his confidence.

"So, Mr. MacReid, where are you taking me for our honeymoon? Or are we just going to stay here in this apartment *kōmman*ing *nana aolep* day and *aolep* night?"

"We are going to Autle," Campbell said.[1] "It's an uninhabited island just around the corner from Matolen, off the far east end of the island. We're going to camp there. I've got food and water all packed up, and we can find coconuts, go spearfishing, and relax."

I peered at him skeptically. I'd grown up camping, which meant I knew exactly how far away roughing it was from my vision of the perfect honeymoon. Room service, a clean hotel room, and a hot shower were far closer to *my* ideal honeymoon.

Campbell was smiling. "*Ri-pālle*, it's the only way we will be truly alone out here." He put his arms around me. "And I need to have you *all* alone," he whispered huskily in my ear. "Where it doesn't matter how loud you get when I "*kōmman nana*" with you."

My stomach leapt. Instantly I could see the wisdom in Campbell's choice.

"All right," I sighed, as if I was still feeling reluctant instead of excited. "What should I pack?"

---

[1] Out´-lay

CHAPTER 23

Autle

My parents showed up hesitantly around ten, but Campbell and I were fully clothed and bringing out our duffle bags, snorkeling gear, and the last few food items I thought of adding to the list of food Campbell said he'd sent on ahead. The town's truck was going to drive us down to the end of the island, where the Rosa family owned a boat that they were renting to us for the weekend.

Once again, my dad and Campbell headed off together, this time to go summon the truck. My mom requested a tour of the clinic, so I showed her my primitive medical set-up.

"Mr. Douglass is leaving this afternoon," my mom said, after she'd tried out my pump faucet. "But your dad and I were wondering if we could stick around until Monday."

"Where would you stay?" I asked. "Still at the Iroij's palace?"

"That's the thing," Mom answered. "We would like to stay here, if you don't mind." She gestured in the direction of our apartment. "Enjoy the quiet, clean and fix things up a little," she shrugged her shoulders. "You know how we like to make ourselves useful."

Mom wasn't kidding. Every time she visited us in Denver, the next time I was in my kitchen my refrigerator would have been cleaned out and my stove top and oven scrubbed.

"We only have the one pair of sheets," I said to her, wrinkling my nose in distaste.

"I could wash them," she said. "But I could also just air them out today. I mean, honestly—last night I saw something a mother-in-law should never have to see, but that means the evidence was mostly there, not on your sheets. And we don't have a black light or anything."

"Yuck, Mom," I groaned, covering my face. "I'm sorry. I should have warned you or sent you away."

"Oh, I knew what was happening," she said. "Besides what I could *hear*," (I buried my face deeper in my hands) "which was an indication that you have married quite an enthusiastic lover, Moneo told me all about the custom, with plenty of time to head somewhere else for a while."

"Why did you *stay*, then?" I whimpered, disturbed by the entire conversation.

"I thought it would be an interesting cultural experience," she said, surprisingly earnestly, "And such an amazing conversation starter when anyone tries to start one-upping their kids' wedding stories at my book club."

"You will *not!*" I exclaimed, coming out of hiding to see her facial expression, obviously pleased with herself for being so hilarious.

"Carlie, I would never," she said, shaking her head and smiling. "Though if Stacy Harrow starts telling me about her daughter's shocking ceremony, I will probably have to work extra hard to resist the temptation to share yours."

I shook my head in embarrassed silence as I ushered my mom out of the clinic.

"Besides," my mom said, "Campbell already set our stay up with your dad. He's got something he wanted us to do while you are gone."

"What's the deal with Campbell and Daddy?" I asked. We could see the pick-up truck appearing from a distance off. "I'm starting to feel like Dad prefers him to me."

"I think he feels like he needs to get to know Campbell. It was so *sudden*, Carlie," My mom ran her fingers through her hair, pulling the curls away from her face. "I just think Daddy couldn't let this happen without checking out your husband. I know you're a grown-up, but you're still his little girl."

"How do *you* really feel, Mom?" I asked. "Was this the stupidest thing I've ever done?"

"Oh, certainly not," she said, hugging me around the waist with a cheeky grin. "You've done plenty of stupider things."

"Is that supposed to make me feel better?" I asked.

"Actually, Carlie," she said, "Impulsive, yes. Sudden, definitely. But stupid, sweetie? I can see the expression on his face when he looks at you, and the way you look at him. I never saw Eric look at you like that. And I don't think you ever felt this way about Eric either, for that matter."

By then I had a lump in my throat that even swallowing couldn't get rid of. Mom hugged me as my eyes filled with tears, and she finished compassionately, "You love each other, baby. And love is never stupid."

I was torn when the time came to leave. I hadn't seen my parents in six months or more, so it was a challenge to say goodbye. But as we were packing up the truck, there were several times Campbell had touched me, just brushing his hand across my back, or stepping close behind me when I was loading something in the truck, so I could clearly feel that he was aroused. Once he leaned over and breathed on my neck beneath my ear, and I about jumped out of my skin. The way he kept looking at me, I felt naked already; and I was beginning to feel quite ready to be naked again.

Fulfilling that desire was delayed by my parents deciding to ride on the truck to see us off; otherwise I had a very strong feeling there would have been some major second and third base action going on in the back of the truck as we rode to the end of the island.

I had a sense of anticipation as we left the dock in Matolen behind and headed across the lagoon in the small silver motor boat. In thirty minutes, we were pulling the boat up to the beach at Autle, and Campbell handed boxes and bags out to me to put on the grassy bank above the beach. Despite taking motion sickness pills before the journey, he was looking queasy; however, he muscled through and helped to carry our luggage to the little sandy clearing where we would be staying.

"The tent is already set up," I said gratefully, "and it's like a little house."

"Ye can thank Graham and Ewan for that," Campbell said. "I couldn't make this trip twice in a day and still be of any use to my wife."

"Did they make the bed, too?" I asked, skeptically peeking in a window of the boxy, tall, room-sized tent.

"Yes," said Campbell, "But we can certainly inspect it before we use it. Unfortunately, lass, I dinna feel very good right now, and I think I should lie down for a time before I do anything else."

"Are you still a little seasick?" I asked. He didn't look like he was feeling well at all.

"Aye," he groaned, kicking off his flip-flops and unzipping the tent flap.

"Well, I guess I can get us moved in and set up our camp," I said, looking around the campsite, feeling a little disappointed and needing to keep myself busy.

"Nah," he said, shaking his head and opening the door of the tent. "*Itōk, Ri-pālle.* You're going to take off your clothes and lie next to me. I want to touch your body wi' my eyes closed."

We went into the tent and Campbell reclined on the air mattress, which despite having been set up by Graham and Ewan, didn't seem to be booby-trapped or poisoned.

"Will ye undress for me? I'd like to watch you." Campbell spoke from the bed, one eye opened just a slit. Somehow having his eyes closed seemed to help his nausea, but there were certain things that warranted using them.

I felt a little shy in the full light of day—the tent did nothing to darken the room. However, I had picked my outfit for the day considering which clothes would look the best coming off, deciding upon a short-sleeved floral dress with buttons down the front. I decided I'd take my time—just to drive Campbell mad—and it worked. When I'd unbuttoned the buttons down past my hips, with my tiny panties and lack-of-bra showing clearly, Campbell groaned.

"I'm not well, lass! Dinna torture me!" He looked at me, grinning, "But dinna take anything else off, either. Just come here now."

I lay down next to him, still wearing the dress. I watched his face as with closed eyes he reached over and slipped his hand inside the bodice of my dress, groaning as his fingertips traced their way around my breast and then closed to surround my nipple.

"Mmmmm. I *like* second base," he whispered, cupping my breast in his substantial palm. I leaned over to kiss him, and he slipped his hand behind my neck to draw me closer to him. "I like *first* base, too, for that matter," he said, yawning.

His yawn was contagious. It had been a long and somewhat sleepless night, so I lay my head on his chest, Campbell stroked my back, and we fell asleep.

When I woke up, Campbell wasn't in bed with me. He'd brought our suitcases inside, and I could hear footsteps moving around in the gravel outside and what sounded like a machete hacking away at something. With a sense of jittery excitement, I pulled something I'd bought in Majuro out of my suitcase, finished taking off my dress and panties, and put it on.

Campbell had his back to me when I slipped out of the tent. He was standing by the stump of a coconut tree, apparently opening a young coconut, evidenced by the pieces of green husk on the gravel at his feet.

"Are you feeling better, Campbell?" I asked. I was disappointed when he didn't look at me right away.

"Aye," he answered with one final hack, then turned around and nearly dropped the coconut he was holding. His eyes told me I had chosen well.

"I'm going *native*," I said. "Look, I'm super decent! My thighs are completely covered!"

Campbell raised his eyebrows in amusement.

In one of the shops, I had found short sarongs meant as cover-ups for swimsuits or bikinis. I had purchased one, but right now I was wearing it alone, tied around my hips, with no top, no bikini, nothing from the waist up.

Campbell watched me with great intensity as I walked over and took the coconut from him, lifting it to my mouth to sip the coconut water.

I handed it back to him, and said, "Okay, what shall we do now? Do we need to go spear fishing for our dinner?"

"No," said Campbell, looking down at my body. He stepped toward me.

"Should we grate up a coconut for cooking our rice?"

"*Jab*," he said.

"What shall we do, then?" I asked, looking teasingly up at him.

"I am going to find out if you're wearing anything under that sarong," Campbell said, bending to kiss me. "And then I am going to make love to my wife."

Campbell was an enthusiastic lover, and so joyful and generous during every part of the process that it seemed wrong to find fault with his technique. I did need him to learn to enjoy going slow, which I managed by spending some time in charge, on top.

After our exhausting afternoon love-making session, we ate a snack of bananas, peanut butter and bread Campbell had baked for us before the wedding. Then we put on our snorkeling gear and went out to hunt for our supper. I wore a bikini without shorts or dress on over it for the first time since arriving, and Campbell again held my hand while snorkeling out to go spear fishing, though on occasion his hands had a mind of their own, straying elsewhere on my body. At one point, he giddily untied my bikini top, stealing it and sticking it in his pocket. I felt irritated, but tried to remind myself I'd married a virgin, and in that respect some teenage-boy behavior was to be expected.

When we'd caught six fish, we headed back to camp. I measured water and rice into the big cast iron pot, and with his knife Campbell scraped mature coconut onto a kerchief, which I then used as I had seen Anni use the cheesecloth. There was something so delicious about the flavor of the coconut with the salty fish that I couldn't imagine cooking the rice without it.

Campbell gathered wood and built up the fire for roasting the fish, gutting them and prepping them while the wood burnt down to coals and the rice started simmering.

The fish were delicious with bites of rice. Campbell had brought along cans of soda from Mr. Ogawa's store, which were refreshing despite being less than cold. After eating, we put the lid on the rice to protect it from flies and set it in the shade where it could cool so we could eat it for breakfast.

I took a breath and looked around the campsite. It was still a little surreal to think that I was married. Yet, here I was on an island on my honeymoon. On a gorgeous day in the tropics, life could not have been more perfect.

CHAPTER 24

The Storm

After our supper, we sat by the fire on a pandanus mat backed up to a large fallen log. Campbell leaned against the log, and I rested against his shoulder. "How long are we going to be able to stay here?" I asked, pulling his arm up and around me, cuddling into his warm side.

"Today's Saturday, so I've arranged for us to be here until Monday. We'll head back in the afternoon. That way I only miss one day of school."

"If we're heading back Monday afternoon, I'm missing Depo Provera day at the clinic," I said, with some concern. "I hope there's not a rash of unintended pregnancies just because the shots are a day late."

Campbell looked at me curiously. "What are *you* using for birth control?" he asked, tossing another log onto the fire.

"Oh, I'm not," I said, with a sudden surge of embarrassment. Honestly, the thought hadn't even crossed my mind. With Campbell being a virgin, I figured we didn't need to use condoms for STD protection, and I hadn't used any other form of birth control for years.

Campbell looked surprised, his forehead wrinkling. "Dinna ye think that's something we should decide together—when we're planning to have children?" he asked slowly. "I ken ye're older than me, so ye might want to try right away, but I thought we'd perhaps have some time as just the two of us."

"Don't worry about it, Campbell," I said reassuringly. "I'm almost positive we won't get pregnant without choosing to." I clarified, "At least not without help. I'm infertile."

"What do ye mean by that?" Campbell asked, staring at me as he randomly poked at a flaming piece of wood with a stick.

"Eric and I didn't use birth control once we were engaged, and in five years we never got pregnant. They call it infertility if you don't get pregnant after a *year* of unprotected sex. So I'll have to do some sort of medical testing or procedures, or else I probably won't be able to get pregnant at all."

Campbell was clenching his jaw. I wasn't certain why, until he spoke. "Now that's *also* something that ye might have found important to tell me, *Ri-pálle*. Did ye not think that I might want to ken that—whether we could have children or no?"

"*Really?*" I retorted. I sat up and scooted slightly away from him on the mat. "I can't believe that in our two-day engagement, we didn't have the chance to discuss birth control, fertility, or children!" I exclaimed irritably. "I was too busy making sure you didn't get moved to another island or sent back to Scotland."

"Aye, but *Ri-pálle*, *children*," said Campbell, eying me seriously. "That's a huge part of the reason for marriage."

"What exactly do you mean by that?" I asked. Campbell wasn't yet familiar with my "calm before the storm" tell, so he probably thought my question was a *question* rather than a *warning*.

"Just that marriage sets up a supportive, committed environment for raising children." Campbell reached gently for my hand, but I pretended not to notice him.

"Is that the *only* reason people should get married?" I asked, deadly calm.

"No, but it's probably the most important one," Campbell answered innocently.

Somehow that was the last straw. I drilled holes into Campbell with my eyes. "Oh, is that what you think, asshole? Eric thought that too, I guess, because I never got pregnant, so he never married me. I thought maybe you were better than that. I guess I was wrong. *Selfish bastard*," I muttered.

"Selfish? And bastard?" he said, rubbing his forehead with a confused expression on his face. "How can ye say that to me, Carlie? Ye know I've been beyond kind and generous wi' ye. I just happen to think that whether or not my wife is on birth control and whether we can have children might be my business, too."

All of a sudden, I felt ridiculously foolish. *What was this kid's problem? What the heck was I thinking getting married so fast?* I stood up and walked to the other side of the fire. Campbell sat there shirtless and barefoot in swim trunks, his red hair in thick ringlets from swimming in salt water. Yes, he was a damn fine specimen of manhood, but he was my little brother's age. I was a grown-ass woman, and this *child* was trying to tell me what I should and should not be doing with my own body!

I started pacing back and forth, rubbing my face with my hands as I monologued. "What the hell was I thinking? Eric, the *man* I was with and loved for seven years, breaks up with me because I was foolish enough to travel halfway around the world without him, and I marry an infant? Why would I even *want* to have a baby with you, Campbell? You're still practically a child!"

"Says the woman who's being irresponsible about birth control," Campbell said condescendingly. "And ye're a nurse, too, Carlie! It seems to me that whether or not you and Eric weren't able to have children, the fault might be his, not yours. And just because your ex wasna man enough to get ye pregnant doesna mean I willna be able to."

He was smiling. *Smiling* as he questioned my knowledge of myself and my profession. *Smiling* as he insulted Eric.

"You think you're more of a man than Eric? Do you think marriage makes you a man? Did sticking your dick in me make you a man? Is that what you think? You just married me so you could finally have sex? What do you need me for now? So you have a warm place to incubate your *spawn*? You're such a fucking misogynist."

"You are being such a vulgar wench!" Campbell's face was flushing, his volume increasing. "Stop talking to me like that! I haven't *forced* anything on you. Ye're the one who *suggested* marriage. And I risked my reputation to let you stay with me that night when that bastard Eric broke up with you... and then I was willing to marry ye to save you from being sent home!"

"*Let* me stay with you?" I exclaimed, glaring at him. "*Willing* to marry me? You *know* you wanted me. You've been trying to seduce me since you first met me. Late nights, putting your arms around me—taking off your shirt when I'm around. You would use *any* excuse to get in my pants. And lucky you, it worked!"

"Oh, dinna be such an icy *bitch*," said Campbell, looking at me derisively. "I wouldna have had to try very hard if I'd wanted to seduce ye. I could see you eyeing me whenever you were around me. You're the horny little *slut*— the one who came to me in the middle of the night in some scanty getup, asking to sleep in my bed wi' me all night, rubbing your round arse against me. Ye're the one who touched ME first, putting your hand on my cock, going down on me... putting your mouth on me... in the *school!*" His tone managed to be both indignant and judgmental at the same time.

"I am not a *slut*," I seethed. "I did it once we were engaged. I did it because I thought you *loved* me. To make you feel good. To make you happy. Well, I *hope* you're happy, you little shit."

I thrust my feet into my flip-flops, grabbed my book from the tent, and stomped off (as loudly as one can stomp in rubber soled flip-flops on shifting coral rock). It didn't look that fierce to be stomping off in a bikini, either, I assumed. However, I headed toward the hammocks on the ocean side, leaving Campbell looking flabbergasted.

I felt furious and embarrassed at the same time, but I climbed into the hammock and tried to read through angry tears. Unfortunately, I was so upset I found reading impossible. I closed my eyes and relived the argument in my mind, trying to remember how it had started and why it had gotten so bad so fast. I didn't like the way this felt, but what made me even more furious was that the only thing I wanted right now was for Campbell to hold me.

"I'm not going to him, though," I declared to the trees.

The thing was, Campbell was right. I didn't *know* if I was the infertile one. Eric and I had never been tested. I *should* have planned for some sort of birth control, or at least brought along the box of condoms for us to use until I could give myself a Depo shot. And he hadn't tried to seduce me. He'd wanted me, but he'd never touched me inappropriately. He'd only been an emotional support and a friend. But his words were so cruel. How could he talk to me like that?

I began to feel it first, a marked chill in the air. My bikini felt completely insufficient. The breeze began to pick up, blowing the palm fronds toward the south. Around me a few large fronds fell to the ground, as well as a coconut or two. I started to wonder if it was safe where I was. I slipped out of the hammock and walked further out onto the beach. As I gazed to the north, I could see a wall of dark clouds moving in our direction. Rain, moving fast enough that I could see its approach.

Storms in the Marshall Islands were impressive and generally brief. Clouds would approach, drop their payload, and move on. They often came from the north and moved south, which meant that from Ine, we could see their approach across the *iar*. But Autle was an east-west facing island, and it had been difficult to see approaching weather.

As angry as I was, I didn't want to be stuck outside in a downpour, so I grabbed my book and headed back to our camp.

Campbell was rushing around, staking down the corners of the tent as well as a tarp over our little food supply area. He started tying the strings of the rain fly out to the bases of four coconut palms, and I went inside the tent and zipped up all the windows, throwing on a dress over my bikini. Then I went outside and pulled our towels off the laundry line, taking another look around the campsite before heading into the confines of our tent.

We made it inside just in time. The rain was just beginning to reach us, rapidly tapping on the rain fly. The wind whipped the sides of the tent around, but so far we were safe and dry. There was really no place to sit, just the air mattress in the center of the tent. Campbell was looking at me, but I didn't meet his gaze. I lay on my side on the mattress, facing away from him. When Campbell joined me, his solid bulk weighed down the bed so that I rolled toward him. I hooked my leg over my side of the mattress to keep myself from touching him and scooched away from him until I was nearly hanging off the edge.

After a while, under the guise of changing positions to be more comfortable, I rolled over but used my book to block my vision of his face. Campbell didn't have a book with him. He was just staring at the tent ceiling. He sighed audibly a couple of times.

"Carlie," he said slowly. "I'm so sorry. My da would never have called my ma any of those names, no matter how angry he was. It was wrong of me. Will you forgive me?"

I took the book from between us and looked at his face. His nose was red. His eyelashes were wet. Campbell was *crying*. It broke my heart. I really hadn't felt so strongly about anyone in a long time, such a deep desire to be with someone, not even Eric, and I'd already hurt him with my words.

"Yes," I said. "You weren't wrong. I *should* probably be using birth control."

"Stop," said Campbell. "I was an asshole, and I'm trying to apologize."

"But, Campbell," I said, tears filling my own eyes. "I'm sorry for being so horrible. You aren't any of the things I called you. Can you forgive *me?*"

Campbell pulled me to his chest. "Goodness, hen, of course." I wept against his chest, tears dripping onto his chest hair.

"I think you need a shirt on," I quavered. "There's no place to wipe my eyes." Campbell pulled up the sheet from underneath us and wiped my cheeks.

"Carlie, talk to me," he said, concern on his face. "I merely mentioned birth control, and it was as if something snapped. What is it?"

"I didn't always know what I wanted to be when I grew up," I sniffled. "But I always knew I wanted to be a mom. I was great with kids; babysat all the time. That's why I stopped using birth control when I graduated. I wanted kids, and it was fine with me if they came anytime. As year after year went by, any time my period was late, I'd get excited. But it was never anything."

"Hmm," Campbell grunted. "So, for me to bring up birth control, it wasn't just me asking about birth control. It was me reminding you about *infertility.*"

I nodded. "That's the first thing Eric brought up when I said I wanted to come out here, you know," I said. "He reminded me that I wasn't going to get any more fertile with time. As if he thought that if I wanted to be a mom I shouldn't even be going out here."

"And you also said," Campbell added, "That ye felt like Eric would have married ye if you got pregnant?"

"It's silly," I said, "But I'm positive he would have. So it felt like somehow it was my fault that he never married me because I couldn't get pregnant."

Campbell kissed me on the forehead. "Well, I married ye, Carlie, and I am glad you are my wife, whether or no' we ever have children." I rolled over and snuggled in the curve of his body as he stroked my hair, hearing the wind howling and rain pelting the tent ferociously.

"And there are good things," Campbell offered. "If you never have babies, I'll never have to share your breasts." He cupped and stroked the part under discussion. "I feel rather selfish about them, already. Can't imagine watching a bairn suckle you and not wanting to do it myself."

"Gross," I grumbled, and Campbell chuckled.

"*Ri-pālle*," he said. "Will ye look at me, please?" I rolled partway over and met his eyes over my shoulder. "I love you, Carlie. I *wanted* to marry ye. And I *was* shamelessly trying, not to seduce ye exactly, but to get as close as I could to ye ever since ye came to Arno."

"Well, I've not exactly been a nun, either," I said. Campbell grinned.

"But I dinna want us to ever call each other names, *Ri-pālle*. Anger is fine. But evil names and bad words—that's hatred."

"I agree," I said. "I'm sorry. You're right—we should only call each other names that are affectionate. So, c'mere, baby boy," I said, reaching my hand out to stroke Campbell's cheek.

"I dinna much *like that* name," he said, making a face.

"It doesn't mean anything bad," I said, turning the rest of the way over to face him. "It's *ironic* because you're big and you make me feel safe. Why does it offend you?" I asked teasingly. "Because you're younger than me?" Campbell's expression told me that was a big part of it. "Because if I tell you to do something, you'll *obey* me?" He grinned. "Because you'd curl up inside me if you could, or because you like to suckle at my breasts?"

He frowned, with a little twinkle in his eye. "All of those *might* be true. Still dinna like it," he said.

"Seems to me you've got a double standard," I responded, tracing his jawline with my fingers, "Your name for me means selfish white person. I hated it at first; now nothing gets me hotter than you saying, '*Itōk, Ri-pālle*,' in that husky voice of yours."

Campbell's eyes twinkled. "Does it, now?" He looked at me through hooded eyes, his lips twisting teasingly. Realizing what I'd just revealed, I rolled away from him. Campbell pushed himself up off the bed, stood up, and reached his hand out to me. "*Itōk, Ri-pālle*." I rolled my eyes, sighed, and put my hand in his.

"C'mon, Mommy," he said. "Let's get your clothes off."

"Now *that's* nasty," I groaned laughingly.

"Is it?" he asked innocently. "I dinna ken. But I do know you got me turned on with all that talk about *suckling* and being *inside* you. I think I know what we're going to be doing soon."

"Dammit, Campbell," I said, a warm flush spreading through my abdomen. "I was going to still be *mad* at you. You're not supposed to be able to turn me on like that!"

He grinned and took me in his arms.

CHAPTER 25

The Drop-off

By nightfall the storm had tapered off somewhat, but in the early hours of the morning it picked up again, thrashing and whipping the tent fabric, breaking off branches and causing the surf to roar. Campbell and I had curled up in bed naked after making love, and when the storm woke us, he gently began stroking my shoulders.

"Your touch wakes me up," I murmured, rolling back toward him slightly.

"I'm sorry," he said, with a kiss on my shoulder. "I just couldn't sleep."

"No," I said, rolling back further, the covers sliding down to expose my pale skin. "I *meant*, your touch wakes me **up**."

"You mean it rouses you?" I could hear the obvious pleasure in his voice, as he began to caress me. "I knew I'd like sex," he said. "That was *never* a question. What I didna ken was how powerful I'd feel knowing I could give you pleasure."

I lifted my lips to him, unintentionally letting out a little murmured whine as he took me with his own, offering his soft tongue. I could feel his mouth pull back in a smile.

"*That*," he said. "Oh God, Carlie, that little noise you make when you like what I'm doing. Feel what it does to me." He took my hand down under the covers; he was so firm, so big, I wanted him inside me right then. I tried to rise off the mattress, but Campbell stopped me with his hand on my shoulder.

"I want to taste you," he said, his lips moving down my throat to my breasts, then my abdomen.

"Campbell, I haven't showered in days," I said, squirming under him as if to get away. He moved to my legs, wrapping his strong arms under them and parting my thighs.

"Open to me, Carlie," he said. "Trust me with your body; ye dinna disgust me. Anyway, you were in the ocean just hours ago," he said, kissing closer and closer. I gasped, and he lifted his head. "More of *that* noise, please," he said. He lowered his lips to me and my body contracted as I felt the warmth of his tongue. This time it was a squeaky squeal I inadvertently released. He laughed. "You taste like the sea, *Ri-pälle*. But you sound like a kitten." I giggled, gasping as he returned to his efforts.

Finally, I ran my fingers through his sleep-tousled curls and lifted his head. "I want to go *with* you," I said. "You're generous, Campbell. But I want to be face-to-face. I need to be closer to you. I need you to fill me."

He drew me off the air mattress. Sitting on our blanket on the tent floor, I faced him, sitting astride his lap. The pale light of morning was approaching as we kissed and caressed each other. I could see his blue eyes, intent on me as we moved together, and I gazed at him, open-eyed and fearless.

We lay in each other's arms on the bed after that, not cradled or spooned, but face to face, our legs intertwined, our arms around each other as if we were trying to melt together. The last thing I remembered was Campbell looking at me, his eyes exploring my face as if to discover all my secrets. I didn't understand why, but I started crying; and he kissed away my tears until I fell asleep.

A couple of times in the past few days while making love with Campbell, I had flashes of thoughts of Eric. Eric and I had dated briefly the fall of my freshman year. He was interested in me, but he was older. It was the first time I had ever slept with someone, so it was a significant relationship, but I wasn't ready to commit. I dated a few other guys, being involved to differing extents based on how much I trusted or liked them. I might have had four sex partners other than Eric. We dated more consistently in the spring, started dating exclusively my sophomore year, and moved in together once I turned 21.

Sex had always been enjoyable with Eric. I loved being touched, loved the way I felt shivers at his fingers on my skin, the way my body warmed up from the inside out. I loved feeling breathless and achy with need. Some of my sex partners had acted like I was supposed to be some sort of porno actress, serving their needs and not even considering mine. When they were like that, they got an instant boot out the door.

On the contrary, Eric was gentle and generous when we made love; but he was never as *hungry* as I was. He could easily go for days without, even a week or more on occasion. I rarely felt pursued; it seemed like I was the one to initiate much of the time. I knew he was older than me, that his family wasn't as touchy or affectionate. Sometimes I had to seek him out for a kiss at night if he was up late studying. If I waited for Eric to approach me, we could go for days without touching at all.

I hadn't realized I was starving.

Being with Campbell was the first time I had ever felt physically satiated. Not sexually—it wasn't that. It was that I was finally being touched enough. A hand on my back or arm. Him pulling me into his side for a quick hug. A brief kiss on the lips, neck, or forehead. Being cuddled in bed, held when I cried.

And when we were together sexually, Campbell was present, enthusiastic, focused on me. If it was light, his eyes were often on me, studying my face, smiling at my reactions. Campbell was a student of my body, in constant learning mode. Maybe that was because of his youth or virginity, but I had a feeling it was just Campbell.

It felt bad to compare, but in some ways, I needed to—to justify this sudden choice to myself. I thought of trying to explain to my friends back home, how to explain it to Greg. I had a horrified thought about having to explain myself to Eric and found myself incredibly grateful that Denver was so far away that I wouldn't need to see him for months, if not years.

So whether it was right or not, I kept remembering how Eric would be distracted during lovemaking, like I was one more chore he had to do. How I could try to message with my body and voice that something was working for me or not, and he either wouldn't pick up on it or would get offended and turned off because he felt judged. How I could need him, reach out to him, and for whatever reason—stress or busyness—he would not seem to need me.

We woke up when the sun was streaming through the trees, making the tent almost too hot.

"What shall we do today?" I asked. Campbell responded by sliding his hand underneath the covers and cupping my butt, pressing me towards his enormous morning erection.

"Oh, Campbell," I groaned. "I'm too sore. I feel like I've been riding a horse for three days."

"Ye flatter me," he chuckled into my neck.

"I'm *raw*," I said. "It's going to sting to go swimming today."

"We've got lube," he said helpfully.

"Seriously. *Hard no.* Never thought I'd ever say no to sex with someone as hot as you, but *no*."

"Not even if I say, '*Itōk, Ri-pālle?*'" He looked quite hopeful.

"Not even then."

"What do I do with this, then?" he asked, looking down sorrowfully and shaking his head.

"What you did every morning of your non-married life," I suggested callously with a grin. "Whatever that might be."

He blushed profusely. "Well, I have two options," he offered.

"Which are?" I teased.

"I dinna much feel like I should be doing the first one on my honeymoon," he said. "So I guess, *think about dead things*, it is!" He gave me a swift kiss on the lips, smacked me on the backside, and got out of bed.

He stood there for a moment, erect in more ways than one, as if to guilt me.

"Campbell, you're gorgeous, I love having sex with you. But remember how fun it was to try to *not* have sex before we were married? Let's do just a little of that today. Maybe say, we can't have sex until 2 o'clock."

"Oooo, I like that," he said. "I'm going to drive you crazy, until you're begging me for it."

"I'll be kinder," I said, crawling out of bed and stretching, well aware of the way my nudity would affect him. "I won't try to drive you crazy," I promised. After my closed-eye yawn, I looked over at him.

"Two o'clock?" he asked, eating me with his eyes.

"Two o'clock," I answered.

"Do you have a long, shapeless dress?" he suggested. "Maybe an ugly hat, some gigantic sunglasses?" I laughed and pulled on a bathing suit and coverup.

When we left the tent, it was surprising to see the damage inflicted by the wind. There were downed coconuts and palm branches everywhere. Thankfully Campbell's preparations had protected most of our things.

"Would you like me to take you to the drop-off?" Campbell asked as we ate cold coconut rice and bananas for breakfast.

"The drop-off, like on *Finding Nemo*?" I asked. "Am I going to get eaten by a barracuda?"

"Aye, that part was too scary for my little brother when it first came out," Campbell said. "My ma had to fast forward it."

"How old were you?"

"Um, if Matthew was like 5, that would make me 8?"

"*Baby*," I said, shaking my head.

"How old were you?"

"Have we not done the math yet?" I asked him. "I'm five years older than you."

"Twenty-seven?" he asked. "Hmm," he grunted.

"You're disgusted. You're married to an old lady," I said, joking but not feeling the humor inside. I'm not sure why it made me nervous to put it out there. It sounded so old in comparison to twenty-two. "You're done being married to me. You want an annulment."

"Unfortunately, Carlie, I'm *quite certain* we've consummated our marriage," he grinned.

"Yeah," I said, wincing slightly as I took a step toward him. "Quite thoroughly, in fact. I think it's too late; you're stuck with me."

Campbell wrapped me tightly in his arms. "Dinna joke about it. I chose ye, Carlie. Don't even think about the things I said yesterday. Given the choice, I'd marry ye again. You do not have to worry about my commitment to ye."

I sighed deeply, and Campbell stroked my back, pulled my hair away from my neck and kissed me. I sighed again. "Maybe I've changed my mind," I murmured, letting my hands meander down to grab his toned butt.

"I can just *hold* you, Carlie," Campbell said quietly. "It doesna have to end in sex."

I couldn't explain it, but I started crying. *Again!* "Oh, my word," I said. "You're going to think I'm crazy! I'm not sure why I keep crying!"

"I dinna think you're crazy. I just think some things were broken in your relationship with Eric," Campbell. "And I may be wrong—it was your life—but maybe you felt like to get the touching ye needed, you had to offer yourself, sexually."

I pushed away from Campbell in shock and looked up at him.

"I'm sorry," he said, eyes wide. "I wasna trying to be rude."

"No!" I exclaimed. "That's it. You're right. I could never get enough, and so I had to make it worth his while." Campbell looked down at me compassionately, his hand still tracing the lines of my back.

"You may be young," I said, "But you've got some wisdom. That's something I don't think Eric ever understood."

Campbell pulled me to his chest again. "*Mo ghràidh,*" he said.

"Oh, that's Gaelic," I said. "I know *mo chridhe* is 'my heart.' What's *that* mean?"

"My love, or my darling," he said.

"Okay, darlin','" I said, drawling the word like a Southerner. "To the ocean side to see the drop-off?"

From seeing teacher Campbell's diagrams, I was aware of the reason there is a drop-off on the ocean side of an atoll. As the extinct volcano sinks under the water, coral works its hardest to stay close to the light since most corals are fed by algae which require sun to produce energy. Therefore coral tends to grow upwards, building upon the skeletons of previous coral formations.

Although coral grows up on both the inside and the outside of an atoll, on the inside the lagoon fills with sediment so there are shallower sections, but the region around the atoll is created by upward-growing corals, which create that drastic cliff.

I knew about the drop-off. I understood it. I even expected it. That didn't change the fact that when Campbell and I swam to the edge of the drop-off and peeked over, my stomach dropped as if I was on a roller coaster ride, as if I was going to fall off a skyscraper. I panicked, backed up (which is harder than you might think with fins on), and quickly stood up on some coral.

"That's terrifying!" I squealed, once Campbell had surfaced with me.

He laughed, continuing to hold my hand, but then his expression changed.

"Hey, Carlie," he said. "We need to get all the way into the water if we're here on the ocean side."

"Why is that?" I asked.

"Trust me," he said. "*Now.* Get your mask and snorkel back on."

I had no idea why, but he seemed serious, so I pushed my mask back on and was getting my snorkel in my mouth when I saw the black-tipped fin moving toward us.

I had to work to avoid hyperventilating once I had my face in the water.

The shark was smaller than I'd expected, probably about four or five feet long. It had been moving toward us, but as Campbell swam toward it with me fiercely clinging to his hand, it swerved and swam away from us. It was graceful and beautiful with a sleek grayish brown body and black tips on its dorsal fins as well as its tail and belly fins.

I had heard that when sharks were in places where there was abundant food, they weren't usually a threat to humans, but despite my knowledge I couldn't get over my anxiety. Campbell could sense it, perhaps in the way I was shaking uncontrollably, so he swam with me to the shore where I stumbled out of the water as quickly as I could.

When we were safely sitting on the sand, Campbell put his arm around me. "They're skittish, unless they think you are food. Here in the Marshalls they know that the best way to avoid a blacktip reef shark bite is to swim instead of wading. The bigger you look, the less likely they are to think of you as edible."

"So when you told me to get in the water you were preventing a shark attack?" I asked.

"*Aye*," he said. "*Aet*."

"That's hilarious!" I said, with a tiny gasp. "The Scots and Majel for yes are almost the same word!"

"Strange things strike ye as funny, *Ri-pālle*," he said.

"Well, that was terrifying," I said. "Can we swim in the *iar* instead?"

"Sure," Campbell replied, hugging me tightly. "But we're not going in the water at all until you stop shaking."

He led me back to camp where we grabbed our fishing spears and he stuck his fish stringer on his belt loop, then we headed across to the lagoon side. It was obvious the waves from the storm had been bigger than normal, as all sorts of flotsam had washed up on the beach—floats, plastic bottles, sprouted coconuts, palm fronds. I was looking at some of the shells scattered about when Campbell swore.

"This is a muckle great pile of shite," he said. "The boat's gone."

CHAPTER 26

The Visitor

How do you think that happened?" I asked, joining Campbell where he stood scanning the horizon, sweeping his vision left and right across the *iar*. Even as he still looked about he put his arm around me, resting one hand on my hip as if he sensed my need for reassurance.

"*Dinna fash*, hen. We willna die." Campbell grinned down at me, pulled me to him, kissed me on the forehead, and then returned his gaze to the lagoon. "I'm quite certain it must have been the combination of the storm with the tides. Sometimes a storm will bring a surge ahead of it, so with that and high tide, plus the waves created by the winds, the anchor rope must have become dislodged."

I could almost swear I saw a metallic glint on the turquoise waters to the west of us, but it was impossible to be certain.

"So, what do we do?" I asked.

"The way I see it," Campbell said, brow furrowed, "We have two choices. The first is to just wait. We have food, water, coconuts if we run out of water. Maybe someone sees the Rosa's boat and figures out. If not, the first day when we dinna come back, they'll think we're being selfish and stealing time together." He grinned at me, "Which wouldna seem that unlikely."

"But will they even notice if we don't come back on Monday?" I asked. "Graham and Ewan won't expect you until school on Tuesday morning."

"That's true," Campbell agreed. "When they do notice, though, it means tracking down another boat, another trip across the *iar*, and picking us up. Sometime Tuesday, probably Wednesday at the latest."

"And what's the other option?" I asked.

"Walk and swim back," said Campbell. I looked at him skeptically. "At low tides, much of the sand between the islets is exposed. For an hour before and an hour after the low tide, maybe a little longer, we could walk through the water if it's shallow, or snorkel on the *iar* side to cross any of the deeper sections. When we got to Matolen, we could walk the last five miles back to Ine or take a truck if we lucked out and one was on this end of the island."

"Is that option dangerous?" I asked.

"Dangerous? Not really. But since it could be anywhere between 8 and 10 and miles back to Matolen, it would be exhausting," Campbell answered, "But definitely more responsible. And definitely less fun." He had an impish smile, and I was quite certain I could guess what he was thinking.

"We already missed two days last week with the trip to Majuro," I said. "If we do want to take any trips to visit your family or mine, we might not want to miss many more work days."

"Aye, *Ri-pālle*, let's think on it," Campbell said. "Far as I can figure, we're an hour or two past high tide. That means we have four hours until low tide, just two or three hours until we'd need to start walking. We would want to pack a bit to take along with us if we chose that option. Enough that if we got stranded on one of the islets we could sleep and eat."

"Well," I said. "While you think that through, I have to go to the little girls' room." Campbell looked confused. "Sorry, that's just one of our Beecherisms from growing up. With three girls and a mom who really liked us to be polite, we didn't say a lot of rude words."

"So, saying going to the bathroom..." Campbell wrinkled his forehead in confusion.

"Bahhhthroom," I echoed him, copying the UK pronunciation.

"Ye think it's any better to say Baaaaathroom?" Campbell teased, in a nasal American accent. "Any way, your ma thinks of that as rude?"

"Not as polite or euphemistic as 'little girls' room.' Couldn't say poop or pee, either. Or shut up."

"Then, *Ri-pālle*," Campbell said, a look of amused surprise on his face as I headed toward the palm forest, "How did ye end up with such a foul mouth?"

"Hell if I know," I joked.

I wandered back through the trees to pee, and when I pulled down my panties, I had to laugh. Of *course*. That would, number one, explain all the crying and mood swings, number two, guarantee that we didn't have to worry about being pregnant, and number three, be just my luck. Of course, I would be shipwrecked on an island during my honeymoon *and* start my period.

"Hey, Campbell," I said as I rejoined him. "I don't know if... What are you doing?"

Campbell had grabbed a stick and was drawing and doing math on the sand.

"I'm trying to figure out the tide schedule and when it will be safest to hike and swim across the underwater sections."

"So you're leaning toward walking back?" I asked.

"Unless you definitely want to stay," Campbell said. "As much as the thought of not sleeping wi' ye in my arms in bed all night tonight pains me, I dinna want to be on Alastair's bad side." He looked at me hopefully. "But maybe you'll make an exception and not make me wait until two o'clock to have ye again."

"Speaking of which," I said, discomfited by the thought of having to disappoint him. "I just... well, I... um..."

Campbell waited, a confused half-smile on his face.

"I guess I'll just say it," I said. "I appear to have started my period."

"*Oh*," Campbell said, good-humored as always, but with a faint hint of disappointment on his face. "Well, now, *Ri-pàlle*, having not been married before, I havena thought about periods very often. But I'm under the impression that this takes sex off the table. Which means we don't need to worry about that. And so I'm assuming... nah, I dinna want to assume anything. What do ye need?"

"Well," I said, "you're right. Definitely don't need sex. The first order of business is figuring out how to take care of it. I wasn't expecting it, so I didn't think to bring along any tampons."

"Are you sure ye even want to come with me, now that's happened? The rumors about menstruating women and sharks haven't proven to be true, so it wouldn't be a danger, but I wouldna want ye to have any extra pain because of exerting yourself. I could go alone instead and travel fast. I might even make it back by tonight, so we could come and get ye tomorrow."

"You're not going without me," I said stubbornly. "I just need something to use as pads in my underwear."

Campbell cocked his head and looked at me with a small smile. "Come along then," he said. "I guess we should do some packing, and I think I have a solution."

He's not fazed by anything, I thought as I followed him. *Not grossed out, not resentful. What hidden evil lurks in his heart?* I laughed out loud.

"What?" Campbell asked, turning curiously to look back at me.

"You're too good, Campbell," I said. "I need you to be selfish and evil every once in a while."

"How do you mean?" he asked, waiting for me to catch up to him.

"Aren't you upset?" I asked. "That my period started? That we can't have sex?"

"That you're a *woman*?" he said, grinning. "I kind of *hoped* ye were. I dinna think I would have married ye if ye weren't."

"You're adorable," I said, grabbing him around the waist and turning my face up for a kiss.

"And if we're married as long as I plan, I figure I have thousands more times I can make love to ye," Campbell said with relish. "Now we can make getting home our priority. And maybe it's a good thing. If I think you're off limits, perhaps I'll stop getting distracted by your luscious round arse in that bathing suit." He reached down to grab my rear and groaned. Then he turned, took my hand, and led me back to camp.

Campbell's solution for my woman problem was to tear one of his old white tee shirts into eight pieces, folding the rectangles into bulky little pads. He gave one to me and packed the rest into a zip-top plastic bag.

I packed our suitcases, so they'd be ready to leave the island whenever we were able to come back and get them again. We each took along a swimsuit in addition to wearing our clothes for walking.

Campbell had a cooler that he could tow when he swam. Into it we put several water bottles, the matches, my pads, some of the leftover rice in baggies, and the rest of the bananas. We figured we could eat fish and coconut as well and that would be sufficient fuel. There was just enough room at the top to shove in his shorts and tee and my sundress and underwear when we needed to swim, and our swimsuits while walking.

The machete and fish spear were going to be more of a challenge. We needed them for opening coconuts and catching fish, but they were a little heavier, both for carrying and when the time came to swim. We finally landed on Campbell carrying the cooler and machete, while I would carry the bedroll of a sheet and blanket in a waterproof sack and the fish spears. Finally, we rigged up a way for each of us to carry our fins, snorkels and masks around our shoulders.

By Campbell's calculations, low tide would be at 3 p.m. So as irony would have it, instead of retreating to our tent to make love at 2 p.m., we found ourselves hiking down the beach to reach the end of Autle as close to the final descent of the tide as possible.

At the beginning it felt like an adventure. We tromped through the calf-deep water over white sand. The tide was going out, so it was as if the lagoon was an overflowing cup and the water was spilling outward, but it wasn't pushing too strongly against us. The depth of the water (or one could say, the height of the sand) went up and down, but as the first hour progressed, I could tell that in general the water level was falling.

Campbell had guessed quite closely, but low tide occurred a little after three. After a while we could sense the water shifting directions again in the open portions of the atoll. We passed a few islets and found it easier to walk around them on the sand than to try to blaze our way through the thick underbrush. By 4:45, the water had risen to the point that it was too exhausting to slog our way through. At this point we decided to rest for a little while on a tiny islet, and then swim as far as we could.

We sat on the sand looking out toward the lagoon, pulled out the rice and bananas, and had them with a bottle of water as we rested in the shade. As we finished, Campbell was gazing at me somewhat longingly.

"Whatcha thinking about?" I asked.

"Dessert," he said wistfully. "Something round, and soft, and sweet."

"You know, just because I'm having my period doesn't mean I'm off limits to touch completely," I said. "I'm not diseased. It's not catching. I still

240

want to be connected!" I stood, peeled off my sundress, laid it on the sand between Campbell's knees, and sat down on it in front of him.

He reached out his hands, and I could feel the barest brush of his fingertips on my skin. He traced the shape of my shoulders and down my arms until he'd raised goose bumps. I leaned back against his chest, my arms propped on his knees, giving him better access to cup his hands under my breasts. When he did, he sighed contentedly, leaning forward to kiss my shoulder. "Softer than baby ducks. Or kittens," he murmured. I giggled, which made him clasp me harder and nip my shoulder. "Don't laugh at me," he complained.

"It's cute," I said, leaning into him as he grabbed my hair to pull it out of the way and nuzzle my neck.

"*Ifrinn*, Carlie," Campbell groaned. "If I thought I desired women when I was a virgin, that's nothing in comparison to the way I feel now. How long do your courses run? How often does a married man die of sex starvation?"

I laughed again. "I want you, too," I said, "But four or five days isn't forever."

"I wonder..." Campbell said, then stopped.

"What?" I asked.

"Do couples ever... *nah*," he said.

"You can ask me, Campbell," I said. I could feel him squirm in discomfort behind me.

"Do some couples still make love during the woman's period?" Campbell asked.

"Yeah," I said, "but usually when they have access to a shower and laundry facilities. And not usually at the very beginning of the cycle. More likely toward the end, when things have slowed and it's been just too long since they've connected!"

Campbell was silent behind me, apparently ruminating over the logistics of period sex.

"It's probably time to continue anyway," I said. "We've got a distance to travel still!"

After changing into our swim wear, we put on our fins as we stood by the water. Campbell tied a rope connecting his belt with the cooler. I held the strap of the bedroll bag in one hand and the spears in the other, and Campbell carried the machete.

"That's our goal," Campbell said, pointing to a medium-sized islet about a mile away, with a good number of coconut palms, what looked like a slight sandy clearing in the middle, and a clear view to Matolen in the distance.

I tried to think of it like a regular snorkeling or spear fishing trip as we swam, though I didn't typically go snorkeling after hiking five miles. Occasionally I would look up to see our progress, but as the exhaustion set in I stopped and just focused on the flurry of bubbles created by Campbell's fins in front of me.

When we finally arrived, I pulled myself from the water and lay panting on the beach in exhaustion. It was close to sunset. Campbell dropped the machete and untied the cooler, then grabbed a fish spear from me.

"Need to catch supper," he said in answer to my confused expression, sloshing away toward the lagoon.

I caught my breath a while longer, then powered through the pain, heading up into the islet to gather wood and dried, fallen palm fronds for our fire. I got the fire started and took the machete into the brush where I found a pandanus tree and hacked off a number of the frond filled branches. While I wouldn't have time to weave a pandanus mat for sleeping like the locals had, it would provide some padding under our thin bedroll to make sleep easier. I tossed the branches into a pile and went back to feed the fire.

We ate the barbecued fish, coconut, and the last of the rice by the light of the fire. "I'm guessing we're over halfway there," Campbell said, looking at the portion of the journey ahead. "But here's the situation. The next low tide will be a little less than six hours away. That means 2, maybe 2:30 in the morning. We do have flashlights, and reef sharks probably won't be prowling in a foot of water, but that does mean hiking in the middle of the night."

"What happens if we don't do it then?" I asked.

"Well, then we have to wait until one or two tomorrow afternoon to start our hike back. That's fine with me, but you'll miss Depo day. And that could be detrimental to your patients," Campbell said.

I sighed. I was already exhausted, but it really seemed like the only option.

After a too-brief respite of sleep on our pandanus frond nest wrapped up in our bedding, we packed up by flashlight and headed, again, across the sand flats. By that point I could do nothing but woodenly put one foot in front of the other.

Suddenly I felt a stabbing, burning pain on my leg. I screamed, "What was that? My ankle! It burns!"

Campbell trained his flashlight on my ankle. An angry red stripe wrapped itself around my leg. "Jellyfish," he said matter-of-factly. "Come on."

"Jellyfish?" I sobbed. The sting in my ankle was worse than any burn I'd ever had. "*Jellyfish?!!*" I was furious and hurt and just plain exhausted.

"We can't stop, Carlie," said Campbell. "We have to keep going."

I stood in the ankle-deep water, crying. "I'm sandy. I'm sticky. I'm gross. I've got cramps. I'm tired. This sting hurts. I can't do it, Campbell."

"Ye *have* to," said Campbell firmly.

"I can't!" I wailed.

If I'd expected a hug, I thought wrong. I was shocked out of my fit by a firm smack on my butt.

"We don't have time for emotion right now, Carlie," Campbell ordered me. "Walk."

"Fuck you, Campbell MacReid," I fumed. "You can't spank me. I am not a child!"

"You're not? Prove it. You're mad, *good*," he said. "Hate me, that's fine. Just keep *walking*."

I muttered under my breath as I trudged through the water behind my horrible husband. "Fucker. Bastard. Shit-faced little asswipe. God-damned fuck nugget..."

When we finally reached Matolen and stepped out onto dry land, I burst into tears. I dropped the load I was carrying on the sandy beach, my exhausted arms and legs threatening to give out at any moment.

Campbell walked a few steps farther to set his burdens down on the grass, but then he returned to me.

"*Itōk, Ri-pālle,*" he said, wrapping me in his arms.

"Campbell, we made it," I sniffled.

"Of course we did, hen," he said reassuringly. He released me to find our bedroll and spread it out over some low beach grass that would create a bit of a cushion. He lay down and reached his hand out to help me join him.

Curled up together, covered with sand and salt residue, we exhaustedly, gratefully, finally fell asleep.

CHAPTER 27

House Warming

"Miss Peachay. Meester Mack," said a little voice. "Miss Peachay. Meester Mack!"

I pushed myself up, blinking my eyes. Campbell and I were still in our little nest in the beach grass, wrapped in the sheet and blanket. Apparently, I'd been using Campbell's chest as a pillow. He stretched as well, opening one eye.

One of the youngest Rosa girls was staring at us curiously. She had dark hair and eyes, was wearing a brightly colored dress, and stood grinning at us. She and Campbell had a quick conversation, much of which I didn't understand, and she went skipping off toward the house we could see through the trees.

"We may be in luck, *Ri-pálle*," Campbell said. "It sounds like Mr. Botla was planning on coming down this direction with the truck this morning, so we may not have to walk all five miles home."

"Ugh," I said. "I just want a shower. Or even better, a bath. Soaking in hot water would be divine..." I groaned, stretched, and caught Campbell's gaze at me. I raised my eyebrows at him.

Campbell grinned at me sheepishly, "Aye, *Ri-pálle*, ye caught me thinking of ye naked. We are still freshly married, ye ken."

We picked up the rest of our things and limped towards the Rosa's house. I hadn't realized that my sandals were giving me blisters as we walked, but now that I wasn't running on adrenaline, I could feel the stinging sensation of sand under the straps rubbing on raw flesh.

When we arrived at their house, we were ushered inside, seated on pandanus mats, and fussed over by several mamas and *bubus*[1] who put coconut salve on my feet and fed us pancakes and papaya with lime. I had always hated the flavor of papayas I tried in the states: floral, almost like perfume, and sickly sweet. With fresh limes squeezed on top, suddenly the sweet was balanced with tanginess, and I actually liked the fresh rosy-orange slices. Maybe it helped that I had burned countless calories slogging through the sand and swimming through the water the previous day and night and was starving. Whatever the case, I was grateful to be fed and fussed over.

Again, I felt jealous that Campbell was able to communicate so clearly with them. I mentally determined that now we'd be living together, he could help me learn even more Marshallese. Although I couldn't understand everything he was saying, his tales of our journey had the ladies gasping in shock and looking at me empathetically as he described our travails in detail.

With rest, company, and a little food in my belly, I felt much better by the time the truck arrived. When Mr. Botla had his cargo loaded up, he stuck his head in the door to let us know our ride awaited.

"Not too long now, *Ri-pālle*," Campbell said, handing me up into the front seat of the truck.

I felt awkward sitting in the front with Campbell in the back of the pickup truck, but did my best to be sociable. "*Kommool tata,*" I said to Mr. Botla.

"You're welcome," he said, smiling as he started the truck.

"You speak English?"

"Yes—educated at the UniServe school and college in Majuro. Unlike others, I actually came home to Arno when I graduated."

"Not everyone does?" I asked.

"The way we live in the outer islands is a dying way of life," he answered, resigned, waiting for a few chickens to strut in front of the truck before he started down the road. "Climate change has impacted us already. We didn't use to get typhoons here, but now our storms are stronger and more

---

[1] *Bubus:* boo´-boos (grandmas)

frequent. With an average elevation of 10 feet, an atoll can't withstand much of a storm surge. Being flooded by salt water ruins the ground for growing, and then as the weather patterns have changed we also have periods of drought. If people who doubt that something is happening were to come here and see how our islands are affected, they'd at least do *something*."

"And so when the kids get educated?"

"They move on. Majuro, Hawaii, mainland United States. There's not work for educated people here. Making copra and perhaps fishing are really the only ways to earn money. Those levels of income can't support the growth of service industries."

I glanced back and forth from the *iar* to the ocean on either side of the road. At this point both were clearly visible, the island narrowing to about 200 feet wide. I imagined a storm surge at the front of a huge squall like Campbell and I had experienced only with winds of 75 or more instead and shuddered at the thought.[1]

I'd experienced typhoons on Guam and knew how devastating they could be. On Guam, building codes demanded that new structures be built of reinforced concrete with poured concrete roofs. Those buildings were immovable fortresses in a big storm—all you had to do was board the windows. Most houses had metal tracks outside the windows, and when storms were impending, you'd go outside and slide plywood securely into the tracks, then retreat into the house ready for the inevitable power outages. But here, the cobbled together structures weren't meant to last through typhoons; they'd never had to in the past.

I was grateful when I saw the clinic come into view. Campbell and I climbed out of the truck and grabbed our few rescued items. As we approached the apartment, I could see our white sheets billowing in the breeze from the laundry lines. I could smell a familiar scent that I couldn't currently place coming from our windows. When I entered the apartment I discovered my mom, hair tied into a knot, on her knees scrubbing the shelves in my kitchen.

At my footsteps she turned.

---

[1] 61 meters, 120 km/h

"Carlie!" She hopped up to hug us. "What a treat!! We thought we'd be long gone by the time you got back."

She pushed me to arm's length away from her. "Whatever happened to you two? You look *horrible!*"

"Thanks, Mom. Long story," I said. "But we're glad to be here."

That's when I first noticed Campbell's wedding gift to me. One section of the kitchen shelving had been sawed away to create space for a shiny white propane stove. "What?" I exclaimed. "There's a stove in the kitchen now!"

In the bustle around the wedding, I had noticed but not noted the strange crate in our yard. Now it was revealed that Campbell had purchased a propane oven in Majuro, and while we were gone, my parents had installed it in our house. And currently there were two loaves of Mom's homemade bread baking.

"Campbell!" I exclaimed, turning to him with tears in my eyes. He was beaming as I threw my arms around him.

"I ken it's not lovely jewelry," he whispered.

"You have no idea how beautiful it is to me," I sighed back.

"Get showered and let me feed you," Mom told us when we let each other go. She didn't have to ask us twice.

Dad was quite proud that he had mastered the wrist flick for perfectly drawing water from the well, so he bustled off to fill the shower bucket for me while I heated a pot of water on my brand-new stove.

A dose of Tylenol, clean water and shampoo, dry panties and clothes, a real tampon instead of a makeshift pad, and I was soon feeling much better. Campbell took his turn after me and emerged from the shower scrubbed and ruddy at about the same time Mom was pulling the loaves from the oven. We ate the soft and delicious slices with peanut butter and honey, and both Campbell and I groaned at the sensation.

"Come see what Dad and I did!" My mom said excitedly when we were done with our snack. In a sunny patch of the yard, they had built up two rectangular garden boxes with wood salvaged from the crate. They had hauled some soil from the jungle across the road, but my mom told me she thought I should get some chickens to provide eggs and manure; the sandy soil wasn't very rich.

Campbell followed us in amusement, listening as my mom and I chattered, interjecting a few comments. It turned out his family were farmers back in Scotland and he knew a bit about gardening.

Mom wrote out the bread recipe for me and helped me make the bed, and then it was time for them to be picked up for the trip to the air field; with a few tears, we said goodbye.

And then Campbell and I turned and entered our house again. "Are ye as tired as I am, *Ri-pálle*?" asked Campbell, heading for the bed.

"Are you just trying to get me into bed, or are you actually going to let me sleep?" I asked.

Campbell answered with a smile, peeling off his tee shirt. "I *will* let ye sleep, but it's probably the other purpose, if I'm being honest," he chuckled. "Though I ken we canna make love yet."

"I guess I don't care which reason," I yawned, crawling into the bed. There had been something on my mind since the middle of the night. "Campbell, I did tell you to be a little more evil yesterday," I said. "But what was with smacking me last night?"

Campbell raised his eyebrows and then frowned. "I didn't say it last night, but I was scared. The tide was coming in, and we were already taking too much time to get across that last stretch."

"But to *smack* me, Campbell, like you were my father and I was a kid?"

"You are right, ye arna a child, and I probably shouldna be smacking you. Even if it was on your luscious little bum." Campbell reached his hand over and stroked my hip.

"Come on, Campbell," I said. "Physical force?"

"Huh," he grunted. "Here were my thoughts last night. We had to keep moving, and you were sleep deprived and in pain. Did I have time to wait for ye to come around to logic? Did I have time to hold ye gently while ye cried? Could I carry ye? I dinna think so. And if not, then tell me, please, what would you have done?"

"Honestly, I don't know," I said.

"Did ye never get spanked as a child?" he asked curiously. "Sometimes that was the only way my ma or da could calm me down enough to get me to obey. That was my intent, *Ri-pálle*—to get you to listen to me and do as I said—to save ye. I didn't do it out of anger. I didna hurt ye; I shocked ye. It stimulated your adrenaline system, which got your brain working well enough and got ye just mad enough to start walking."

"I guess," I said, "I just had a controlling, abusive boyfriend in high school, and I don't want that sort of relationship again."

"I understand that," Campbell responded, pulling me closer. "Back in Scotland there was a girl..." he paused briefly, as if remembering. "She was very possessive. She didna want me talking to any other girls, didna like me doing things wi' my friends. She wanted to own me. Leaving Scotland, the relationship with her was something I was glad to leave behind. So I *ken* what ye are talking about, and I understand your concern."

"Was she your other second base?" I asked teasingly.

"Aye, though the way you were talkin' to me just then, I was feeling a little afraid I was never going to get there wi' ye again," Campbell smiled. He took one of my hands in both of his. "I willna say every single decision I've ever made has been the right one. But marrying ye? I think it was the most *important* decision I've ever made. We MacReids are a loyal lot; you and I are married now, but more importantly I've vowed *myself* to you. I will fight for you, protect ye with my life, sacrifice myself. I promise I willna hurt ye."

I was quiet, considering.

"Come, now. Can't ye forgive me, Carlie?" Campbell asked. "Can ye please trust me?"

I met Campbell's gaze. This was not the face of a manipulator, and by the light of day I could empathize with him. I had been distraught, tired, and impossible to reason with. "Maybe there would have been a better way, Campbell," I said. "But your intentions were right, and we're here safely now." I stroked the back of his hand.

"Can I make it up to ye, then?" Campbell asked, a tiny smile quirking the edge of his lips. "If I hurt you, I should make ye feel *good* as penance." My eyes must have questioned his motives, so Campbell explained, "I saw Mrs. Botla putting the coconut salve on your feet. Ye liked it—I could see it on your face. If ye had any oil or lotion, I could massage your feet for you."

I looked skeptically at him.

"Dammit, *Ri-pālle*," he said with a shamefaced grin. "You're like Wonder Woman and her golden lasso! If I can't make love to you, can I at least see your body and touch ye? Of *course*, I plan to massage more than your feet. But I had to start *somewhere!*"

"Well, I haven't had a decent massage in forever, and I do have some aloe vera massage oil," I conceded, though I wasn't reluctant at all at the prospect of getting a massage from a muscular man. I located the oil, spread a beach towel on our bed, stripped to my bra and panties, and lay face down.

"Are ye keeping this on then?" asked Campbell, running his finger across my bra band.

"You need some practice unhooking it," I said cheekily. When he succeeded, I shrugged the bra off and tossed it over toward the laundry basket.

True to his word, Campbell did start with my feet; his strong hands, just a little rough from physical labor, gently rubbing the oil into my skin. He then moved gradually upwards, first working from the left side of the bed until he'd massaged my left thigh, then kneeling on the bed beside me to massage my right leg. By the time he finished my back and shoulders, I felt a combination of hyper-alertness and relaxation.

"Well," I sighed. "I think that more than made up for your sin. Now I think it's my turn to touch you!" I looked up at his eyes and could see how that suggestion affected him.

I didn't put my clothes back on. Wearing just my panties I massaged Campbell's muscular legs, though it was hard to get him to relax since he kept turning to watch me at my work.

"Stop watching me," I scolded, finally making it impossible by climbing astride him and kneeling as I massaged his shoulders and back. Touching him was pleasurable, his muscles defined under his smooth, tanned skin. He was more ticklish than I expected, wriggling especially when I got anywhere near his sides.

"I'm going mad wi' desire," Campbell groaned finally, as with my hands I traced the length of his arms which were bent above his head, once again letting my breasts drift across his skin. He reached back with his right hand and gripped my right ankle, then in one smooth motion rolled himself over underneath me.

I was feeling my share of arousal from being touched, from the silky feel of lotion on Campbell's smooth skin, from knowing I was giving him pleasure, and from seeing his gorgeous masculine body. Now I could feel his desire as well, hard beneath me. As I saw the look of hunger on his face, I bent to kiss him.

"Oh, God, Carlie," Campbell groaned, thrusting his hands into my hair and pulling me down to him. "I dinna ken how I'm going to wait."

In answer, I took one of his hands and placed it on my breast, and then started moving over him, rubbing myself against him. "I wish I was done, too," I whispered in his ear. "I can't wait until I can have you inside me again."

Campbell flipped us over and pressed his body against me, kissing me with enthusiastic urgency—my lips, my neck, and breasts. I wasn't surprised when it happened, as aroused as I was, but it shocked Campbell.

"Did you just...have an orgasm?" Campbell pulled back from me, looking stunned. "So, it doesn't take..."

"Intercourse?" I said.

"No, I ken it doesn't take that—remember the shower?" Campbell smiled. I definitely remembered, too. "No, I mean it doesn't take direct contact?"

"That pressure was pretty direct," I said, looking up at him. "Now, I'm not going to make you go without. Lie back and let me take care of you."

CHAPTER 28

Feels Like Home

We had napped an hour or so when a knock came on the door. "You are coming, Miss Peachay?"

I shot bolt upright. "Yes, Sharbella, I'm coming!" I slithered into a loose-fitting dress, then noticed Campbell's toned bare backside, which I admired before covering it with the sheet.

Even in sleep he looked satisfied, tousled red hair framing a half-smile. Because he'd waited so long for sexual activity, there were many things Campbell had never done; or had done to him. After the massage he'd given me, I'd made use of the aloe lotion to give Campbell another first experience and had enjoyed watching his incredulous response. "Sweet boy," I said, as I left the apartment.

There was a short line of women between the ages of 15 and 50 outside the clinic. "*Jolōk bōd*," I said, apologizing.

"*Ejjelōk bōd*," the women responded. Campbell had told me I should ask him sometime about the true meaning of the Majel words for "I'm sorry" and "it's okay," so I made a mental note to ask him at dinner.

I was about to head inside the clinic when two familiar figures came slouching down the road.

"Ewan! Graham!" I exclaimed, trotting over to them. It would have been the most natural thing in the world to hug them as well as greet them, but I reminded myself I was only recently forgiven by the locals for my terrible manners.

"We're not talking to you anymore, Miss Peach," said Graham, looking away.

"Or Campbell, either," agreed Ewan.

"Aye, but it's mostly Campbell we're angry with." The guys nodded at each other, agreeing on that opinion.

"Why?" I asked.

"You were our friend, too, Miss Peach, and now he's stolen you away," Graham said grumpily.

"And," added Ewan, "I never got a chance to invite ye to the jungle...*or* to get to see ye changing."

"As well," Graham added, "Campbell was the best cook of the three of us. And you stole him."

"Ohhh," I murmured empathetically. "Well, we can fix that! Come over for dinner tonight! Campbell got me a stove."

"Are ye serious?" Ewan asked. "Can ye ask us over wi'out asking your husband's permission?"

I made a face at him. "The two of you will always be welcome in our home," I responded.

For the entire afternoon, I was subjected to merciless but good-natured teasing by the local women as I gave them their contraceptive shots. One particularly beautiful young woman asked me, "You have Depo? Or you make baby?"

I had Sharbella help me say "*Ij jab kōnaan bōroro kiiō*," meaning I didn't want to get pregnant right now.[1] "*Kōttar jidik*," I added, trying out my memory of the phrase 'wait a little.'[2]

---

[1] *Ij jab kōnaan bōroro kiiō:* ee-jab´ coe-non´ boh-row´-row key´-yoh (I don't want to be pregnant now.)

[2] *Kōttar jidik:* coat´-tar chee´-dick (Wait a little while)

They agreed that I should wait, but only a little, and quickly began to describe the children Campbell and I would have. "*Lukkuun kilep niñnin*," said one.[1]

Sharbella giggled as she translated, "Extremely big babies."

"With curly red hair," chuckled another girl. "*Būrōrō bōrañañ.*"[2]

Various jokes centered around Campbell's large size. "Meester Mack is *lukkuun kilep. Ej kilep aolep lilik*[3]?" Sharbella shook her head in embarrassment as she explained they were remarking that Campbell was extremely big. The question meant "Is he big all places?" They were asking whether his large size was true of him *everywhere*. I couldn't help but blush, which made the ladies roar in laughter.

What I noticed, though, was that my marriage made them more comfortable with me. They were joking, laughing. A few were brave enough to ask questions about uncomfortable menstrual cycles or how long they should wait between children.

After the women left, Sharbella smiled at me. "They like you," she said. "They are happy you marry Meester Mack. You too old to not be married. Some girls, not so happy that Meester Mack has a wife; but the mamas are very happy. They don't want their daughters to marry him and move far away."

"Do *you* need birth control?" I asked Sharbella as she was about to leave. She was probably in her mid-to-late 30s, and I knew she already had a couple of kids. She was a little heavy, and always moved about wearily.

She smiled shyly. "No," she said, "I don't need it. The other day when I went to Majuro on the Jolok boat? I saw the doctor and found out I'm *pregnant*." She waved to me and headed down the road.

After she left, I brought out one last syringe. I stared at it, then set it down on the counter. For an infertile woman, there was something sad and

---

[1] *Lukkuun kilep niñnin:* loo´-kwoon key´-lep ning´-a-ning (very big babies)

[2] *Būrōrō bōrañañ:* boo-row´-row boh´-rawn´-yawn (Red and curly)

[3] *Ej kilep aolep lilik:* Edge key´-lep all´-lop lil´-leck? (Is he big all places?)

senseless about putting a hormone to prevent pregnancy into my body; I wanted to talk to Campbell first.

When I entered the apartment, Campbell was sitting at the kitchen table naked, grading papers and making lesson plans.

"You're adorable," I said, squeezing his buns and nuzzling his neck. "But you need to get dressed. We're having company over for dinner."

"On our honeymoon?" Campbell asked skeptically. "I wanted to see you naked again!"

"We will need to have friends when you're impotent and I'm fat, Campbell," I said, laughing as he leaned back and pulled me into his lap. "However, right now there appears to be little danger of either," I added, wide-eyed, as he kissed me thoroughly.

Finally, I pulled myself away and set about the task of making pasta, delighted that I had enough burners for pasta, sauce, and a vegetable, as well as the ability to toast up some fresh bread with garlic powder and Parmesan cheese on it in the oven at the same time.

"Open the windows, Campbell," I suggested. "And could you make the bed, too? It smells like bodies and sex in here, and Graham and Ewan don't need to be any more jealous than they already are."

I pulled out my cellphone to take a picture once I'd set the table with our mismatched plastic plates and silverware. Despite the complete uselessness of virtually every other app on the phone, I continued to maintain a charge simply for the camera.

Campbell came up behind me and hugged me, looking over my shoulder at the table and my phone. "First dinner in the new home?"

"And first houseguests," I said. "Who, from the sounds of it, are arriving as we speak."

When we sat down, there was a bit of awkward silence. Campbell was staring at Ewan rather harshly and finally Ewan cleared his throat. "Miss Peach, it wasna very nice to call Alastair on the two of ye. Though it all worked out well in the end, didn't it?"

Campbell continued to stare at Ewan threateningly.

"And, I'm sorry. I hope you will forgive me," he finished. Campbell finally seemed satisfied.

"I understand where you were coming from, and I can forgive you, Ewan," I said. "It seemed cruel at the time, though."

"Aye," he said, shamefacedly. "Sorry, lass."

It was good to have Ewan and Graham around again, and they were adequately impressed with my culinary skills, limited as they were. Mostly they were surprised by the abundance of the food; I had to encourage them to eat more so we wouldn't have to throw anything away.

"That would be a good reason to get pigs or chickens," Campbell said, then grinned. "Your *daddy* thought that maybe if we built a pen, we could use the manure to enrich the garden beds."

"Animals wander freely on Arno," Graham said. "The locals might look at you funny."

"Well, it would probably be better than trying to run around behind them to collect the manure," retorted Ewan.

After we finished eating, Graham and Ewan looked around the room.

"I dinna think we should sit on their bed again," Graham said. "I'm sure there are all sorts of germs in it."

"And ye havena got a couch," complained Ewan.

"Let's just stay at the table," I suggested. "You boys all have to teach tomorrow anyway. And if you figure out a way to build me a couch, I'll take it in payment for future dinner invitations." Graham and Ewan nodded in agreement.

"Campbell," I said, scooting a little closer to him on the bench. "You told me there was an interesting way you found out about the Marshallese words for 'I'm sorry' and 'It's okay.'"

Campbell nodded, sitting up straighter as if the story-teller in him was waking up.

"You know how teachers sit down before the school year begins and plan out the rules and so forth? The three of us did that, thinking we had all the possible rules we needed. So, we start teaching last year, and it's the first recess. Graham and Ewan and I are watching the kids play outside, when all of the sudden one of them starts crying."

"It was one of the little guys," said Graham, "So I went to see what was wrong..."

"Well," said Campbell. "He said that one of the other kids had thrown a rock at him."

"We thought it was a pretty bad thing to do, though the rock he showed us was more like a baby pebble," said Ewan, "so we had the person who threw the rock have a time out from recess."

Campbell continued. "And later that day, we go over the rules, adding 'Don't throw rocks at people,' as one of the rules. But the next day, recess time, two different kids start crying because two different people threw rocks at them. We ask a few more questions, and it turns out the crying kids had been teasing somebody or breaking the rules of the game. We reiterate the rules."

"But the next day," said Graham. "More rock throwing. We were totally at our wits' end with these kids. Wondered how in this incredibly gentle culture they were being raised to be such violent human beings."

"Then," Campbell said, leaning forward, "We decided to go *bwebwenato* that first weekend— you remember, Carlie, how you just stop by and visit people? And we're sitting on a mat in someone's yard, and a dog across the yard goes sniffing at some food."

"Just like that," exclaimed Ewan, "The dog yelps and runs away. We looked around, wondering what happened."

"And then, one of the bigger boys is teasing his younger brother. We glance over at the mama to see if she has a problem with it, and to our surprise," said Campbell, his volume increasing, "She picks up a pebble, and with complete accuracy, she hurls the pebble at her bigger son, who says 'Ouch,' or '*Emetak*!' or whatever as she hits him in the leg!"[1]

Ewan and Graham both smiled as Campbell finished. "We realized that day that we were **never** going to be able to combat the rock throwing at school. Not if a beautiful, calm, kind Majel mother uses that as one of her forms of getting after her kids."

"It worked awesome, though," said Graham. "She didna have to yell or anything,"

---

[1] *Emetak*: Eh-meh´-talk (It hurts!)

"So what does that have to do with 'I'm sorry'?" I asked.

"Oh, I'm not done yet," said Campbell. "There are also dogs that run wild here on Arno. We were on a longer walk, heading toward Matolen, and a dog came out of the jungle, baring its teeth."

"It looked pretty fierce," agreed Ewan. "I nearly pissed my pants!"

"So, we didna have any weapons," said Campbell. "The only thing I could think of was to lean down and pick up a rock. So I did. And the dog yelped and ran the other direction. All I did was *pick up* the rock. I didna even have to throw it!"

"The Marshallese have crazy-amazing throwing skills!" exclaimed Graham in conclusion. The three boys all stared at me expectantly.

"*Okay*," I said hesitantly, not knowing what they wanted from me. "The Marshallese are great at throwing. And?"

"Here it is, *Ri-pālle*. Guess what *jolok bōd* means, literally," Campbell said.[1] His eyes were alight; he was obviously excited.

"There's the Jolok boat," I said, hesitantly. "But I don't know what it means."

"*Jolok* means *throw*. *Jolok bōd* means... throw... away... my... mistake!" Campbell ended triumphantly.

And I finally got it, where all Campbell's lead-up was going. "That's *awesome!*" I laughed. "You ask them to throw away your mistake, because you know they're really good at throwing things."

The boys all nodded, smiling. "So then, *ejjelok bōd*, what you say back.[2] What does that mean?" I asked.

"*Ejjelok* means 'nothing,'" Campbell said. "So you see? You tell them to throw away your mistake, then they say, 'there is no mistake'— 'there's nothing here.'" He grinned at me. "It's one of my favorite Majel translations."

---

[1] *Jolok bōd:* joe-lock burr, with a rolled 'r' (I'm sorry)

[2] *Ejjelok bōd*; Etch-chel´-lock burr (There's no mistake here)

I looked over at my grinning guests. Then, even without turning to look at Campbell I could tell he must be hinting to Ewan and Graham that it was time for them to go, from the way they were wordlessly communicating with their own eyebrows. I rolled my eyes and got up from the table.

"Who is going to help me with the dishes?" I asked, successfully inspiring Ewan and Graham to realize they needed to be getting home.

As they left, Campbell grinned at me admiringly, grabbing the water bucket and heading outside to the well. "You could totally be a teacher, *Ripālle*," he whispered as he passed me. "You're so clever. Getting boys to do what you want without even ordering them."

"Hey, Ewan," I called out from the doorstep at the retreating figures. "I'm not that good at throwing, but just in case you needed to hear it, *Ejjelok bōd!*"

"*Kommool tata*," he said back. "Thanks, Carlie."

Evening chores complete and the water prepped for morning showers, it was time for bed.

As Campbell closed all the curtains, I stood in front of my dresser. It seemed rather cruel to wear any of the lingerie I'd bought since I still wasn't interested in having actual intercourse, but somewhat unfriendly to put on regular pajamas.

"If I dinna like it, I can take it off ye," Campbell said, as if reading my mind. "And if ye wear those itty-bitty shorts and tops, I can finally do all the things I thought of when I held ye on my lap and in the swing, and when you slept wi' me."

"God, you're adorable," I said, grabbing a tank top and shorts from my drawer. Campbell watched as I pulled the shorts on and put my tank top on over my bra. "Don't get so disappointed, baby boy," I said at the look on his face, skillfully removing the bra from underneath the tank top.

Campbell wrinkled his forehead at me. "Baby boy, adorable? Is this what I get for marrying an older woman? Isna that what you say about puppies?"

"Come to bed," I said, reaching for his hand.

He stopped and pulled off his shorts. "I dinna care what you're wearing; I'm sleeping naked."

Lights off, tucked into bed, I snuggled next to Campbell as he slipped his hand under my tank top, grunting contentedly when he had my breast in his palm.

In the darkness I felt braver somehow. "When I say you're adorable, Campbell, I mean I *adore* you. I look at you, strong and handsome, wise and likeable, and I can't believe you're *mine*."

My compliment was met with silence, and I felt foolish. But then Campbell moved next to me, exploring me with his hands until he found my face, then leaning to press his lips to mine.

"Nah, Carlie," he said huskily. "I'm the lucky one. You're so clever. And that I get to hold you, to touch your body. And that you do what you do for me." Laughter rumbled in his chest, and I could feel him shaking his head. "You amaze me, *Ri-pálle*. I'm just grateful that you're here, that you're with me."

"Well, Campbell," I said kissing him gently in return, "that makes two of us."

CHAPTER 29

Division of Labor

Tuesday morning, Campbell got dressed and tossed his things for school together. "So, lunch?" I asked him. "Do you usually pack a lunch or eat with Ewan and Graham?"

"I dinna ken *what* I should do," he said, wrinkling his forehead. "We excuse the kids at lunch time for an hour. I would usually eat at home with Ewan and Graham, but that's not home anymore." He leaned over and kissed me on the forehead. "What if I want to see my wife?"

"Well, you could come home," I said coquettishly. "Though the travel to and from the school would take a good percentage of your lunch break. From the way they talked last night, I think they miss you, Campbell. We've got bread, peanut butter, honey. You could make a sandwich or two, eat there at lunch, and then just come home after school."

"*I* could make a sandwich, is it?" he said. "My *wife's* not going to do that for me?"

"Your wife has plenty to do without also making you a lunch," I retorted saucily.

"Truly? My ma always made lunch for my da," Campbell said. He appeared to be serious about this expectation. I had thought he was joking; realizing he wasn't, I started to feel irritated.

"Well, in the *Beecher* household," I retorted, "My 'da' was the one who made breakfast *and* lunches for us all, and when we started to complain about what was in them, we started making our *own*."

I could see that Campbell was sorting his thoughts. Finally, he smiled. "Okay, *Ri-pálle*. I can make myself a sandwich. But I think this evening perhaps you and I should spend some time sharing how things were in our own families and creating our own roles and expectations." He paused. "I dinna like earning frowns from you." He stepped into the kitchen, pulling the peanut butter off the shelf, and then turning to look at me. "Would ye like me to make you a sandwich, too?"

His offer completely diffused the irritation that had been rising in me, and I sighed. "Yes, that would be nice, Campbell," I said. "I'm sorry. I was being selfish with my time. And I agree. They say that expectation is the enemy of happiness. A lot of what Eric and I dealt with when we first moved in together was just not communicating and expecting things to be a particular way."

Campbell frowned. "D'ye think about him a lot, Eric?" He had taken a cutting board from the shelf and cut six even slices of bread, laying them down in pairs of two.

"Less than I think I should," I said. "But life here is a million miles away from the way things were in Denver." I pulled the honey from the pantry and handed it to him. "There's barely anything that reminds me of him here. I'm drawing water from the well, doing laundry by hand, cooking, and working. In primitive conditions like these life feels more urgent and immediate. And I'm so focused on *now* that I've not thought a lot about what's gone."

He nodded, concentrating on drizzling the honey on the sandwiches. I grabbed three plastic sandwich bags from the pantry and after closing one piece of bread on top of the other, put each sandwich into a bag.

"Do *you* think about Eric much, Campbell?" I asked.

"Aye, a little." Campbell met my eyes with an uncertain grin, scrubbed the peanut butter off the knife at the sink and set it in the drainer. "I dinna understand him breaking up with the woman he's loved for years. And I dinna understand how he could let you go so far away from him. He should have set the date then and there. I see that ye are a woman who kens her own mind, so maybe he is just a man that knew well enough to give ye space. But I do wonder what he's like. He's older than me, I know. And more successful, more knowledgeable."

I chuckled, "But ironically, also a teacher." Seeing the look on his face, I walked over to him and wrapped my arms around his waist. Looking up at him, I said, "Though I can say that you're my *favorite* teacher ever. You manage to demonstrate and explain without making me feel stupid. But babe, that's over now. It's done. You and I are *married*. Don't worry."

"It's hard, though," Campbell said, looking down at his feet. "I know you wouldn't be married to me if he hadna broken up wi' ye." He took the two sandwich bags from me, lifted my chin with his finger and kissed me on the lips.

"But he did. And we are," I responded.

Campbell smiled down at me. "Aye, we are married, aren't we? Sometimes I canna believe it."

"Every day it will feel a little more believable," I suggested.

"And every day we will figure married life out," Campbell agreed. "In fact, I've learned something just today. That in the MacReid household, we can make lunches *together*."

"The Beecher-MacReid household," I corrected him. I reached up and pulled him to me more firmly, his sweetness suddenly causing me to be overcome with a desire to make out with him. Campbell set the sandwiches down before they could get squished and squeezed some of my softer bits enthusiastically. Finally, he pushed me away with a grin. "Ye sure ye dinna want me to come home at lunch today?"

"No," I said. "I need to focus on clinic, and you should spend some time with your friends."

"Any idea on when..." Campbell indicated my pelvic area with a vague hand gesture, "*that* will be over? I dinna ken how long I can wait until we can be together again."

"It's slowing down," I smiled encouragingly. "Maybe tomorrow. And in the meantime, there are many other things we can still do."

"Aye?" Campbell said, a look of curious anticipation on his face. He picked up his backpack, slipped the sandwiches inside, smooched me firmly on the lips, and headed out the front door. "See ye around four then."

"Have a good day at work, MacReid," I said.

He blinked at me and came back to squeeze me again. "Oh Carlie, the day I thought you called me '*mo chridhe*'," he said. "I was already head over heels wi' ye."

A few people meandered in during the clinic hours when Sharbella was there. One little girl had been cut on coral and the cut had gotten infected. Another mother brought in her son who had a boil on his leg. One of the older men, who Sharbella called Jimma had a hacking cough that had been troubling him for a while. [1]

I asked her what Jimma's last name was to try to find his file, and Sharbella laughed. "*Jimma* means Grandpa. We call all the elder men *Jimma*, in respect. His *name* is Toko Bwelok."

When the clinic hours were over at one, I bid Sharbella goodbye, left a little note on the white board of where to find me, grabbed the seeds from the pantry, and headed to the garden boxes. Reading the instructions as to depth and concentration for planting the seeds, I planted a row of tomatoes, one of peppers, one of cucumbers, and one of long beans. I thought I'd try a short season root crop as well, so I also planted some radishes and carrots. Next, I used the shovel to build up two mounds in the ground beside the boxes. Moneo had told me that squash was one of the things that grew naturally in the Marshall Islands, so I assumed the soil would work fine.

It took three trips to the well to get enough water to saturate the beds and the two mounds to make sure my seeds would have the best chance of growing. Finally, I tossed the netting we were using to keep the chickens and other birds out of the beds over the top of the boxes.

Around that time, the pick-up truck came rattling by. Two men got out and grabbed things out of the truck bed. I had to walk halfway across the yard to see it was our suitcases and other supplies. I repeatedly thanked them, in both English and Marshallese. "How much do we owe you?" I asked.

"*Ejjab. Ejjelok.*" They said, shaking their heads and waving their hands. Even if I hadn't recognized the words as *No* and *Nothing* I would have understood them.

---

[1] *Jimma*: She´mah (Grandfather)

I smiled at them in gratitude and said, "Thank you so much! *Kommool tata*," as they went on their way. Since there weren't any patients waiting, I grabbed the suitcases and lugged them into the house. Glancing at the clock, I tried to calculate the hours until sundown. We hadn't done laundry this weekend, so I imagined we'd be running out of underwear at some point. Looking into the laundry hamper, though, I realized that the only thing in it was our clothing from the previous day. *My mother had done our laundry.* Hand-scrubbed our shirts and shorts, my dresses and the sarong, my panties and Campbell's briefs, dried and folded them, and put them away.

"Mom!" I sighed, shook my head, teared up, and promptly sat down on the bed, staring at our closet. Her actions had reminded me *that* was how you divided labor— by serving other people because you *loved* them. I had known for years that Acts of Service was one of my mom's love languages— that she expressed her love to people by *doing* things for them. And that gave me an idea for our planned discussion.

By the time Campbell came home, I had scribbled some notes out on a pad of paper. Without the help of the internet, I had to depend on my memory, but I thought I had summarized the five love languages decently well. I was all ready to start giving him my relationship quiz, but Campbell had other things on his mind as he came in the door and locked it behind him.

"It is *near impossible* to teach with a hard-on," he said, taking me in his arms.

I laughed in response, smiling empathetically up at him.

"You're so beautiful, I couldna get ye out of my mind all day," Campbell groaned. "Can't we please? We can put a towel down. Ye can shower after. I *need* you."

"I don't mind," I said. "I just hadn't imagined you would want to. I didn't want to gross out a virgin during his first week of sex."

"Aye, but I haven't *had* a week of sex," Campbell responded. "Just..." he counted on his fingers, "Friday, and Saturday, and...oh, we didna do anything Sunday morning because ye were *too sore*," he smiled suggestively. "And then your period started and we hiked back from Autle. Yesterday we had a little fun in the afternoon, and ye let me feel ye up last night. But Carlie, I'm dying here."

"Fill the shower bucket and take my towel out there," I said, smiling as I handed the towel to him. "I'll get some water boiling."

"I'm going to make it worth your while," he said, nodding earnestly.

"You don't have to convince me, Campbell," I said. "I want you, too."

Afterwards, Campbell lay flat on his back, staring breathlessly up at the ceiling. "I think it's a good thing I didn't know what I was missing all these years," he said.

"Yeah," I said. "Kind of hard not to want it once you've had it."

Campbell turned toward me, admiring my body as he stroked me gently. "I dinna ken whether knowing I could have ye next to me this afternoon made my day harder or easier," he said, sighing at the feel of soft skin on his fingers, and smiling at the way his touch raised goosebumps and made me shiver. "The day seemed very long, to be honest, but I did feel that in the hard moments, I could encourage myself by thinking, 'Ye can get through this. Ye've got something to look forward to.'"

I reluctantly pulled myself away. "Can you take the hot water out? I need to get to the shower quickly without doing anything that slows me down."

Campbell kissed me firmly on the lips, grabbed his sarong to wrap it around himself, stuck his feet in his flipflops, and took out the water pot.

When I was finished with my shower, I came inside to find Campbell dressed in his swimwear. "Fish and rice tonight?" he asked. "I can go out spearfishing."

"That sounds good," I said. "I'll see if Anni will teach me how to use her grating bench. Though I think I need a coconut."

Campbell showed me how the mature coconuts were often blown down from the trees by the wind. He walked over with me to Kona and Anni's house and showed me how to jam the coconut husk onto the flat metal coconut husking bar protruding from the ground, then twist it to get sections of the dry husk off. Campbell used their machete to give the coconut a sharp rap to split it in half.

Then he headed off while Anni demonstrated how to sit on the bench and lean on the coconut husk to grate it into a bowl. I felt like I was getting as much coconut on the ground as I was into the bowl, but Anni and I laughed and she continued to show me how to hold the coconut better and not accidentally grate my hands.

By the time Campbell returned, the rice was simmering on the stove. Campbell used the oven to bake the fish instead of a fire for barbecuing, but we found that using the broil function created a crispy seared finish to the skin.

"Now, is *this* the first dinner in our house with just the two of us?" I asked, as we sat across from each other.

"Aye," said Campbell, grinning at me. "And I think I *like* being a married man."

After doing the dinner dishes together, we slipped on our flip-flops and went for a walk down the main road and back on the beach. When there was no one around, Campbell held my hand, or threw his arm over my shoulder to draw us close. "Isn't it rude to be physically affection in public?" I asked.

"They know Americans are different. But we should probably be at least a wee bit respectful of their culture," Campbell agreed reluctantly, taking his arm off my shoulders.

We visited with several children, and I tried out my Marshallese on them, asking them their names and what they were doing. They chattered so fast I couldn't understand, but Campbell would cheerfully translate.

The sun was setting when we got home. We piled up our pillows at the head of the bed. Campbell was about to grab a book when I stopped him.

"You know how we talked about expectations this morning?" I said. "I had an idea. I've got a test I want you to take, and I think it will help us understand each other better."

I'd designed a little questionnaire, trying to narrow down Campbell's primary love language. When he started reading the questions, though, he laughed.

"Five love languages, right?" he asked.

"*Oh,*" I said, realizing I'd spent a good hour on something I could have just asked him about. "Do you know what yours are?"

"Can you guess?" asked Campbell, putting his arm around me.

"Physical affection?" I asked.

"Aye," Campbell said. "That's my highest."

"What's the other one?" I asked.

"Guess," said Campbell. "Think about the day I hung out with you while you did laundry."

"Acts of service?" I asked.

"No," said Campbell. "Though, I dinna mind helping people. There's a different reason for it, though."

"Quality time!" I exclaimed. "You were just hanging out while I did laundry to spend *time* with me."

"Aye," said Campbell. "I have one more that was nearly as high as that."

"Words of affirmation?" I guessed.

"*Aet!*" Campbell said. "And ye do say nice things to me. Makes me feel good," he said.

"Hmmm," I said, looking at him quizzically.

"So, let me guess yours," Campbell said. "Physical Affection. Quality time. Words of Affirmation."

I stared at Campbell with wide eyes.

"*That's* why!" I exclaimed.

"Why this feels good?" Campbell said, looking down at me adoringly. "Why there's just a rightness in us together?"

"I think so," I said. "The things that feel loving for me to do are things that you interpret as love," I said.

"So the name calling," said Campbell, "Which is *completely* the opposite of affirming words, that argument killed both of us. We canna be mean like that."

"You're right," I agreed.

Campbell smiled at me, his forehead wrinkled. "Ye know I felt connected to you from early on," he said. "I wonder if that's why."

"From the *very beginning*, Campbell," I agreed, "You walked me home. You came back and hugged me, you hung out with me, you spent time with me. You held my hand when we went snorkeling." Overcome with affection, I leaned over and kissed him on the shoulder.

"I love you, too, wee one," he said.

"So when it comes to household chores," I said. "Should we divide the labor?"

"When we need to," said Campbell. "For dinner tonight, ye did the rice and I got the fish, and that worked. But I ken that we would both do best when we work together if possible."

"Because that means spending time together," I said. "I guess when we're doing the dishes, doing the laundry, if we can, we should work together on it."

"And if we can't," Campbell said. "We'd better be prepared to compliment and share appreciation after."

"*Or* be prepared to make out a little," I said, getting off the bed. I knelt over his legs, facing him.

"*Excellent* idea, Mrs. MacReid," he said huskily. "Now, get ready to feel loved, Carlie."

CHAPTER 30

Love Notes

D *ear Uncle Ferguson,*

    *I've got some news to share with you! I think I've told you about the beautiful UniServe nurse Carlie Beecher who stitched me up when I fell on the corrugated tin boat. How much I admired her, how bonny she was, and how I hoped I'd find someone like her to marry someday. Nah, that's not the whole truth. What I wanted was **her.***

Though she's a brash American who is clueless about many things, she's also the first woman I've known who made me feel like I was seeing the best qualities of my mother again. My da always said when the right woman came along, I would just know. And I just knew it the first day I met Carlie. Surprisingly, she happened to be stitching up a rather large wound on my arse, but that's neither here nor there.

So here's my news. I married her!

You read that correctly. I'm married, incredibly, to the woman I've been pining for over the last six weeks. It's a good thing I didn't know how amazing sex was, because I would probably have been as bad as a wild boar, rutting with every female I could. I am grateful, though, that I didn't; grateful for my ma's advice and for your encouragement.

My wife (how strange to say that!) has said several times how delighted she is to have been my first, and how special it is to not be competing with countless other women in my memory. Somehow I doubt that there'd be much competition—she's generous, this one. And hungry for contact, eager to be with me, and enthusiastic in many ways, including... you ken. I know a gentleman doesn't talk. Suffice it to say that I can have no complaints in that department.

I remember you saying that Alana was well enough to hang out with, but she wasn't the kind of girl I needed to marry, and because of that I should not bed her. You said I should marry an equal. I did not know what you meant at the time, but now I do. Because Carlie is an equal. Intelligent, funny, interesting, and passionate. She's a nurse practitioner, also serving in UniServe International here on Arno. And through a strange set of circumstances, she ended up proposing marriage to me. And because I am not <u>that</u> much of a millennial, then I proposed to <u>her</u>. ☺ She can have a sharp tongue, but knowing my sister as ye do, and having known my mother, you know I'm used to quick-witted women.

I mentioned she's an American. Her parents live on Guam—her dad is a chaplain, a major in the US Air Force, and we plan to visit there for Christmas. She has said she wants to visit Scotland. I believe that by that time, I should have completed my community service hours, and I may be able to have my record expunged since I have not only completed my college degree but will have also taught two years by then. I should be able to enter the country without incident, but I may need you to make certain for me. I wouldna want to get there and not be able to see family; nor would I wish to be embarrassed in front of my wife.

If you are able, I would so love for you to make a visit out here. I wouldn't be generous enough to let you stay in our apartment with us, though. A man must have his boundaries, and may I just say, you would not be able to sleep very well anyway. Graham and Ewan still have my bed in their apartment, so there would be a place for you to stay.

As always, know you are in my thoughts often, and that when I pray, you are in my prayers. Sometimes living out in such a beautiful place, walking and breathing are as much praying as anything. You feel close to both nature and God.

I miss you deeply.

Love,

Campbell

Campbell and I sat in bed, each with a pad of paper. Campbell wrote his tight printing with a black pen, and my loopy script was in purple.

"So, who are you writing to tonight, *Ri-pálle?*" Campbell asked.

"My best friend Greg," I said.

"A guy best friend?" Campbell asked curiously. "How long have you been friends?"

"Since college," I answered. "Freshman year we were lab partners in General Biology. Cheated on the lab final together because it was too damn hard, and that cemented the friendship. We chose classes and studied together through all of nursing school, and that went so well, we went through the nurse practitioner program together, too."

"Dinna hate me for this, Carlie," said Campbell. "Ye say he was your best friend."

"Yes," I said.

"And you studied together for years..."

"Pretty much every day," I confirmed. "We even ended up both being hired at the same clinic in Denver. Of all the people I know, he's the one I want to tell about you the most."

"But you never dated... or wondered whether you should be wi' *him* instead of Eric?"

I laughed. "Are you jealous? Nervous?"

Campbell looked at me sheepishly. "Aye. Maybe a little."

"*Dinna fash*, Campbell MacReid," I said, in my worst Scottish brogue. "Handsome as he may be, Greg never thought of me like that."

Campbell still didn't understand.

"He's *gay*, Campbell," I explained.

Campbell nodded, finally, a light coming on in his eyes. He looked like he was about to start a sentence but appeared to re-think it. "I'm glad ye have a friend you can write to, though," Campbell said, "Not just family." I nodded in response.

"Who are you writing to?" I asked, peeking over at his paper. Campbell blushed, turning the pad away from me so I couldn't see it.

"My uncle, Ferguson MacReid," Campbell said. "I'm telling him about you, and I'm not really ready for you to hear what I think about you."

I tried to overcome my extreme curiosity to know what Campbell could possibly be saying that he didn't want me to see. "Where does your uncle live?"

Campbell set the pad of paper down.

"Oh, I didn't want to interrupt you," I said. "You just hadn't mentioned him before."

"Ferguson is my da's older brother. From the way he talks about my ma, I wonder if maybe he was in love with her too."

"But your dad got the girl?" I asked.

"Aye," Campbell chuckled, "Heather Douglass, fiery in both hair and temperament."

"And your dad?" I asked.

"Handsome, kind, romantic Gordon MacReid."

"So, what is your sister Isla like?" I asked.

"Same hair as me and ma, with ma's spunky disposition." Campbell grinned. "No' so tall as me, though. She's closer to your height."

"You haven't told me, Campbell, what happened to your parents and Matthew," I said quietly. "You don't have to right now, but I hope you'll trust me enough to share that part of your life sometime."

"Well," Campbell said, "Mail doesn't go out until Monday. I'll have plenty of time to finish my letter to my uncle..." He looked down at the page. "I'm just singing your praises," he said bashfully. "It's nothing bad at all. But he kent I was a virgin, and he's a man, so maybe I'm sharing a little more than I want you to hear."

I set my paper aside as well, curled up next to Campbell, and leaned on his shoulder, but he adjusted his position to put his arm around me. I sighed once I was leaning against his chest, and he chuckled. "I like cuddling, too, Ri-pālle," he said. "Well, where do I begin?"

"Maybe with the happy part," I said. "Tell me about your family."

"I grew up in the Highlands of Scotland, in a region called Elrick—it's on the outskirts of Inverness. Have you heard of Inverness?"

"Can't say that I have," I said. "Sorry. Self-centered American... isn't that your name for me?"

"Then, have you heard of Loch Ness?"

"Yes, that I have," I chuckled. "Nessy, the Loch Ness monster..."

"Inverness is on the River Ness, and Loch Ness..."

"Must be a lake on the River Ness..." I said. "It's okay, Campbell. You probably don't know much about Guam— I'll show it to you. And you can show me Scotland. Then I'll be able to place all your stories."

"Aye," he said, seeming satisfied. "Small town, and Da was just a small farmer, and he had a stable where he boarded and trained horses. I learned to ride and helped him with the chores around the stable. My ma, Heather, she was a teacher. I suppose that's what made me think of teaching when the time came. I was just used to seeing the projects my ma had planned for her students, and she would test things out on Matthew and me before she tried them at school."

"So Isla was two years older than you, and Matthew was three years younger?"

"Aye," said Campbell. "I was sixteen, and Isla was eighteen, and Matthew just thirteen, when he and my Ma were killed in a car accident. They were just driving home from school, in some torrential Scottish rain. Sometimes it would get so bad, the wipers on the car just couldn't wipe fast enough. We're not quite sure how it happened, but it was on a tight corner. The car skidded off the road and tumbled down a steep embankment. They both had their seatbelts on, but it wasn't enough. Someone called 999, but by the time the ambulance service got to them, they were both gone."

"I'm so sorry, Campbell," I said. I felt, suddenly, like I should be holding him instead of him holding me. But he started stroking my hair, running his fingers through the haphazard curls and occasionally pressing his lips to my head.

"Her hair was red, and it was curly just like yours. You remind me of her, a lot, Carlie."

I turned and looked at him. His eyes were moist. "Oh, Campbell," I said, sympathy tears filling my eyes. I kissed him, then settled back against him.

"When she died, my world fell apart," he said. "I had always been a good student, hard worker, responsible son. And I didna understand why God would let a perfect woman die. And Matthew, too. He looked like me, ye ken, but he was the sweetest of us. Isla and I fight and butt heads wi' each other, but Matthew didna fight. He had a kindness in him that neither of us had. So I didna understand. And I was angry."

"Of course, you wouldn't understand. Of course, you would be angry," I said. "I certainly hope no one ever told you it was part of God's plan. I don't think that's ever true of death."

"Ye know, some did. And that was when things turned south for me. An angry boy fell in with some angrier, older boys. Boys who used drugs to escape their anger and turn off the pain for a while. Boys who needed money to support their habits and ended up breaking and entering, and eventually getting caught."

"You can't blame yourself," I said. "You were young."

"Aye," said Campbell. "But I do blame myself for driving away my da."

"How?" I asked. "How can you?"

"Because after my sentencing hearing, after my da had heard the charges against me read, he went home, packed his bags and left. He didna kill himself, but depression over losing my ma and Matthew, and devastation at seeing what I'd become was just too much for him to stay. I lost both my parents and my brother in the course of two years." Campbell was speaking almost woodenly now. "And Isla will *never* forgive me for the part I played in making our da leave. We havena heard from him in four years now."

"Babe, can I hold you for once, please? You've comforted me so many times, can't I comfort you?" I turned and pulled him into my arms, maneuvering until he was resting his head on my chest. I stroked his hair, whispered my own words of comfort, and let him grieve.

Dear Greg,

When I first brought up the idea of serving in UniServe International, I remember you encouraging me to go, saying to me that you were tired of seeing me without a sparkle. I guess I didn't know what you meant. Or I thought I knew what you meant, and now I really understand. My life was comfortable, familiar, sanitary, affluent, organized, and entirely unsatisfying.

Coming out here to Arno was a ridiculously unsettling choice. My first few days I felt like I was constantly crying, whether from being overwhelmed, missing Eric, questioning my choice, or pure exhaustion from having to draw every bit of water I used from the well. I wasn't eating very well, either, but I'm doing much better now.

Now? I feel alive, Greg. I feel useful and needed. And I also feel like I have no idea how to say what I have to say next.

*I am **married**. And not to Eric—who broke up with me by letter about a week ago. I met and fell in love with a gorgeous red-haired big-hearted guy named Campbell MacReid. He's Scottish. He's five years younger than me. He's an elementary school teacher, and he is... I'm afraid to say it. I'm afraid if I admit it, put it into words, that it will all fall apart. But I've always been honest with you, so I guess I just better spill it.*

Campbell is my soul mate. There it is. Without effort, without hours of couple's counseling and lists and reading books together and reminders, he gives me what I need because it comes naturally to him. And what I can give him is enough. He's not constantly scolding me for my irresponsibility or making me feel like I can never live up to his standards.

He is young. I mean, younger than me. Is five years a huge amount of time? It doesn't feel like too much. I feel young when I'm with him. Adventurous. Alive.

So, I don't know what the future holds, Greg. While I certainly may return to working at the clinic with you, I have a husband who is Scottish and a teacher, and where we settle will depend on him, too.

Write me soon. Don't use all caps or scold me too much. Remember, you were the one who told me you wanted to see me sparkle again.

Love ya,

Carlie

CHAPTER 31

Date Night

Y ou seem happy today," I remarked, as Campbell squashed me in a big hug on Wednesday morning. He did indeed seem to be especially buoyant. He had cheerfully made breakfast, packed us lunches, swept the kitchen floor, and even watered my garden for me.

"I am," he said. "Today is *the day*, and I have *plans*."

"You do?" I said. I knew exactly what he meant. I don't think I'd ever been so glad to have my period end. Already I felt a sense of anticipation.

"Aye, ye better prepare yourself to be romanced, *Ri-pälle*." Somehow his words made me feel all shivery inside, and he chuckled at the way I squirmed.

"What in the world do you mean?" I asked.

"Well, I realized I've never taken ye on a date," Campbell said. "That didna seem right to me. So, as I said, I have plans." He grinned, appearing extremely proud of himself.

"A date?" I asked, raising my eyebrows at him. "How shall I dress for this date?"

"I think..." Campbell pretended to be contemplating, glancing over at our closet. "I think, um, dressy island wear might be appropriate."

"And when should I be ready for this date?" I asked.

"Let's say, 6 o'clock? Half hour before sunset?"

"Do I need to stay out of the apartment today, or at least this afternoon?" I asked him.

278

"What kind of man do ye think I am?" Campbell said, indignantly. "I take ye on a date to our *kitchen?*"

"It wouldn't be horrible," I said. "It's not like there are any restaurants or theatres to go to."

"Nah," he said. "I have better plans than that." He was giddy, and it was adorable.

Just then there was a knock on the door. Campbell answered it, and we saw a small boy with long black hair flopping in his eyes, shyly looking downward. Campbell squatted down to his level so he wouldn't look so terrifying. The little boy spoke so quietly that I couldn't hear him at all.

"*Kommool*, Abner," Campbell said as he stood up again.

"*Kon jouj*," the little boy said.[1]

Campbell turned back to me. "Looks like you may have to use sign language or the Marshallese-English dictionary today. Sharbella has morning sickness and Abner says she's not going to make it for clinic today."

"That's okay," I said. My heart had sunk momentarily, but I realized it was probably good for me. "You and Sharbella keep on teaching me words, and I made out my cheat sheet for medical terminology, anyway. It'll be good practice for me." Campbell cocked his head and smiled at me admiringly.

Right before he headed out the door for school, Campbell turned back to me, a playful gleam in his eye. "Just so you know, though, with all the work I'm putting into this, I'm *probably* going to expect you to put out tonight."

"*Put out?* What decade were you born in again? That is not gentlemanly at *all*," I retorted indignantly, but then added with a suggestive smile. "But, just so you know, I probably will be very... very... *very...* grateful." It made me laugh when my words appeared to make him shudder as well. "And I imagine I will want to show you."

He stopped and narrowed his eyes at me. "Now that is not fair, Carlie. How am I supposed to make it through the school day thinking about the ways ye might demonstrate your gratitude?"

---

[1] *Kon jouj*: con-zhush´ (you're welcome)

"The same way I'm supposed to make it through the day wondering what you have planned for us," I smiled.

Campbell had been gone about ten minutes when I looked on the kitchen counter and realized he had left his sandwiches behind.

I had been struggling through my patient interviews for about an hour when there was a light tap on the clinic door. It was Riti Botla, Campbell's bright little student.

"Riti!" I said. "Are you okay? *Emetak?*"

"No, Miss Peachay," she smiled. "Meester Mack ask me to come help you a little. He say translating for you will be good practice for my English."

I would have hugged her or at least patted her on the head in gratitude, but Campbell had recently told me (after I'd already made the mistake) that pointing at or touching people on the head is offensive in the Marshallese culture.

Things went much more quickly with Riti's help. I still tried to pay attention to her questions and their answers, but it wasn't nearly as stressful or time consuming. A few times an embarrassed adult would ask her to leave and we'd struggle through the words and definitions for their more grown-up issues, but in general it was much easier with my young translator.

I was finishing up with my last patient when a chuckled murmur passed through the little crowd of ladies gathered under the tree in front of the clinic.

"Why are they laughing?" I asked, trying to remember the Majel words. "*Kōn ta ettōñ?*[1] Is that right?"

"Good, Miss Peachay!" Riti exclaimed encouragingly. "You ask why they are laughing. They say Meester Mack *an lukkuun mōkaj neōm.*[2]"

"Muh gus?" I asked. I knew 'loo-koon' meant very.

"*Mōkaj* is **fast**," smiled Riti.

---

[1] *Kōn ta ettōñ:* cone tah et-tong´ (Why do they laugh?)

[2] *An lukkuun mōkaj neōm:* on loo´-koon muh´-gus nem (has very fast legs)

"And 'nem'?" I asked.

"Legs," Riti said.

"So, they're saying Mr. Mack has very fast legs? That he runs very fast?"

"*Ayet,*" Riti answered. "And the mamas say Meester Mack *kōnaan ipādwaj.*[1] He wants to be with you," Riti was blushing, visible even through her tan, so I assumed there may have been some double entendres in their statement. "*Joñan wōt e maroñ*...As much as he can," she finished.[2]

I couldn't help but smile. We might speak different languages, but they had a good grasp of my husband's intent. I began to wonder whether he'd left his lunch at home on purpose.

"*Iiokwe,*" the ladies started to say, grinning and getting up from their places. "*Kommool tata,* Miss Peachay."

"*Kon jouj,*" I said, waving to them, then locking the clinic door.

I felt hyper-alert as I went into our cabin. With my last glance down the road I had seen that Campbell was nearly to the clinic, loping along on his 'muh gus nem' towards me. I had a feeling sandwiches might not be the first thing on the agenda; in fact, I *really* hoped they weren't. I tossed my panties into the hamper just as I heard the door knob turn.

"Well," Campbell said, shutting the door, looking at me with a question in his eyes.

"Well," I said, turning to him with an inviting smile and a nod.

"I'm trying to make up my mind whether to do it really slowly and savor every second or follow my instinct... which is to eat my sandwiches right here in the kitchen." He grinned as his joke slowly sunk in, the look on my face registering confusion as I realized what he'd said.

"*Sandwiches?*" I asked dryly. Campbell laughed, but then smiled sweetly.

"Oh, I misspoke," Campbell said huskily, stepping closer to me. "To slowly savor every second of making love to my wife, or to ravish her right here in the kitchen."

---

[1] *Kōnaan ipādwaj:* koe-non´ ee-pod´-wadge (He wants to be with you)

[2] *Joñan wōt e maroñ:* sho´-non what ee mah-rong´ (As much as he can)

"How about a compromise?" I suggested, boosting myself up onto the counter behind me. "*Itōk*, Campbell. Come here."

Campbell stepped between my knees, pushing my skirt up as he did, his hands traveling up my thighs.

"Your skin is so soft, Carlie," he murmured into my lips, his fingers stroking circles toward the sensitive skin of my inner thighs.

I gasped unintentionally as he brushed his fingers against my abdomen, and Campbell drew away, eyes wide. "Ye arna wearing any knickers," he grinned, then kissed me more hungrily as he explored further.

"Wait," I whispered. "Too soon. Make me wait. Make me beg for it."

"Aye?" He drew his hand away, circling underneath my skirt to clasp my buttocks, but stepping closer, so I could feel his hip bones pressing against my thighs. I pulled his shirt off over his head and put my hands on his chest, warm and soft with curling hair.

His lips were on my neck, and I squeaked a little as he nibbled on me.

"I think I might have you for lunch instead," he said, chuckling with a deep rumble as I shivered at his words, meeting my lips with his and pressing himself to me as he dug his fingers into the hair at the back of my neck. I started feeling lightheaded.

"Campbell, oh hell, it's time. I can't wait any longer," I said, reaching down to undo his shorts.

He stepped away from me, breathing heavily. "Sorry," he said, with a glint in his eye. "We're saving it for tonight."

"Really?" I said skeptically, drawing my dress off over my head. I wasn't wearing a bra, either.

"Oh, *ifrinn*," Campbell said, looking at me in stunned appreciation. "You're right. I dinna have that much self-control." He unbuttoned his shorts and dropped them to the floor.

Except for our wedding day, I hadn't put makeup on since coming to the island. Sweat and humidity made makeup uncomfortable and impermanent, and the fact that no one else wore it rendered it completely unnecessary. The fresh-faced look made me look younger, but the thought of a date had me bringing out the makeup bag. After that I looked through my clothes, feeling surprisingly jittery as I tried to decide what to wear, even though I was going on a date with my *husband*. There was one slinky wrap sundress that crossed at the bust with a plunging V-neck, and I decided to skip the bra. Even though we'd already had a lunchtime quickie, I had a feeling we weren't finished for the day.

The hair. That was the last, challenging, frustrating thing. Humidity made it curl up more than ever, so I'd take to twisting it into a bun most days. I rarely had time to fuss with it, but today, I felt like it was worth it to take the time. I got my hair wet and pulled out my curling cream, expensive stuff that it was, and worked it through my hair. It had a way of binding the curls together into ringlets instead of crazy frizz, giving them enough weight so they drooped down instead of standing out wildly all over the place.

As I looked at myself in the mirror, I felt only a faint sense of recognition of the girl I saw, but I was quite confident that Campbell would appreciate my efforts.

Six o'clock brought a knock at the door. I hadn't realized Campbell had taken clothes with him to school, but he was dressed in khakis and a nice shirt. His eyes widened at the sight of me and he smiled. I did notice his eyes drift downward and his face flush slightly.

"You look *lovely*, Carlie," he said.

"And you look quite dashing yourself," I responded.

"*Itok, Ri-pālle*," he said, holding out his hand to me and helping me descend the steps, as if we were heading down the stairway into some grand ballroom instead of our coral rock side yard. He led me down the road to the fishing dock on the ocean side. At the end of the dock stood a small table and two chairs, lit by hurricane lanterns set on wooden crates. Campbell pulled out my chair for me, and shortly after we were seated Anni came grinning down the dock carrying two plates which she set before us with a flourish and then left.

On the plates were barbecued chicken, a rice and squash dish, and roasted breadfruit. I felt shy suddenly, and I was grateful to have something to do with my hands, and a place to look other than Campbell's intense gaze.

"Tell me about yourself, Carlie," said Campbell, as if this were a first date. "What brought you out to work for UniServe? And particularly, how did you decide on the Marshall Islands?"

"Well," I said, after uncomfortably finishing the bite of food I'd just taken, also like a first awkward date. "I am a nurse practitioner. From an early age, I always thought I would volunteer for USI. And after feeling like I was in a funk for six months, I decided that now was the time."

"And how did ye choose Arno?"

"I browsed through the options, and honestly, I chose the most primitive, most remote location that happened to also be in the islands."

"Pardon my asking, but why would a young lady such as yourself want *primitive* conditions?" Campbell asked. "You look incredibly stunning tonight."

"Did I dress up too much?" If we had been in character before this, now I was definitely breaking character. "Should I have skipped the makeup?"

"Oh, Christ, no," said Campbell, taking me in with his eyes. "You look gorgeous. I guess I just feel overwhelmed by ye, and for the first time I realize how far up I married."

I scoffed. "As long as I had crazy hair and didn't wear makeup, you felt like we were in the same league?"

"I wasna trying to be *insulting*," he chuckled. "It's just, ye are a *woman*. A *grown* person. And next to ye, I must seem a wee child."

"Don't say that," I said. "There are times I feel like an irresponsible baby next to you too. No need to feel unequal."

"Aye, but ye look so classy!"

I laughed. "Come now. You've met my parents. We're very down-to-earth people."

"I guess I'm not making my question clear," Campbell said, wrinkling his forehead. "I'm just surprised that ye ended up here. That you *chose* the primitive surroundings. There are a lot of nicer UniServe locations. I only ended up here because I'd gotten in trouble wi' the law. It's been good for me, but I dinna ken whether I would have chosen it."

"I wanted the year to *count*, if that doesn't sound too strange," I explained. "It wasn't likely that I'd be able to volunteer again. If I was in a place that was just like a different city, a different America, with accents... that just wouldn't have been enough. Though I have to admit, if there had been a posting in Scotland, I might have actually considered it."

"Would you have?" Campbell asked, appearing pleased.

"I think many Americans find the incredible green of Scotland and Ireland attractive," I responded. "We don't live in a place with so much history; with castles and faeries or leprechauns. I've always considered Scotland kind of *magical*."

We were finishing with our food when I heard a faint sound. Turning toward the island from my seat facing the ocean, I saw a little procession of school children. Several were playing ukuleles and guitars, and four of the little girls wore the grassy skirts of the native dancers. They paraded shyly out onto the dock, and then performed an adorable song and dance for us. Then, just as quickly as they had come, they disappeared into the darkness.

The lamps still lit the area around us, but the sky had darkened and the stars were becoming visible. I was feeling a little chilled as the cool ocean breeze rippled the water and headed over the land.

"Come here, Carlie," said Campbell, reaching for my hand. He led me to the edge of the dock where he sat down and had me sit between his legs. The tide was low enough that our toes barely touched the water, and I leaned back against his warm chest.

"I have a gift for you," he said. I could feel him reaching into his pocket and watched as he brought out a ring box. I was confused, since we already had simple gold wedding rings we'd found in Majuro. He gently opened the lid, holding the box up to catch the light. Inside there were two silver-colored rings with writing on them.

The script did look remarkably *Lord-of-the-Rings*-like, but I resisted the urge to say, "*One ring to rule them all.*" The way Campbell gently picked the smaller ring up out of the box, I realized now was not the time for jesting.

"This set of rings were my ma and da's wedding rings," he said quietly. "My da couldna bear wearing his after she died, and he said she would want for me to have them for my wife one day. Uncle Alistair brought them out after our wedding, and I was just waiting for the right time."

I held my left hand out, but Campbell reached for my right hand instead. "The one on your left hand," he explained, "That one is my ring for you. A humble ring to remind us that we can be both humble and happy, as long as we have each other."

I lifted my right hand to him and Campbell slipped the smooth silver circle onto my third finger. I took the wider ring out of the box and after inspecting the writing, which I discovered was on both the inside and the outside, slid it onto his finger.

"What does it say?" I asked.

"'*Is ann le mo ghraid mise*' on the outside," Campbell said, "and '*Agus is leamsa mo ghràidh*' on the inside." He took a breath. "In Gaelic it means, 'I am my beloved's, and my beloved is mine.'"

"That's from the Bible, right? From the Song of Solomon?" I asked.

"Aye." Campbell traced the circle on my finger, then intertwined the fingers of his right hand with mine so the two rings touched. "I dinna think I'd ever find someone I could love as much as my da loved my ma." He paused. "I'm so glad I was wrong."

I could barely see the rings any more, my eyes swimming with tears as I whispered, "I love you, Campbell."

He wrapped his arms around me. "I love *you*, Carlie."

We sat in silence for a few minutes. I felt overwhelmed by the depths of emotion I was feeling, trying to blink away the tears and swallow to rid myself of the lump in my throat.

"Let's go," I said. "I need you to make love to me."

He stood and helped me up, and we walked hand in hand back home.

The door of our apartment clicked closed behind us, and we were in utter darkness. Campbell was behind me, and with a single step forward he was close enough that I could feel his breath on my hair. I reached toward the light switch, but Campbell stopped my hand firmly.

"No lights," he said. "Let's just do it by touch it this time."

"None?" I asked. "I fixed myself up!"

"And I can remember how lovely you look," Campbell said. "But I want to feel you." As the skin on my arms pricked with goosebumps at his words, he kissed my neck, sending shivers up my spine.

"Come on," he said, leading me through the apartment until we were by our bed.

"How does this dress fasten?" he asked, his hands traveling down my arms.

"It's a wrap dress," I explained. "It ties in the front, and the ties wrap around."

Campbell's fingers found the bow at the front, and he deftly untied it, letting the ties drop so the dress slowly unwrapped and hung from my shoulders.

It was interesting to go by feel. Eric had always wanted lights on; he needed to see me to get turned on. Without light this time, I wasn't worried about how I looked and I was able to focus on sounds and sensations. I found my way to the waistband of Campbell's slacks; instead of unbuttoning them, though, I gently ran my hand down his fly.

A sharp intake of breath told me he liked it. I could feel how excited he was, too, which made me groan slightly.

"Ye like that, do ye?" he asked.

"Yes," I whispered. "I like knowing you want me."

"God, yes, I do," he said. I took my fingers back to the button and undid it, then unzipped his fly, taking advantage of the easier access to lightly stroke him once more.

Campbell gently removed my hands, returning his attention to the front of my dress. Now that the tics were loose, he was able to gently slide the dress off my shoulders.

"I am going to kiss every inch of your body," Campbell murmured, laying me down on the bed. I heard his clothing drop on the floor, and then the mattress sinking down under his weight as he knelt over me.

Starting at my neck, Campbell made good on his promise, kissing, licking, and nibbling my skin until I was panting and writhing in arousal.

"Campbell," I begged. "Babe! Please. *Please.*" I reached down and touched him with my hand, which only made me gasp with anticipation.

He lingered with his lips at my breast, slowly lowering his body onto mine, his abdomen between my legs. Then I heard a chuckle.

"Don't laugh, Campbell!" I groaned. "Are you taking pleasure in torturing me?

"No," he whispered huskily, "It's just that I can actually feel how much you want me."

"What?" I asked, confused and slightly disturbed.

"You are very..." he kissed my breast, "very..." moving upward, he nuzzled my throat, "very..." he kissed me on the lips "wet." With that, he entered me.

Though we had been married barely a week, Campbell and I had been intimate numerous times. This time, however, was different. Despite not being able to see each other, our connection was palpable; I felt almost too much.

The evening had been lovely, his time and attention making me feel open and adored. To receive the gift of his mother's wedding ring demonstrated how much I meant to him, especially considering the beautiful, spiritual sentiment attached to the simple white gold circle.

But for all the times we'd made love, for all the times I had *felt* loved, I had never before said "I love you" to my husband. There had been so many times that it was at the tip of my tongue, or I'd felt like I *should* say it. Campbell had already said it numerous times to me. To say it now didn't feel like pretending, didn't feel like lying.

I didn't know if Campbell had really noticed, but I could feel the change in the way Campbell touched me. He could easily vary between tenderness and taking charge in bed, whichever he sensed I enjoyed the most at the time. But this time he made love to me with such bare intensity that I could sense he *must* have heard.

Afterward Campbell collapsed next to me with a final gasp of amazement. "Carlie," he groaned, "that was *incredible*."

I struggled to dwell in the discomfort of vulnerability and intimacy. "Darn it, Campbell," I said in faux irritation, "I have a policy of *never* sleeping with someone on a first date."

"Well, I *am* your husband," he reasoned.

"Guess I'll have to forgive myself," I chuckled, tucking myself into the comforting crook of his arm.

For a few minutes it was quiet. I could hear the lap of ocean waves from outside, the sound of Campbell's heart rate and breathing returning to normal. But then, he tensed slightly.

"Ye *said* it, Carlie," he murmured quietly.

"I did," I answered. He took in a deep breath.

"I love you," I repeated, and Campbell pulled me close once more.

CHAPTER 32

Getting Settled

W e had fallen asleep in the nude, with Campbell's arm heavy over my side, his left hand cupped around my breast. In the middle of the night, Campbell pressed up against me, quickly making it very clear what was on his mind.

"Campbell," I whispered.

"Hmmm?" He grunted back.

"Are you asleep?" I asked him.

"I thought I was," he said sleepily, nuzzling my neck, "But my body seems to think otherwise."

"Sorry. I thought you were trying to start something," I whispered back, realizing that by waking him up, I was the instigator. "Go back to sleep."

"How can I, wi' your beautiful body next to me?" he groaned, moving even closer to me. "It's like, we've barely finished before I want ye again. I'd have ye now, if ye said yes."

I chuckled. Truth be told, his nearness, the way his leg hair brushed against my thighs, his chest met my shoulder blades, and his erection pressed against my tailbone, I wasn't feeling very sleepy either. When he kissed the tender hollow of my shoulder, breathed across my skin, and then caressed my breast, I felt *completely* awake.

I rolled toward him. "Yes," I whispered.

"*Ifrinn, tha,*" he murmured, pulling me toward him.

"What's that mean?"

"Hell, yes," he chuckled, meeting my lips with his.

Being married to a young, amorous virgin was eye-opening, to say the least. I'd always felt that sex two or three times a week was sufficient with Eric. I couldn't climax every time with him because he didn't respond well to direction or advice during sex. I had calculated that if we achieved that level of frequency, I could be satisfied with one or two orgasms a week.

Campbell woke something up in me. My brain might say, "Oh, I've already had sex today. One time is plenty." But my body plainly disagreed, as I was walking around with the female equivalent of a constant boner. It didn't matter what I was doing, what I was thinking about, or whether I'd just been sleeping; if Campbell put his hands on me, swept my hair aside and kissed my neck, or just suggested with his eyes that he'd like to see me naked, I was powerless to resist him.

The days began to fall into a semblance of routine. Campbell's morning desire often acted as a pleasantly affectionate and arousing alarm clock, followed by shower and breakfast. Sometimes we would pack lunches, but if we hadn't been intimate in the morning, Campbell would head out the door with a grin, saying, "See you at lunchtime." The day was filled with patients, and if none came, research or charting. I made sure I was home at lunch, and then in the afternoon I tried to get in a well child home visit or two each day, trying to walk in one direction or the other—towards Matolen or toward Jabo. And in the evening, we would eat dinner, walk together, write letters, make love, and then sleep.

On our second weekend of marriage, we did laundry together, went spear fishing, showered, and then lazed around in bed all afternoon, alternating between intimacy and sleep. We aired out the house with an hour to go until dinner time while Campbell made pizza dough, and then we had Ewan and Graham over for dinner, finishing up by playing a rousing game of Five Crowns at the kitchen table. Having never played before, I reached the massive score of 340, and good-humoredly suffered through multiple jibes about the inferior female mind.

Sunday morning, Graham and Ewan proudly arrived at our apartment hauling a couch, if you could call it that. They had taken the wooden frame from the single bed they'd removed from our house and assembled it into a couch-like shape. They were very proud of the cushions, which were a joint effort between them and the local mamas, scrapped together from old sheets and fabric. The couch took up a place of honor on one section of wall close to the kitchen table, and after sitting on it, I realized it was a nice addition to our home.

That evening, Campbell and I hung out on the couch, Campbell lying on his back with his head in my lap as he read to me. I loved playing with his vibrant ginger curls, and he practically purred like a cat while I did it.

I nearly had a heart attack when the author mentioned a syringe. "Campbell!" I gasped. He sat bolt upright.

"What?" he exclaimed.

"Sorry," I said. "I just keep forgetting to have the birth control discussion with you."

Campbell lowered his eyebrows. "I thought we already had that conversation. It's one of the less pleasant memories from our honeymoon and as far as I can remember, we decided that was *your* choice and *your* business," he said.

"No," I said, "As far as I remember, we realized that for me, birth control was about more than birth control, that it raised insecurities about infertility. I think we'd be able to have a civilized discussion now."

"But," he interjected, lying his head back down on my lap again. "It *is* your body. I dinna have a right to tell ye what to do."

"You have a right to share your opinion," I said, stroking his forehead. "Because this is also your marriage and your future."

"Hmmm," he said. "Well, can ye lay out your options, then?"

"So, I could use Depo Provera. It's a progesterone shot that lasts about three months. After a time of using it, it can actually cause periods to stop temporarily."

Campbell couldn't hide a small smile. "I canna say that would be bad," he said. "But what are the other side effects?"

"It can cause weight gain, acne, mood changes, and osteoporosis," I said.

He frowned, shaking his head. "And then, how does it affect fertility?"

"Well, fertility can take time to return, even after the medication is supposed to be out of your system. Anywhere from six months to two years."

"And, what has your experience with birth control been?" Campbell asked. "What have you used? Did they cause those side effects?"

"Different ones," I said, "I used birth control pills for a time, and I'm not sure why but they caused sex to be painful for me. I didn't know that was why until I stopped using the pill."

Campbell's wrinkled his forehead, obviously thinking furiously. "Well, I dinna like that," he said. "I couldna have fun knowing it you wouldn't enjoy it as much."

"I mean, Depo Provera might not, but since it lasts for three months, it would be a risk we'd have to take if we chose it."

"What other options do we have?"

"Condoms?" I said, shrugging.

"Where would we get those?" he asked. "I wouldna want to ask Alastair to buy some and send them out here."

"I... *have* some," I said. Campbell wrinkled his nose and looked up at me in surprise. "I didn't *plan* to have sex with anyone," I said, "but Eric thought I'd have trouble staying faithful to him, and I didn't want to risk an STD."

Campbell sat up and stared at me.

"Okay, stop with the judgment, baby," I said.

"Dinna call me names, hen," Campbell said, putting his arm around me. "I know how hard it would be to stop after ye'd had sex. I'm more surprised at Eric. Did he *really* say that to ye? That he thought ye couldna be faithful?"

I nodded. "And in some ways, he was right. I fell in love with you before he broke up with me."

"But ye didna actually *do* anything wi' me," Campbell insisted.

"Well, ye didna actually *try* anything wi' me, either," I said back, trying to mimic his Scots accent. He squeezed me closer to him.

"So, *Ri-pàlle*, none of these sounds good. And ye *do* want to have kids."

"I always have, yes," I said. "And I *am* 27."

"Well, I just ken I want to *make* babies," joked Campbell. "Whether or not I have kids doesna matter."

"No, Campbell, really," I said. "What do you want? You'd mentioned giving it time—six months or a year. I left Eric behind, completely realizing I was putting off pregnancy for 18 months to two years, at least. We could wait the same length of time."

Campbell took my hand and held it in both of his. "Honest truth? I don't want any of those side effects at all. If we were to have a baby, that would be a pretty beautiful side effect. In fact, that's the only one that makes me feel good inside."

I wasn't sure I was interpreting him correctly. "So," I said. "No birth control at all? Will that make you want me less?"

"I dinna think so," said Campbell, standing up and taking me by the hand. "Thank you for asking me, though, Carlie." A small smile played about his lips. "I don't want to make the choice for you, but I'm glad you asked me. So, do ye feel better now?"

"Yes, Campbell," I said, stepping into his embrace. "I think I do."

On Monday at noon, Campbell came dashing through the door, flushed from his noon sprint.

"Campbell," I giggled. "You're so obvious. What excuse are you using with Graham and Ewan for leaving at lunch time? Surely telling them you forgot your lunch only worked once."

"Oh," Campbell said blandly, "I just tell them *Carlie* wants us to eat lunch together. That ye miss me when I'm away." His eyes sparkled, and he tried to hide his grin as he started hiking my skirts up and guiding me toward the bed.

"So you're blaming it on me, then?" I laughed through his eager kisses, as I undid his shorts button and zipper. "Do they believe you?"

"Absolutely not," Campbell exclaimed, gripping the sides of my panties with his hands and pushing them downward. "Especially when I say, 'Carlie gets really *really* hungry at lunchtime."

"You did *not* say that!" I exclaimed indignantly. Campbell lowered me to the bed and slipped my panties off the rest of the way. I propped myself up on my elbows. "That's not fair. I won't be able look them in the eyes now!"

"Aye?" Campbell asked, kneeling by the bed, placing his hands on my hips, and quickly making it clear that *I* was on the menu. "Do ye want me to stay at school for lunch time, then?" He gently kissed my knee, and then traveled up my inner thigh.

"No," I squeaked, lying on my back, eyes wide open. "It's nice when you come ho-oome!"

Just before sunrise on Tuesday morning, I woke up with a strange feeling of foreboding in my gut. I'd forgotten to draw water for my shower, so I was about to head out to the well, wearing my regular night time attire of shorts and tank top.

"Carlie," Campbell said, seriously, "Ye willna go outside wearing that."

"What?" I asked. "It's dark. No one is going to see me."

"Someone might. It's disrespectful to the culture, and I am telling ye that you will not go outside wearing only that."

"It'll be five minutes. I'll be out and back," I said, about to head out the door.

"*Ri-pälle.*" He spoke calmly, but this time he got out of bed and stood to his full height. "Come now. Put on a dress."

"Are you *seriously* trying to tell me what to do?" I stared at him skeptically.

"Aye," he said, stepping forward. Damn, he really was big. And muscular. And he wasn't wearing any clothes. I put my hand on the doorknob.

"Carlie," he sighed. "You are still new to the culture. You are still warring against the things you perceive as backward. But ye are my wife and *I* care whether or not you respect their ways."

"What are you going to do about it?" I scoffed, "You think you're my boss? Think again."

"Well," he said thoughtfully, "I may no' be your boss, but ye arna very big, and I believe I could keep ye from leaving the apartment dressed like that."

"You wouldn't," I said, lifting my chin defiantly.

"Test me," he said, coming up to me with one final step. "You're small enough that I believe my odds of winning are quite high."

The argument between us was stirring something in me. Seeing him fierce and confident, flushed and naked was having the opposite effect I thought it should have. The feminist in me thought his domineering behavior should rouse defiance in me. Instead, it was making me want him. My heart was pounding, not from anger, but desire.

I was pretty sure I knew what would happen if he took hold of me, and it involved nudity and a bed. "*Jiddik niññiñ*," I muttered, testing him.

"I'm a tiny baby?" Campbell responded, an amused expression on his face. "Huh. Ye didna seem to think I was so tiny last night. In fact, I think I heard ye groaning something quite the opposite when you were on top of me."

Just the memory had me going to jelly inside, but I tried to steel my expression and head out the door. When I looked up into Campbell's face, though, I thought I might be in trouble. When I glanced about three feet lower, I *knew* I was.

"*Itōk, Ri-pālle*," said Campbell huskily, reaching his hand toward me.

"I've got to get to work on time," I protested, though I knew it was an empty argument. There was no such thing as "on time" in the islands. A half hour, an hour late—it was still considered fine in the laidback Marshallese culture.

"It won't take very long," Campbell assured me. "I'm ready, and I ken ye will be too, the way my voice keeps making ye shudder and wriggle like that."

He was right, too. Just hearing his voice was enough to make me shiver inwardly. Often when Campbell called me to bed, he didn't even have to touch me before my body started to respond. I was beginning to feel as if I didn't own myself.

"*Kwon itōk ippa, Ri-pālle.* Come wi' me." He took my hand and drew me toward the bed.

I sighed, shook my head, and followed him.

"It's not fair, Campbell," I said, when he had thoroughly made love to me and I was resting in his arms, flushed and satiated. "I'm *powerless* against you. You have the advantage. You make me feel so weak." I was teary; not angry, exactly, but frustrated. I wiped away a tear with a perturbed fist. "It's not fair that you can just *talk* to me and I melt into a puddle." I bit my lip. "It doesn't feel right that even when I've made up my mind to defy you, all you have to do is look at me, reach for me, and I'm your *slave*." I blew out my breath and shook my head in confusion.

Campbell propped himself up on his elbow and looked down into my eyes. "Oh, Carlie," he said, "Do ye not know how much power you have? You could break me with a word. If you denied me yourself, I would shrivel up and die. My mind is filled with ye all day, and any time I wake, ye're the first thing I think of. I want you, yes. I need you. And I'm grateful I can rouse ye so easily," he smiled wryly.

Then Campbell crushed me to himself, kissing me on the forehead. "But as for power, *Ri-pālle?* I have *none.*"

CHAPTER 33

The American

D on't worry about it, Carlie," Campbell urged, out of breath. We'd gotten distracted mid-way through our afternoon letter writing and Campbell was currently practicing his bra-removal skills. But the persistent knock continued, and the little female voice kept calling out "Miss Peachay!"

"It's no use, Campbell," I said, extracting myself from bed and pulling my bra the rest of the way out of the arm holes of my dress. "I can't focus right now." With a discontented grunt, Campbell quickly re-wrapped himself in his sarong and sat back down on the bed as I walked over and opened the door, to find Mina standing there, the little girl who belonged to Jibon and Kabua, our next-door neighbors from across the clinic yard.

"*Amedkan* come," the little girl said.

"What do you need?" I asked in Marshallese.

"*Amedkan atok*," she said, pointing down the road.

"You want me to come?" I asked. I was ready to reach for my shoes.

"No," Campbell corrected me casually, looking up from the book he had picked up. "She's saying an American *is coming.*"

"I just can't get the grammar straight," I laughed. "What American?" I asked, turning back to Mina. "*Won en ej atok?*"[1]

---

[1] *Won en ej atok:* wan en edge a-talk´ (Who is it who comes?)

"A man," she said. "He look for *Carlie Beecher*," she said, enunciating all the sounds. "That you, Miss Peachay, right?"

"Who is he?" I asked. "*E metak? Is he hurt?*"

"No, he no hurt. He say him name *Edik*."

"Ed dik?" I asked

"She can't mean Eric, can she, *Ri-pālle?*"

I felt like I'd been punched in the gut, like I was going to vomit; nauseated and terrified and guilty. "*Eric* is here? Why is Eric *here?*"

I looked out in the road, and I saw him, walking with his familiar lanky stride, looking around curiously. He appeared to be in no huge rush, but he saw me, and he lifted his hand in a wave, a wide smile brightening his face.

Campbell had come over and was standing behind me. He put his hands on my shoulders.

"Oh, my God, Campbell," I said. "Stay here."

I descended the three steps and walked toward Eric as quickly as I could. He didn't have a suitcase with him. He was wearing a hat, loafers, shorts, and a tropical print shirt. What a *ri-pālle*, I thought with a chuckle, and then I felt sick again.

"Carlie!" Eric exclaimed, rushing to me. He put his arms around me and bent to kiss me; I turned my cheek to him. My heart was thudding in my ears.

"Why are you here, Eric?" I asked, though I already knew why.

"Carlie," he said, holding me about the waist. "I am so sorry. I was *such* an asshole."

I couldn't think of anything to say, so I stood there dumbly, my heart pounding. Back in the house behind me was my husband of 12 days; in front of me my fiancé of 5 years. Well, ex-fiancé. No matter what happened, this was not going to end well. I was breathing shallowly. I wasn't certain my legs were going to keep working.

"It was a shitty thing to do, breaking our engagement. I'm so sorry." He suddenly looked worried, as if perhaps I didn't even know why he was there.

"Yes, I got your break-up letter," I said. I took a breath. "And I'm assuming the reason you're here, having travelled thousands of miles, is that you got *my* letter?"

"Carlie," he said. I met his repentant, familiar eyes, and my heart broke. "When I got your letter, I realized I couldn't wait for another letter to get to you, and then for your response to get back to me. I needed to talk to you. I needed to *see* you."

"Eric, I love you," I said. "And I have loved you for years, but..."

"Babe," he said earnestly, "if you were serious in your letter, and I think you were..." He took my hand. "I'm here to ask you two questions."

I started shaking my head, whether in disbelief or to try to stop what was coming next. I turned woodenly toward the apartment, and Eric walked with me.

"Will you please come home?" he asked, reaching to take my hand as we walked side by side. "Life just isn't right without you." He pulled us to a stop, turned to me, and looked in my eyes, "And will you please let me finally exchange your engagement ring," he lifted my hand, kissing my fingers, but not breaking eye contact to notice the change on my hand, "for a wedding ring?"

How had he not noticed the horrified expression on my face? "It's *too late*, Eric," I said.

"How can it be too late, Carlie?" Eric responded, clasping my hand to his chest. "I've never known you to hold a grudge before. In your letter, you said you recognized how wrong this choice had been—that it was cruel and selfish to leave me. How is it too late?"

I shook my head. I was trembling. "You're *too late*," I repeated, gesturing up at the door of our apartment, where Campbell stood, arms crossed over his muscular chest like a red-haired bouncer at a tiki bar.

"Who the hell is that?" asked Eric.

"That's...*Campbell*," I said, in a tone that said of course Eric should know who he was.

"Who the hell is Campbell?" Eric asked, looking up at Campbell, shirtless, sarong-clad. Realization started to flush over his face. He looked at me, then back at Campbell.

Now Eric looked as horrified as I was feeling. "Damn, Beecher, you can't keep it in your pants, can you?"

"You will not talk to my wife like that," said Campbell, taking a step down the stairs, his eyes glinting blue and angry.

Eric stared at Campbell, open-mouthed. "You are fucking kidding me. Tell me he's kidding me." He turned to me again, eyes wide. "You got *married*?" I stood there dumbly, still astonished that he was on Arno, that he was next to me. I wanted to run away, leaving the two men to work it out between the two of them with their fists, but that would be cowardly.

"When? *When* did you get married?"

"You *broke up with me*, Eric," I started.

"*When* did you get *married*?" he repeated, desperation creeping into his voice.

"A week and a half ago," I said.

"You *just* wrote me, Carlie. I *just* got a letter from you five days ago where you asked me to forgive you and you told me that I was the most important thing in the world to you. I found someone to teach my courses, made plane and hotel reservations, and headed out here. Explain yourself, please." Eric's jaw clenched, and a blood vessel in his temple was visibly throbbing.

I couldn't think clearly, but I tried to get some words out. "Almost two weeks ago I sent that letter in the morning. I was ready to commit to us again. I was willing to forgo my friendship with Campbell for the sake of our relationship. But then your break-up letter came that evening. I was devastated, but your choice was clear. I didn't have any reason to believe you would change your mind."

"That still doesn't explain it," Eric insisted. "I *still* don't understand it. I broke up with you, and you got MARRIED? I broke up with you, and days later you get fucking *married*?" He was shaking his head in astonishment, staring at me with disgust.

"It's not that simple, Eric," I said.

"No? It could have been *way* simpler, Carlie. Couldn't you just suck his dick or let him fuck you without having to *marry* him?"

The words had barely gotten out of Eric's mouth when a ruddy blur passed me on my left and Eric was on his back on the ground, Campbell standing beside me, shaking his hand in pain.

"I *said*," he intoned fiercely, towering over Eric, "Ye canna talk to my wife like that."

"You bastard," said Eric, pushing himself to a seated position and wiping blood from his nose. "She's only been here for weeks. She and I have been together for years. You have *nothing* in comparison to what we had. You're taking advantage of a woman who's suffering from culture shock."

"Seems to me, ye're the one taking advantage of the woman," Campbell said sternly. "Keeping her hanging on, not marrying her, year after year. A woman deserves stability and commitment. You werena willing to provide it for her. I am."

"I'm right here, dammit!" I exclaimed.

Eric was working on standing up. Campbell offered him his hand, and Eric warily grabbed it, stood, took two steps back, and then said, "Would it be possible to talk to you, Carlie, without this ginger giant punching me in the face?"

"I just helped ye up, man," said Campbell, scoffing. "I'm no' a monster. If you can keep yourself civil, ye needna worry about any more violence." He looked at me. "Do ye want me to stay, Carlie, or would you like me to give the two of you a chance to talk?"

"Thanks, Campbell," I said. "I think it would probably be better if you weren't here."

"Do ye want the apartment?" Campbell asked. "I can go visit Ewan and Graham. Or catch fish for supper."

"Supper," I said, thankful for his forethought. I turned to Eric excitedly. "The fish here is the best stuff ever. Better than any seafood restaurant you've ever been to."

I realized how quickly my sense of familiarity towards him had come back, but Eric did not look equally warm and welcoming.

"I don't want to visit you in the apartment where you've been fucking this man," hissed Eric.

"*Stop*, Eric," I said.

"Making love with... her *husband*," corrected Campbell, his hand on my back a centering source of calm. He looked fierce and angry, but he was gentle with me even in his fierceness.

"Please," I said quietly, urging Campbell back into the apartment.

"*Husband*," scoffed Eric. "What do you do to get married out here? Run around a coconut tree three times and throw some sand over your shoulder?

"No," said Campbell, stopping in the doorway and turning back to us, a clear look of confidence and a vindictive glint in his eyes. "Carlie's parents came over from Guam, and Jeff married us." I winced at his words, knowing how much they would wound Eric. He hadn't even said, 'her dad,' or 'Major Beecher.'

Eric turned to me. "The Major married the two of you? Your mom and he approved?" He was dumbfounded and stood there, mouth gaping like a fish. Suddenly a light came on in his eyes. "You're pregnant," he exclaimed.

"No one gets married just because they get pregnant anymore," I said. "And, no."

Before he closed the door, Campbell raised his eyebrows at me. "You okay?" he mouthed. I nodded.

"Shall we sit?" I asked. I would have taken Eric's hand and led him, but I couldn't touch him right now. I walked toward the lagoon, leading us to the grassy area above the beach. I tucked up my skirts and sat, leaving a spot for Eric next to me. He wouldn't sit, though, and stood staring out at the gorgeous turquoise water.

"Carlie," he said, closing his eyes, breathing slowly. "What the *fuck?*"

I shook my head. "Go ahead, Eric, talk," I said. "I can't even think right now."

"Seven years, Carlie. Seven years." Eric stared out toward the islands on the other side. "We weren't married, no, but I was committed. Did it really matter so much to you that we weren't married, that you run into the arms of this infant?" He saw the look on my face. "Sorry. I'll try not to be insulting. What *happened?*"

"It wasn't just that we weren't married, Eric," I said. "You *broke up* with me." I looked at him, hoping he could read my heart. "I don't hate you, but you were *cruel*. And those had already been my hardest few days out here, even before I read your letter. Who was I supposed to run to but Campbell? He was my best friend out here."

"But, marry him?" Eric said. "Did you not still see a chance for us?"

"Your letter left me in little doubt that you didn't."

"Still," Eric was shaking his head in bewilderment. "People don't get married that fast. They date. They get to know each other. They get intimate."

"I was going to be fired," I said, "because I spent the night at Campbell's house. It went against UniServe cultural guidelines, and the head wanted to send me home."

"So, I broke up with you, you slept with him, got in trouble for it, and then you married him?"

"I didn't sleep with him," I insisted. "Whatever you think of him, he's not like that."

"You expect me to believe that a young guy like that wouldn't take advantage of a beautiful woman who needed comfort?"

"He was a virgin when we got married, Eric," I stated quietly.

Eric seemed truly taken aback. "You had never slept with him and you married him? So this is like a green card marriage, isn't it? You just married him to save yourself. So, get the damn marriage annulled, and come home and marry me." He started walking toward the road and I followed him.

I was feeling confused. Seeing Eric was bringing back countless memories of years together. Vacations, dinners with friends, both of us pursuing our educations, homework at the kitchen table. Watching movies on the couch, sharing secret jokes, making love, arguments, resolutions. Six New Year's Eve kisses, six Christmases, four engagement anniversaries, countless times sitting in the bathroom together while we waited three minutes for results. Shared purchases, shared pictures, musicians we both liked, concerts we'd attended. *I didn't even know what kind of music Campbell liked.* I felt like I was going to hyperventilate.

"I need to think," I said, finally.

"Well, I feel like a fool," said Eric turning back toward me as we reached the white gravel of the road. "But I'm not leaving until we really talk this through. I'm going to walk back to the Iroij's house, where the truck dropped me off. We will wait for you for an hour, then we're going to go back to my hotel in Arno Arno. Come and meet me, pack a bag and you can stay with me if you want. The room has two twin beds. We need to talk about this in a place where I don't feel like he's looming over me."

I watched Eric walk away down the white coral road, fell on my knees, and vomited in the grass.

"*Mo ghràidh*," Campbell said. He was holding me in his arms, running his fingers through my hair. He helped me stand up, and then he lifted me, carried me into our apartment, lay me down on the bed and curled himself behind me, wrapping me in his arms.

I pulled away, stood up, and peeled off my clothes. "Make love to me please, Campbell," I begged. "I feel like I'm going to break."

Campbell looked pained, though he did unwrap his sarong and pulled it over us as he curled up with me. "Wait just a minute," he said, as I reached for him. "What's in your heart right now? What has he said? What have you decided?"

"I can't talk, Campbell, please," I said. He understood me then, and gently moved over me, whispering and caressing me, until I urged him inside. Even then he moved inexorably gently; but slowly both of us clung to each other with more desperation, as if trying to convince ourselves that we were still together, still okay. Even when we finished I held on to him tightly, not letting him go.

"Carlie, you're crying," Campbell whispered. "Why?"

"I don't know," I sobbed.

"Your tears tell me you feel guilty and torn. You're afraid that ye're going to hurt one of us or the other. Ye canna base your choice on not wanting to hurt anyone. It's impossible. And Eric's right, ye ken. He has a far greater claim on you. Ye might actually be married in the eyes of God. On Arno, too," he said, with a faint hand gesture indicating the island. "Common law marriage is accepted, expected even. Sometimes young couples don't get legally married until they have a child."

"But, Campbell," I protested. "We have something special together. How can you say I should even consider leaving you, losing this?"

"He probably considers our relationship a kind of *affair*," said Campbell. "Affairs often feel good and special. And ours may be a hallowed, blessed, *married* affair, but an affair nonetheless. I confess I wanted ye. So badly I was blind to the truth that it might not truly be over with Eric. So selfish I would keep ye here; tie ye down."

He shook his head. "I should have sent ye back. Or at the least," he smiled wryly, "encouraged ye to take yourself home. I know by now you're a woman that willna be ruled by a man. But perhaps you should have waited or gone back to Eric—to see what was salvageable."

"Maybe," I said. "Maybe I should have given it more time. But I didn't have that time if I wanted to stay here."

"Carlie," said Campbell, holding me closer. "You have to stop justifying it and truly think—have ye made a mistake?"

"*This* is not a mistake, Campbell," I wept. "*We* are not a mistake. And we're married, anyway. That's a legal contract."

"I've been thinking, and there is a way out for you," said Campbell. "You didna enter this marriage truly thinking we would have children. And if ye also entered the marriage without the intent of eternal commitment, it can be annulled by the Catholic Church. The Catholic marriage covenant is taken when both parties enter with the commitment to be together forever, with an openness to creating new life."

"Campbell," I said. "I don't...I can't..."

"Carlie, *I* need you to go to Arno Arno with Eric. You need to talk to each other, far enough away from me that ye don't feel the burden of this place where we connected, and that Eric doesna feel the pressure of my presence."

"But..."

"If you choose me, then come home. If you decide to go back to the States with Eric, send word. I will pack up your things and send them to you on Majuro, or to Denver. Dinna come back. I canna imagine my heart could stand seeing ye again."

"But, Campbell," I interjected.

"You need to decide with a clear mind, Carlie. Now that ye know Eric wants ye still, you must make the choice knowing both that I love you, *and* that Eric wants ye, too. And he has the greater claim."

"What if I don't want to?"

Campbell leveled his gaze at me, grasping me by the shoulders. "I canna stay married to ye in good conscience if you don't at least think this through. I dinna want you to resent me in years to come for holding you back. But Carlie, I love you more than anything. And I vowed to love you forever." He closed his eyes, then, and leaned his forehead to mine. "I dinna want to lose you," he whispered, "but I love you enough to let you go."

CHAPTER 34

The Hotel

Eric and I didn't talk on the trip to Arno Arno. Campbell had packed my suitcase for me as I sat dumbly on our bed. A couple of dresses, panties and bras, a swimsuit, shorts and tank tops. As I watched, Campbell had hesitated in front of the dresser. "What do you wear to bed with him?" he asked quietly. My heart nearly broke.

"Don't make me go, Campbell," I begged.

"I'm no' *making* ye go," he said. "It is your choice. But ye'd regret it if ye didna go."

"Campbell, we are married now," I said. "Shouldn't that trump everything else?"

"Carlie," Campbell said quietly. "Think about it. Would you have married me if Eric hadna broken up wi' ye?"

"Not a fair question, Campbell," I said, shaking my head in distress.

"Isn't it? Just because I ken the answer, doesna mean it's a bad question to ask. Because now he's taken it back," Campbell said. "Now he doesna *want* to be broken up. And now you need to decide—do ye want to not be married?"

I shook my head sadly. I knew he was right; I had to think it through and truly make a choice.

Now I winced at the memory and turned away from Eric so he couldn't see my tears. *Campbell would have seen,* I thought. *He would have moved next to me. He would be holding me by now.*

I looked out across the vivid blue water of the lagoon, thinking about how Campbell had stuck in my snorkeling gear. "You should take him snorkeling," he'd said. "Give him a taste of the islands since he's come out here."

"Who *are* you?" I asked him. "Eric's trying to steal me away from you!"

"Lass," Campbell said, an ironic smile on his face, "I canna fault the man, and I really canna hate him. He saw the same thing in ye that I have, and he's finally acting as I thought he should this whole time. *I'd* follow ye to the gates of hell, ye ken," he said, shrugging.

"Just to the gates?" I asked, unable to let a joke pass by.

"Well, ye dinna think I need to enter hell to *experience* it, do ye?" Campbell asked, turning away from me, choking out the last few words. I had gone to him then, wrapping him in my arms and crying with him. We held each other in a rocking dance of goodbye.

I had suddenly noticed my clutter everywhere and I had cleaned compulsively, putting everything back in order, straightening the bed, putting books back on the shelf. I even organized the shoes, matching each pair and putting them next to each other by the door, Campbell's worn flip-flops, my sandals, the tennis shoes Campbell had started taking to school so he could jog home at lunch. I couldn't rid myself of the lump in my throat.

With ten minutes to spare, I stood next to my suitcase at the door. We were both red eyed. I was panicky, breathing heavily; I felt like I was going to throw up again.

I had put my hand on the doorknob when Campbell let out a guttural, "No, Carlie!" He pulled me into his arms, clinging to me, pressing me to his heart.

"I canna let ye go yet," he wept. He lifted me and carried me to the kitchen counter. I needed him, he needed me; we both knew it. With my panties hanging around my ankles, he dropped that damn sarong on the floor and took me again. No foreplay, just his mouth desperately on mine, and him filling me, claiming me.

"Harder, Campbell," I begged. He lifted me, lay me down on the wood floor. With the increased leverage of his weight and gravity, Campbell obeyed me, driving himself into me until the sensations removed anything from my mind but him. I couldn't tell when it started, so lost in the urgent 'us,' but when Campbell cried out, I was already clenching and spasming around him.

Campbell offered me a towel when he finally pulled himself away, but I rebelliously pulled my panties back up, as if insisting "I'm yours, and here's the evidence."

He had clutched me to him for one final embrace. "I love you," I had sobbed.

"I love *you*," he had insisted, eyes wet as well.

He had picked up my suitcase and carried it for me the half mile to the Iroij's house in Ine, almost until we reached the truck. Then he stopped, and turning toward me, took my face in his hands, kissed me firmly, and then leaned his head against mine. With one final kiss on my forehead, he had turned and walked away.

Turning back to the truck bed I sighed, seeing Eric's loafers. I glanced up at him then. He was watching me, eyebrows lowered.

"Are you okay, Carlie?" He asked. "It's just to talk. I'm not kidnapping you."

I wanted to throw myself off the truck and start walking back home, but I'd promised Campbell I would go through with it. I would talk. I would listen to what Eric had to say. And then I would decide.

The nine miles to Arno Arno took a half hour to drive. With the ruts and bumps, speedy travel was impossible.

The hotel was a very plain little box-like building. Eric carried my suitcase in for me, and we climbed the stairs to a stark room with a kitchenette and three single beds, made up with plain white sheets. My first thought was to ridiculously muse, "Oh, there were enough beds for Campbell to come." Incredibly the bathroom had flush toilets and an actual shower.

"I'm not ready to talk, yet," I said. "Would you like to go snorkeling? We have probably an hour until sundown."

I pulled my swimsuit and swim shorts out of my suitcase and retreated to the bathroom to change. (The ugliest swimsuit, I noticed with a grin, the one that didn't show *any* cleavage—and the longest shorts). When I came out, Eric was just pulling up his shorts. He turned, and I commented without thinking, "Oh, have you been working out?" His chest and abdominal muscles had lost some of their academic softness. He smiled and his shoulders squared.

We went out to the *iar*, where I gave him an impromptu geology lesson on the formation of atolls, showed him how to spit in his mask and rub it with leaves, and then we sloshed out until the water was deep enough to submerge our faces. I reached for Eric's hand, and there was something comforting about having him next to me as we swam, something special about showing him a part of my world. I inwardly blessed Campbell for his forethought and suggestion, grateful that Eric and I were currently incapable of talking. I tried to calm and center myself, listening to the raspy Darth-Vaderish echo of my breath through the snorkel. And I tried to think—what the hell was I going to say to Eric?

After snorkeling, I stood in the shower for a delicious five minutes of warmth, luxuriating in the ability to shampoo and condition my hair without doing countless squats to scoop up lukewarm water to pour over myself.

In the hotel dining room they served us a simple supper of fish and coconut rice. I described to Eric how the rice was made, and told him a little about Anni, the coconut grating bench, and even the "Come see the miracle," story. Of course I left off his break up letter waiting at home for me. And then we went back upstairs.

Eric sat down on one of the beds, and I sat on the one across the room from him. His hair was still wet, and there were small dark circles on his tee shirt where he had missed spots with his towel.

He looked at me sadly as I hugged a pillow to my chest.

"I already fucked this up, didn't I? I've been harsh," he said. "I've been insulting. I'm sorry. I just... this has not been anything at all like I thought it would be."

For a moment, I considered what Eric had probably expected. That he would come out to the island and I would be overjoyed to see him. He imagined finally setting a date and my delighted response. Perhaps he thought I'd be relieved to be going back home with him; I'd said it was so much harder than I'd expected when I wrote him. He could have anticipated

311

many things: a flurry of wedding plans, making love again, no longer being alone.

Eric had never been one to cry. I might have seen him tear up once or twice in the seven years of our relationship. But he was weeping now. "Carlie," he said, the lines on his face deepened by emotion. "I miss you. I miss *us*. My life is not right without you there. What did I do that made you leave me? What was missing? What was *I* missing?"

Looking at his familiar face, the face of a man I had loved for years, I longed to comfort him. And I realized I could probably do it. I could walk over to him, undress, and stand in front of him, let him kiss me, touch my body...I could easily go down on him...I would probably even enjoy it. For the first time in our relationship, though, my heart knew it was wrong. I didn't want to be unfaithful to Campbell. And so I sat where I was, and I didn't get up.

"Tell me, Carlie," said Eric finally. "Tell me what it is that this kid has that I didn't."

"He's twenty-two, Eric," I said. "Can you just stop insulting him? When you do, you're insulting me too, and it's *not* going to help."

"Dammit, Carlie, I'm sorry," he said. "I feel *emasculated*. He's so big and muscular, and that sarong didn't leave much to the imagination. I know I broke up with you, but it feels like you cheated on me. What is it, then? What would make you marry someone you'd known such a short time?"

"Campbell satisfies my *soul*," I said finally.

I pictured him then, his good-humored face, eyes twinkling at me, his muscular chest where I'd rested my cheek many times. His arms wrapped around me, the way I felt in his embrace, as if nothing could harm me. I sighed.

Eric laughed bitterly. "Your *soul* is satisfied? That just means he's giving you lots of oral."

I rolled my eyes. "Oh my god, Eric, don't be an ass. Campbell was a virgin when we got married. He didn't go down on me before I married him. And I *didn't* marry him based on sex."

"You know I can tell when you're lying, Carlie, don't you?" Eric said, the corners of his mouth rising slightly.

I shook my head. "I didn't say I wasn't *attracted* to him. But I didn't marry him because he impressed me sexually. We did nothing before we got engaged, and even then it was pretty benign over-the-clothes stuff."

"Good for you, staying celibate for the *three* days you were engaged before you got married..." Eric's voice was laced with scorn; which I probably deserved, thinking about a certain desk in a certain classroom.

I looked directly at Eric. "Eric, you need to know that in no way is this a referendum on you as a sexual partner. You're an excellent *lover*, Eric. You were always generous and skilled."

"Then what is it about? Because you seem to think you have some deeper, *real* reason you married this boy...*sorry*." He shook his head in apology; it seemed impossible for him to restrain himself from name-calling.

"The real reason, Eric? I didn't realize it at the time Campbell and I got married, but I have realized it since then. You may have been a good lover, but I didn't feel *loved*."

Eric stared at me.

"I can tell this hurts you, and I'm sorry," I said. "But can you really tell me that our relationship was enough for you? Did you truly feel loved and fulfilled?"

"Our life was fine, Carlie."

"It wasn't fine for me," I said. "I felt empty. I needed something more."

"This is just like you," Eric said. "You make decisions with your heart instead of your brain. So he fulfills you... physically. I'm trying to believe you that it's not about sex. But you really think that's enough to base a relationship on? A marriage? You'll have to spend a lot of time hugging and holding each other—because you'll make decisions based on your feelings and everything will fall apart when you blaze into every decision too fast. You'll have all the hugs you need, but there'll be no one to be the voice of reason, the calming, measured influence."

"Did you *like* being the voice of reason for me?" I asked.

"No. I hated it. It *sucked!*" For a single instant, it looked like something was getting through to Eric.

"Well, maybe I don't *want* you to be my parent, to look down on me. I don't want being with me to be a burden. Because I am not a burden to Campbell."

Eric was silent, considering me with serious eyes.

"The question is, Eric, did I fill your soul? Did you feel complete with me, or just better? Just not lonely? Because with Campbell I finally feel satiated. Full."

"That's hard to believe. You were always so damn needy," said Eric. "Always wanting so much. 'You need to hold me more, Eric. You need to touch me more, Eric. You need to make love to me more, Eric.'"

"Needy?" I said. "Do you consider it being needy for humans to need oxygen?"

Eric looked at me skeptically. "No. Because humans need oxygen to stay alive."

"Well, I need affection and attention and time for my heart to stay alive," I replied. "And no matter how many times I reminded you or asked for what I needed, you wouldn't, or couldn't, give it to me. But with Campbell I don't even have to ask him. For him affection comes as naturally as breathing or eating."

Eric was glaring at me. "He'll cheat on you, you know. If he's this physical you won't be enough for him. You're older than him. Someday he'll decide you aren't young enough or beautiful enough or adventurous enough for him."

"Not fair, Eric," I said. "You can't know the future. And sexual faithfulness matters enough to Campbell that he stayed a virgin until he was twenty-two."

Eric scoffed. "What does virginity mean nowadays, anyway? There's still oral and hand jobs and masturbation and porn."

I cocked my head at Eric. It wasn't worth arguing with him; he wouldn't believe me anyway.

We talked for hours, rehashing the same few points—why wasn't Eric enough, and why did being with Campbell fulfill my needs? Finally, exhausted, I put on a loose dress to sleep in. I was about to crawl into bed, when Eric came over to me.

"I want to kiss you, Carlie," Eric said. "So kiss me, and then tell me you feel nothing for me anymore."

He pressed his lips to mine, his palm firm on the small of my back, his pelvis tilted toward me, clearly indicating he still desired me. When he gently licked my lips with the tip of his tongue, I pulled away.

"I love you, Eric," I said, through tears. "Just not the same way anymore. I'm married to Campbell, and I love my husband. I wish you all the best, and I hope you find someone who fills your soul."

"Okay, babe," Eric said wearily. He hugged me tightly for a minute more and then released me. "I'll accept it. Now, just sleep, Carlie," he said. "The truck is scheduled to return in the morning and I'll take you back tomorrow."

I tossed and turned restlessly, but it wasn't very long before I heard the soft, even breathing that meant Eric was asleep. I rolled over onto my side.

When it first came to mind, I couldn't tell whether it was a dream or a memory.

Eric had raised his eyebrows at me. "Again?" he had asked. "We just did it yesterday."

I had been wearing an adorable lace camisole with boy short panties underneath. Before coming downstairs, I had looked in a mirror. I looked damn fine, my perky breasts heaped up above the lacy bodice, the boy shorts cheekily showing just enough of my fabulously round booty, if I said so myself.

"I've really got to focus on this chapter, babe," he had said. "My deadline is a week from today."

*I had gone upstairs muttering to myself bitterly, "How do you say no to **this**?" But after I'd spent a little time appreciating myself in all my adorable sexiness and I didn't feel frustrated anymore, I changed into pajama pants and a tank top.*

I hadn't finished the dishes from dinner, so I headed downstairs. Standing at the sink, I'd heard voices coming from Eric's office. Voices, and sounds. Whimpering, panting, grunting, groaning sounds.

I felt nauseated as I padded barefoot down the hallway.

Eric was in front of his computer screen, his face contorted, eyes closed.

"Babe?" I said quietly. He slammed his laptop shut, as if that could hide what he was doing.

And he had the same excuse as always. It wasn't me; he was stressed about his deadline. It was too much work to have sex; he just needed the stress release. Never mind that I was about as active and generous a partner as a man could get. Never mind that I needed the connection, the touch. Never mind that if he'd told me how he was feeling and that he needed a stress release, I could have made his eyes roll back in his head with the things I could do with my mouth and hands.

I couldn't judge. After all, I masturbated, too. But it was never a replacement for being with him, never as fulfilling, and I would never choose it over being together.

I wanted Campbell, then, desperately. His innocence, his devotion, his faithfulness, his wisdom, his kindness, his strength. Tomorrow would not be soon enough.

So I strapped on my sandals, and crept downstairs.

CHAPTER 35

Hey, Uncle Ferguson!

I can't write, Uncle...I can barely even think clearly, so I hope you'll be fine with a tape recording. That these things even exist anymore is a wonder, what with phones and iPods. But with no way to send a digital file, this is what you get. Break out the tape player and prepare yourself...it's a rambling mess!

Campbell

.....*static*... Hey, Uncle Ferguson! Man, I wish ye were here. I need someone to talk to, so this will have to do. I thought... that when my ma died, *that* was the hardest I could cry. But then Da left, and that seemed even worse, because I blamed myself, and I didna have anyone to hold me... or hug me..... *sniffling... nose blowing....* Uncle, the pain I'm in right now... I can scarce believe I'm still alive. Like... pain like this should kill me. *This. Pain. Should. Kill. Me.*

I dinna drink very much out here. There's no' much to drink, first of all... Arno's officially a dry island, meaning they don't sell it here. People bring it over from Majuro or make their own version of moonshine. But I'm a teacher, and I canna spare either the poor decisions *or* the hangovers.... we didna even have champagne at our wedding. Something about Carlie's parents not drinking? Not sure.... but I found some of this whisky ye gave me when ye visited.... maybe it'll help me forget...... *swigging drink... sharp intake of breath.... cough, cough...* wow, I really canna handle my liquor anymore......

Wi'out Carlie, it's like my heart is gone....... *footsteps heading away, then coming back......* Sorry, thought I heard something..... Have ye ever been in love, Uncle? I don't know if ye've ever told me about being in love.... I thought I loved Alana.... hell, that was just my cock talking..... I don't think I was ever in love before this. Not this gut-deep, love-sick longing. Not this feeling that I would sacrifice life itself to be with someone... cause I would, I'm serious... if she needed a blood transfusion and it would kill me to give it... *chuckle*.... well, that doesna make sense...maybe I'd risk my life as long as it meant I could be with her *longer*... but really, even if it meant I would die, I would sacrifice myself for her sake.

Hmmm, I canna decide whether this is more like confession or talking to myself, except at confession I was usually just telling Father Kelly about how many times I'd had impure thoughts... *countless*... and how many times I'd abused myself... *fewer than that, but I always cut the number in half*... as far as confessions go, here's one.... I've spent the last hour since Carlie left curled up on the floor, sobbing my heart out. I dinna feel like a man right now. Men are stronger than this. Aren't they?

Carlie's gone. I ken she loves me, or I thought she did. And I want to believe that tomorrow I'll see her coming down the road, coming home to me. But that wouldna be right. So I'm preparing myself for the worst... *cough... sniffling... cough*.... God, I'm not doing very well at keeping these emotions in check. Maybe if I just talk about getting to know Carlie.....

So I told ye a little about Carlie in my last letter, and I mentioned her before in passing. I told ye there was a new UniServe nurse, and I ken I've told ye how I lusted after her... *sigh.... groan.... A Dhia*. I wanted her so bad.... *chuckle*.... Ye ken, she had her hands in my trousers in the first ten minutes after I met her. I told ye about that, didn't I?... *laughter*.... How I was wearing swim trunks when I had that horrific boating accident?... clumsy arse that I am.... She offered to cut them off, but I've told ye how hard it is to get clothes out here. I tried to get my shorts off, but it hurt too bad. So she offered to help me, all casual, like, (*high pitched, sexy*) 'I'm a nurse!' ... *laughter*... And I could see the way she looked at me, too. She reached for the drawstring and suddenly I realized it was double-knotted. So she knelt down in front of me, her hands in my shorts practically, and I prayed, 'Please, God, don't let me get a hard-on right now. Not with her face so close to me.' Good thing I was in so much pain....

Can you believe I hugged her? Dinna ken if that's typical doctor patient behavior, but she was sad and lonely. Oh, wait, that wasn't until *after* she took out my stitches... *hmmmm*.... I'm telling this all wrong, Ferguson. The hug was the next day, I think. Or was it that night? It all gets mixed up in my mind. She came to check on me, and brought us dinner, some strange salty American dish. We've had it since, and I kinda like it, but I would have even eaten *dog food* if she'd cooked it; I was so gone on her already...

Ewan and Graham were arses and wouldna walk her home, even with me injured. But I wouldna have missed it for anything.... I walked her the mile back to her house that night, and when I said goodbye to her at her door, I could see this fragility in her eyes. She was lovely and lonely and hurting. I'd walked away from her apartment after saying goodnight and I was kicking myself, thinking, 'Campbell, ye bastard, she needed a hug!'..... (I'm pretty sure it was the day I was hurt, because my arse was still hurting something awful.) But I turned myself around and walked back to her house, thinking this was stupid and she was going to laugh at me.

But I knocked on her door and asked if she needed a hug. And her face just crumpled, and she collapsed into my arms... this perfect sweet thing. And I knew she needed to be held, so I went inside her apartment (going completely against UniServe guidelines) and I sat down and I took her in my arms while she cried. And she was wearing these tiny shorts, barely more than underwear, and a tank top.... *deep breath out...* I got *so* turned on.... she saw me looking at her boobs, too, man... that was bad... But I was so turned on that she totally noticed and got off my lap. And of course by now, she'd told me she was engaged. So I was sitting in her apartment with a raging erection wearing a sarong, of all things. I'll have to tell ye about the sarong another time. But she made this silly joke, and she didna seem offended, didna seem disgusted by me..... *chuckling* ....."sarong time to be wearing that".... *hmmm.... sigh* .... She's a witty one.

Ewan and Graham like her, too. They were a pair of numpties, though, determined to embarrass me by telling Carlie I was a virgin. They pushed us together, and then when it worked, tried to pull us apart.... *bastards....*

Not that it's just about sex, Uncle, because it isn't.... *swigging drink...* But damn, she is sexual. I told ye that in my last letter. Did I also tell ye that she's decided she's going to do everything people do that have sex before they get married for me..... Like, ye ken...*everything*?? She says it makes her happy, especially because I stayed a virgin. I wouldna have thought it would be a turn-on for a woman.... but anytime I use that as an excuse for not knowing something—*oh, sorry, I dinna know how, because I was a virgin*, she gets all handsy and smoochy and takes *over*.... So far, she's used her hands, and her mouth, and we did it over the clothes.... what did she call that? Dry humping? We did that when she was on her period.... I think I'm getting drunk, man. Ye dinna want to hear all this... Mm-maybe I should cover that part up.... *Campbell, you arse—rewind and delete that bit....*

Two minutes of silence......

So, like I was saying, what I feel for Carlie is more than just desire... I love her, more than anyone. Ever. I told her the other night about Ma and Matthew, and Da. I've comforted *her* often. Curled up in my arms, she starts to relax, and I can just feel the sad go out of her... But, Ferguson, like, *she* held *me*. And with my cheek on her soft, soft, breast, my head tucked by her neck, it was like nothing could hurt me. God, I miss her........ *silence.... soft snore...... snort.... hiccup....* Damn. I think I'm falling asleep. I'm going to go lay down... *Click.*

Remind me never to drink again, Ferguson. I feel like a pile of shite. I apologize for anything I said in the last half hour of this tape. There's no way I'm going to listen to it, though, so I hope you'll forgive me or that you'll at least have a laugh at my expense... oh, I completely forgot we were making bread. I'm going to the kitchen.... *footsteps, plastic on wood, slapping, pounding sound....* You can hang out with me while I make this into loaves...

So where was I? Carlie had a fiancé... did I mention that? And that's where she is right now... With him. At a hotel... *swig of drink... grunt...* And I told her to go, to hear him out? What kind of eejit am I? Anyway, while she and I spent time together when she was just new to the island, I didna try to make him look bad, exactly, but I kept asking her why he let her leave, why he didna marry her. I asked her if she loved him. And she didna say yes...... *metallic clunk...* Okay, two loaves... how long do they have to rise? Sorry. Talking to myself. It's getting late... but I need to finish this bread, so I'll talk to ye a little longer.

There was gossip going around about the two of us. Guess some people heard us talking late at night, thought we were sexually active. Well we werena having sex. Except in my dreams every night. I hadna had that happen to me at night in a long time. I try to keep my self-abuse to a minimum, even if I dinna have a priest to confess to. But it had still been since I was a young teenager that I woke up having been so wrapped up in a dreamed fantasy that I... ye ken... But it was happening more than I care to admit as I got to ken her. Oh, the *thoughts* I had...

This one day, I hung out wi' her while she did laundry. We were talking, and she was hanging up all these bras and knickers. We hung out that whole afternoon... *chuckle*... I think I kept stretching it out, just trying to spend more time with her.

Then a storm came. You've never lived until you've seen an approaching storm on Arno. We rushed around, getting her clothes off the lines. And afterward she danced around in the rain like a little girl. Till her dress was clinging to her body...till she was cold and I could see her nipples, sticking out like... sorry, I'm acting like I'm just talking to myself again. *I should probably erase that bit, too... Let's see... which button do I push?...*

Thirty seconds of silence.

Well, I hope that worked...Where was I? So she came up and squeezed next to me on the stoop. I put my arm around her... she was shivering and cold. I could have kissed her then. She was looking at me like she wanted me to. She invited me in, just to get out of the rain, ye ken... but I felt so lustful, looking around her apartment, at her bed, seeing her hang her bras to dry. I kept imagining peeling her clothes off and making love to her. And I felt guilty and awkward.

Even now I realize though, Ferguson... none of those fantasies can stand up against the reality. Christ, she's amazing.... I miss her so much, and she's only been gone...... eight hours... it's like 1:30 in the morning. The bread should be ready to go in the oven now... *clanging noises, feet walking back.*

Where was I? I set the timer for the bread to come out. It should be done by 2:05 or so. So with the rumors going around about us, and with Graham and Ewan urging her away as strongly as they'd pushed her toward me... I think she realized how she felt about me, and it was like she broke up with me because she felt like she was cheating on her fiancé. Wouldn't let me comfort her, wouldn't come to me for friendship. Even when one of her little patients died. God, I could see on her face how much she needed me.

Until... until Eric broke up with her. I think it was the next day, or the day after that, after the funeral. I'd been in agony wi'out her. My students thought I was sick. "Are you sad, Meester Mack? Meester Mack, you are *nañinmej*? Go home, Meester Mack."

That night, there was a knock on my bedroom window. And it was Carlie. Wearing those sexy little shorts and a tank top. I held her while she cried. And then she asked if she could sleep with me.... *groan*.... Not in a sexual way.

She just couldna be alone. Have ye ever slept next to a woman you're attracted to, Ferguson? Talk about torture. Her round arse pressed up against me? Her breasts, barely covered... I kept waking up with my arm around her, my hand nearly on her breast, my cock erect and pressing against her... restraining myself took herculean effort!

So he hurt her, but then she came to me broken and open to be loved. The man was a fool and I benefitted because of it. And today Eric showed up here. Apologized. Proposed to her... this time for real.... *scoff*.... Not sure why any man would propose without the intent to actually *marry* a girl... *gulp... ahhh....* I punched him in the face, though... that was good. Basically, he called her a *hoor*, my wife... that *bastard*...

Uncle, she'sh *got* to come back. If she doesna, I'm not sure what I'm going to do... I need to lay down again. The timer for the bread will wake me up.... *click...*

I'm back. I sink I'm drunk... I dinna want to be up, but the bread needs another five minutes before I can take it out of the oven... *wooden rapping noise...* Someone's knocking at the door. What the...? It's two fifteen in the morning. I'll be right back..... *footsteps... metallic rattling... squeak of a door...*

CARLIE?

Campbell, I'm home.

Oh, Carlie. God, Carlie!

I choose YOU...

Get *in* here!... *laughter...* oh, Ri-pālle, you look like hell, woman... *female sobbing, then silence...* Itōk, Ri-pālle, let me hold you.... *approaching footsteps... sounds of kissing... bed squeaking... more kissing... Much more kissing...*

Ha! Uncle Ferguson! Ye shneaky wee bastard. Thought ye'd listen in, did ye? Talk to ye later, man... *cough, sniff...* all ish well in my world tonight... *click.*

CHAPTER 36

I Choose You

My heart was singing as I began to walk. Campbell. I was going home to Campbell. I imagined his face when he saw me, how his eyes would light up. I thought of making love to him, of how much I wanted to be one with him again. The gravel crunching under my sandals was a repeated chant, "Campbell, Campbell, home to Campbell."

After an hour on the road—an hour in near pitch darkness—I began to question the wisdom of my choice to walk home in the middle of the night. I had tried to jog at the beginning, but after landing firmly on a sharp rock that had lodged itself in my sandal, followed five minutes later by stubbing my toe, I decided it was best to be a tortoise.

Math occupied my mind for a time. I had left a little before 11. If I kept a steady pace of about two-and-a-half to three miles an hour, it would take me over three hours to get back to Campbell. Could I walk until two in the morning? Or later? I was already tired; it had been an emotionally exhausting day.

To keep myself from discouragement and exhaustion, I knew I needed to distract myself. I tried to recall the different times I had interacted with Campbell, and how each one had led to falling more in love with him. There was a common thread, as most of them were him being compassionate and ended with him hugging me, holding me, or sleeping with me, so I decided that was ineffective at helping me stay motivated or awake. I wanted to be home already, in his arms already, and I didn't want to start crying.

I thought of singing my favorite songs, but realized that in the silence of the islands, I'd forgotten a lot of them. I did remember Journey's "Don't Stop Believing," from the countless times my dad had played it for us at home, so

I sang as much of it as I could. I tried to remember the soundtrack for the *Sound of Music*, though I did question whether singing was the best of choices. I didn't want to attract the attention of any wandering drunk men.

By one in the morning, I was exhausted. I was past the point of wondering whether I was developing blisters on my feet and now wondering if I would be able to keep my toes, and a nagging thought in the back of my mind made me think I might just fall down and die of exhaustion and get eaten by coconut crabs. Or mosquitoes. I hadn't put on bug spray after snorkeling, and they were finding me delicious.

But then the moon came up, a slivered crescent of light in the sky. I could see it slowly moving and it provided just enough light that I didn't feel like I was walking in circles. I could see the pale channels of coral gravel with a grassy divider in between, and I doggedly put one foot in front of the other. My new mantra was "One more step...one more step..." (during which I could actually walk eight steps). Occasionally I would close my eyes, but I found myself veering to one side of the road or the other and decided that was ineffective.

Passing the air strip was a significant landmark, and when I walked through Jabo I knew it was just a little more than a mile until I would be home.

On the outskirts of Ine, I nearly started to cry in relief. The trees occluded my view of the moon, but there were finally outlines of houses added to the never-ending coconut palms of the previous miles. Occasionally I would get a glimpse of the *iar*, silvery slivers of moon reflecting off the ripples of water.

And then I heard it. A low growl, coming from my left. I figured it was just someone snoring, but then I heard it again. It was definitely a growl, and it was coming closer.

I had nothing on me. I was wearing a dress and sandals. But I remembered Campbell's rock story, and I dropped to my knees on the road, scrabbling around to see if I could find a rock. The growl came again, and out of the shadows slunk the lithe form of a wild dog, his hackles raised, white teeth visible. He started to move toward me and I drew back my hand, gripping the medium-sized rock I had found. This dog wasn't as skittish as the one in Campbell's story; he kept moving forward. As he came closer, from somewhere deep in my throat came a guttural, primal sound. "AAAaaaa!" I screamed, running toward the dog, as I hurled the rock with all my might at his head. "I am going home to my husband, you beast, and you are not stopping me!"

I don't know if I hit him with the rock or terrified him with my voice, but that dog turned tail and ran, and so did I, not caring about the way the rocks jabbed into the bottoms of my feet, the way my blisters stung, and my sweaty legs chafed together. I was going home...

The faint solar light was lit on the exterior of the clinic as I stumbled across the yard to our door, up the steps, and tried the door knob. It was locked, and my key was back in my suitcase in Arno Arno. I knocked quietly; I didn't really want to bother Campbell if he was sleeping. But looking at the curtains through the louvers, I thought I saw a hint of light. The lights were on? Campbell was up? I knocked louder.

I heard a low male voice and the hollow echo of footsteps across the floor, then the rattling sound of the lock being unbolted. Why was it taking Campbell so damn long?

The door opened, and there he was. Still wearing the blue sarong, still shirtless. His eyes were bleary and red, his hair was a mess. His fingernails were rimmed with white and there was a smudge of flour on his cheekbone. The bread?

He stared at me, then said in shock, "CARLIE?!!" He stood there dumbly.

"Campbell, I'm home," I said, as if I needed to declare it to myself as much as him.

"Oh, Carlie," he said, "*God, Carlie*," he stepped outside and wrapped me in his arms.

"Campbell," I whispered into his chest, then lifted my chin to look at him. "I choose *you*."

"Get in here!" he exclaimed, ushering me into the house. As I came into the light, he laughed at me, looking me up and down. "Oh, *Ri-pālle*, ye look like hell, woman!"

I'd held it together until then but dissolved into tears. It took Campbell a moment to realize that I felt like hell as much as I *looked* like hell, and the smile disappeared from his face, replaced by a look of compassion.

"*Itōk, Ri-pālle*," Campbell said, leading me toward the bed. "C'mere, let me hold you." He sat down and pulled me onto his knee, kissing me soundly.

325

We pressed ourselves together like we hadn't seen each other for years, kissing as hungrily as if we were starving.

Campbell picked me up and rolled us onto the bed, continuing to cover my lips and face with ardent kisses. Then my hip bumped something in the bed, and I picked it up.

"Ha, *Ferguson!*" Campbell exclaimed, taking the tape recorder from me and talking to it. "Ye shneaky wee bastard. Thought ye'd listen in, did ye? Talk to ye later, man." He almost looked like he was about to cry as he looked at my face, and smilingly said, "All is well in my world tonight," before he hit the button on the side of the player.

It didn't take long to realize Campbell wasn't acting like himself, more like a big goofy four-year-old who wanted to touch my body. When he tried to kiss me again, now that our first eager greetings were done, I could tell why.

"Campbell, you *reek!* Have you been drinking?" I grimaced, pushing his face away.

"Aye," he said. "Whisky... fromFerguson..." he slurred his words together and pointed at a bottle of amber colored liquid on the table. "D'ye wanssum?"

"No thanks," I said, pulling myself out of bed and going over to my dresser. I was sweaty and dirty, and I needed something clean to wear before going to bed. There would be no passionate love-making that night for several reasons, among them that I was exhausted, it was past two in the morning, I had blisters on my feet, and my thighs were chafed from walking nine miles in a dress. And add to that, my husband was totally and completely *drunk.*

I grabbed panties, shorts, and a tank top, then went into the kitchen. Campbell followed me with his eyes; the rest of him didn't appear to be coordinated enough to stand upright.

Plugging the sink, I poured some water in. Peeling my clothes off, I grabbed a washcloth and soap and hopped up to sit on a hand towel on the counter, sticking my poor sore feet into the sink. Just being able to wash the dirt off my legs felt good, chilly as the water was.

At the sight of my naked body, Campbell roused himself, stumbling across the apartment to join me. "Oh, Carlie," he said, as he leaned on the kitchen counter, watching me. "Ye're so bew-ful. I just want to touch your body. B'cause I love you soooo mush... mush.... so *much*..."

"Really, now?" I said dryly. "You do know I came home for you, don't you?"

"Aye," he said. "I washdrinking because I didna ken if you would. I cried a *lot* today."

I had a hard time reining in my laughter. "So is whisky like truth serum for you?" I asked.

"I dinna want pancakes," he said, closing his eyes. "Even wi' serum."

"Go to bed, Campbell," I said, laughing. "If you talk much more, I'm going to turn around and walk back to Eric."

Campbell's eyes instantly looked five times more sober. He walked over and put his arms around me and his forehead on my shoulder. "Ye canna leave me now, Carlie. You chose me."

As sore and tired as I was, I could see my husband was in much worse emotional condition. I swiveled my legs and lowered myself off the counter, put Campbell's arm over my shoulder and my arm around his waist, and helped him back to our bed.

"S'like when we first met, *Ri-pálle*," he slurred, shaking his head. "'Cept, I was bleedin', and you werena naked."

I turned, took his face between my hands to kiss him, and then lowered him into the bed.

"Lie wi' me, please, Carlie," he said, not letting go of my hand. "Just until I fall asleep? I need you in my arms." He was teary, and it made me misty-eyed in sympathy. "Today was the *worst*," he sighed. "I love you... I'm so glad you're back." Looking at him, I realized bathing was the last thing my sweet husband needed me to do. I turned the apartment lights off and tiptoed back to our bed, lifting the sheet to crawl in.

"I love you too, baby boy," I said, curling up in front of Campbell. He wrapped his arm over me, palmed my breast with a contented grunt, and swiped my hair out of his way so his forehead rested at the nape of my neck, his curls blending with mine.

I felt him whispering then. I wasn't sure if I heard him correctly or not, but I thought I heard him say, "Oh, God, thank you... *thank you* for bringing her back to me."

I woke to a touch as soft as a paint brush, Campbell tracing the lines of my face with one finger. I breathed in deeply and sighed as I exhaled, as Campbell drew my cheek, my eyebrow, the bridge of my nose. I stretched and smiled without opening my eyes, and Campbell touched my lips with his.

"I'm sorry about last night, *mo ghràidh*," Campbell whispered. His breath was minty, his skin cool and hair wet. He'd showered and brushed his teeth.

The touch continued, a light whisper against my skin...my jaw, down my neck, up the slope of my breast, and a chilly circle traced around my nipple, echoed by the warmer whisper of breath and lips. I gasped and my body contracted in response to him.

I opened my eyes to see him beaming down at me. This morning his eyes were cloudless blue, crinkled at the corners, his mouth a constant smile.

"Oh, Carlie," he said. "I dinna ever want ye to leave me again."

I could feel myself opening to him, first as an ache of affection in my chest, followed by a growing warmth between my legs.

"Will ye say it again for me?" he asked, closing his eyes and lowering his lips to mine.

"Say it?" I asked, confused. "I love you?"

"No," he answered. "You told me last night, I think, but I was pretty drunk."

"Oh!" I said, realizing what he meant. I raised my hands to his cheeks and looked him in the eyes. "I choose you, Campbell MacReid."

He groaned. "Oh, Carlie, I need ye so bad. But I've got to go teach. And I think a quickie at lunch won't be satisfying enough. I promise that this afternoon or evening after school, I will have recovered from my hangover and you'll have rested enough. I need to spend some time on you." The promise in his eyes made me shiver.

"Please. Because I need you, too," I said, pulling him down to kiss me. "Probably a good idea to delay, but you still may need to be gentle. I walked nine miles yesterday, and my upper thighs are chafed."

He got an impish look on his face. "I've got a few minutes before I have to leave, so I can do something about that... Let me start by massaging you with some lotion, then."

"So *kind* of you," I teased. "But somehow I have a feeling I wouldn't let you leave once you got started."

I slept almost all day. Campbell had scribbled "Miss Peach *enañinmej*," on the clinic sign before he headed wearily off to school, kissing me soundly before he did. Hopefully there wouldn't be any terrible accidents and I could just rest, after the emotional and physical upheaval of the last 24 hours.

Partway through the day, I heard a knock on my door. When I pulled myself from bed and opened it, there was my suitcase, with a curt note from Eric saying it would have been nice for me to let him know what I was doing—he was terrified when he woke up and didn't know where I was. I shook my head wearily and went back to bed.

I had thought Campbell would come home and want to spend time with me immediately after school, but instead, he had brought a stack of tests he needed to grade with him, so he sat down at the kitchen table to try to finish them up. I had slept the day away, and was feeling stir-crazy and bored, having only achieved one goal—taking a thorough shower. I stood behind Campbell for a while, rubbing his shoulders, but not managing to distract him, I started wandering around the apartment.

"Do I get to listen to this?" I asked him, pulling the portable tape recorder from where he'd set it on the bedside table the previous night. "Drunk Campbell could prove to be *very* interesting."

At the look of terror on his face, I teasingly held the tape recorder and ran to the door of the cabin, out to the shower, and locked it with the hook. Campbell, having been in a sitting position on the heavy wooden bench at our kitchen table, was at a distinct disadvantage.

"Carlie!" Campbell's voice thundered out through the louvers. "Ye shouldna hear the awful things I said about ye."

"Awful?" I said. "I was under the impression that you loved me and wanted me to come back..."

"No, just *lustful* things. The things I thought and the way I felt before we were married."

"Oh, now I'm even more interested," I said, pressing rewind so the recorder made a metallic squeaking sound.

"Carlie," his voice was lower now, pleading. "Dinna embarrass me, please. I was drunk...I think I said some things I wouldna want you to hear."

"Okay," I sighed. I unlocked the door and headed back into the house, handing the recorder to Campbell as I entered.

"What if I *want* you to talk a little dirty to me?" I said. "What if I want to hear those lustful thoughts? What if they make me want you as well?" I grinned at him.

"Okay," he said, one corner of his mouth lifting in a smile. "Just one. For now."

"And?" I said helpfully.

"But ye have to play along," he said. "So ye need to be wearing a tank top, and no bra, little knickers, and tiny shorts."

"And what will you be wearing?" I asked.

"A sarong," he said, biting his lower lip. "And a tee shirt."

"I think I like where this is going," I said, as I retrieved the suggested clothing items from my dresser and started to change. "But no peeking!" Just for jollies, I left off both the bra *and* the panties.

"So," I said. "I'll be Carlie, who has just newly moved to a tropical island. She's lonely, and this guy...let's call him..."

"Campbell," said Campbell. "A really handsome, nice guy, great smile, hot body." He grinned.

"He just walked her home. And he dropped her off at her house, and he headed back to his, leaving her all alone," I narrated sadly.

"But he started thinking, she looked so sad. She maybe needed a hug. So he turned around, thinking, *she's going to think I'm stupid.*"

"Really?" I said. "Oh, Campbell, I *didn't*. It was the sweetest thing!"

"Oh, I ken," said Campbell, confidently. "Because when Campbell knocked on the door, and asked if she needed a hug,"

"She said yes. And started crying," I said, stepping into his arms.

"He felt her body against him, all those luscious curves."

"How did he *ever* restrain himself?" I lifted my face to him.

"By the grace o' God," Campbell replied with a grin. "But he was toying wi' God's grace when he took her into her apartment," he led me by the hand, "and sat down on her bed. And took her on his knee."

"He was holding a crying woman. What could he have *possibly* been thinking?" I asked innocently. Campbell looked shy for a moment, until he realized I was just fishing for more details.

"Aye," he chuckled, "What *indeed?* Just that she had the roundest arse he'd ever seen, and he wanted to put his hands on it." With that, Campbell made me squeal by dipping his legs as if to drop me; but he saved me by firmly grasping the part under discussion. "And what of Carlie? Was she having holy thoughts about her fiancé?" he asked.

"I don't think she remembered she had a fiancé right then," I admitted honestly. "What she *did* notice, was that Campbell was looking down her shirt."

Campbell complied with my directive, grasping the neckline of my tank top and pulling it outward slightly. "Oh, Carlie," he breathed, looking up at me with dilated pupils. "I dinna ken how much more of this I can stand!"

"Restraint is sexy, babe," I said, and then squirmed on his lap slightly. "Oh, I remember this part, too."

He flushed in embarrassment at the memory and his current state. "God, I was horrified. It isna fun to be a man sometimes. Your body betrays what's in your head and heart, even when you're trying as hard as ye can to be respectful."

"I received your gesture in the spirit it was meant, Campbell," I said seriously. "You were being so sweet to me."

"Can we stop now? And move on?" Campbell asked, eyeing the bed. "I think we're both adequately roused."

"You need to tell me what you were *thinking* of doing," I said. "Once you've confessed, I'll let you *do* it."

"Now, that's an odd kind of confession, *Ri-pālle*," Campbell said. "I'm used to feeling guilty for what I confess because it's wrong."

"You need to reeducate yourself," I said. "Because now, with me, it's right."

"Aye, marriage is a sacrament, isn't it?" He wrinkled his forehead. "After years of confessing my impure thoughts, I dinna ken if I'll be able to freely share them."

"Shall we listen, then?" I said, eyeing the tape recorder.

Campbell scoffed. "Maybe if I tell ye quietly, in your ear."

He perched his chin on my shoulder, his rumbly voice and the tickle of his breath on my ear and through my hair giving me shivers even before I registered what he was saying.

"I thought about coming back in after we said goodbye. I thought about standing with you, taking you in my arms, and kissing you. I imagined peeling off your tank top and pulling down your shorts and your knickers. I wondered if ye might take off my shirt and unwrap my sarong," he blushed. "I wondered if ye would touch me, too. I thought of laying ye on your back and lying on you between your legs. I wanted to take your breasts in my hands and in my mouth. And when you invited me, when you asked me to, *if* you asked me to, I was so ready to make love to ye, to give myself to ye."

"Even though you were committed to being a virgin?" I turned to look at him. "Even though you'd kept yourself from it all those years?"

"Oh, Carlie," Campbell said. "I knew I loved you that first day. When you cried, and I held ye; I couldna imagine ever letting anything hurt or harm ye. And I didna want any other man to have ye. I waited, yes, but I think I was waiting for you. You are my match, Carlie, my perfect fit. Say it to me again, *Ri-pālle*."

I smiled into his eyes. "I choose you, Campbell MacReid."

He kissed me. "I choose you, too."

CHAPTER 37

Love Making

I couldn't stop touching him. I was massaging his shoulders again, naked, standing close enough that my breasts and stomach were brushing against his back.

"*Ri-pálle*, I'm trying to finish grading," Campbell said. He paused, and then I could feel his muscles tense under my hands. "When we made love," he said hesitantly, "and I...touched ye while I was inside, I thought...well the noises ye made...and what I felt, I thought you..."

"Oh, yeah, I had an orgasm," I assured him.

"But...ye aren't satisfied?" He paused but he didn't turn to look at me.

"Sexually, yes. Emotionally, no," I admitted honestly. "Campbell, I was one decision away from losing you forever. Just yesterday. Will you come back to bed and hold me? Are these tests that important?"

"No more important than my wife," Campbell said, reaching back, grabbing me around the waist, pulling me next to him, and quickly nipping at my breast. "But the lads and lassies were very worried about their science test grades, and I promised them I'd have them graded before tomorrow. You would have me be a man of my word, would ye not?"

"Definitely," I said, with a sigh of resignation. He was right, of course. The things that made me love him were also the things that obligated him to others as well. I wrinkled my forehead in thought. "Is there any part I could grade *for* you? I'm happy to help if it means I can have your attention back sooner."

Campbell smiled at me, an endearing lopsided grin. "Aye," he said. "But will ye put something on? I canna focus wi' your naked body so close."

Obligingly I found the tank top and shorts next to the bed where Campbell had flung them an hour previously after removing them in just the way he'd promised. When I stood back up after bending to retrieve them, though, Campbell looked away quickly, his face flushing.

"You know, you *can* look at me," I said. "I'm your wife. This..." I indicated my body, "is yours to enjoy."

"Aye?" Campbell said, directing his gaze back at me.

"Definitely!" I said. "It makes me feel beautiful to know you want me."

"That I *do*," Campbell said, his voice dropping nearly an octave as he cocked his head to the side, staring at me as I pulled my shorts up. "Hmm," he said, eyes twinkling. "Why don't ye stop wi' just that. Once we're done, I *will* come back to bed wi' ye, but I canna promise it will be just to hold ye."

"Whew!" I fanned myself, looking away. "Is it hot in here?"

"Actually, it is," Campbell said, grinning, "But I dinna think that's what ye meant."

I sat down at the table, and Campbell handed me a small stack of papers and a red pen. Riti Botla's name was at the top of the first test.

"She got a hundred percent," Campbell said, with a fond smile. "Use her work as the master key to grade the other students' matching sections."

"Can I use purple pen?" I asked, looking with distaste at the red one. "It's just a friendlier color."

"D'ye want your husband to get teased more than he already is by his students?"

"Do you get teased on a regular basis?" I asked, wondering what his students would tease him about.

"Aye," he said, "And it's all your fault. The boys tease me by asking me if I touch your body and *kōmmon nana* wi' ye; the girls tease me by asking me when I'm going to have a baby wi' ye, and they all tease me any time I accidentally get distracted by thoughts of ye; which, sadly, happens more than I care to confess."

I leaned my chin on my hand and stared adoringly at Campbell. "Dammit, I have *such* a crush on you," I said.

"Do ye now?" Campbell asked, looking pleased at the thought. But then his eyebrows furrowed pensively. "But you *love* me too, don't ye?"

"Yes," I said earnestly. "That's why I'm *here*. And there are things I want to say to you, things that I realized as I talked to Eric about my decision, things that *you* need to hear. But, I really want it to be distraction free, so let's finish this up first." Campbell nodded, and we turned to the pages in front of us.

As I began to grade, I realized that the sheets looked handwritten, and the ink was blue. "You don't have electricity at the school. Or a copier," I said. "How did you make copies?"

"Have ye heard of a mimeograph?" Campbell asked.

"I might have heard the word," I answered, shaking my head, "but I don't know what it is."

"It's a machine, run by crank, that creates copies of documents when ye dinna have electricity."

"How does it work?" I asked, as I moved on to the next test.

"Well, ye use special paper and write really hard to create a carbon copy. It makes a mirror image of the writing, so it's backwards. Then you use the mimeograph machine, tucking your original into a slot on a large metal barrel and using a special solvent that allows the blue writing to be imprinted on paper. Then ye crank, once for each copy, and it will make a good number of copies, up to 50, I think."

"Neat," I said. "I hadn't really thought about the lack of computers, tablets, printers, and copiers out here. It probably makes it a little harder to teach."

"I dinna think so, actually," said Campbell, shaking his head. "Wi'out those things to distract the children, they actually find us teachers very amusing and they enjoy school. And here in the islands it helps that education is respected and teachers revered."

"But still teased?" I said, stretching my back while his eyes were on me. I tried to look nonchalant, but the stretch wasn't only for my benefit.

"Aye," said Campbell. "Still teased." He looked at me hungrily. "Perhaps we should work more and talk less, lass. I'm beginning to feel a little hot myself."

I finished grading, but Campbell still had a few short-answer questions to read over. I used his calculator to total points and figure percentages, but finally I had done everything I could.

I sighed deeply, and caught Campbell eyeing me. "Ye arna very patient, wee one," he said. "So I'm going to give ye an assignment."

"Now, what would that be?" I asked curiously.

"I confessed the dark desires I had for ye before we married," he said. "Now it's going to be your turn."

"Is it?" I asked, eyebrows raised.

"Aye," he affirmed. "Get to work. Make a plan and take care of anything ye need to get it ready." He chuckled. "Or to get *yourself* ready."

If Campbell had first thought of making love to me when he first walked me home and held me, my first lustful thoughts about him were when he hung out with me on laundry day. When the storm came, after pulling the laundry off the line I stayed in the yard and danced in the rain. Then, soaking wet to the skin, I joined him under the awning. The two of us huddled there and he put his arm around me as I shivered, apparently not caring that I was getting him wet. He looked at my lips, and I wanted him to kiss me, or more.

Watching my face as I was thinking, Campbell smiled broadly. "*Oh*," he said. "I've a feeling this is going to be good."

"But I haven't said a *word*," I said.

"Your face told me plenty!" Campbell chuckled and turned back to his grading with a new intensity as I went and started a pot of water boiling, then searched through the closet for my clingiest sundress.

How am I going to do this? I wondered. I didn't want to attract attention by being inappropriate outside, but I thought that's at least where we should begin. When it appeared that Campbell was on his last test, I took the pot outside to the shower.

Campbell looked up as I was leaving. "Am I joining ye?" he asked.

"No. Just wait. I'll let you know when it's your turn to enter the scene."

I felt a little ridiculous and not a little horny as I changed into the sundress, sans underwear, then poured warm water over myself. The dress clung to my curves, my hair hung down in droopy ringlets, and I was soaking wet. I stood in the shower for a minute, letting the excess water drip off, then shook my head, rolled my eyes, walked to our door, and knocked, standing there dripping.

Campbell came to the door. When he saw me, he almost gasped. I could tell from the instant softening of his expression that it meant something to him that I'd chosen this moment.

"Your face just said something," I said to him. "Can you tell me what you were thinking?"

He looked down bashfully. "I thought... That day I *thought* you might feel something for me. But then I talked myself out of it. It made me doubt myself. Made me think I was a fool, reading something in your eyes that wasna there."

I pulled Campbell down to me and kissed him on the lips. "I was ashamed of it then, because I felt like I was cheating on Eric emotionally. But let's not focus on that. Quick, put your arm around me, and then let's go inside."

"Just a minute," Campbell said. He looked down at my body, his gaze focusing on two particular points. "Mmm," he grunted appreciatively. "I remember that afternoon quite vividly. But I think ye've cheated a little. I think ye were wearing a bra that day. Ye arena wearing one now."

"But I'm wet like I was that day," I said.

"*Itōk, Ri-pālle*, and we'll see if ye are or if ye aren't," Campbell replied naughtily, guiding me inside with his arm around my shoulders.

As we came inside, Campbell turned off the main lights and pressed me against the door with his body, kissing me as he gathered up my dress with both hands. The dress warred against him, attempting to stay fused to my wet skin.

"Just a minute, Campbell," I said, pushing on his chest. "I'm *engaged*. So we can't actually have sex. Are you okay with that?"

He pulled away briefly, looking down at me. It took a second for him to register that I was playing Carlie back then instead of myself, but then he got an impish grin.

"Aye," he said. "Then, we should slow this thing down." With that, he knelt in front of me, and put his hands on my hips, while I rested my arms on his shoulders. "Carlie, you're like a Silke," he said, looking at me, running his fingers through strands of my still-dripping hair. "All shiny and wet, like ye just came out of the sea. Are ye 'eternally lustful' like the Silkes? Because I think I've already lost my heart to ye. If ye leave me, I ken I would be lovesick forever."

"When I'm around you, yes, Campbell, I am filled with lust." I responded. He leaned down slightly and took my nipple in his mouth, biting just enough to make me squirm, then sucking until I could hear the water flowing through the fabric. He gripped me tighter, his fingers digging into the soft flesh of my hips and hindquarters.

He put his mouth on my other breast and groaned. "A Dhia, Ri-pàlle, I want to see ye naked. But my da said a good policy to keep your virginity is to never be naked together."

"But I can't keep these wet clothes on," I said innocently. "I need to change."

Married Campbell grinned as he sorted through the possible responses Virgin Campbell might have had, and then slowly stood up. "Aye. Ye *should* change. I will turn my back and give ye privacy."

I chuckled as his adorable British pronunciation—prĭ-vacy instead of prī-vacy—went to my dresser and pulled out a peach satin chemise. So far, we'd pretty much gone the route of clothing straight to naked when we had sex, and I hadn't bothered much with lingerie. I turned to see if Campbell was peeking, which I completely expected, but he had his back to me, chin up, looking away from me.

"Okay," I said, once the chemise had fallen over my body. Campbell turned, and his eyes widened.

"God, Carlie," he said, "Just when I dinna think ye could be any more beautiful, there ye are." He stood and stared at me. "I dinna feel like I'm worthy to touch ye."

"Are you *acting* right now, or serious?" I asked.

"*So* serious," he said. He stepped forward and took me in his arms. He rocked me, back and forth, one hand on my hair, the other one around my back.

I looked up at him. "I don't want to pretend anymore," I said. "This is real, and my feelings for you are real, and I want to make love to you, so that you don't wonder whether what you're feeling is really me."

Campbell stroked my back and my hair, continuing to weave back and forth as he held me. It was curious, but my desire started to ease away. Instead I just felt comforted.

"I'd like to hear what it is you wanted to say to me, Carlie," Campbell said.

"Like this?" I asked. "Not lying down in bed?"

"Like this," he said. "What did you tell Eric that ye havena told me?"

"I told him that you are my soul mate, that with you..."

"Not like that," Campbell said. "Talk to me, not to Eric."

I suddenly felt vulnerable, as I looked up into his piercing blue eyes, darkened by dilated pupils.

"Campbell," I said. "I don't know if you believe in soul mates, but I have never felt this way about anyone. I'm so comfortable in your presence, and yet you wake my body like no one ever has. I've never been so satisfied being with a person, and yet ached so badly when we're apart. I've always thought that there was something wrong with me—that I was too needy—like I was asking for more affection than anyone could ever give me. But with you I feel satiated and full."

Campbell's eyes were moist as he pulled me to him and kissed me on the forehead, wrapping his arms around me again. He sighed, his muscular chest and abdomen expanding, pressing against me. He started crooning in Gaelic into my hair.

"*Mo chridhe*...oh, Carlie," he said. "I've been so afraid. That I love you more than you could ever love me; that I want you more than you could ever want me. Do you know how much it means to hear ye say this, *Ri-pàlle*?"

Wordlessly I hugged him in answer.

"This may sound strange, Carlie, but I want to *not* make love to you," Campbell said, almost in disbelief at his own words. "What we have isna just about sex, *Ri-pàlle*. Because love will last even when we're too old and feeble to make love to each other anymore. Tonight, I just want to fall asleep with you close to me."

We turned off the lights, climbed into bed, and wrapped in my husband's arms, I fell asleep to the steady sound of Campbell MacReid's beautiful heart.

The End

Island Fever Calendar

October

Sunday	Monday	Tuesday	Wednesday	Thursday	Friday	Saturday
1	2	3	4	5	6	7
8	9	10	11	12	13	14
15 *Arrive* **#2 Miss Peachay**	16 *Well child checkups* *Campbell* **#3 Alone** **#1 Meester Mack** **#4 Pain in the Arse,** **#5 Tuck-In Service**	17	18	19	20 *Night time visitors* *Campbell the night watchman* **#6 Night Noises**	21 *Laundry Bwebwenato Visit Anni* *Graham* **#7 Dirty Laundry**
22 *Ewan*	23 *Well low, new moon* *Campbell bores Carlie to sleep* **#8 Poor Me, Bore Me**	24	25	26 *Campbell gets his stitches out* **#9 Stitch Removal**	27	28
29	30 *Eric sends break-up letter*	31 *Samhain bonfire with the boys* **#10 Geckos The Huntsman and Campbell, Oh My!**				

The events of <u>Island Fever</u> happen at a rapid pace over a mere six weeks. I found it helpful to have a calendar to refer to and thought my readers might enjoy it as well.

November

Sunday	Monday	Tuesday	Wednesday	Thursday	Friday	Saturday
			1 *Matolen trip Something's Different* **#11 Sunshine**	**2**	**3** *Fish & Pizza* **#12 A Beautiful Doughy Ball** **#13 Scar Stories**	**4** *Baby Maxson/ Funeral* *Carlie Recommits* **#14 The Break-Up**
5	**6** ***Come See the Miracle!*** *Mail Day-Carlie sends a letter & there's one from Eric, too* **#15 Consolation**	**7** *Alastair Calls Boat to Majuro* **#16 The Proposal** **#17 Getting to Know You**	**8** *Majuro Tasks Calling the Parents* **#18 Phoning Home**	**9** *Back to Arno* **#19 Restraint**	**10** *Parents Arrive* **#20 To Have and To Hold** **#21 First Blood**	**11** *Trip to Autle* **#22 The Morning After** **#23 Autle** **#24 The Storm**
12 *Snorkeling Walking Back* **#25 The Drop-Off** **#26 The Visitor**	**13** *Truck Home Good-bye* **#27 House Warming** **#28 Feels Like Home**	**14** **#29 Division of Labor**	**15** *Eric Gets Your Letter* **#30 Love Notes**	**16** *First Date* **#31 Date Night**	**17** *Campbell takes up jogging Carlie is on the menu*	**18** *Spearfishing Dinner Guests*
19 **#32 Getting Settled**	**20** *Eric Flies into Majuro*	**21** *Eric on Arno* **#33 The American** **#34 The Hotel** **#35 Hey, Ferguson!**	**22** *Carlie Goes Home* **#36 I Choose You** **#37 Love Making**	**23**	**24** Book 2: # Island Hopper **#1 Lukkuun Lakatu**	**25**
26	**27**	**28**	**29**	**30**		

343

AFTERWORD

IN THE 90s, I VOLUNTEERED as an elementary school teacher through my university and spent a year on Arno teaching grades four through six. I was there with two other girls, who taught the other grades in the little school in Ine.

Living on Arno was such a vivid experience. So many of the little details of life—the stories told within this book—came from reality, among them gargantuan spiders, mating geckos, jellyfish, the moon-controlled well, nighttime troubadours, boils, crazy storms, handwashing laundry, and the constant but incongruous presence of disease and death in such a beautiful place.

My adorable fourth through sixth grade students were the ones who were constantly asking "What mean Be-Nice? What mean Ba-Shinah?" And of course, I was the teacher who so skillfully played dumb and thwarted their efforts to entrap me. There was indeed a woman who had lost her three previous children in infancy, and we brought soap and dollar bills to her fourth baby's funeral, sitting sadly with her as she fanned the flies from his face, his mouth covered with a sheet to keep his spirit from escaping. Our cycles readjusted to the moon. We were perplexed by our sweet students constantly throwing rocks at each other and had the ah-ha moment of observing a sharp-shooting Majel mother discipline from a distance when we visited one of our students. Our young neighbor took us on a nighttime run to "Come see the miracle" ending with a beautiful view of the moon from the oceanside dock. I was constantly (if unintentionally) offending people, so "*jolok bōd*" was my most frequently needed Majel phrase, and my students frequently laughed at my efforts to speak Majel, telling me I talked like a "*jidik niñnin*" (tiny baby).

For years I've wanted to write about Arno, but it was such an intimate experience, so close to my heart, so intense, so immense that it seemed impossible. In addition, because I shared the experience with friends I didn't want to steal their stories to tell mine. As wonderful as they were and as

345

imperfect as I am, I would have unfairly cast myself as the heroine of that story and it could never have been "true."

So for years this incredible place and these vivid experiences have lived on only in my memory, waiting for the right place and time to be shared with a larger audience.

Using Arno as a setting for a love story and beginning it as *Outlander* fanfiction was a crazy combination of irony and serendipity. Volunteering on an island without running water or electricity was indeed as close to time travel as any real-life experience could be.

It was *after* I began to write the story that other delightful little ironies and similarities emerged. Marshallese is one of a few languages that uses the rolled "r"—just like the Scots do. Scots wear kilts? Islanders wear sarongs.

In *Outlander*, Jamie nicknames Claire "Sassenach." A Sassenach is an outsider, an Englishman (or woman) in Scotland. On Arno, I absolutely hated their word for us Americans—"*Ri-pālle*," which did indeed mean "selfish white person." It's amazing that when those words come out of a muscular Scotsman's lips, suddenly "*Itōk, Ri-pālle*" is a sexy come-on!

In searching for pictures of this beautiful place and catching up with my island home some 20 years later, what I found broke my heart. The beaches on Arno are still as pristine, the children just as joyful. But even a few centimeters of ocean rise caused by climate change is enough that it is slowly decimating the atolls. If a king tide coincides with a tropical storm, the storm surge can wash over the islands, many of which have a maximum elevation of 10 feet (3 meters), killing plants and the coconut palms that supply the main source of income, destroying homes, and contaminating water supplies.

Changing weather patterns also mean that there is less fresh water deposited in catchments, and times of drought are more and more common.

At the 2017 G20 summit, the Fijian Prime Minister Frank Bainimarama called on the United States to offer climate change refugees from the Marshall Islands permanent status in the US. Said Bainimarama, "We have not caused this crisis, your nations have... We have trodden lightly on the earth whereas you have trodden heavily. And those carbon footprints pose a threat to us in the Pacific and to all humanity" (Climate Change News).

It is my hope that this book will remind each of my readers of the global community with whom we share our earth, and that each one of us will do what we can to allow the people of Arno to continue to live and love on their gorgeous island home. Though my American background sometimes made it hard to understand their culture and social norms, I had never met such happy people, for whom the simple was enough to satisfy them. As I wrote, I found myself homesick for blue sky, white sand, turquoise water, and the kindness and generosity of the people of Arno.

—Sarah Carrell

Chapter Notes

My own experiences informed most of this story, but I was also inspired & influenced by other people as well as the Outlander sagas, both the novels by Diana Gabaldon and the Starz TV show. These chapter notes will provide a little insight into the details that are completely true as well as the ones that have been altered or emphasized for the sake of story.

Chapter 1 & 2—Meester Mack, Miss Peachay

Carlie Beecher is an anagram of "Claire" with a last name that is a variant of Beauchamp. After creating "Miss Peachay" in the fan-fiction version, I just couldn't completely get rid of Claire Beauchamp's name. I considered "Carlie Vietz" briefly, but somehow "Miss Pizza" just didn't have the same sweet connotation as "Miss Peachay." I'm still getting over not having "Meester Shamie" as my male lead (the Marshallese pronunciation of Jamie).

When my friends and I first arrived on Arno, we came by boat. It's not as impressive an approach as coming in by plane. When you approach a skinny little shoestring that looks like it could sink into the ocean at a moment's notice, viewing it in an airplane from above is terrifying!

We were also only given a very short tour and introduction before being left. I think the superintendent came out with us and went back to Majuro after a half hour, but as there were three of us, at least we didn't feel quite so deserted.

Chapter 3 – Alone

I loved watching the sun rise over the islands on the other side of the atoll more than almost anything. I relished a quiet start to every morning, slipping out to the beach before sunrise and reading or journaling while I watched the sun come up.

It was curious to me that people chose to do their morning bathrooming on the beach, but my students told me they found it strange and disturbing that we peed into a toilet full of water that made such a loud noise, so...

Breast-feeding was a non-issue there. No awkward attempts to cover themselves; women would just pull out a boob and go for it. It makes a lot of sense; Americans have sexualized breasts to the point that sadly something as natural as breastfeeding is viewed with disgust by some.

And we had our own little Katie, who did indeed know just one sentence in English and who would follow us around asking us "What's you name? What's you name? What's you name?"

Chapter 4 – Pain in the Arse

For a time, I considered changing the location of the story to add a level of anonymity and protect the identities of the residents of Arno (though I have changed names). The "there Arno" (are no) conversation between Ewan and Graham is probably the main reason I couldn't bring myself to change islands...as well as the fact that it was what I know...

Chapter 5 – Tuck-In Service

People who serve in the Peace Corps take part in a month-long training and language boot camp before they are placed in a host country. Because the organization I went with employed college students who had raised the funds to support themselves through the year, we had a one-week orientation in Hawaii. Although we did a good job and had a great experience, we were *woefully* underprepared.

Marshallese sexual mores were the hardest cultural difference for me to understand. I do remember being indignant that these "backward islanders" would consider me walking alone at night a sexual invitation. It was a challenge for me to accept that *different* wasn't *wrong*, but eventually I admired so many things about their culture that I had a more open-minded view of the parts that seemed odder to me.

Chapter 6 – Night Noises

The one cash crop in Arno was copra, the smoked meat of coconuts; which was processed and made into coconut oil for suntan lotion, shampoo, and other toiletries. The men would pick the coconuts, strip off the husks, split the shells by holding them in one hand and giving them a sharp blow with the blade of their machetes, and then stack them on the smoking trays.

As for the nighttime visitors? Seriously. Scariest thing ever is being awakened by the sweet voice of a Majel man singing "I want to talk to you!" outside your window at night. They'd run through all three of our names and then start again. Tell us we were pretty (*likatu*), ask us if we wanted to go to the "shungle" with them. We learned enough Majel to tell them to go away. I sometimes would say "*Kwon nana*," which means "you are bad." That phrase more than any seemed to hurt their feelings the most. "*Ejjab nana*," they would sing-song back ("We're not *bad*...")

Oh, and Carlie's moment of terror with the sound at her door comes from a time when our door knob wasn't working, and the door would occasionally un-latch and come open in the middle of the night. One night after our singing visitors had come, a little while later I heard the doorknob rattling and then footsteps walking across the house toward me. I sat up in bed and let out the most primal, guttural scream I've ever heard, only to discover it wasn't a rapist coming to attack me—it was one of my housemates who had gotten up to check the door; she was just walking back to her bed!

Chapter 7 – Dirty Laundry

Laundry was one of the chores I loved doing on Arno. The other girls ended up hiring people to do their laundry for them, but I didn't because I enjoyed it so much. I got good at drawing water from the well, and there was something calming about sitting in the shade after school on Fridays listening to Enya's *Shepherd Moon*, scrubbing my clothes and then hanging them up on the line. On still days our laundry would end up crispy; on windy days it was like the tee shirts had been tumbled dry. Through the year our clothing got softened and worn from being scrubbed with a scrub brush and sun-bleached from being dried on the line.

I give Archive of Our Own user "*FaerieChild*" credit for the accurate info on Scottish literature. I appreciated the helpful responses of readers who were from Scotland or the UK, as there is a limit to what one can discover with online research.

In the Marshallese language *bwebwenato* means "story" or "talk" and "visit" as well. The people on Arno are incredibly hospitable, and as we went and visited we would speak as much Marshallese as we could. Sometimes all we could do was smile and eat what they fed us.

And the see-through curtains! We didn't realize until a few months into our time there how translucent our curtains were at night when the lights were on inside the house. The nighttime troubadours had realized we weren't going to the *shungle* with them by then, so at that point we started to have visitors that just stood outside our back window and watched us. One time I was sitting on my bed and I looked out the window and noticed a hand holding on to the shortwave radio antenna right outside. That had barely registered in my brain when I saw the outline of a head barely four feet (1.2 m) away from me. Creepy! Whenever we noticed a peeping Tom outside, we would wonder whether we'd remembered to turn the lights off before changing, how long they'd been there, and how much they'd seen!

Chapter 8 – Poor Me, Bore Me

I was never as aware of the moon as I was on Arno. I hadn't realized before then that during a full moon, you will actually see your shadow at night. We especially appreciated the full moon when we had to take trips to the outhouse in the middle of the night.

As for the science: There are two high tides per month—one when the sun & moon are on opposite sides of the earth (full moon) and one when the sun and moon are on the same side of the earth (new moon.) The quarter tides, when the moon is a waxing or waning crescent, the moon and sun are at 90-degree angles with each other, so they each counteract the gravitational pull of the other.

We very quickly tired of the same foods over and over again. I missed fresh fruit and vegetables so much; there were days I would just have died for a salad.

The one break in monotony was mail day. Usually we got mail once a week, though there were a few times when bad weather or a plane or boat being broken down meant we went two weeks between mail deliveries. Mail day was so precious that sometimes we would even excuse the kids from school early. We would read and re-read the letters from family and friends. I still have that box of letters from Arno under the eaves in my house somewhere. Never could get rid of them...

Chapter 9 – Stitch Removal

Long distance relationships are hard when all you can do is communicate by letter: trying to figure out what they really mean by what they say and wishing they said things that they didn't. The hardest thing was the length of time it took for mail delivery. At the very fastest, we'd get mail that had been sent a week previously. At the worst, letters were post-marked two to three weeks before. By the time you got a response to a question you asked, it could well have been two to four weeks since you'd asked it.

Arno still doesn't have cell service. There are a few satellite phones on the island and short-wave radios, but if you want to make a phone call you have to take the Jolok boat to Majuro.

Chapter 10 – Geckos, the Huntsman, and Campbell, Oh My!

AO3 user Peg had lived on Kwajalein, an atoll on the eastern side of the Marshalls, and she reminded me of those huge spiders. I must have blocked them from my memory...were they ever creepy! A couple of times in the night I felt something run over my face. Not sure if it was a gecko or spider. Not sure if either would be less terrifying...

It was fun to research Samhain traditions. Considering that every family is different, I doubt that any Scottish family does all of these things, but I chose the traditions that sounded the most fun to me.

Of all of them, I loved the recitation of poetry most, particularly because the Robert Burns poem I found is meaningful considering the *Outlander* storyline that first inspired this plot. When Claire and Jamie meet they ride on a horse together for hours in the rain, and Jamie pulls his plaid loose to wrap around her. It's such a sweet moment, one of my favorites in episode one of the TV series. She says she's fine, and his response is, "You're shaking so hard it's making *my* teeth rattle."

When Campbell reads the line: "My plaid to the angry airt, I'd shelter you; I'd shelter you," it works as a beautiful metaphor for the care and concern he has for Carlie as well as the physical comfort and warmth he provides.

Chapter 11 – Sunshine

Chapters 8, 10, and 11 were all added after the initial daily posting of this story. There was more to be done to develop Carlie and Campbell's relationship before their sudden engagement, and many more distinct island experiences to share. *Sunshine* is the final chapter added to the story. On reading through as I was working on final edits, it still seemed too sudden for the boys to be telling Carlie to stay away. There was a chapter missing— something that moved their relationship forward even further, something that would convince both her and Campbell to back off on their friendship.

Our last day on Arno, we took the truck down to Matolen. A few of my favorite students lived there, smart studious little girls who amazed me with their love of learning. As the other teachers talked to the parents, I went with the girls and sat out in a field of delicate pink flowers. They showed me how to take off a petal, lick it, and then stick it on a fingernail. I hadn't had a manicure since going to the island, and there was something beautiful and natural about the lovely pink nails.

We climbed into the pick-up truck bed to ride back to Ine, and as we drove away, one by one the petals blew off my fingertips. I cried at that loss of beauty, a metaphor for the beautiful stories of this place that have disappeared into the recesses of my memory. What a blessing to discover as I have written that the memories have still been there all along.

As I wrote this chapter I remembered several things for the first time in years: the jacks game we played, the limes that came from Matolen, and the tradition of salting limes and sucking on them (so delicious, but terrible for the teeth!)

Campbell and Carlie's awkward moment is semi-autobiographical. When I was in high school a good guy friend accidentally called me his girlfriend's name. We'd been getting closer; she lived far away, and people had begun asking him if we were dating. During an emotional phone conversation, her name slipped out as he was talking to me. After that call, things were never the same. I think he finally realized how much he cared about me and how much it was like cheating for him to continue our close friendship. I couldn't understand why he didn't recognize our friendship as growing love and choose me instead of her. At the time, it hurt like a break-up.

Chapter 12 - A Beautiful Doughy Ball

Diana Gabaldon says that leading up to writing *Outlander*, the image she held in her mind was of a man in a kilt. My leading man mental image is a shirtless guy making pizza dough by hand.

During Spring Break, we traveled to Majuro to meet up with other volunteer teachers. The three of us girls went to the apartment of a couple of guys, who made us parmesan cheese pizza with homemade pizza crust. After months of not seeing American men, the fact that one of them was shirtless and gorgeously muscular impressed itself very vividly in my memory. This particular chapter title is in Matt's honor. As he lovingly described each step of the process, he ended by saying "and knead it until it forms a *beautiful doughy ball!*"

Growing up on Guam, I had frequent opportunities to snorkel. I could never get over how isolated I felt underwater, though, and found that if I held hands with someone (one of my sisters or later, my boyfriend) I could better relax and enjoy the view.

Chapter 13 - Scar Stories

Arno was indeed rumored to have a love school. Needless to say, the three of us teachers received plenty of teasing about that detail from friends and family. In the Marshallese dictionary I frequently used during the writing of this story, one of the example sentences about Arno is, *I kid you not*: "She performed the Arno sexual technique so well that he passed out."[1]

Because their language doesn't have words for private parts (as far as I can tell they refer to it as "down there,") I never could get a good answer

---

[1] *Marshallese-English Dictionary*, quoted on Marshallese.org.

about what exactly they learned and how they learned it. It had something to do with the feel of the ocean waves, and one of the learning experiences was for a woman to lie on her back in a canoe drifting on the ocean for hours.

From watching the local style of dance, I know that the Majel women have very limber hips; I have a hunch the technique involves intricate hip movements.

Chapter 14 – The Break Up

Death was incongruous in beautiful Arno but a constant presence in our lives. I remembered the death of this baby boy, whose empty-eyed mother would wheel him around in a wheelbarrow. Sitting and "being sad with" the mother felt like a beautiful thing to do. Soap and dollar bills I didn't understand, but I'm guessing it was just a way to give the family a token of kindness that didn't cost too much.

It seemed almost wrong that the funeral was like a party. They served donuts and Kool-Aid with ice in it, and I remember realizing that it was the first cold drink and the first dessert I'd had in months.

Chapter 15 – Consolation

Come see the miracle! Our crazy teenaged neighbor came running over to our house one night, just as described here. We ran with her, arriving out-of-breath at the oceanside dock, only to have her point up at the brilliant full moon.

It was such a simple thing that brought us such joy. I still use that phrase sometimes when I've done something simple that makes me happy—like organize the kitchen pantry—when I'll tell my husband and sons, "Come see the miracle!" It's good to remember that if you appreciate the simple things they can seem miraculous too.

Chapter 16 – The Proposal

I went on the Jolok boat and terrified myself with thoughts about the entire invisible world under the black ocean surface... that's about all that came from my own experience in this chapter! Didn't propose marriage to anyone, never got punished for bad behavior on Arno...

Chapter 17 – Getting to Know You

When we visited Majuro after being on Arno for several months, I was delighted to finally be able to order a salad at a restaurant. As exciting as it was to eat fresh vegetables, they treated my system as badly as the veggies treated Carlie!

Chapter 18 – Phoning Home

Initially I regretted not killing off Claire's family in my fan-fiction version. (Her parents are both dead in *Outlander*). However, having ways I already diverged from the inspiration fiction was helpful in making this story distinctly my own.

Guam comes from my experience as well. My parents lived there for 13 years, though my dad is not a chaplain or in the air force. My parents flew over to visit us on Arno once during the year and all three of us girls flew to Guam for Christmas along with the other service volunteers.

Carlie's family will be featured more heavily in book 2, "Island Hopper."

Chapter 19 – Restraint

This chapter felt incredibly familiar, and it's one of my favorites. Funny how *not* having sex can be so sexy! I grew up conservative and virginity until marriage was a goal of mine which I achieved... barely. Being a sensual person, whose love language is physical touch, I'm still surprised I waited as long as I did (we dated over four years). I remember how desperate waiting could feel at times, so this was easy writing.

Now, I wasn't as forward as Carlie before marriage, but then *she's* not the virgin in this story and I felt like I needed to reflect current culture, not that of the 90's...

Chapter 20 – To Have and To Hold

With my body I thee worship. I've always loved that line and I like writing poetry, but nothing from this chapter really comes from life. I didn't get to attend any Majel wedding ceremonies, and I didn't get married on a beach...

Chapter 21 – First Blood

I took *tremendous* liberties with truth in this chapter to create wedding night awkwardness and to echo both the forced consummation and the blood vow of the original *Outlander* story. In that story, Claire and Jamie take part in a wedding ritual where they each receive a small cut on their wrists, which are then tied together so that their blood mingles. In my head canon this is one of the reasons their love transcends time.

In my research on island wedding traditions, I discovered that the "red cloth" ceremony was a common tradition in Kiribati, a Pacific island miles away from the Marshall Islands. On their wedding night the bride and groom make love for the first time on a white sheet. If there is blood on the cloth, the bride's family celebrates and tosses the cloth to the groom's family as evidence that their daughter/ sister/ granddaughter was still a virgin when she married their son/ brother/ grandson. If the family knows she isn't, they skip this part of the tradition. Even in Kiribati, I doubt that there would be any expectation that residents from other countries would carry on the tradition at their weddings. For the sake of story, though, I'm running with it. And "nuknuk" is simply the Majel word for "cloth" or "clothes."

I felt there was something beautiful and bonding in the situation I created. For Campbell to offer his own virgin blood to cover Carlie's "shame" in that culture was precious, and particularly deep considering his spirituality and Christianity. I especially love the way it connects him to his new wife and endears him to Carlie's dad.

Chapter 22 – The Morning After
The "true" parts of this chapter? Acclimatizing so that 72° felt so cold I had to wear a sweatshirt and trying to pre-plan for showers so that it didn't take so long in the mornings.

Such a bummer none of this other stuff happened out there...

Chapter 23 – Autle
We went to Autle during Spring Break, just for a day. It's much closer to Ine than I chose to make it, but I wanted Campbell to get seasick and there were other reasons in future chapters to have it farther away.

Enedrik is an uninhabited island in the Arno Atoll that can be rented. You'd definitely be roughing it if you went there, though!

Chapter 24 – The Storm
If I could choose anything to experience again, an Arno storm would be one of the things I would love. There was raw power in a storm out there. You could often see it approaching from the north across the atoll and it would move so quickly that you could see the water roughened under the clouds by rain moving across the lagoon toward you. The rain would fall in drenching sheets with incredible power, and then almost as fast as it had come it would be gone again.

Now that the climate is changing, so are the storms. They can be more powerful, more destructive, and last longer.

It was when writing this chapter that I made the decision that there wasn't going to be a "bad guy" or assault in my story, two things that feature heavily in the *Outlander* novels. I realized that when we were on Arno there were enough terrifying and tragic things that happened without there being an actual antagonist. Death, disease, and weather are fierce enough forces. And a new marriage between two people who barely know each other creates challenges of its own! So instead of having some drunk sport fishermen discover a topless Carlie wandering on the ocean side of island, I had an argument and a storm... and I felt that was drama enough.

Chapter 25 – The Drop-off

Scariest thing ever, snorkeling on the ocean side on Arno. I did it exactly *once*. Between the gut-dropping sensation of going over the drop-off to seeing a blacktip fin shark, I was done after one time. There are also tiger sharks found around Arno on the ocean side which are much more dangerous to humans. We were able to see beautiful fish and coral when snorkeling on the lagoon side, so that was good enough for me.

I didn't have the "a-shark-is-swimming-toward-you-get-in-the-water-right-now" experience like Carlie and Campbell in this chapter. My shark was gracefully swimming below me through crevices in the coral reef. However, Wikipedia mentions that Marshall Islanders choose to swim instead of wade as their best method for avoiding reef shark bites!

Chapter 26 – The Visitor

This title is an evil play on words. One of the American euphemisms for having a period is saying you have a *visitor*. By titling this chapter this way, I assumed I'd make people think that Eric would be showing up soon.

Jellyfish stings are almost the most painful things I have ever experienced. There was a particular time of year on Arno when there was an influx of little 3-4 cm jellyfish with long trailing stingers that would beach themselves on the lagoon side. One night I was jogging on the beach and ended up getting jellyfish stingers around one ankle. Worse than any burn, it stung for more than an hour.

For those familiar with the *Outlander* books, one of the things that occurs because Claire steps back in time to the 1700s is that Jamie punishes her when she endangers the lives of his men (and then he promises to never do that again when he realizes he's endangered his continued relationship with her). Campbell's reaction in this situation comes from me being a mother of boys. Many people don't believe in corporal punishment, but sometimes an irrational mind needs additional stimulus to start working again.

The polite family thing is me, too. I'm one of three girls, and we didn't say poop, pee, or shut up.

Chapter 27 – House Warming

In researching and looking up pictures of Arno, I ended up at the website of Philip Jessup, who has written a photo book chronicling the challenges of the current islanders on Arno. His pictures were so beautiful they brought tears to my eyes. But I was also devastated to learn how even a few centimeters of ocean depth is having life-altering consequences for the islanders that I loved.

Philip's beautiful pictures can be found at https://www.jessup.ca/atolls/

Chapter 28 – Feels Like Home

"*Jōlok bōd*" and "*Ejjelok bōd*" were my favorite Marshallese phrases (bod sounds more like "burr," as you roll the d like an r). The other girls and I were unintentionally rude so many times, it felt like we were constantly apologizing. But there was something comforting in asking the islanders to throw away our mistakes and in hearing them answer that our mistakes were nowhere to be found, accompanied by a wide white smile in a beautiful brown face.

Chapter 29 – Division of Labor

The full five love languages are 1) Quality Time, 2) Acts of Service, 3) Physical Affection, 4) Words of Affirmation, and 5) Gifts. You can find the book by Gary Chapman online, as well as take quizzes to figure out what your primary love languages are. Most people have more than one love language, but if you ever find a friendship or relationship developing with almost no effort at all, it's often because you both have similar love languages. In the beginning stages of most relationships, people will show every one of the love languages—spending time together, doing nice things for each other, being affectionate and complimentary, and giving gifts. Once the blush of newness wears off, people tend to revert to their own preferred love languages. This is when understanding what makes your partner loved and expressing what makes you feel loved is especially helpful.

Physical affection and quality time happen to be my primary love languages, too. When one has different love languages than their partner, it's a little harder to connect; for example, my husband's primary love languages are acts of service and words of affirmation.

If your love languages are different than your partner's, it doesn't spell doom for your relationship. For me, realizing that when my husband does the dishes he's demonstrating love for me helps me receive it in the spirit it was meant. I'm just guessing that if two people had the exact same love languages, it would be easier to translate into feeling loved...and might contribute to feeling like soul mates.

Chapter 30 – Love Notes

Can I admit the part that's true in here? Um, that my Bio lab partner and I cheated in Freshman biology? Shame on us, though we were both "A" students, so if we found the lab final hard, maybe it *was* just too damn hard.

I really love the moments we see into Campbell's mind. The challenge with writing first person is that typically you get a very one-sided view of a story. And Campbell has such a good heart that hearing from him is just uber-sweet.

Chapter 31 – Date Night

I purposely chose primitive when I went as a volunteer teacher to Arno. There were plenty of trendy, cushier places (Scotland, for example!) but I wanted to break out of my comfort zone. No running water? *Sign me up.* No electricity? *Awesome.* And though the culture shock was extreme, and the first weeks of adjusting to our new life somewhat stressful, I was so blessed by the amazing people, beautiful surroundings, and most of all the decluttered life I experienced.

Wish I could move my family someplace like that—get my sons to unplug, just go snorkeling and play on the beach. . .

Chapter 32 – Getting Settled

Carlie's infertility journey is close to home for me. I stopped using birth control after our first year of marriage, but never got pregnant. It was stressful to anticipate getting pregnant monthly, but I hated the side effects of pills so much that I couldn't bring myself to use them. We ended up adopting our sons, so I did get to experience the joy (and the challenge) of parenting. But through the years there were many "do we or don't we" discussions about birth control.

Campbell's "I want to make babies" comes from my friend's high school-aged son. He announced to his mother, a OB nurse, that he wanted to make babies. "You want to have kids?" she asked. "You're really young for that."

"Oh, I don't want to *have* kids," he said, grinning. "I just want to *make babies.*"

Chapter 33 – The American

My current husband (well, my only husband... my husband currently... or just... my husband?...) was my boyfriend at the time of my year overseas. He was great at regularly writing letters to me, and I wrote to him, but at times it felt very frustrating to know that mail would take a week to get to him and then a week to get back to me. I wouldn't receive a response to any of my thoughts for two entire weeks and by the time I did hear back (about something that felt incredibly important at the time), it was *just too late*. Never as important as the letters between Eric and Carlie, but definitely it felt important at the time...

Chapter 34 – The Hotel

I had horrible writers' block for this chapter. So much energy had gone into the last one that this was a struggle. I've only had one real breakup in my life, but plenty of painful conversations. I could just feel the awkwardness and guilt as I wrote the conversation between Carlie and Eric.

I had a lot of compassion for Eric and could only imagine how terrible it would be to sever a long-term relationship. But the natural affection that Carlie and Campbell have for each other, the passion, the gentleness? I can't imagine Carlie choosing to lose that. It also seemed that she had left home and Eric for a reason. Deep down there *was* something broken in their relationship.

And I do wonder at a person who would choose to just remain engaged and never commit to marriage when their partner so clearly longs for it to happen. By the time Eric came around and realized the error he'd made, it was just too late.

Chapter 35 – Hey, Uncle Ferguson!

When we were on the islands we couldn't call, but we missed our family's voices. As a remedy we would sometimes record audiotapes and send them through the mail. I suppose nowadays you could send a little USB drive, but that would assume electricity. An old-fashioned tape player used good old-fashioned batteries.

This was a stream-of-consciousness chapter with an occasional sound effect. It may not have been your thing, but it was fun to write. And again, it was a sweet opportunity to hear from Campbell. He's so honest to his uncle, and so obviously in love with Carlie that it just breaks your heart for him. In the *Outlander* story, there's little that's as heartbreaking as Jamie leaving Claire at the stones, truly believing that she is never coming back to him.

Chapter 36 – I Choose You

In the previous chapter and this chapter, it was fun to peek inside Campbell's mind. So much of this story comes from Carlie's perspective that you don't really know how he feels, as you only perceive him through his words and her eyes.

To hear Campbell's thoughts was fun, and I loved Carlie's reassurance to him that he was the one she had chosen. And drunk Campbell was *adorable*. So needy, so honest...

Chapter 37 – Love Making

On Arno, we had to use a mimeograph machine to make copies for teaching. I got so used to using it, that when I thought about coming back to the States, I wondered what I would do without it. How would I make copies of worksheets for my students? Ummm, copy machines, maybe?

I felt like it was important for Carlie to tell Campbell exactly what she'd realized when she was with Eric—that Campbell was her soulmate. It also felt right to end the book with affection instead of sexuality. Because truly, there is more to love than just passion. There is also comfort and affection, and the simple joy of being close to each other and falling asleep in each other's arms.

Thanks for reading! Feel free to visit www.carliebeecher.com, leave a review on Amazon and share the book with friends.

The story continues in *Island Hopper*, coming Fall or Winter 2018.

77374576R00222

Made in the USA
San Bernardino, CA
22 May 2018